THE MEMORY JAR

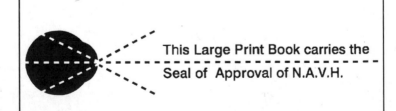

This Large Print Book carries the
Seal of Approval of N.A.V.H.

THE MEMORY JAR

TRICIA GOYER

THORNDIKE PRESS
A part of Gale, Cengage Learning

GALE
CENGAGE Learning®

Detroit • New York • San Francisco • New Haven, Conn • Waterville, Maine • London

GALE
CENGAGE Learning

LIBRARY OF CONGRESS CATALOGING-IN-PUBLICATION DATA

Goyer, Tricia.
    The memory jar / by Tricia Goyer.
        pages ; cm. — (Thorndike Press large print Christian romance) (Seven brides for seven bachelors series ; #1)
    ISBN-13: 978-1-4104-5516-1 (hardcover)
    ISBN-10: 1-4104-5516-5 (hardcover)
    1. Amish—Fiction. 2. Montana—Fiction. 3. Large type books. I. Title.
PS3607.O94M46 2013
813'.6—dc23   2012043360

Published in 2013 by arrangement with The Zondervan Corporation LLC

Printed in the United States of America
1 2 3 4 5 6 7 17 16 15 14 13

Dedicated to my sweet daughter Alyssa.
You are a gift to us,
and I enjoy making memories
with you day by day.

The Lord God fashioned us for mighty ends, and nothing less than following that for which He made us can heal our restlessness of heart.

— ARTHUR JOHN (A. J.) GOSSIP

GLOSSARY

ach — an exclamation
appeditlich — delicious
bensel — silly child
blappermaul — blabber mouth
brieder — brothers
bruder — brother
brutzing — pouting
boppli — baby
danki — thank you
dat — dad
dawdi house — grandparents' house
demut — humility
guder mariye — good morning
gut — good
in lieb — in love
ja — yes
kapp — head covering
kind — child
kinner — children
maut — hired girl
mem — mom

9

ne — no

oma — grandma

opa — grandpa

Ordnung — unwritten set of rules and regulations that guide everyday Amish life. Meaning "order" or "discipline"

Rumspringa — running around. A time when Amish youth are encouraged to experiment and explore.

wonnernaus — a polite way of saying "none of your business"

wunderbaar — wonderful

PROLOGUE

Sarah Shelter didn't know her friend was going to die that day at the lake. If so, she would have looked into Patty's smiling face and determined once and for all if her eyes were more blue or green. She would have captured Patty's laughter in her memory. And held her friend's hand as they walked down to Lake Koocanusa, like they used to when they were ten.

Instead, Sarah settled onto the quilt they'd spread upon the rocky shore and plopped the last bit of strawberry cupcake into her mouth. The texture was fluffy and sweet. The vanilla frosting, good.

"So yummy." Patty's eyes widened. Sarah's older brother Jonathan, Patty's brother Michael, and their friend Jebadiah chimed in their agreement. Their kind words warmed Sarah even more than the bright sun in the cloudless Montana sky.

Patty licked frosting from her fingers.

"The best cupcake yet. You really should open your own bakery, Sarah."

"You want to open a bakery?" Jebadiah asked.

Sarah eyed her friend. *"Blappermaul."*

Patty tucked a stray strand of hair back in her *kapp.* "Don't call me a blabbermouth." She laughed. "Everyone knows yer the best Amish baker in all of the West Kootenai. Why would anyone be surprised?"

"I'd be a customer." Michael eyed the basket of extra cupcakes.

Sarah took out one and handed it to Michael. "Amish women don't run businesses, as *Mem* says, our jobs are to keep our husbands' bellies full." Heat rose to her cheeks. "Not that I have one, uh, yet . . ." She let her words trail off, hoping she didn't sound too desperate. She trusted God would bring her the right bachelor at the right time. At least mostly trusted. Sometimes she wondered why God was taking so long. Wondered if there was a reason she'd been passed by.

"Besides," Sarah quickly added, "even if I were thinking of having my own business someday, I'm still fine-tuning my cupcake recipes. Got to get each jest perfect like."

Michael took a big bite and swallowed. "How could you possibly do better than this? *Appeditlich!*"

Sarah didn't know if Michael was the man for her, but she hoped that someday an Amish man would make his intentions known. If not a young man from one of the twenty families that lived in the West Kootenai, then maybe one of the thirty Amish bachelors who visited their corner of Montana every year.

Patty's dog, Monty, snoozed with his chin resting on Sarah's knee. Gray and scraggly, he'd followed at Patty's heels for the last eight months.

Sarah stroked his paw. If a dog like this — that looked more like a mangy squirrel with a dog's legs — could find love, couldn't she?

The call of an eagle interrupted her thoughts as it swooped over Lake Koocanusa. It glided over the dark blue waters. Stately pines and white-trunked birch trees lined the lake's shore.

From their place on the colorful quilt, Sarah eyed the tall bridge that crossed the wide lake. It sparkled in the summer sunshine like silver. Yet the bridge's beauty and complexity were no match for the small pinecone she'd picked up. The pinecone wasn't much longer than a green bean, but it was perfectly intricate. Sarah needed something for her memory jar to remember this day — the day when Michael's eyes had lingered on her longer than ever — but not a pinecone.

Sarah tossed it into the lake. It bobbed for a minute and then rose on a gentle wave, most likely caused by a speedboat out there somewhere. Then a glimmer of white on the rocky shore caught Sarah's attention. She scooted to the edge of the picnic blanket and picked it up, turning it over in her fingers. It was as lily white as marble, so different than the gray stones and gravel that covered the beach. Holding it up to the bright sunlight, she saw a cross shape etched into the stone.

Deep laughter rose from behind her. Sarah touched her *kapp* and then glanced over her shoulder. Michael was standing, circled up with the two other men. Yet his eyes weren't on them, but on her. He smiled. Heat rose up her cheeks and she quickly looked away.

"The fish was so large she broke the line!" Jebadiah exclaimed. "*Gut* thing. I would have been pulled into the water had she not."

"Look at that." Patty pointed across the lake. "Those trees on the other shore look like eyelashes. They're all fringed and full."

"The lake is an awfully big eye," Sarah's

brother Jonathan teased.

They didn't understand. The guys saw a lake, but Patty saw a masterpiece.

If the lake was an eye and the trees lashes, the mountains in the distance, white capped and pointed, made impressive eyebrows. It was Patty who'd helped Sarah see things in such a way.

Sarah took her friend's hand and squeezed. "*Ja,* I can see it. They are beautiful lashes, aren't they?"

Sarah rose and slipped off her shoes and stockings. Sharp rocks poked the soles of her feet. Lifting her skirt, she stepped into the cold water near where Jeb's canoe was tied to the shore. Patty joined her. She stood by Sarah's side, holding her skirt to her knees, and then took one step deeper.

"Yesterday this water was snow," Sarah said just loud enough for Patty to hear.

"It's a *wunderbaar gut* day when you can splash in snow, isn't it?" Patty kicked softly and water splashed into the air. Sarah pictured a school of trout swimming closer to see what the commotion was about. Then Patty quieted and stared into the expanse, taking it all in. The only sounds were the lapping of the water against the shore, the distant buzzing of a motorboat, and the guys' voices as they moved on to hunting stories.

Sarah fingered the stone in her pocket, letting her thoughts flit back to Michael. What things would he be interested in talking about beside fishing and hunting? Anything that would interest her? Would it be too bold to approach Michael and start up a conversation?

Patty scurried up the rocky beach, shoes in hand. Sarah followed her, and then the two friends sat on the quilt, side by side.

"I have an idea," Patty called to the guys. "Let's head across the lake in Jeb's canoe. My cousin's place is jest on the other side. We can stop fer a quick visit."

Jeb and Jonathan quickly agreed, but Michael remained silent.

Undaunted, Patty turned to Sarah. "You hafta come unless . . ." Patty leaned closer. "Unless you want to stay behind with Michael."

Sarah turned the stone over in her hand, and then tucked it into her pocket.

"Michael's not going?" Sarah whispered.

"*Ach,* heaven's no." Patty lowered her voice. "He almost drowned in the river back behind our home as a lad. He's terribly afraid of water. Besides, you don't want my poor brother to sit alone, do you?"

"But I'm comfortable with *you*. I don't know where to start with . . . *him.*"

Patty placed a hand on Sarah's shoulder. "Every man is looking fer someone who will listen to his dreams. Ask Michael what he thinks about. What he hopes for."

"When did you grow so wise of love's ways?" Sarah asked, glancing at Jonathan. He stood in the water with his handmade denim pants rolled up to his knees, guiding Jeb's wooden canoe into the water.

Patty didn't respond, but Sarah knew the answer. Patty and Jonathan were *in lieb.* She wouldn't be surprised if by this time next year they'd announce their wedding.

"I know what it is to be falling fer a dear man," Patty answered in a low voice. She took Sarah's hands in her own, squeezing them tight. "We'll be sisters if I marry Jonathan, and if you and Michael find love in each other — double sisters."

Sarah's stomach trembled in soft waves. "It would be nice to talk to him some."

"That does it," Patty called to the others. "Jonathan, Jebadiah, I'm crossing the lake with you. Michael, you won't mind staying with Sarah, will you?"

"*Ne,* I'll stay."

The simple answer brought a double patter to Sarah's heart. Patty rose and hurried down the shore.

The three climbed into the wooden canoe, taking the paddles and beginning to move across the lake. Wide-brimmed hats shadowed the men's faces. Patty sat between the guys, her grin as bright as the sun reflecting on the water.

A speedboat zipped across the other side of the lake. Sarah thought about calling out to her friends, telling them to wait until the boat left. But it would do no good. When Patty's mind was set on something, there was no changing it. Besides . . .

Sarah turned to Michael. This was the chance she'd been waiting for.

As the canoe continued farther out into deep water, the passengers' voices carried back to shore. Even from this distance, Patty's laughter was clear.

Patty's dog, Monty, trotted along the shore, whining for his master.

"Come here, boy." Sarah snapped her fingers. The dog curled up next to Sarah, but his eyes stayed fixed on the canoe.

"Do you mind if I sit closer?" Michael asked.

Sarah patted the quilt beside her. He sat down near enough to show Sarah he was interested, but far enough to be proper.

"So I hear your *dat*'s finished with yer

family's new house."

"Yes, *Dat* finished the porch today." She chuckled. "It'll be better than staying in the old camper. It's been mighty tight. Tonight's the big night. We'll be sleeping within real walls again."

The speedboat zipped by and the occupants waved. One of them yelled something. Sarah thought she heard the word *bonnet* but couldn't be sure.

Sarah lifted her hand and waved back. As summer warmed the Montana air and more tourists arrived, the peculiar Amish became as much of an attraction as the lakes, mountains, hiking trails, and bears.

Michael shook his head at the passing boat, and then turned his attention back to her. "So I heard you got a job at the West Kootenai store. I heard yer cookies —"

A scream filled the air. The speedboat had turned and now bore down on the canoe. Sarah's mouth opened to call a warning, but no words emerged. The sky faded to gray. She couldn't move, couldn't speak.

Michael rose and sprinted to the water. "Stop!" He waved his hands at the speedboat. "Stop!"

It was too late. With frightening speed, the boat caught the end of the canoe. The canoe flipped and tumbled like a dry leaf on the wind.

Michael rushed into the water up to his knees. He turned back to her. "I can't swim." Panic twisted his face. "Patty cannot swim either."

Her friend . . . her brother . . . Jeb. Sarah clenched her hands. "Dear God, please let them be all right. Please."

"Patty!" Michael called. "Patty!"

Sarah moved to Michael's side, clutching his hand. The canoe righted and two heads bobbed up — hatless now. Breath escaped Sarah's lungs. *Jonathan.* Her brother was all right.

Jebadiah swam around the canoe, searching the water. Patty was nowhere to be seen.

The speedboat circled back. Cries of panic carried over the water. Life jackets were thrown into the lake. Two men jumped in. Minutes passed, but still no Patty.

"Go!" Michael turned to her. "Run to the . . ." His words fumbled. "There's a house close. Call fer help. Send someone fer my *dat.*"

A cry escaped Sarah's lips. She slipped on her shoes without taking time to tie them, then ran. Her legs felt as solid and heavy as the pine trees around her. She hurried up the hill. Her heart pounded. Her lungs ached. She looked back. Michael had sunk to his knees in the gravel. There was still no sign of Patty in the water.

Sarah knew she should pray more, pray harder, but only one prayer scrolled through her mind.

Unser Vadder im Himmel, hallowed be
thy name.

The words of the Lord's Prayer mixed *Englisch* and Pennsylvania Dutch in her mind.

dei reich loss komme.
dei wille loss gedu sei,
uff die erd wie im himmel.
Give us this day our daily bread.
And forgive us our trespasses
as we forgive those who trespass against
us.
And lead us not into temptation, but
deliver us from evil.
Fer dei is es reich, die graft,
un die hallichkeit in weicheit.
Aemen.

It seemed like an eternity until Sarah reached the closest house. She pounded on the door until it opened. An older Amish man stood there, eyes wide. *"Ja?"*

"We need help," she panted. "An accident! At the lake."

"Come." He motioned to her. "My neighbor down the road, he has a phone."

The man hitched up his horse. Sarah climbed into the buggy, her body trembling like an aspen leaf in the wind.

How much time had passed? Too much.

Something weighed her pocket. She reached inside, pulling out the rock.

A cloud moved in front of the sun, and a sinking feeling weighed in Sarah's gut. "It's too late. We lost Patty. My friend is gone."

Only a miracle of Christ could save Patty now. Sarah's thumb followed the etching. All hope slipped from her heart.

Dear Lord, what now?

CHAPTER 1

Two years later

With one motion, Sarah Shelter pulled her apron over her head. The garment smelled of fresh-baked bread, ham, and onions from the French onion soup she'd put on to simmer before leaving the West Kootenai Kraft and Grocery. Her *Englisch* friend told her once that the way to a man's heart was through his stomach. If that were the case, Sarah should have been married off years ago. She'd cooked for plenty of Amish bachelors, every year befriending the thirty or so men who came to Montana for a season. Problem was, their eyes were more on the wild game that filled the hills than on finding a wife. Typically, girls waiting back home had already captured their hearts. The bachelors appreciated Sarah all right — to fill their stomachs until their western adventure came to an end and they returned to their farms, their families, and their waiting brides.

Tossing the apron into a wicker basket filled with tomorrow's wash, Sarah moved to her bedroom window and opened it. Warm, afternoon air that smelled of sunshine and pine wafted in. She paused, staring up at the trees and the green pasture beyond, but mostly at the large mountain that rose in the distance. Eve Peachy had come into the store earlier to tell Sarah they'd been invited to hike Robinson Mountain. Sarah had laughed, thinking it was a joke, until Eve announced it was a bachelor who'd planned the outing.

"Amos is planning it yet," Eve had mentioned with a twinkle of her eye. Though not the most handsome bachelor, Amos had an outgoing, playful side. Eve knew if anyone could get Sarah to put on hiking boots to climb a mountain, it would be Amos.

Sarah placed a hand over her heart — which danced a double beat at the mere mention of Amos's name — and smiled. She supposed it was time to hike the mountain. Her older brothers had both hiked it, even her father and mother had. Spring had brought plenty of sunshine and had already cleared the snow from the mountain trails. She had no excuse really. And maybe . . .

24

maybe she'd even get a chance to get to know Amos a bit better.

She removed her *kapp,* placing it on her bed. She'd bathe early and spend the evening quilting on the porch. She never liked the sticky feeling that spending all morning baking at the store brought about. More than that, if one of the bachelors happened to stop for a visit, she'd look proper.

Sarah moved to her dresser and stopped short. Two large jars — previously used for pickles — sat there, filled with all types of curious things. Pretty rocks, old pennies, a rusty nail, and a hand-carved whistle, each with a memory attached. But the third jar . . . she rested a hand on her hip. Its contents had been spilled out and the jar itself was gone. She picked up the white rock that had been dumped with the other items and fingered it. Then she set it back down.

She balled her fist. A rush of anger tightened her shoulders. How could someone treat her things so carelessly?

Stomping out her bedroom door through the living room, Sarah let out a shout. "Andy!"

Hearing his name, her twelve-year-old brother rose from where he'd been sitting on the front porch and darted into the woods. Through the open front door, Sarah spotted what she'd been looking for. Her jar. It sat there covered with what looked like tin foil and . . .

Sarah stepped forward. A snake was inside! Her brother had dumped out her things to keep an ugly ole brown garter snake?

She picked up the jar, crumpled the foil, and slipped her hand inside the jar.

"Well, I'll be." The man's voice caused Sarah to start, and she nearly dropped the jar.

There, striding up the wooded path leading from the road, was Amos Byler with another of the bachelors by his side.

Sarah looked at the jar in her hand and, with a quick grip of her fingers and a flip of her wrist, tossed the snake into the yard. It bounced slightly and then slithered away into the tall grass.

The two men stood staring. Amos ran a hand down his smooth face.

Then she remembered. *My* kapp. Sarah placed a hand on top of her head. The silkiness of her blonde hair felt foreign. Since a small girl, she'd worn a *kapp* by day and a sleeping kerchief at night.

"I was 'bout to change," she explained. "And then I noticed my memory jar was

26

missing."

Amos cocked an eyebrow as he nodded. A hint of a smile spread on the other man's face.

"My *dat*'s not here, if that's who yer looking for, and I best get inside." She clutched the glass jar to her chest and hurried to the front door. The wooden planks of the porch squeaked under her feet, and a blue jay twittered from the top of the porch railing, as if chiding Sarah for her improper presentation.

"Before you go!" Amos called.

She paused and turned, heat rising to her cheeks.

"We didn't come fer yer *dat*. We came to see you, Sarah. We're hiking up Robinson Mountain next Saturday — all the way to the top. Care to come?"

"*Ja,* sounds fun," she called over her shoulder, and hurried inside, her knees trembling. She rushed to her room. Good thing no one else was around to witness that. She hoped no one would find out, especially *Mem.* Sarah's mother spoke quietly, but her words had impact. Sarah grabbed up her clean clothes and hurried into the indoor bathroom.

Would Amos tell?

She had a feeling he wouldn't. He seemed

too kindly for that. But that other man. What was his name? Jathan. Yes, that was it. He stood at least six inches taller than Amos and his shoulders appeared twice as wide. He'd been smiling, and his eyes twinkled as if he enjoyed seeing her embarrassment.

As she unpinned her sleeve, Sarah decided right then she didn't like Jathan one bit . . .

The cabin wasn't much more than four bunks, but it had enough room in one corner for a small kitchen with a wood-burning cookstove and a handmade table with two chairs. Jathan Schrock had straightened it up some when he first arrived. His guess was that the guys who'd most recently stayed there hadn't tidied up much. Nor the group of guys before that.

He supposed the accommodations weren't what beckoned most bachelors to the West Kootenai. It was the promise of high mountains, endless forests, and abundant game that called to the outdoorsmen.

"A haven for single Amish men." *Mem* had read about the bachelors' cabins in *The Budget.* Sawmill and carpenter jobs were aplenty in the West Kootenai. Wouldn't Jathan like to go to try his hand at hunting too?

Jathan was excited to come face to face

with elk, mule deer, and moose. But he also wanted time to get away and think about his future. He'd snuck two books on running a small business into his suitcase and had been reading them late into the night. Someday, he wanted his own retail shop — he liked that idea much more than working at a mill or factory. He liked people too — finding out about their lives, meeting their needs. Jathan had worked one summer in his uncle's cheese factory as a salesman, and he'd been hooked. The idea of offering people something they valued while also providing for a family appealed to him. He could see himself doing that rather than working in the garage-door factory like most of his friends did.

Being in Montana wasn't just about what he came for — but what he ran from. He'd be in the door factory this very moment if he hadn't spent his savings on a suitcase and a train ticket out west. And although finding a wife wasn't one of his motives, he'd thought more about having one here than he ever had elsewhere.

Thought more about her — Sarah Shelter.

Yet she hadn't paid him any mind, except to offer another cup of coffee at the West Kootenai store. She'd also scowled his direction when she'd been caught this afternoon without a *kapp.* But that didn't count as romance, right?

Jathan got the cookstove going. After being here two months and missing some of his favorite dishes, he'd decided to cook his own dinner tonight and had stopped by the store for supplies.

The food at the West Kootenai Kraft and Grocery was good, but his favorite part was watching Sarah work. He liked the open kitchen that was visible from the dining room. Liked her broad smile as she kneaded bread dough or whipped up batter for cakes. He especially liked the way she chatted with the customers as they entered.

He'd learned a lot about Sarah by her conversations with others. She had a married brother and three married sisters; one older brother, Jonathan, who wasn't married yet; and younger siblings too. She liked baking more than cooking and liked cakes and cupcakes best of all.

What Jathan didn't know was why there was always a hint of sadness in her eyes. Something pained her, and he wished he knew her well enough to ask what it was.

Sarah.

The memory of her blonde hair glimmering in the sunlight as she stood on her front porch today caused his neck to grow warm.

He chuckled under his breath, remembering how she'd picked up that snake and flicked it into the yard as if it were a twig. He couldn't think of one woman he knew back in Ohio who'd do that.

Jathan opened the front door, letting in a cool breeze, and glanced down the walking path that led to the main road, and beyond that, Sarah's place. Maybe he'd get a chance to talk to her before another two months passed.

His stomach growled, and he grabbed the paper sack he'd brought home from the store. First out was a cooking pot. Jathan hadn't been surprised that there wasn't one to be found in the cupboards of the cabin. Instead of cooking pots, he'd found coils of rope, a knife sharpener, and bullets.

He wiped down the countertop, and then chopped up an onion, carrots, and potatoes. With that done, Jathan melted shortening in the pot on the stove and added boneless beef cubes. When they were browned, he tossed the vegetables into the pot and added water, salt, and a tablespoon of sugar. Then he pulled a few more items from his grocery bag: Worcestershire sauce, paprika, allspice, clove. A dash here, a splash there, and within a few minutes, the room smelled like his mother's kitchen back home rather than

31

sweaty socks and gun oil as it had before.

He pulled out one of his books on small business ownership, writing notes in the margins as the stew simmered.

An hour later, just as he'd tested to see if the stew was done, a pounding of footsteps sounded on the front porch — Amos stomping mud off his boots. Jathan's eyes widened. Would Amos think any less of him for his ability to cook? Tension tightened Jathan's gut.

Amos entered through the front door and stopped in his tracks. He looked over at a bunk and then crouched down and peered under it. "Okay, where is she?"

"Who?"

"The woman. Someone's been cookin' in here. It smells amazing." Amos chuckled.

Jathan shrugged. "Nothin' special. Jest something I cooked up." He took out two clean bowls and ladled up the stew.

Amos grabbed a spoon, sank onto a lower bunk, and dug in. *"Ja,* this is really *gut,"* he said between bites. "You should give the recipe to Sarah at the West Kootenai Kraft and Grocery."

"No." The word shot from Jathan's mouth. He took a bite from the stew but was suddenly no longer as hungry. He wanted to talk to Sarah — get to know her better —

but not in that way. Wait until he brought in the prize elk. Then he'd make a proper introduction.

"Don't go jabbering about things unknown to you," Jathan said. "Have another bowl, but don't eat yerself full. I'd like to head over to the store later fer some cake."

"A piece of Sarah's cake no doubt?" Amos cocked an eyebrow. "It wonders me why you haven't asked her to go on a walk." He combed his fingers through his dark hair and straight bangs. "From the way you keep glancing her direction while she works, well, yer interest is clear. Why don't you ask her to walk down to the lake or something? Jest to be friendly."

"*Wonnernaus.* There's no reason really." Jathan narrowed his gaze as if trying to convince Amos it really was none of his business.

The fact was, he did want to get to know Sarah, but what did he have to offer if she showed her affection back — talk of a door factory job waiting for him? No, he had to figure out some business plans first.

Most people thought he'd come to Montana for the hunting, and while he enjoyed that, Jathan had another reason. He was running — running from being the youngest son who, no matter how hard he tried, couldn't live up to his brothers, who lived the perfect Amish lives and always obeyed *Dat,* always made *Dat* proud.

Amos served himself another bowl. "This really is *gut* stew."

Jathan finished his stew and stood. He placed his bowl on the counter and then stuffed his hands into his pockets.

"Are you sure you made it?" Amos asked.

"No, yer guess was right the first time. There's an Amish woman here. I stuffed her into my pillow."

Amos laughed and then placed his dirty bowl on the counter. "Hit the spot."

Amos eyed the pot. "But it looks like there will be enough for breakfast afore we go out shooting in the morning."

"*Ja,* leftovers are always better." Jathan tried to hide his disappointment. As much as he looked forward to target practice, doing so would mean he'd miss sitting in the restaurant and saying hello to Sarah Shelter.

CHAPTER 2

"Sarah had two bachelors over today, and when she was talking to them, she didn't have on her *kapp*." The words spilled out of twelve-year-old Andy's mouth as soon as the members of Sarah's family lifted their head from silent prayer after thanking the Lord for their supper.

"Sarah!" Her mother's small blue eyes widened and her jaw dropped. The spoon she had poised to scoop up mashed potatoes hit the table with a thud.

"That's not how it happened," Sarah hurried to explain. "I was gonna bathe after work and noticed one of my jars missing." She narrowed her gaze at her brother. "Andy had gotten into my things, and I'd already taken off my *kapp*. I'd jest gone outside to get my jar when Amos and another bachelor walked up. I didn't even see them coming." She glanced from *Mem* to *Dat*. Instead of shock, she noted humor in *Dat*'s gaze.

"Now children —" *Dat* leaned forward and rested his elbows on the table — "we mustn't bicker like this."

Sarah wrinkled her nose, understanding how foolish she must appear, tattling like she was ten or twelve, not twenty-four years as she'd turned in March.

Twenty-four. That was something to be embarrassed about. Her older brother and sisters had been married for years at this age. And even though Jonathan hadn't found a wife after the heartbreak of losing Patty, their younger sister Beth — barely twenty — had gotten married and moved back to Kentucky to be near her new husband's family. Where did that leave Sarah?

Though no one spoke it, she felt like an old maid who had everyone's pity. Either that or she was lumped as a child with her younger siblings, twelve-year-old Andy and Evelyn, who was almost five years old. She supposed arguments like today did nothing to prove her maturity in *Dat* and *Mem*'s eyes.

"It's not like you meant to parade before them bareheaded," her mother finally said with the releasing of her breath. "I jest hope that doesn't make them question yer worthiness as a bride in their eyes."

"Mem, please . . ." Sarah salted her potatoes and then took a big bite.

Debra Shelter released a heavy sigh with the familiar wistful look. Knowing her mother as she did, Sarah guessed what her mother was thinking: *If only Patty hadn't died. If only her family hadn't moved back east after the funeral. If only Michael had stuck around. If only Sarah had fallen in love with one of the other bachelors who had come and gone since. There had been lots of other bachelors after all.*

Dat told Sarah she'd closed up her heart after Patty's dying. Sarah believed this to be true for the first year. Mourning her friend had been harder than she'd thought it would be. Yet now? She was ready to love, wasn't she?

Sarah ate her dinner in near silence as her mother chatted about all the community news from the quilting circle. Yet Sarah's thoughts drew her into the lonely journey of "if onlys."

If only Patty hadn't died. From the moment her lifeless body had been pulled from the lake, Sarah wished things could be different. If only she had Patty to talk to, to get advice from. But life didn't work that way. God chose who lived and died. His way was perfect, she'd been told.

Yet how could something be considered "perfect" when it still jabbed her heart like a knife?

Sarah helped *Mem* wash the dishes and then retreated to her room. With Patty still heavy on her thoughts, she moved to the three jars lined up on her dresser. If Patty were still alive, Sarah had no doubt she'd be on that hike — first one in line, leading the others. When Patty was alive, it had been easy to follow her — to be brave. Now it was Sarah's turn to step out.

She needed to talk to *Dat* about climbing Robinson Mountain despite the dangers. Although it was mid-May, snow still clung to high mountain peaks. Even though she hadn't been up there herself, she'd heard the trail was narrow in spots, and bears roaming the hills were always a concern.

Yet Amos's smile filled Sarah's thoughts, pushing away those worries. She'd never find a husband if she kept to herself.

That's why she wouldn't tell *Dat* about her plans quite yet. Telling him too early would give him a week to ponder his concerns. She'd talk to him on Friday. One day would give him plenty of time to fret and to remind her of a hundred things about hiking these hills before she headed out.

She picked up one jar and pulled out the

small pinecone lying on top of its contents. After all, one never knew what gift could be found in the shadow of tall Montana pines.

Some way to spend my tenth birthday, Sarah thought, as she kicked a clump of dirt on the ground. Here they were, living in a small cabin, her sharing one room with all her brothers and sisters, no friends to play with. Only the trees outside the back of the cabin waving their birthday wishes as the branches twisted and shuddered in the wind. Only the forest floor to occupy her. Then again . . . she found things here she'd never seen back home.

Sarah looked down at her apron. Pine needles, a clump of moss, a golden leaf. She'd never found such things in Kentucky. Well, maybe she had, but they seemed extra special here.

Back home, flat land stretched out from her farm in all directions. Here they were surrounded by trees and bushes, except for the narrow dirt road that took them to the main road where the store was. And even the main road was more pothole than path — or at least that's what *Dat* said.

"*Mem*'s not gonna like my dirty apron," she scolded herself. Placing her items on the porch, Sarah ran into the cabin and opened the cupboard under the kitchen sink. There was a jar of clothespins, some cleaning rags, and a bottle of bleach. She moved to the next cupboard over and found pots and pans. The next one had bowls and . . . there. Sarah pulled out an old jelly jar, unscrewed the lid, and raced back outside.

In the distance, she could hear *Dat* and her brothers Joe and Jonathan cutting firewood. *Mem* had walked to the store with Sarah's little sister, Beth, toddling by her side. Sarah dropped her findings into the jar and then looked around. A pinecone would be a good find for her collection. She moved to the stand of trees away from where her father and brothers worked.

She picked up one pinecone, but half of it looked crushed, as if someone had stepped on it. Or *something* had stepped on it. Another one was damp and moldy on one side. Still keeping her eye on the house, Sarah stepped farther into the stand of trees. The air was cooler under the shade of the limbs and leaves. It smelled moister, too, like the muddy pond on their Kentucky farm that she and Jonathan used to throw rocks into.

She found two small pinecones and was

40

examining them to see if they had any flaws when a crashing erupted in the forest. It sounded like a wild horse . . . or a bear. Sarah's heart raced. The pinecones tumbled to the ground.

In Kentucky, children were taught to stay out of horse corrals, but here . . . where could one go in Montana to keep away from bears? Sarah turned and was prepared to run with everything in her when a singsong voice belted through the trees.

"There ya are! I heard a new Amish family was in town. Wheredja come from?"

Sarah turned, slowly. There, through the trees, she saw something unexpected, something wonderful. An Amish girl jogging her direction. Well, at least Sarah supposed she was an Amish girl. The girl wore a *kapp,* but it was tied by the strings around her neck and hung down her back. Dirt streaked her cheeks, and she wore boots far too large for her feet, as if she'd stepped into her father's boots while running out the door.

"Come on," the dark-haired girl called without so much as an introduction. She motioned to Sarah. "What are ya jest standin' there for?"

Sarah glanced over her shoulder, positive the girl was talking to someone else.

The girl paused and put two hands on her hips. "I said, 'What are you jest standing there for?' "

Sarah's eyebrows folded. "Whoever are you talking to?"

"I'm talking to you, silly."

"Me? Well, I can't go anywhere. I . . ." She pointed back at the house. "I was told not to wander off."

The girl brushed brown, wispy hair back from her face and jutted out her chin. "*Ja,* but is it really wandering when I know where I'm going? I won't get you lost."

"Maybe not, but who are you? A stranger, that's what."

"*Ne,* not a stranger, jest a friend you don't know yet. That's how things are up here in the West Kootenai. Our neighbors are jest folks we're working to get to know better."

Sarah smiled. "I like that. I'm Sarah Shelter. And you?"

"Mossy Weathercreek." The girl's eyes widened as she said that name, as if liking the way it rolled off her tongue.

"I've never heard of an Amish girl named Mossy or the last name of Weathercreek. What's yer real name?"

"Today?"

Sarah placed a hand on her hip. "Today

42

and all the days you've been born."

"Today it's Patty Litwiller, but ten years from now, when I turn twenty, it's going to be Patty Beiler. *Mem* says that's how long I have to wait until I marry Jebadiah Beiler. He lives not far from us and has the prettiest green eyes. As green as the moss you have in that jar."

It wasn't until Patty mentioned the moss that Sarah remembered she had the jar in her hands. She glanced down at it, but now the things she'd picked up weren't nearly as interesting as the girl who stood before her.

"Does Jebadiah know you'll be marrying him?" Sarah asked.

"Not yet." Patty smiled. "*Mem* says I need to wait eight years to tell him. She says that to do so now would scare him away faster than a fox chases away a rabbit."

Sarah took a step closer. "Do you have rabbits here?"

Patty nodded so hard Sarah was sure Patty's chin was going to bounce off her chest. "Wild ones. Foxes too. They're small and red and spook easy. I haven't seen one in a while, but they're around. Wanna go look?"

"Tell you what. Why don't I get a jar like

this one, and we can fill it with interesting things."

"Like spiders?" Patty's eyebrows arched into two peaks.

"If you want."

"All right then. The foxes can wait."

"One thing . . ." Sarah pointed to Patty's *kapp.* "You better put that back on."

Patty gasped and pulled it by the strings, back onto her head. "*Gut* thing you said something. If *Mem* saw, I'd be hanging all the laundry fer the next two weeks. You saved my life, Sarah Shelter. Honestly, you did."

CHAPTER 3

Jathan held the hunting rifle in his hand, feeling its weight. One hundred and eighty days. It was how long one needed to reside in Montana before he could be considered a resident and hunt. It was the reason so many bachelors came. Many Amish men from Jathan's hometown of Berlin, Ohio, had gone on this great "out west" adventure. They'd returned with large antlers, but more than that, with stories of rugged mountains, large lakes, raging streams, and abundant wildlife. One of his former schoolmates told Jathan he'd hiked through knee-high snow for a whole day in search of elk without seeing another human. Even though Amish didn't believe in taking photos of themselves, his friend had a photo of the mule elk he'd finally taken down.

Jathan guessed if he got an elk like that, he'd have a photograph taken too. Jathan had hunted plenty of times, and along with the chase and the thrill, he enjoyed the solitude. Growing up the youngest of three older sisters and five older brothers, quiet wasn't something he'd ever known. Not in their house. Not in the barn, as they worked together on chores. Not in their family's woodworking workshop behind their home. Not even in the fields.

Like most Amish farms in their community, land had been divided and shared among families. The expansive farms of his grandfather's day were now small farms insufficient for providing a living for large Amish families. Even in the fields, there were houses nearby, eyes on you, people expecting things. Expecting you to behave as any Amish man should.

Jathan ran his hand down the smooth stock of his rifle. He'd bought the .270 Winchester from Amos's brother. It shined as nice as any of the rifles Jathan had seen thus far. He smirked as he looked around the cabin. A half-dozen other guns hung on gun racks. Many nights were spent chatting about flat-shooting cartridges with punch for mule deer and .32 caliber magnums for grizzlies. They discussed hunting grounds, tags, and gear. What would the others think if Jathan admitted he was just as familiar with the kitchen as a gunshop?

To him, the 180 days meant something else too. It was a break from having to decide about working at the door factory. It was a time to be able to remove the yoke of following in the footsteps of his brothers, who each provided for their families by working in the factory while also tending a small farm. Well, except for his oldest brother, Yonnie, who worked with their father in their workshop. To some, Montana meant adventure, but to Jathan, it meant planning out a business that would make sense even to *Dat.*

Jathan ran his hand down the gun's stock one more time, then slumped onto the wooden chair. At twenty-two years old, he'd worked for enough *Englisch* men to know that the comforts of their life did not bring happiness, but he wouldn't shy away from getting their advice on how to run a business. Maybe he could even talk to Annie at the store.

He rose and stood at the window of the small cabin, looking down the trail that he'd just journeyed the thirty minutes prior. Not more than a mile down that path lived the pretty Amish woman Sarah. Only problem was, her eyes were more focused on Amos. Jathan had lived his whole life being compared to his five older brothers; he should be used to it.

A man walked up the trail, and Jathan recognized him as Edgar from the store. His gray hair was trimmed short and he had a clean-shaven face. His cheeks hung in heavy jowls and his forehead was a map of wrinkles. Amos had mentioned that an experienced mountain guide would be stopping by today. Could this be him? Surely not.

The door swung open, and Edgar stalked in. He looked to be about seventy, but he had a quickness to his step that proved age hadn't slowed him.

"Amos said to drop the trail map off with you."

Jathan rose and set the gun on the gun rack. *"Ja, danki."* He stretched out his hand.

Edgar looked at his hand and paused. "But I'm worried. Have you ever hiked these mountains before?"

Jathan glanced out the window, eyeing the majestic peaks. "Not those."

Edgar cleared his throat. "Have you hiked any mountains?"

Jathan glanced back. "Not really."

The disappointment in Edgar's gaze was clear. "That's what I thought. Don't know why I'd expect anything else."

Even though the man hadn't been in

Jathan's temporary home but two minutes, the words cut to Jathan's heart like one of the sharp-edged hunting knives in the cupboard. With Edgar's whispered accusation, more words swirled through Jathan's head — words that had been spoken long ago but stung as deeply as if they'd been said just yesterday.

"Didn't know a boy could take so long with a little bit of wood and some nails."

"Didn't know deciding on a decent job at the factory could be made into such a big deal."

"Didn't know you were the hiking type."

That last one was one of his father's most recent comments, which came after Jathan had told him he was heading off to Montana for the good part of a year to figure things out. Jathan needed to find a glimmer of hope in the life planned out for him. It was like walking down a tunnel he knew he had to get to the end of without a candle to show him the way. Without even a voice, soft and encouraging, to tell him he was headed the right direction. Was 180 days enough time to figure it out?

Sarah hoped she wasn't too obvious, showing up at the shooting range with a basket of cupcakes swinging at her side. Her excuse was that it was Jonathan's birthday, though she knew he'd be home for dinner and she could have waited until then to give him his favorite snickerdoodle cupcakes.

Her second excuse was that she'd baked far too many cupcakes for Jonathan alone and knew he'd want to share.

She'd waited on the front porch, working on embroidered pillowcases for her hope chest, until she heard the gunshots die down. Then she'd left her handiwork on the porch bench, taken up her basket, and headed out.

The men stood in a circle, gazing at the bits of soda cans, milk jugs, and flowerpots that lay in pieces around their feet.

She approached with slow steps, noting their bright eyes and large smiles. She'd wait until they noticed her and then show them her offerings.

"Whoa, look at this." Amos grabbed a brown beer bottle and held it up. "The top's been shot clean off."

"Who's that good of a shot?" one of the others asked.

The men glanced around at each other and then Amos's eyes landed on his tall friend.

"Jathan, I think it was you."

Jathan readjusted his black hat on his head. "Suppose so. Lucky shot, I guess."

"Luck has nothing to do with it, friend. I have a feeling it'll be a good year fer you, *ja*?" Amos grabbed his friend's shoulder.

Jathan shrugged and, instead of commenting, turned to Sarah as if he'd known she'd been there all along.

"Are those fer us?" He arched his eyebrows.

She narrowed her gaze at Jathan, noticing he wore the same half smile as when he'd seen her without her *kapp. He's not going to let me live that down, is he?*

She ignored him and turned to Jonathan. "They're fer my *bruder* — fer his birthday. I thought he might like to share with his friends." She stepped forward and offered the basket to her brother.

"Snickerdoodle! *Wunderbaar!*" Jonathan took the basket, pulled out a cupcake, and then passed around the basket.

Sarah crossed her arms over her apron and couldn't hide the hint of a smile as she noticed the joy on the men's faces as they dug in.

"These are the best I've ever tasted!" Amos exclaimed. "Sarah, yer going to make some man a great wife someday." The others chimed in agreement. All except Jathan, who still eyed her with humor. She looked away, but from the corner of her eye, she

51

noticed him approaching.

"These really are wonderful," Jathan said, pausing before her. "Have you ever considered opening yer own bakery?"

"Has she considered it?" Jonathan stepped forward, wiping frosting from his upper lip. "It's her dream."

"*Was* my dream." The words spouted from her lips before she could stop them.

"Was?" Jathan stroked his jaw.

"Things have changed. There are more important things I'd rather do. Fulfill the dreams of every Amish young woman." She glanced over at Amos, but instead of listening, he was again picking up shattered objects from the ground.

"It used to be Sarah's dream," Jonathan stated simply. "Used to be all she talked about. She and her friend used to jabber about it late into the night, forgetting that my bed was on the other side of a thin curtain, and I could hear every word, every wish between them."

Sarah glanced at her brother and a knowing look passed between their gazes. Her throat constricted, and she attempted to swallow the emotion away, but it stuck like a shard of broken glass.

"*Ja,* well, sometimes it's the hard things in life that make one realize what matters.

And what doesn't." She picked up a cupcake and took a bite. "A bakery would take time away from a husband and family. People are more important than sugary sweets that only bring joy fer a short time."

Sarah glanced at Jathan, hoping he'd let the matter drop, hoping he'd turn his attention back to the other guys. Instead, his look said he'd wait for her to continue — wanted her to continue. She brushed a stray strand of hair back from her face. What did this Ohio bachelor care about the former dreams of a young girl?

Nothing, she told herself. *Don't let his interested gaze pique yer heart.*

Dear *Dat* and *Mem,*

I hope this letter finds you well. Things are good in Montana. I went target shooting with some friends today. They were impressed with my shot. I have to admit I was too.

The weather is cold here. Even though it's May, frost still covers the ground. Our cabin isn't much more than a shack, and it's not insulated real *gut.* In fact, I woke up to find ice on the inside of the windows this morn.

Mem, I was sorry to hear Aunt Kay is having trouble with her allergies. Will she still be able to help at the bakery? Surely you can't keep up with everything on your own.

It's *gut* to hear *Dat*'s doing well with the woodshop at least. He and Yonnie always made a great team. And to answer your question, *ja,* there are single Amish women in this area, and *ja,* they are pretty. Well, at least one is. That's all I'll tell. And please apologize to *Dat* ahead of time for little sleep tonight as you toss and turn with worry of just what type of young woman your son is falling for. If I can ever get her to look my way for more than twenty seconds, I'll be sure to tell you all you need to know.

Your son,
Jathan

54

CHAPTER 4

"Yer heading up Robinson Mountain today?" *Mem* stood by the large front window
and wore a troubled frown. Her steepled
fingers rested against her lips. "I heard we
have a storm coming."

Dat rocked back and forth in the rocking
chair next to the wood stove with a sleepy
Evelyn on his lap. Evelyn was nearly five.
When Sarah had been that age, she remembered gathering eggs, feeding the chickens,
and even greasing the pans for *Mem*'s
famous carrot cake. Evelyn cuddled on *Dat*'s
lap most mornings and still didn't know
how to muck a stall. Youngest siblings got
off easy, Sarah determined. Evelyn and
Andy grew up in a home where age had
slowed their parents. Time had also softened
them as they realized that there was more
to life than working to look as good as one's
neighbor. Or putting up more canned
goods, baking more pies, and sewing a more

intricate quilt just for the pleasure of offering yourself an invisible pat on the back.

Dat leaned his head back against the rocking chair, readjusted Evelyn in his arm, and then ran a hand down his beard. "No storm today. Should be fine. Supposed to have a cold front come in tonight though. Rain, possibly snow." His words were lazy, slow. He'd be talking differently if he were outside chopping wood. The scent of Evelyn's morning skin and starched sleeping kerchief had apparently brushed worries from *Dat*'s mind.

Sarah put on her hiking boots, thankful *Dat* had insisted on buying them for her years ago. She'd heard of one woman who'd taken quite a fall last year trying to hike in her slick-soled Amish shoes and she'd broken her arm. Sarah shuddered, considering how long it would take — half a day at least — to get good medical care. There wasn't a medical clinic in the West Kootenai and only a small one in Eureka, forty-five minutes away by car. Someone with bad injuries had to go all the way to Kalispell, which was over an hour and a half away. Thankfully, the Amish had *Englisch* drivers who would transport the Amish as needed. Otherwise, medical attention would be completely out of reach.

Mem hurried around the kitchen, pulling out her canisters and jars that held wheat flour, honey, yeast, and other ingredients. Even though breakfast had just finished, *Mem* was already working on *Dat*'s favorite rolls for dinner.

Sarah walked to the kitchen counter, picked up her backpack, and slung its strap over her shoulder. It held her lunch and water bottle.

Mem turned to her. "Do you have enough food? You know how hiking grows one's appetite."

"It's not a long hike. We'll be back by dinner."

Dat pointed to the row of hooks hanging by the front door. "Make sure you take a jacket. Don't want you to catch something."

"*Ja.*" She knew better than to argue. Instead, she offered him a smile, thankful for his attention and care.

Her father, Will Shelter, was one of the most hardworking men in the community. He worked at Montana Log Works on the peeling machine and doubled the production of any man half his age. Because of his broad shoulders and bushy beard, some of his friends called him Will Bear, but *Dat* had a gentleness he expressed when he was with his family.

While he didn't tell Sarah too often that he loved her, she saw it in *Dat*'s eyes. Knew it from the way he continually pestered her. *Dat* always wanted to know she was safe, cared for, and protected, and he ensured she was, not only with his actions but also his prayers. Sarah had seen the warm glow of the lantern light especially early this morning. Her guess was that *Dat* had been up reading his Bible and saying a special prayer for Sarah's hike. She'd not only have her jacket to protect her from the nippy morning air, but she imagined his spoken words going before her up those mountain paths, flowing over each rock, each creek, each ledge.

Her warm breath hung on the chilled air as Sarah walked down the dirt road leading to the store. She was the last one to arrive. A small cluster of her Amish friends had already gathered on the wooden front porch of the West Kootenai Kraft and Grocery. The building was made of logs and had a planked walkway leading up to it, like something from the old west. Sarah's favorite feature was the tall log post near the store. On it were arrows that pointed toward various locations. Each arrow had the name of a place and the distance to it crudely painted on. North Pole — 2,750 miles; South Pole — 9,500 miles; Honolulu, Hawaii — 3,912 miles; Canada — 2 miles. If she had to pick a place to travel to today, Hawaii would be it. Even though it was spring, the mountain breeze was cold.

"Guder Mariye." Sarah smiled at Amos as she approached.

"Good mornin' to you too," he answered.

The others also greeted her with warm hellos, and Sarah readjusted the backpack on her shoulder and offered them a wave.

"Beautiful day fer a hike," Jathan commented.

"Oh, yer coming?" Amos playfully punched his friend's shoulder. "I thought it was jest me and the ladies."

Jathan nodded, and his eyes flashed the same sparkle Sarah had seen the last time they met.

"Well, if you don't want me to come, I can help Annie in the kitchen." He chuckled. "The place is busy today."

Amos scratched his chin, eyeing the business that was part restaurant, part grocery store. One room inside was dedicated to crafts too.

"This log-style building reminds me of yer *mem*'s shop back home." Amos glanced over at Jathan. "Looks almost the same from

59

the outside anyway . . ."

"Ja." Jathan nodded. His lips puckered slightly, and Sarah's heart sank. Did he miss his family? And what kind of shop could his mother have? She eyed him, for the first time realizing that though she saw him in the restaurant every day, she hadn't thought to get to know him — to ask about his family back home.

As if reading her thoughts, Jathan stepped closer. "*Mem* has a bakery back in Ohio. She's been working there since I started school. She's a *gut* baker, like you —"

The rumbling of an extended-cab diesel truck interrupted, diverting Sarah's attention. Sarah knew the sound of the truck as well as any other in these parts. She waved at the older driver, whose trademark cowboy hat was set firmly in place. Millie Arnold parked and jumped down from the cab with the same energy as someone thirty years younger.

"Good morning, crew!" Millie called as she approached. "Where are you youngins off to this early on a Saturday?"

"Robinson Mountain," Hope Peachy announced first. "Just waiting fer our ride."

"Now you be careful up there, especially this time of year." Millie pursed her bright red lips and shook her head. "I wouldn't be surprised if there's still snow clinging to the trails. Not only that, the bears are waking up and they're hungry." She turned and pointed her finger at Jathan's chest. "Tell me, son, you'll do all you can to protect these lovely ladies?"

"*Ja,* of course." His shoulders straightened. "You have my word."

Satisfied, Millie offered them a parting wave. "If you'll excuse me, I need to get my morning coffee and find something to rile up Edgar." She chuckled. "It's been too long since I got him blowing steam, and I need some entertainment." With quick steps she headed inside.

"That's something I'll never get used to," Amos said when the door shut behind her.

"What's that?" Sarah asked.

"The friendships between Amish and *Englisch* here. A conversation like that would never happen in Ohio. Isn't that right, Jathan?"

"*Ja,* but I find it refreshing." Jathan tugged on his gloves and gazed in the direction of the lake. "Jest this morning Edgar told me he's lived in these parts his whole life. And yesterday he brought me this —" Jathan pulled out a piece of paper with some type of hand-drawn map. His brow furrowed. "Don't really understand the chicken scratch, but I appreciate his help."

"Did you know Edgar had family who'd homesteaded here on land that's now underwater?" Eve Peachy interrupted. "When the Libby Dam was built, Lake Koocanusa formed in the valley between the mountains. It's creepy to think that old buildings are still there under the water. In fact, that's not the only creepy thing about the lake. Sarah can tell you something even worse. Can't you, Sarah?"

The guys' gazes turned to Sarah and an image filled her mind. The log store before her faded and was replaced by the image of a beautiful summer day and a canoe in the middle of the lake. She heard Patty's laughter, followed by the scream.

Sarah reached for the pole supporting the porch, but her hands found only air. Her knees softened, and the only thing holding her up was a large hand around her arm. Jathan's hand.

"You all right?" Jathan took a step forward.

As quickly as the image filled her mind it was gone. "Oh, *ja.* I'm sorry." Sarah grabbed her apron, twisting it in her hand. She'd never been so embarrassed. Yet she also refused to talk about Patty's death as if it were just another part of local folklore.

The front door opened, and with a trembling hand, Sarah pointed to the middle-aged man emerging from the store.

"Look, there's our ride. I think it's time to load up." She pulled back slightly, and Jathan released his grip. Then, with quickened steps, Sarah turned and hurried to the waiting van.

If only she could run away from the painful memories as easily.

CHAPTER 5

The thirty-minute drive carried them up the mountain. The road grew narrower as they went along. The ride, bumpier. A locked gate announced they were at the trailhead. An old yellow truck was parked there — other hikers who had beat them to their trek up the hill, no doubt.

With bright faces, the young Amish friends unloaded themselves and their backpacks, and with hardly more than a declaration that he'd be back in six hours, their driver drove away. Sarah kicked at a rock on the road, trying not to watch Amos, who was taking a swig of his water.

Amos returned the water bottle to his pack, tightened the straps of his backpack, and then glanced up, winking at Sarah. "Eager to hike to the peak?"

Sarah tried to ignore the fluttering in her gut brought on by his simple wink. "Eager to be with friends, *ja,* but I'm afraid of how

64

winded I'll get. Baking loaves of bread and plates of cookies isn't the same as hiking mountain paths."

Amos adjusted his wide-brimmed hat. "I'm not worried about the hike, but at that mention of bears . . ." his voice trailed off. "Wish I would have had enough foresight to pack a gun." A small gasp escaped Eve's lips and her face wrinkled up in concern.

"Don't worry." Sarah placed a hand on her friend's shoulder. "God is with us. He watches our every step. I prayed this morning that we'll all be safe. I know my *dat* was up this morning praying too."

Eve nodded but didn't comment. Even though they lived in the same community and attended the same Amish church services, the Peachy family was far more traditional than Sarah's family. While the Peachys spent most of their time with other Amish families, Sarah's parents had forged friendships among the Amish and *Englisch* alike. They'd even occasionally attended prayer meetings with their *Englisch* friends, and if Sarah had learned one thing while living in Montana, it was that God's love extended to all people. One did not need to be in Amish dress to also love God with all of his or her heart.

They started down what looked to be an

old logging skid trail for about a quarter of a mile before their path led them into a heavily wooded area.

Jathan walked beside her, his shoulders drooping as he stared at the ground.

"I have some advice fer you," Sarah dared to say.

He lifted his head and glanced over at her. "You talking to me?" His eyes widened in surprise.

"*Ja* . . . I'm not talking to him." She pointed up at the eagle whose wings were spread wide as he flew in a lazy circle over the trail.

"*Ja,* okay then."

"When you hike, make sure you don't stare at the ground the whole time."

"Excuse me?"

"When you walk . . . I've seen it done many times. One gets so focused on the steps, so worried about stumbling, that he forgets to look up — look around. I know what I'm talking about. Someone told me the very same thing once."

"Good advice." Jathan lifted his head. "I didn't see that eagle until you mentioned him. He was beautiful."

"*Ja,* and I bet you missed the meadowlark back there too."

Jathan nodded. "I did. But I know better

66

now . . ."

They continued on, and the trail soon led them between two rivers. Young Creek and the Yaak River was Sarah's guess. Every now and again, the trees thinned, and Sarah got an occasional view of breathtaking vistas. Small alpine meadows were also scattered along the path.

At one clearing, Amos lifted his gaze to the mountain peaks, a gasp escaping from his lips.

"Amazing," he whispered, taking in the view. "Hard to imagine I grew up not knowing places like this existed." He brushed his bangs back from his forehead. "Nothin' like this near us in Ohio, is there?" he called to Jathan.

"The Yoders' barn is high with a tall peak," Jathan joked.

Laughter spurted from Sarah's lips, and she was pleasantly surprised. Maybe Amos wasn't the only one in their group with a good sense of humor.

A bird chattered in a tree overhead and then flew up to the next tree as if following them.

Sarah pointed. "He's telling all his bird friends to come see these women hiking in dresses and *kapps*." She chuckled and the others joined in.

Soon the trail was only wide enough to go single file, and they fell into line. Amos took the lead. Hope followed right behind. Eve and Sarah walked behind her, and Jathan brought up the rear.

"Yesterday, when I told Edgar we were heading up here, he said this trail was originally used by tribes of Salish and Blackfoot Indians," Jathan said, only loud enough for Sarah to hear. "He said they used this trail to reach the south fork of the Flathead River."

"Really?" Sarah glanced around, trying to imagine Native Americans walking here, carrying all their gear, their little children following.

She glanced over her shoulder, catching his eye briefly. "So is this what you expected?"

"Of the trail?" Jathan asked.

"Of Montana."

"Some."

"Look at that!" Amos pointed ahead. "Wow, amazing!" Sarah looked where he pointed. A black bear stood at the edge of a thicket of trees. They all stopped.

Sarah leaned down, placing her hands on her knees, peering under the tree branches to get a better look. "It's just a small one. Maybe a yearling." Seeing it, the fear that had mounted in Sarah's chest dissipated. "It's a good thing. If that small bear's hanging around here that means the larger, more dangerous bears aren't around."

Jathan and Eve exchanged glances, and Hope hurried past them to get a closer look. Amos let out a whoop, tossing his hat into the air. "I jest can't believe it. My first bear."

Hearing the commotion, the bear lifted its head, turned, and lumbered up a hill. They all watched until it disappeared into the brush.

Amos turned to Sarah. A sly grin filled his face. "You must think I'm pretty silly, don't you?" He readjusted his wide-brimmed straw hat on his head.

"Not at all. I was the same way when I first came. I remember seeing my first moose. I went out to hang the wash one morning with *Mem,* and there it was, sniffing our clothesline." She bit her lip, remembering that Patty had stayed over the night before that event. She and Patty had danced around the porch in excitement until the moose lumbered away.

Amos nodded, and they continued following the rest of the group. When the trail narrowed again, he again took the lead with Sarah right behind him.

She studied the back of Amos's head,

wishing he'd turn around. Her emotions were the same as they'd been that day on Lake Koocanusa. She'd wanted Michael to look at her, pay attention.

Time had passed and the surroundings had changed, but inside, Sarah felt as needy as ever. An ache grew in her chest.

But maybe this day shouldn't be about trying to catch Amos's eye. If nothing else, she'd at least build better friendships and find a few special discoveries to tuck inside her memory jar. She didn't know what — she had enough stones and pinecones already — but there'd be something, she guessed, since sometimes the best treasures were unexpected.

"Are you sure we should be wandering off this far?" eleven-year-old Sarah asked as they walked through the woods behind Patty's house. It had been a long winter, something Sarah hadn't been used to in Kentucky. The snow had piled up to the bottom of the windowpanes. Instead of on buggy wheels, most of her Amish neighbors traveled through the wooded wilderness roads in horse-drawn sleighs.

Yet the snow had melted now, and the ground was only slightly muddy. Sarah looked down at her simple flat-soled shoes. Mud clung to them, but she wasn't worried. She could wipe it off with a damp cloth. It was her stockings she worried about. They were splattered with mud. Thankfully, she and Patty wore the same size. More than once, Patty had given Sarah clean stockings to wear home, tossing the dirty ones into her mother's wash basket. Patty's mother didn't seem as worried about dirt as Sarah's mother was.

They continued on, stepping over fallen logs, pushing low tree branches out of their way. A hint of chill was in the air and a light wind caused the new, spring leaves to sway.

"So where are we going again?" Sarah pushed her kapp off, allowing the sunlight filtering through the trees to warm her head.

"Shh, I'm concentrating."

Sarah paused. "Concentrating? Are we lost?"

Patty turned around in a slow circle. "Not lost. Jest need to find my path."

"Yer path?"

"*Ach,* I came out here the other day. I put markers down. They were leading . . ." Patty's voice trailed off. She shielded her eyes with her hand, like an explorer in one of Sarah's storybooks. "They lead to a hill."

71

"A hill?" Sarah didn't see a hill, but to the right, the ground rose up slightly. She pointed. "Like that?"

Patty clapped her hands, and then raced in the direction of the "hill." Her *kapp* bounced on her back as she ran. Her dark hair pulled out from her pinned-up bun.

Sarah had no choice but to follow.

Her legs pumped as she moved through the forest. The moist air smelled like spring. Overhead, two birds chattered and flew along, as if joining them. Finally, Sarah's legs carried her up the rise to where Patty stood. Sarah stopped in her tracks. On the other side of the rise was a large pond. Tall green trees circled it. The water was still and deep green. A turtle skimmed across the surface. Sarah sucked in a breath.

"You found this place?" She turned to Patty.

Her friend's wide smile was the answer.

"And this isn't even the best part." Patty waved a hand. "Come on."

Sarah followed Patty around to the other side of the pond, and they headed back into woods.

"Are you sure we should be doing this?" Sarah asked again. Patty didn't answer, which meant the answer was *no.* Sarah had known the answer was no even before she asked.

They slowed their steps as they walked. The trees were thicker here, closer together and taller. Less sun filtered through the trees, and the whole forest took on shades of gray. Sarah reached out and took Patty's hand. Patty squeezed it and pulled Sarah forward with her.

Just when Sarah was about to urge Patty to turn around, an image appeared before her. It was an old cabin.

The log walls were gray from age and moss grew on the roof. One of the windows was broken. There was no front door, but the door hinges were there, almost as if someone picked up the door and hauled it off.

"Did you go inside?" Sarah paused her steps.

"I looked inside, but I was waiting." Patty turned to her and smiled.

"Waiting?"

"For us to explore together."

Sarah squared her shoulders. "I'm not going in."

"*Ja,* we will together." Patty tugged on her arm. "There are pretty things inside fer yer memory jar."

Sarah tilted her head at those words.

"Like what things?"

"There's a shelf of things. I saw an old clock. A jar of coins. Books."

Sarah's brow furrowed. "Yer making that up."

Patty jutted out her chin. "Check fer yerself."

Sarah released Patty's hand and stepped forward toward the cabin. The closer she got, the more light flowed into the clearing, brightening the area around her. She stopped before the door and looked inside. Sarah's jaw dropped. She glanced back at Patty and her friend's eyes glowed with excitement. Patty leaned forward eagerly, and Sarah felt Patty's eyes on her as she stepped in.

A layer of dirt, mud, and dead pine needles covered the wooden floor.

"See, I told you," Patty called from the doorway.

Sarah stepped closer to the shelf. There were the things Patty had mentioned and a few other items too. She reached her hand forward, hovering it over the jar of coins, and then paused. No, she wouldn't touch those. They seemed important, like they would be valuable, and if Sarah brought old coins back, her mother or father would want to know where she'd gotten them. Instead, Sarah reached for a key. It was thin, with a circle on one end and a little knob on the other. Dust covered it. Sarah blew off the dust, watched it float through the air.

Her heart pounded. She turned around and held up the key for Patty to see.

"Do you think it's okay to take this?" Sarah asked.

Patty nodded. "I don't think no one's gonna come lookin'. 'Specially since there isn't no door fer that key to go into."

Sarah grasped it in her hand. "What about you? Are you going to take something?"

"I don't know." Patty shrugged. "My memory jar isn't like yers." She tapped the side of her temple. "I carry my memories up here." Then she tapped her chest, right over her heart. "And here."

"I carry my memories in those places too." Sarah puckered her lower lip. "Are you saying I don't?"

Patty sighed, then she reached out and grabbed up a matchbook. "I wasn't saying that. Just saying we're different. You like to find things; I like to search fer them."

"*Ja,* I know, but maybe you'll change yer mind. Maybe later, when yer old, you'll hold that matchbook up and remember this time we had together."

"Yer right." Patty pointed back out the door. "We should get going before my *mem* starts to worry."

Sarah nodded, but something else caught her attention. It was a rock. It looked like a large chunk of gravel, but there were all types of glittery things inside. The glittery bits were pieces of white rock mixed into the chunk like huckleberries mixed into ice cream. Sarah put it in the same hand as the key and then followed Patty out. As they walked back, she thought about what Patty had said.

Am I all about the finding? she thought.

She supposed so. Maybe she should be more like Patty, who found just as much happiness in the searching. Then again, the small items Sarah tucked away reminded her of the journey. They reminded her that no matter how far she'd wandered off, she always returned home with another treasure to tuck into her jar.

CHAPTER 6

It seemed like the trail would never end, and the blisters on Sarah's toes made it all the worse.

God is with us. He watches over our every step. Sarah had said those words to Eve just a few hours ago, and here she was fretting. She needed to enjoy the journey. Needed to appreciate this time with her friends, not just feel satisfied on the peak.

Yet the words had barely replayed through her mind when Sarah felt her next step go wrong. The toe of her right boot caught on a rock, and her left foot jerked forward to catch herself. Her left ankle twisted, and Sarah felt a sharp pull. The world around her turned gray, and she grabbed Eve's arm to steady herself.

Eve paused, grasping Sarah's shoulders. "You okay?"

Sarah nodded and grimaced. "Oh, *ja,* jest a bad step." She stepped on it again. Another pain shot up her leg. Sarah hobbled forward.

Jathan's eyes narrowed in concern. "Maybe we should go back."

Sarah waved a hand at him and forced a smile. "Jest a little twist. I'll be fine in a moment." She nodded her head as if doing so would convince herself it was true. "Besides, we should be at Lake Geneva soon. Isn't that what yer map says?"

Jathan eyed the piece of paper. "I'm not sure. I know this must make sense to Edgar, but I don't think it's helping much." He tucked it into his pocket.

Sarah did her best to continue on without a limp.

Her act must have convinced Amos, Eve, and Hope, because they continued on without much of a pause. But Jathan stayed by her side.

Sarah smiled. This time it wasn't for show. She appreciated Jathan's obvious attraction but hoped he wouldn't be disappointed. After all, it was Amos who captured her interest, wasn't it?

After thirty minutes, Sarah could finally hear the sound of rushing water. She rounded a corner, and there was a creek . . . not beside the trail, but over it. Beyond that, the shore of the lake.

Amos paused beside her, looking down at the water they had to cross. "Looks deep."

"Spring runoff does that to the rivers in these parts. I jest never expected we'd have to cross one," Sarah said.

She eyed the rocks that jutted up from the water, knowing they'd be how the group got across the creek. Her ankle offered a gentle throbbing that matched the beating of her heart. *How am I going to do this?* One slip and she'd be in water up to her waist.

The others crossed with no problem, jumping from rock to rock. Sarah stood at the water's edge, knowing it wasn't possible for her.

Without being asked, Jathan hopped back to the rocks in the center of the creek and held out a hand. "Grab my hand and I'll help you." He pointed to the rock she should step on. "I promise I won't let you fall."

Sarah took his hand. It was large and wrapped around her smaller one with tenderness. Jathan's eyes met hers, and he smiled. His chin jutted out slightly and his shoulders straightened as if helping her wasn't a chore, but an honor. She stepped out, clinging to his hand. He guided her with gentle motions and then released her hand on the other side.

"Thank you." She looked up at him, noticing for the first time what beautiful, kind eyes he had.

"My pleasure, Sarah."

She'd never heard anyone say her name like that, like a rose blooming from his lips. The ache of her ankle felt dull compared to the heat spreading through her chest.

Jathan . . . Is he the unexpected gift of this day?

The view opened up as Sarah approached the lake. It sat in a large bowl with mountains on three sides. Numerous waterfalls fell from the rock on the other shore. Sarah bent down and brushed her fingers over the surface of the water, but even this beauty didn't distract her from Jathan's closeness.

"What are you doing? Testing the water before you jump in?" Jathan chuckled as he squatted beside her.

"Oh *ne.* Just splashing in the snow." She offered a smile, remembering Patty saying nearly the same thing.

Twin peaks rose straight ahead. Amos pointed to one farther left. "That is Robinson Mountain."

"How do we get up there?" Eve asked.

"According to Edgar's note, we go to that rock slide on the other side of the lake and climb it." Jathan's eagerness to find the trail in the rock slide was clear, and Sarah didn't want to disappoint him — or disappoint the others.

She took a long drink from her water bottle, and then took the lead.

"I've never climbed a rock slide before . . ." She tried to sound cheery.

"Don't you want to eat lunch here?" Amos called after her.

Sarah shook her head. "Why don't we wait until we get to the top? Then we can really relax!" She spoke more from fear than eagerness. If she paused, it would be impossible to get up.

The climb wasn't as hard as she thought it would be. As long as she led with her good foot, she was able to scale the rocks fairly quickly.

"Well done." Amos grinned when they reached the top. "I'm going to have to call you Sarah Mountain Goat from now on."

Sarah crossed her arms and pretended to scowl. "Why, thank you. How flattering."

They continued on. The trail became steeper, more dangerous. Snow clung to the ledges, and the path gave way to drop-offs on both sides. The rocky trail was made up of what looked to be quartz. It sparkled beautifully in the sunlight but made the trail slippery, especially where there was snow.

Sarah paused, picking up a large nugget of quartz. It looked like a large piece of gravel with shiny specks.

"So this is where it came from," she said between ragged breaths.

"What?" Jathan paused beside her.

"Oh, there's an old cabin . . . deep in the woods behind . . . where the Sommer family lives now. A friend and I . . . came upon it years ago, and I found . . . a rock like this." The elevation was high. Even though she was sucking in large breaths, the breaths didn't satisfy her lungs. "It makes me smile to think that an occupant . . . from years and years ago hiked this same trail."

Her ankle burned as if it were on fire. Tears rimmed her lower lashes. Sarah knew they were partly from the pain and partly because it had been Patty who had led her to that cabin.

Jathan placed a hand on her arm, and she paused.

"Is it yer ankle, Sarah?"

She limped toward a large boulder. "It really smarts. You better go ahead."

"We can't leave you behind." Jathan's voice rose an octave. Upon hearing his words, the others paused and turned.

"No, really, I'll be fine." She waved her hand toward a vista as pretty as had ever been painted. "It's not a bad view to have to sit and take in."

"But if there's another bear . . . No, I'm not going to leave you. I promised . . ."

"A bear up here? Above the tree line? *Ach,* I don't think so." She pointed. "Look, I can see in all directions. No bear is going to sneak up on me." She wiped away a tear and tried to hide the pain. "Besides, if I see one, I'll sing really loudly. That will scare him away."

The others circled around her, looking unsure.

"Look, the top is jest right there." She pointed up the trail. "It'll probably take you only fifteen minutes to get up there. I'll be fine." She pulled up her backpack and set it on her lap. "I'll jest be sitting here eating my lunch."

Amos stroked his jaw. "You sure?"

Sarah turned to Jathan, knowing he was the one she had to convince. "*Ja,* really. I'll be all right."

Jathan eyed her. He looked up the trail and then back to her again. "If you think so . . ."

"Yer wasting time. See, if you hadn't argued so, you'd already be up and back." She playfully slugged the taller man's arm. "And then on the way down, we can talk,

83

ja? I'd like to hear more about yer *mem*'s bakery. And yer dreams too." Sarah glanced up at him, ignoring the stares of the others. "I'm sure you have some ideas for yer future, Jathan. But get on yet or the darkness will be here and we'll miss our ride!"

The trail was longer than it had looked when they'd left Sarah. Jathan had thought it would only be a ten-minute walk, but they'd been gone at least thirty. Worry caused his heart to pound even more than the exertion. Then, just when he'd convinced himself he needed to turn back, the trail opened up to a small plateau and there sat an old lookout cabin.

"Wouldja look at that." Amos picked up his pace, and Jathan joined him. Almost the entire face of the cabin had been carved with people's initials. As he paused before it, Amos pulled out a pocket knife and set to work carving. Jathan thought about joining him, but it wasn't his name he wanted to carve. It was Sarah's. And now, standing here at the top without her, he wished he would have stayed by her side.

"We shouldn't stay too long," Jathan said.

"*Ja,* well, tell them that." Amos pointed to Hope and Eve. They'd passed the top of the trail and were heading over the other side.

Jathan's jaw dropped. "Where do they think they're going?"

Amos shrugged. "Canada? I hear the border is only a half-mile from here."

Jathan didn't wait for Amos to finish carving his initials. He quickened his pace and caught up with Eve and Hope. They'd stepped down to a rocky area that overlooked a majestic view. Hills rolled down from where they sat — slopes covered with trees arrayed in fresh green leaves. In the distance, snow-covered mountain peaks jutted into the sky.

As Eve and Hope ate their lunch, they chatted about some of the other bachelors, and Jathan found himself forgetting about Sarah for a moment. Instead, his heart leaped in awe of God's handiwork. For a strange reason, he wanted to grab both girls by the shoulders and say, "Look at this. Look what God has done!"

Instead, he walked a short distance away and sat on an outcropping of rock. A warm sensation flooded over him. One he had never felt before. It was as if God had moved from "out there" to right in the middle of his chest.

Jathan blew out a long, slow breath, never

wanting this knowing of God's nearness to leave, but fearful of it all the same.

He'd grown up knowing about God. His people spent their whole existence ordering their lives with God at the center, but at this moment, it was as if a curtain had been pulled back. Reality replaced knowledge. The heat grew within Jathan and filled his chest and limbs. It was as if his heart had swallowed up some of the sunbeams that hit his shoulders and then radiated them through the rest of his body.

Dear God, his soul whispered. *I know I'm running. Maybe I've known all along that it's also what I'm running to. Maybe I came to Montana because I'm running to you.*

The thought grew and took root in his mind like a small acorn in dark rich soil. He'd brought his Bible and had read it every day. He'd attended the church services and had really listened. And when he had sung, he'd paid attention to the words. He'd prayed about more challenging things, like how to handle returning home. But at this moment, another prayer touched his lips. Jathan needed to pray for Sarah.

God, be with her. Watch over —

The words had barely pulsed through his mind when fear crashed over the peace in his soul.

86

He jumped to his feet and turned. Amos was already there, standing just behind him on another rock. Amos glanced at Jathan. His smile fell. "You all right? Yer face is as white as Eve's *kapp.*"

"We need to head back. I have a bad feeling about Sarah."

Amos narrowed his gaze. "A bad feeling?"

"Jest . . ." How could he explain it? He shook his head. "We've been gone too long already, that's all."

When they passed by the lookout cabin, Jathan sent up a silent vow that he would return. He didn't want to get his hopes up, but he did like the idea of carving Sarah's name into that building . . . especially with her by his side.

CHAPTER 7

The sun moved toward the western horizon, and Sarah scanned the trail. *Where could they be?* She strained to hear their voices, but the only sound was birdsong from a distant tree.

What could be taking them so long? Should she hike up to find them?

No, that wasn't possible. Not with her ankle.

She gazed up at the sun and tried to guess the time. Two o'clock, maybe? Three o'clock? She wished she'd borrowed *Dat*'s pocket watch.

She could start down the trail, and they could catch up with her. Maybe that would be better, since she was going to have to walk slower than the rest of them.

But if they came to the rock and didn't see her, they'd worry.

She looked through her backpack, wishing she had something on which she could leave a note. She had no paper, no pens, but . . . she thought of something else.

As quickly as she could, Sarah picked up nuggets of quartz and formed an arrow on the path.

The wind picked up. Dark clouds gathered in the south and moved Sarah's direction. Just seeing them made Sarah shiver.

She pulled her jacket from her backpack and put it on. She hobbled down the hill, and the pain shooting out from her ankle caused her stomach to lurch. Tears filled her eyes. She brushed them away with the back of her hand.

She walked on, but there was no sign of the others behind her. Had someone slipped off a snowy part of the trail? Had they come across a bear? She doubted it at their elevation, but one never knew.

Sarah's shoulders quivered. She wasn't sure if it was from the breeze, the thought of bears, or the greater worry of what had happened to her friends.

She hobbled on until the open ledges were behind her, and trees lined the trail once again. It meant she was getting closer to the lake, but the pain in her ankle was almost too much to bear.

At least another thirty minutes passed. The storm darkened the sky, and soon the clouds began spitting speckles of rain.

Sarah tried to pray for help but no words came. Yet something caught her attention. Just as the trail turned, she noticed a path leading into the trees. It was wide enough for two people to enter. Was it another path from the lake they hadn't known about? It made sense. There had to be a better way to get from the rock to the trail than by climbing down a rock slide.

She looked down the new trail, noticing that it wound gently down the hill. It looked easier to go down. Easier than jumping down the rock slide to get to the lake.

"Lord, I think finding this trail was from you. Please watch my steps. *Guide* my steps." She moved forward, thankful the ground was softer on this trail.

She continued on, step by step, hurrying as fast as she could while hoping the others weren't as worried about her as she was about them. She walked farther and the trail narrowed. The trees pressed in. Instead of looking to the left and right as she had coming up the mountain, Sarah focused her eyes forward. If something was out there, she didn't want to know.

Then, just when she thought she should be upon the lake, the foot trail disappeared before her. The trees had grown thicker, darkening the sky around her. Snow clung to their bases. Sarah turned in a slow circle, eyeing the ground. If the trail was here, it was hidden under a layer of snow.

Suddenly, she wasn't sure why she'd headed off the main trail or even what direction she'd headed. Even the trail she'd just walked down seemed no more than a steep, narrow path when she looked back up at it.

She could have been walking in the opposite direction of Lake Geneva for all she knew. She cocked her head and lifted her ear, listening for the roar of water from the waterfalls and creek. Only silence met her ears.

To make things worse, Sarah's ankle was past the point of only throbbing.

She looked around and noticed a fallen log. Part of it looked dry. She sat on it, and as she did, the pain radiating up her leg caused her heart to pound harder. Sweat beaded on her forehead, and she considered rolling down her stockings and checking her ankle for swelling and bruising, but fear changed her mind. She didn't want to see. Didn't want to know how bad off she really was.

Stupid, stupid, she'd told herself. She pressed her hands over her white apron, smoothing it. She pressed and smoothed it over and over again, while her heart pounded in her chest.

She'd lived here long enough to have heard many stories of people who set off by themselves in the woods only to get lost. It wasn't like she was a tourist. It's not like she didn't know better.

The cold wind picked up again, and Sarah pulled her arms closer to her chest.

She also thought about her friends, but instead of worrying, anger heated her cheeks. Why had they taken so long? Didn't they know she couldn't wait all day?

A sick feeling settled in her heart — the same feeling as when Patty had paddled out onto the lake.

"Ach, ne." Maybe the feeling came not because something was going to happen to her friends, but because something was going to happen to her. Who was she fooling? She was lost and injured and afraid. Something had already happened.

Don't be afraid. It wasn't an inner voice that spoke to her, but rather the memory of what she'd told Eve.

Sarah lowered her face into her hands and shook her head. Then she lifted it up quickly, eyeing the trail — the path she'd just struggled down.

Maybe this was a path worn down not by

humans but by the animals that called this mountain home. She studied the trees as if expecting a bear to lumber through the forest at any moment.

Don't panic, Sarah. Think, think.

What had Jonathan told her about his hunting trips? Ah, she remembered. An expert hunter was like a detective, searching for clues. She hadn't spotted any animal footprints on the trail, even though the ground was soft. That had to be a good sign. She looked around, searching for any sign of freshly broken limbs or old, dead leaves that had been disrupted on the forest floor. She didn't see any signs that an animal had used this path in a while. Sarah breathed out a sign of relief and then bit her lip.

That didn't mean one wouldn't come this direction though.

She considered heading back up the trail, the way she'd come, but the pain in her ankle made that impossible. Besides, what had *Dat* told her to do if she ever got lost? Don't move. The people who tried to find their way out were often the ones who were never found alive.

Something didn't seem right to Jathan. They walked the dirt path down the mountain, but the path seemed slightly different than before. Wider maybe. He also noticed dried horse manure on the trail. Had he seen that on the way up? Maybe it *had* been there, but he'd been focused on other things, or rather people — Sarah.

"So Jathan, what type of game are you hoping to hunt for this season?" Hope stretched her legs as she walked beside him, trying to keep up with his long-legged gait.

"Deer, elk, not sure."

Their pace was quicker than when they'd headed up. The slope helped with that. His eagerness to see Sarah and make sure she was safe had something to do with it too.

"Oh, *ja.*" Hope gave a simple reply, most likely guessing he didn't want to talk.

They continued on for what seemed like thirty minutes, forty. The sky to the south darkened and at each turn Jathan was sure they would come across Sarah.

Where was she? He picked up his pace to a jog now, worry flooding over him.

"Hey, what are you doing?" Amos called behind him.

Just ahead, something on the trail caught Jathan's attention and he paused. It was a log. He rushed up to it and looked down. It wasn't a new log, but one that had been there a while. One he surely would have seen on his way up. Fear stabbed his heart like a hot knife, and suddenly he knew why he hadn't seen it. Why they hadn't come upon Sarah yet.

His hands balled into fists at his sides and he kicked the log. Bits of wood splintered off and scattered on the trail. Jathan removed his wide-brimmed hat from his head and tossed it to the ground. How could he be so stupid?

"Hey, Jathan . . . ." Amos bent over and picked up the hat, handing it to him. "What's wrong?"

"We took the wrong trail. It's my fault. It's my fault."

Eve and Hope rushed closer. Their cheeks were red from exertion. They stood silently, unsure of what was happening.

Jathan pointed to the log. "That wasn't here. And where is all the snow we trudged over? I've been noticing horse manure on the way down that wasn't there on the way up. This isn't the right trail. We went the wrong way."

Amos's eyes widened and a gasp escaped his lips. "Sarah."

"*Ja!*" Jathan ran his hand through his hair. "And it's my fault."

Amos sank into a squatting position and shook his head. "Come to think of it, we faced the cabin when we climbed the hill and we walked parallel to it when we left."

"Oh *ne.*" Hope's hand flew to her mouth. "Oh *ne,* oh *ne.*" She looked to Jathan. "It's not yer fault, it's mine."

Her sister grasped her arm. "What? What is it?"

"*Dat* told me something important this morning when we were leaving. You were still putting on yer hiking boots, but when I walked outside, he paused from chopping wood and told me to watch ourselves. He also told me to watch the trails, because there are two that go to the summit of Robinson Mountain. One for people, one for horses. He said horses can get jumpy, so it's best not to take the horse trail up . . . or down." She looked to Amos and then Jathan. "I'm so sorry. I was upset with my sister fer going so slow and was not paying *gut* attention. I forgot he mentioned it until now."

"That means Sarah's on the other trail," Amos spouted.

"It also means we have to find a way to get back to her, and fast."

"Look!" Eve pointed through the trees. Jathan followed her finger and noticed a glimmer of light blue. It was the lake. It was farther down than he thought it would be. He doubted they were even halfway down this trail. Who knew how it wound around to the lake? It could take another hour — time they didn't have.

"I'm heading back up." Jathan rolled up his sleeves, adrenaline pumping through him.

"Why up? Don't you think it would be better to go down? Maybe Sarah has already started that way." Amos looked to the sky. "Surely if she saw the storm coming she would have started down."

A stirring in his chest told Jathan otherwise. "Maybe not. Maybe she's still waiting. Maybe she headed up the hill looking fer us." He blew out a breath. "I'd rather run up this path and find the right trail than go all the way to the bottom and have to climb back up the other side. And also, what if we get to the lake and she's not there? We won't know if she continued on to where our driver is going to pick us up or if she's still on the hill. If I go to the top and head down, I'll be able to check the path she was on all the way from the top."

"*Ja,* that makes sense." Amos crossed his arms over his chest. "Should I go with you?"

Panic widened Eve's eyes, and Hope clung to her sister.

"*Ne.*" Jathan shook his head. "Make sure these two get down safely. If Sarah's not at the lake, keep going. Go all the way to the van."

"And then what?" Eve asked. "Should we ask the driver to wait, or should we go back to town and get help?"

Jathan rubbed his eyes, unsure of the answer.

"I doubt you'll get there before three o'clock, and the driver will already have been waiting for a while."

"Wait a while more, I suppose. Maybe thirty minutes. And if we don't come by five o'clock . . . or it gets too dark because of the storm . . . then go for help. Sarah's injured, and I don't want her trying to walk down a dark trail. If worse comes to worst, we'll have to stay the night in these woods . . . but I want to make sure Sarah won't have to do so alone."

Twelve-year-old Sarah turned over on her side. Not hearing Patty's breathing, she stretched out her hand and felt the bed next to her. The mattress was warm, but just barely.

Sarah sat up, rubbed her eyes, and then opened them. "Patty?" she whispered into the dark room. No one answered, and Sarah kicked off the covers and then stood.

The door to Patty's room was partly open. Sarah checked her sleeping kerchief to make sure it was still in place and then hurried through the door into the living room.

Sarah's toes curled up as she walked on the cold, wood floor. A crackle snapped in the woodstove as the flames died down. Sarah looked in the kitchen first, checking to see if Patty had gotten up to get a drink of water. She wasn't there. Then Sarah looked at the stairs, wondering if Patty'd gone up to her parents' room. She doubted it. Sarah checked the bathroom, but still no Patty. Then Sarah got an idea and hurried to the mat beside the front door. Sure enough, Patty's shoes were missing.

Sarah opened the door and stepped outside. The air was cold. She looked to her left and then to the right. There . . . Patty sat on the porch swing, a quilt wrapped around her shoulders.

"Sarah. What are you doin'? No shoes, no blanket? Hurry now." Patty opened the quilt. Sarah gladly sat beside Patty and pulled one side of the quilt all the way around her, tucking it under her chin.

"What are *you* doing out here?" Sarah dared to ask. "It's the middle of the night."

Patty looked at her. The moonlight lit

Patty's face.

"Don't you get up at night jest to look at the stars?"

Sarah shook her head and a soft laugh slipped from her lips. "Can't say I do."

"*Ja,* me neither, but I thought it would be a good time to start, now that we're getting older."

Sarah playfully punched Patty's knee under the quilt. "*Ach,* we're far from old."

"I disagree. Nearly thirteen and only a little more than a year left in school. We need to pay attention to things."

Sarah rested her head on the back of the porch swing and kicked her feet against the porch so they rocked. "Like those stars up there? Is that what we're supposed to pay attention to?"

"*Ja,* and the sounds of the forest. Do you hear that?"

Sarah listened but didn't hear anything other than the chains of the porch swing creaking. She was just about to tell Patty when she heard what sounded like crying.

Sarah's eyes widened. "Is that a baby?"

"*Ne,* a coyote."

"Will it hurt us?"

Patty shook her head. "No, *Dat* says they're special. When there are coyotes here, we know it's safe and the wolves aren't around. Or bears either."

"That's good. I'll have to remember that."

"Yer special too, Sarah." Patty turned to her and smiled. Then she pointed to the ground. "See, even yer moon shadow is pretty-like."

Sarah followed Patty's gaze. The moon had cast their shadows onto the porch. Sarah touched her sleeping kerchief, noticing the way it stuck up. She chuckled. "Speaking of coyotes, it looks like I have coyote ears in that shadow."

They sat and rocked a bit longer, and Sarah looked at the stars that filled the velvet-black sky. It amazed her that a God who made all of the stars — filled the sky with them — would think of her, make her.

After a while Sarah's toes felt like ice. "Can we go inside yet? I'd hate to have yer *Dat* and *Mem* come out here in the morning and find us frozen solid."

Patty yawned. "*Ja.* All better now." They rose and scooted together toward the front door, the quilt still wrapped around them.

"What's better?" Sarah smiled when they stepped into the house and shut the door behind them. Even though the fire had died down, the inside was much warmer than it was outside.

"I'm better." Patty shook her head. "I

woke up after a bad, bad dream. I was lost up on the mountain. It was cold, and even though I screamed and screamed, nobody came fer me. *Mem* always told me to think of *gut* things when I have bad dreams, so I thought of God and the stars and my best friend."

Patty hurried back to her bedroom and climbed under the blankets. Sarah followed and realized that if she'd had a nightmare, she would have thought of the very same things.

She also trembled, thinking how horrible it would be to be lost and alone like in Patty's dream. Thankfully, she didn't have to worry about that. She could push those thoughts from her mind and fall back to sleep to the sound of Patty's soft breathing.

CHAPTER 8

"Wake up, Sarah. Yer jest dreaming," she whispered into the cold forest. "Jest like Patty used to have nightmares about being lost in the woods, maybe this is jest a dream." The only problem was, this wasn't a dream. It was real. Yet knowing that, Sarah also knew Patty's solution to pushing bad dreams out of her mind would work in this situation as well. *I'll think of God and the stars and my best friend.*

So she did that. She thought of God, who was with her now. Who had brought glimpses of peace even when her heart ached most.

She thought of the stars. So far away, yet glowing because God made them. If he created universes like that, couldn't he control the bears in one square mile around her?

And when she thought of a friend, the strangest thing happened — it was Jathan's face that filled her mind. She hadn't tried to impress him, instead she was impressed. He was gentle, kind, easy to talk to. He was handsome and full of humor. Why hadn't she noticed it before?

Just like with Patty, Sarah hadn't realized what she needed — whom she needed — until God stepped in. She just hoped God would step in again and help Jathan find her. Deep down, she knew he was looking. "Hello? Help! Somebody!" she called as she had been for the last hour. "Somebody? Jathan!"

It was mostly dark now because of the storm. Only a gray glow through the clouds told her the sun hadn't completely gone down. She was frozen. Her skin was numb, and it would only get colder as the night pressed in. Why hadn't she thought about putting some essentials in her backpack like matches and warm socks and more food?

She had a few cookies left over from earlier. She'd packed extras for her friends. She ate two and saved one for . . . for when? Later in the night? Or morning? She hoped it didn't come to that, but guessed it could. Had the others made it to the driver and the van? Were they heading back to the West Kootenai even now to call for help? Surely they weren't lost on this mountain too.

Her guess was they'd already made it

down and would call search and rescue, but living in Montana as long as she had, she knew a few things about search and rescue. They had to come from Kalispell, which was over an hour-and-a-half drive away. They also never launched search parties at night, but waited until morning to keep members of their own team safe.

Sarah looked in her backpack again, as if wishing something else would show up. Even her water bottle was empty. She'd finished that off earlier when she was hiking, thinking she was almost back to the lake and the spring.

He is with me. God is watching over me. He knows where I am. He's sending someone to find me even now . . .

As those thoughts looped in her mind, Sarah started to sing as loudly as she could. She hoped it would scare away any wildlife. Or maybe someone on the trail might hear her. But mostly, she hoped it would calm her own pounding heart.

"Sweet are the promises,
    Kind is the word,
    Dearer far than any message man
        ever heard;
    Pure was the mind of Christ,
    Sinless I see;

He the great example is, and pattern
   for me.
"Where he leads I'll follow,
   Follow all the way.
   Where he leads I'll follow,
   Follow Jesus ev'ry day.
"Sweet is the tender love
   Jesus hath shown,
   Sweeter far than any love that mortals
   have known;
   Kind to the erring one,
   Faithful is he;
   He the great example is, and pattern
   for me.
"Where he leads I'll follow,
   Follow all the way.
   Where he leads I'll follow,
   Follow Jesus ev'ry day."

Sarah sang her mother's favorite hymn two times through, and after the second time, just as she was about to sing again, she heard the sound of movement. Large movement, like something clambering through the forest. She thought about calling out. After all, maybe it was Jathan or Amos. Yet as the sound grew louder, Sarah wrapped her arms around herself, fear freezing her like a statue. A scream rose in her throat but stuck there. Just when she thought for certain she'd see the snout of a gigantic bear, something appeared. The form moving down the pathway was a man!

Sarah rose and waved her arms. "Jathan! Here! I'm here!"

Jathan tried to stop in his tracks, but his momentum slid him forward.

She expected a scolding for going off the trail. She waited for his explanation for why they hadn't shown up. But instead, Jathan rushed forward and stood before her, taking her hands in his. His hands were warm, and she resisted the urge to step into his embrace and let his whole body warm her.

"Sarah, I'm so sorry. Will you forgive me?"

"Forgive you?" She tilted her head back. Surprise arched her eyebrows.

"First, that I left you alone on the trail. And second . . ." He squeezed her hands tighter. "Second, it's my fault yer here. At the top, I was in such a hurry to get down, to see you, that I led us down the wrong trail. There are two trails leading down from the top," he explained. "We had no idea until it was too late."

Sarah thought about asking about the second trail, but something else he said mattered more. "You were in a hurry to come back fer me?"

Jathan's mouth dropped open slightly, and

he released her hands. "I, uh, I was worried about you. The view was amazing, but I felt bad you weren't there. I felt even worse that I'd left you. I should have gone with my inner feelings and stayed by yer side."

"*Danki,* but I have to know . . . how did you find this trail, and how did you know I went down it?"

Jathan glanced around, as if sizing up where they were. He nodded. "I will tell you, but first we need to start a fire while we have even a little light left. It'll be a long, cold night if we don't." He turned to find some wood.

"We're going to be here all night?"

"We can't hike out in the dark. It's too dangerous, especially with you injured." He looked over his shoulder at her. "But I'll make you as comfortable as I can, Sarah. I promise."

Dark clouds blocked out most of the fading sunlight, and Sarah blew a heavy breath, as if that alone could push the coming rain the other direction.

Jathan dug under a pile of dead branches, looking for dry wood. When he found enough, Sarah knelt beside him and they layered the sticks. She also brushed aside other branches or foliage to give them a wide, clear ring — not that she thought a forest fire could start in this damp place, but it was better to be safe than sorry.

Moisture from the ground seeped through her skirt and chilled her legs.

Jathan pulled a match from his pants pocket.

"Wait, before you do that." She rose and hobbled over to a tree, peeling back layers of moss until she found a large, dry piece.

He eyed her.

"It'll be easier to light the moss than the wood." She handed it to him and then sat on her log, rubbing her ankle.

Jathan packed the moss around the wood, lighting it.

"I'm so thankful you brought matches." Sarah rubbed her hands together.

"*Ne,* Amos did. All the others emptied their things into my backpack jest in case we couldn't make it down to the bottom of the mountain before dark."

The small flame flickered and danced. A cold wind swirled, nearly blowing it out. Jathan hunched down, cupping his hands to shield the flame from the wind. A moment later, the flame grew, igniting the wood.

"There." Jathan sat back on his heels. "That should knock off a bit of the chill."

"Too bad we don't have a steak to cook

over that fire. I'm starved."

"I have half of Hope's sandwich and an apple from Eve if yer hungry."

"Famished . . . but I'll only eat if we share."

Jathan nodded, and they divided what was left of their food. They shared the half of sandwich, and she ate the apple while he finished off her last cookie.

When the food was gone, Jathan's stomach growled. *It must take a lot of food to fill up such a big man,* Sarah thought.

He rubbed his stomach. "I should have thought to bring more supplies. These are the mountains of Montana, not a local park."

"It's not that you knew."

"Yer right. I've never been in the mountains before. I should have been more prepared." He lowered his head.

She stood and moved closer to the fire, kneeling before it and opening her hands in front of the flames to absorb the warmth. "You didn't know I'd get lost and we'd have to stay overnight."

"*Ja.* I thought I'd have some months to get used to these forests before I had to find my way through them." He chuckled. "Somethin' to write home about fer sure."

"Do you have forests like this back in

Ohio?" she asked, even though she had a feeling she knew the answer.

"There are wide-open spaces, and it's very hilly where I live in Berlin. But there are no high peaks or mountain ranges that expand as far as the eye can see. Not like this. Not at all."

She fiddled with the string of her *kapp*, a thousand needles pricking her skin at his closeness. Suddenly, she couldn't remember one thing she liked about Amos at all. But Jathan — he was someone special.

What had Patty told her? To show someone you care, ask about his life. Listen to his dreams.

"Why don't you tell me about Berlin? I'd love to hear about it. I have an aunt who lives there, my mother's sister. It'll make the time pass faster."

He cocked one eyebrow. "I suppose . . . I mean, if it'll help pass the time."

"*Ach,* I didn't mean fcr it to sound like that. I'm interested too. Really I am."

He smiled and focused on her. The glow from the campfire danced over his face and Sarah tilted her head. How handsome he was. Again, how had she not noticed that before?

She also thought about how easy it was to talk to him. Here she was lost, in pain, cold, and hungry, and they were chatting as easily as if they were sitting in the restaurant of the West Kootenai Kraft and Grocery.

"Berlin is a beautiful place. Expansive fields and roadways lined with flower beds of tulips. We have *gut* fishin' rivers, and in the fall, the trees turn all colors of yellow and orange." Jathan looked around. "The trees aren't the same. We don't have forests of pine like here. We have black cherry, sugar maple, black walnut, white ash, and red oak. The oaks, as a group, are the most common forest tree species and are predominant. My favorite is the maple though."

"Maple is pretty wood."

Jathan chuckled. "Oh, I like the maple fer its syrup most. There's nothing like pure maple syrup over buckwheat pancakes. And I have the recipe fer the best maple nut twist rolls."

"You have the recipe?" Sarah straightened, intrigued.

He glanced to the left and shook his head. "Uh, no. I meant my *mem.* She has so many *wunderbaar* recipes. I've never seen anyone who found such joy in the kitchen . . ." He dared to glance over and look into her face. "Well, other than you."

Sarah fanned her face, not because she was hot, but because she hoped to distract

112

him from the embarrassment that was surely tingeing her cheeks. She wasn't used to someone being so bold with his compliments.

Jathan cleared his throat. "But that's getting off the subject now, isn't it? Before I tell you more about where I came from, there's something else I need to tell you about."

"*Ja,* what is that?"

"I want to answer yer previous question. I want to explain how I found you. How I knew you headed down this trail." Jathan sighed. "I've never experienced God as I have today, Sarah, and I'll never doubt how real he is. He's with us here now." He tapped his chest. "I can feel it." He tapped the side of his head. "I know it as clearly as I know my own name."

CHAPTER 9

Jathan studied Sarah across the fire. She sat on a log they'd pulled up close, and even in the woods, she sat proper-like, back straight, like any Amish woman would. When he first found her, he'd expected they would hike out. Yet the weariness on her face and the way she'd favored her ankle told him it wasn't possible. He hadn't expected having to stay all night. Now they had no choice. Now it was up to him to care for her, protect her.

Part of him felt foolish for being inept with his survival skills — he should have known about the moss. The other part of him was overwhelmed, thankful, that he'd found her at all.

"We realized halfway down that we were heading down a different trail. I climbed back to the top and found the right one, and then on the way down again I was praying. I was praying the whole time, but my prayers increased as I neared where I expected you to be. I wasn't surprised you weren't there." He paused, remembering the arrow of rocks. "I liked the arrow. That was smart. In fact . . ." Jathan reached into his pocket and pulled out one of the rocks. He placed it on his palm and then stretched out his hand. "I picked up this rock fer yer memory jar."

Sarah's eyes sparkled as if he'd just offered her a pearl of great price. "You remembered." She took it from his hand and then unzipped her backpack and reached inside. She pulled out another rock and held it up. "I thought of the same thing — even though I already have a piece similar to this. A piece I found years ago." She lowered her head and looked up at him from under her lashes. "Now I'm certain I won't forget, although it would be impossible to forget this day anytime soon."

The fire crackled and the woods around them grew darker still. Sarah shivered, and Jathan removed his overshirt and handed it to her. He was thankful *Mem* always urged him to wear an undershirt no matter the weather.

"Danki." She smiled as she took it, wrapping it around her shoulders and then tucking it under her chin. "And . . . then?"

"Oh, *ja,* the rest of the story. I was walking along, and I heard a rumbling from the hillside next to me. I never saw what happened, but suddenly a large rock was bouncing down the hill. It was heading right toward me. I jumped into the trees to get out of the way." Goose bumps rose on his arms, even now as he told the story. "The rock hit my boot, and I'm sure I have a bruise, but it could have done so much more damage."

"That's amazing."

"It's not the best part." He leaned forward. Even as he prepared to tell her, sweet warmth flooded over him. It was the same sensation he'd felt on the summit as he looked over the view. It was as if God's presence was touching him down here too.

"When I pushed off the ground, I noticed something. I had leaped into an open area, and there was a small piece of blue fabric snagged on a tree branch."

Sarah eyed her skirt, and sure enough, there was a small tear near the hem. "I had no idea . . ."

"There were also footprints, oh, about yer size," he continued. "I called yer name, and I didn't hear a response, but I knew they had to be yer footprints. They were fresh, and it looked as if you were favoring yer left foot. I wasn't sure where you would have been heading going down this way, but after five minutes of walking, I heard something." He leaned forward and his eyes widened. "It was the voice of an angel."

"*Ach,* it was not!" Sarah laughed and picked up a stick to toss it at him. "Yer teasing me now."

Jathan chuckled at her surprised expression. He enjoyed seeing her so flustered. "*Ja,* I guess I am. I jest guessed you were doing what you could to scare away the bears." He stuck his fingers in his ears.

Sarah's mouth dropped open, as if she didn't believe what he'd just said. She balled her hand into a fist and leaned forward to punch his shoulder.

As she stood to reach him, a look of pain replaced the playful smile of a moment before. Her ankle gave out. As if in slow motion, she began to crumple, heading right for the fire.

Jathan stood and lunged. He stepped into the fire pit to do it, but he caught her, pushing her back. She fell to the ground with a cry. Flames rose around his foot, and he quickly stepped out of the fire pit. Moving around the fire, he hunched beside her.

"Sarah, that was close. You all right?"

"Oh . . ." Sarah moaned and opened her

eyes. They looked slightly glazed over as she peered down at his foot. "Are you all right?" she gasped. "Did you get burned?"

"Nah." He shook his leg. "My boots are tough."

"Is that the same foot the rock hit?" she asked, slowly standing up and returning to her spot on the log.

"*Jah,* a little burned, a little bruised. I'll be fine."

"You sure?"

He nodded. It did feel a little hurt, but not burned.

"That — that was an amazing story. I know God was at work there." Sarah attempted to keep her voice steady, but she winced and rubbed her ankle.

Jathan scooted closer. "Do you mind if I take a look?"

Her eyes widened. "I don't think that's needed. I'm sure it's jest sprained."

"We won't know until I look. May I?"

Sarah nodded and bit her lip. Jathan sat crossed-legged in front of her. Then, ever so slowly, she stretched her leg out to him.

Jathan's heart pounded as he untied her boot. He had to wiggle it back and forth to get the boot off. Her breathing quickened and he paused.

118

"Am I hurting you? Tell me if I'm too rough."

"Uh, *ne, ne.* Yer fine."

He glanced up at her. She was blushing. *Why, I think Sarah might be enjoying this . . .* Even though it was obvious she was in pain, there was a spark of interest in her gaze he hadn't seen before.

He set her boot on the ground and then looked at her sock.

Sarah bent over and lifted up her skirt slightly to find the top of the knitted stocking. Jathan saw a flash of the skin on her knee and looked away, pretending to watch the fire.

"Ouch! Oh." Sarah gasped. He looked back. She was rolling the stocking down and had almost gotten it over her ankle when the pain made her stop.

He reached for her hands and covered them with his. "Let me help you."

She nodded and removed her hands. Jathan gently slid his thumbs under the sides of her stocking, stretching the fabric. Then, as carefully as he could, he slid the stocking the rest of the way off.

He cupped his hand under her heel, helping her hold it up. Her skin was snow white, except where there was swelling and discoloration. Jathan swallowed, and then cleared his throat. He was just trying to help her, but the moment felt intimate.

"Do you feel any numbness?" he asked.

"*Ne.* Not numb, jest hurts real bad."

He studied the sides of her leg, running his fingers down each side. She trembled. Was it from the pain? The cold? His touch?

"It looks like it's still aligned. I don't see any unusual angles."

"You seem like you know what yer talking about. Are you a doctor, and I didn't know it, Jathan?"

He liked the way she said his name. "Not a doctor, but every Amish man knows how to care for horses." He stated that with confidence, because out of all the ways he'd failed to live up to his father's expectations, he did know how to do that.

"First you tell me I'm a poor singer, then you compare me to a horse!"

"Uh, I didn't mean . . ." he hurried to explain and then noticed her smile.

"*Ja,* but horses aren't so clumsy and don't make such a big deal out of a simple sprain," she added.

"Sprains aren't simple. I've heard they're more painful than breaks. My *bruder* Otto had both and told me that was a fact."

"You have a *bruder*?" She pulled her foot from his hold.

"Five *brieder* and three sisters. I'm the youngest."

Sarah nodded and cast him a smile. "That explains it."

"Explains what?"

"Why yer so kind and accommodating. The youngest ones in a family are used to tagging along with everyone else. They're happy to jest be included."

Jathan took his handkerchief from his pocket and stood, then walked over to a small pile of snow. He scooped some up in the handkerchief, tied it off, and then brought the bundle back to the log. "Here, we need to put this on yer ankle. It'll help the swelling."

"But I'm cold already."

"You have to." Jathan put it on her ankle and then motioned for her to scoot closer to the fire. "Sit with yer side to the fire and yer ankle farther away so the snow doesn't melt too fast."

She did. When she settled, Jathan walked to the side of her that was open to the cold air. He sat beside her on the log and scooted close, positioning himself so his body protected her back from the cold. She stiffened at first, and then slowly relaxed until finally leaning her head back against his shoulder.

Sarah's *kapp* smelled of laundry soap and

121

sunshine. He wished she would take it off. Wished he could see her blonde hair as he had that day on the porch. But no, it would be improper. Even though they were alone, God would want him to respect Sarah. Jathan vowed to treat her just as he would if their whole community were watching, for God was greater than even their community . . . and he was watching.

As much as Jathan hated having to spend the night in the woods, he was thankful he'd found Sarah. Thankful for the fire.

Tomorrow, they'd be able to make their way up the trail and down the hill . . . but tonight he would enjoy Sarah's closeness, even if they were in the middle of the cold, damp, dark woods.

Then again, maybe he should be thankful she'd gotten lost. How else would he and Sarah have gotten this close so quickly? And they had a long night stretching ahead of them still.

CHAPTER 10

Sarah thought about that old cabin Patty had found. What she wouldn't do to have even a simple structure like that to protect them from the cold of the night. Their fire crackled in the flat open area. The area wasn't much bigger than *Mem*'s kitchen. There were no ledges or outcroppings on the hillside to protect them from the cold spring wind, but the pines offered a bit of protection, despite the snow still heaped around them. Sarah sighed, realizing their small fire was all they could count on for warmth.

Well, not quite the only thing she could count on.

Sarah leaned her head against Jathan's shoulder, thankful for his support. Thankful for his protection from the cold. She felt bad in a way. She had his shirt wrapped around her, and he was still taking the brunt of the cold air. She thought about offering it back or urging him to scoot closer to the fire, but she knew it would be no use. Jathan took his role as her protector seriously.

"So tell me about yer family," she said, accepting the fact that hours stretched ahead of them. "I'm especially interested in yer sisters. To have six *brieder, ach*!"

"My sisters are great. In a way, they mothered me more than *Mem.* Until recent years, we had a dozen milk cows on the farm. My earliest memories are of summer evenings with my sisters milking the cows in the yard. The cows weren't tied up. They let my sisters milk them while they happily chewed their cud."

She heard the smile in his voice even though she couldn't see it. She guessed there was a brightness in his eyes, too, but was afraid to look up to see. Their faces were too close. She didn't want him to think she was having any affectionate thoughts . . . even though she was. The thoughts crackled within her mind just as the fire crackled by her side.

"My sisters love singing," he continued. "They sang old hymns, and I can remember the words of many of them. They even sang as they milked."

Jathan cleared his throat, and she sat up and turned to face him.

124

"There were ninety and nine that safely lay in the shelter of the fold, but one was out on the hills away, far off from the gates of gold. Away on the mountains wild and bare, away from the tender Shepherd's care, away from the tender Shepherd's care," he sang, and then let his voice trail off. His voice was strong and clear. In a way, it surprised her that he'd just start singing like that since they hadn't really spent much time together before this. But on the other hand, he obviously felt as comfortable with her as she did with him.

Sarah glanced around. " 'One was out in the hills . . . the mountains wild and bare'? I wonder what made you choose that song." She wrinkled her nose and grinned.

Jathan shrugged, picked up a stick, and stirred the fire. "I'm not yet sure. It jest came to me."

"Poor lost sheep." Sarah stuck out her lower lip. "I feel so bad." She motioned to him to turn toward the fire so she could see him better, and he did.

"Oh no . . ." He waved his hands over the flames. "Do you not know the rest of the song?"

"I heard it long ago, when I was jest a child. My *opa* used to sing it. And even though I have an idea of what the words

125

are, I'd love to hear you sing."

Jathan didn't hesitate. He cleared his throat again. "And all through the mountains, thunder riven, and up from the rocky steep, there arose a glad cry from the gate of heaven, 'Rejoice! I have found my sheep!' "

Goose bumps rose on Sarah's arms as he sang. She closed her eyes as he continued, feeling safe and protected, as if his voice were setting up a shield around them.

"And the angels echoed around the throne, 'Rejoice, for the Lord brings back his own! Rejoice, for the Lord brings back his own.' "

Sarah sat quietly for a moment, aware of the damp log under her. She heard the hoot of an owl and the sound of the wind through the trees. The crackling fire warmed her, but inside she was warmer still.

She opened her eyes and looked at him. *"Danki."* It was all she could think to say.

"That song was one of my sisters' favorites — probably still is."

"And yer *brieder?*"

"*Ach,* we'd get into so much trouble." He pointed to a nearby tree. "I don't think there was a tree within two miles in any direction that I didn't climb." He winked. "And I fell out of jest about all of them . . ."

126

His voice trailed off, and she could see that a memory played in his mind.

"Oh *ne*. Why?"

"I was the little one trying to keep up with my *brieder,* remember?"

"Sounds like a *gut* Amish family. Perfect, if you ask me."

"No family is perfect." His words sliced through the air like the late-spring wind, sending a chill down her spine. "I think we all know how some folks appear — as if everyone is fine on the outside, but deep . . . Well, inside there's more pain than anything."

"You sound like you know this from experience." She scooted back slightly. This was a side to Jathan she hadn't seen yet. It surprised her.

He forced a smile. "I was jest getting warmed up with happy thoughts. Don't wanna ruin that."

"No family's perfect," she said, hoping it would show him she understood. "I'm here to listen if you'd like to talk."

"*Ja,* well . . ." He got up and walked around her to adjust the snow pack on her ankle. "That is kind of you."

When he returned to his spot on the log, they sat silently for a few minutes. She wanted to hear what he had to say, but was sure if she asked anything more about his family he would change the subject.

A grinding stirred in her chest, like sandpaper scraping over her heart. What was he hiding? Surely it must be painful if he couldn't share. Had he lost someone like she had? She considered that question and realized loss comes in many forms.

"There's one family story I hear retold at nearly every family gathering that I think you might like," he finally said. "The story starts in the Great Depression. So many men and sometimes women were out of work after the 1928 stock-market collapse."

"*Ja,* I remember learning about that in grade eight. Men took to walking the country seeking work. Most worked fer food or a place to stay." She looked around. "I guess sleeping out like this wouldn't be unusual fer them."

"And that's what happened to Lewis Barkley." Jathan took a tone that reminded Sarah of her father when he launched into one of his stories.

She smiled and made eye contact, letting Jathan know she was listening.

"Well, Lewis was wandering in Ohio after his wife died," Jathan started, "and he found solace among the Amish. He spent seven years working fer a young woman who'd

128

lost her husband. After the seventh year, he approached the bishop and asked to become Amish. Only after he got approval from the church did he ask the widow to be his wife. They had three daughters . . . one of whom was my *oma.*"

"Really?" Sarah's eyes widened.

"*Ja.* I can still remember a tune my *oma* always used to hum. One day I asked her and she shared the words, 'May I sleep in yer barn, Mister? It is cold lying out on the ground, and the cold north wind is awhistling, and I have no place to lie down . . .' " Jathan sang.

A shiver traveled up Sarah's spine, and she looked around. "I'd give anything to be sleeping in a barn tonight — even a stinky one."

Jathan nodded and laughed. "Ain't that the truth, Sarah. Ain't that the truth."

They talked about their grandparents and extended families. They talked about their schooling and laughed because they'd learned some of the same poems and rhymes.

"So what was it like when you first moved to Montana?" he asked. "Was it lonely? Did you miss yer old community and friends?"

"*Ne,* jest the opposite. I wouldn't have believed it if I hadn't seen it with my own eyes. When we first moved, *Mem* wasn't prepared for the stream of visitors. For a while, we saw our friends from back east jest as often as when we were still back home — or so it seemed. Everyone wanted to come and see our place in the wilderness. Some stayed for a day, others a week. I didn't like visitors so much, because it meant I had to stay and play with the other children. It was less time I could play with Patty."

"Patty?"

Sarah stiffened. She readjusted herself and reached for her stocking. She didn't know why she'd mentioned her friend's name. Things had been going so well. She didn't want to talk about Patty. Couldn't talk about her. *Mem* had tried talking to Sarah at various times, but each time, Sarah broke down in tears.

"Jest a friend. She doesn't live around these parts anymore."

"You sound sad about it, and if I were to guess . . . Is it the same Patty who passed away jest a few years ago?"

Tears sprang to Sarah's eyes. She blinked quickly before they could break through. Her lips compressed with emotion and heat rushed into her chest.

"I'm so sorry, Sarah. I didn't mean to

make you cry."

"*N-ne,* I know. I jest . . ." She blew a breath out through her circled lips. "H-how did you know?"

After a long silence, Jathan placed a hand on her shoulder. "People talk. The first time I heard of the drowning was when the van driver took us over the bridge."

"I don't like that." She crossed her arms over her chest. "I don't like that people are talking about it as if it's jest a story. She was a person. A real, living . . ." The tears came then. More tears than Sarah had cried in a long time. They dripped down her face, falling and dropping to the forest floor. Jathan didn't tell her to stop. He didn't say a word. He simply placed his hand over hers to let her know that, when she was ready, he could be trusted with her words.

Sarah wiped her face and sucked in a breath. "She w-was my best friend. We did everything together. It seems every good, childhood memory I have is attached to her. Sh-she . . ." Sarah swallowed, knowing she was acting like a fool, but did it matter? She was lost, injured, and cold. She'd already made a fool of herself by going off the trail. What difference did a few tears make?

"Patty laughed at my jokes and got me lost in the woods too. She was the first to

131

encourage my baking, to really encourage me. She told me I made better cupcakes than anyone on the earth."

Jathan smiled. "I have to agree."

Sarah wilted, slumping her shoulders and realizing the heaviness of sharing her heart. How was it possible to feel so relaxed, yet so tense? To feel so open, yet so fearful of losing control of her emotions all at the same time?

"I want to tell you more, like the time we almost burned down the whole West Kootenai Kraft and Grocery. I want to, but I can't. It jest hur . . ." She covered her face with her hands.

"It's all right, *ja*? Yer tired. It's been a long day. Why don't you lie down for a while? You can use my shirt for a pillow. Close yer eyes for a time, Sarah. I promise I'll keep watch."

Sarah didn't argue. She climbed off the log, lay down with her back to him, closed her eyes, and listened as he rose to add more wood to the fire.

People have learned to live with loss. What's wrong with me? She brought her knees closer to her chest. More tears came, and she was tired of them. Tired of crying. Even more tired of holding them in.

Let him in. Talk to him. You can trust him,

her inner voice told her. Sarah didn't listen. Couldn't listen. Jathan wouldn't understand.

The ground was cold underneath Sarah. She was aware of dead leaves and twigs poking through her clothes and tickling her skin.

Time passed, five minutes or ten, she wasn't sure which, when a voice broke through her sleepy mind.

"It wasn't yer fault."

Sarah stirred and turned slightly. She wasn't sure if Jathan had actually spoken or if she'd fallen asleep and the words had come as the start of a dream.

She sat up so she faced him. He still sat on the log, trying to peel a burned piece of rubber off the bottom of his boot.

Sarah cleared her throat. He lifted his eyes and looked at her. Compassion filled his gaze. Seeing that, the woods seemed less scary. Her emotions less scary.

"Did you say something?" she asked.

"I said it wasn't yer fault."

Her brow furrowed. "But that doesn't make sense . . . why would you believe I'd think it was?"

"My *bruder* Yonnie lost a friend in a buggy accident they were in. They were hit by a drunk driver. There was nothing Yonnie could have done, yet he felt guilty because he survived. It happens. It's a common emotion. Besides . . ." He leaned closer so the firelight fully illuminated him from the shoulders up. "I saw the guilt all over yer face."

"*Ja,* well, you don't know anything then." She closed her eyes. She didn't want to see his disapproval when she said the next words. "You don't understand then, because it's true . . . it *is* my fault."

"Sarah, how can you say that? Were you driving the speedboat? We both know you weren't."

"I might as well have been. I saw the boat on the lake. I thought about warning them, but I didn't." She bit her lip. "I was interested in Patty's *bruder.* I'd liked him for a while, but we'd never really had time alone to talk." The words spilled out, tumbling out of her mouth like rocks down a rock slide. "I didn't warn them as they paddled away. I didn't warn them, because I was looking forward to time to get to know Michael better."

She squeezed her eyes tighter, unable to believe she'd just confessed that. In the two years since Patty'd been gone, she'd never told that to another soul. Even though she thought it every day, she never told.

He didn't say anything.

Shame crawled over Sarah, like ants on an anthill, sweeping down from her head to her toes with accusations.

Now that he knows, he's not going to be so friendly. He'll get you out of these woods, but that will be that.

"Sarah, do you think you are more powerful than God?" His words interrupted her thoughts.

"Excuse me?" The question caused her to look up into his face as it glowed in the firelight.

"Do you read the Bible often?" His voice was steady and quiet and somehow made the hairs on her arm stand on end.

"*Ja,* how dare you —"

"Have you read Psalm 139?"

She jutted out her chin. "I've read all the psalms, more than once."

"Well, in the middle of that chapter, it says something that goes like this: 'You, God, saw my body while it was being made, and all the days you'd planned for me were written before any of them happened.'

"Sarah, God wasn't surprised by the accident. He doesn't point his finger at you fer not warning Patty. Besides, even if you had, who knows if she would have even listened?"

Sarah watched his lips as he spoke. Was that the truth?

She thought about it for a moment. An image of her friend's plain features and determined stance filled her mind. More than anyone, Patty was hard to sway when she'd set her mind on things. She was the most willful and stubborn Amish woman Sarah had ever met. She'd never really considered before that Patty may not have listened . . . she'd only focused on the fact that she hadn't warned them as she thought she ought to have done.

"The way I see things, Sarah, God knew the day Patty was going to die even before she was born. I know you know this . . . but maybe you should *believe it.* Believe deep in yer heart where all that pain lies."

Sarah nodded. Could she believe that? Really believe it? By accepting that God knew the day of Patty's death, she also had to accept that he'd allowed it. To Sarah, taking someone from the earth during the prime of her life — when she was filled to the top with so many dreams and hopes — didn't seem like a loving thing to do.

She wished she were more like *Mem. Mem* accepted everything that happened as God's perfect will. She trusted God even when she didn't understand.

Maybe that was Sarah's problem. She was trying too hard to understand. Maybe she needed to listen to what her mother had been trying to tell her. Maybe she needed to pay attention to what Jathan was saying now. God knew every one of Patty's days . . . and he'd chosen when to call her home.

Sarah curled back up on the ground, her hands under her cheek. It made sense, what he said. Jathan was right. It was something she had known, in her mind at least.

She considered something else. God had given her Patty. He'd forged their friendship. He'd been part of their relationship as they'd spent years seeking God together.

And for what purpose? So Sarah would keep all other relationships at bay? So she would hold her pain close to her, like a porcupine cradled to her chest?

God, why did you bring Patty into my life? The question filtered through Sarah's mind. *More than that . . . what can I do to show you that giving me the gift of her friendship wasn't a waste?*

CHAPTER 11

Sarah didn't know she'd drifted off until she heard someone stirring behind her. She thought it was her brother Andy coming to wake her to tell her *Mem* needed her help. Then, all at once, her senses pulled her from her sleep.

She smelled the dampness of the earth and the scent of decay from the forest floor. She smelled the smoke from the campfire and even the sweat from Jathan's shirt.

Jathan.

Sarah sat up with a start. She opened her eyes and then rubbed them, trying to clear her vision. "Is everything okay?"

She glanced around. Was it morning? The sky was still dark. She thought she saw a twinge of gray sky in the east, but she wasn't sure.

Jathan's eyes were wide. "I heard something." His breathing was quick, shaky.

Sarah sat up straighter. "Like a bear?"

He shook his head. "No, not like a bear. It was crying. If you listen . . ."

"Like a baby crying?" As she said the words, her earlier memory filtered through her mind. She was back on the front-porch swing; the night had been dark and cold like this one. Only then, it'd been different. Back then, Sarah had been able to see the stars. Now, here, the cloud cover made that impossible.

"*Ja.*" Jathan nodded. "It did sound sort of like a baby."

"Coyotes," she whispered. "It's a good sign."

"How do you know?"

Sarah yawned and then smiled. Her eyes felt sticky, but her mind was alert.

"My friend . . . Patty told me so. I was twelve. I remember very clearly."

Sarah continued with her story, telling Jathan about waking alone in Patty's bed and then searching for her. Telling him how she'd found Patty outside, and their conversation on the porch. Just as she prepared to tell him about how her sleeping kerchief had looked like coyote ears, a sound filtered through the trees. It was a coyote all right, and it wasn't a coincidence.

When she finished, Jathan launched into a story about an injured red-tailed hawk he'd once found. Sarah tried to listen, but her mind wandered.

For so long, she'd taken her memories of Patty — the memories they'd created together — and held them outside of herself, protecting herself from the pain of carrying them deep within. It was as if she carried all the memories in her jars. But in doing so, it was as if she'd also kept everyone else — those still in her life — at arm's length too.

But now . . . now she'd shared about the porch swing, and instead of pain, it brought joy to invite someone else into that memory. Sarah felt full, as if by opening her heart, a bit of happiness was stuffed inside.

Sarah didn't know when the jar had transformed from a celebration of their experiences into a way to keep thoughts of Patty from pricking all the tender places deep within, but it had.

Afraid of the pain missing Patty would cause, Sarah hadn't let memories of Patty fill her mind or journey through her heart. But what if she did? What if Sarah took the lessons she'd learned from her friend and applied them to her life? What if she took the joy, the wisdom, and the laughter and made the memories count? Could Patty's memories grow within and better Sarah's life now?

Sarah felt a rush of energy wash over her. Her chest tingled, and she found it hard to breathe. Did it take getting lost to discover what God had wanted her to find — the truth that Patty's life would serve its purpose through her if she'd let it? That God's Spirit would serve its purpose too?

Tingles danced up Sarah's arms, and she released a long, slow breath. Jathan was still talking, and she attempted to focus on his words, but the joy filling her made it hard to concentrate. It was a joy Sarah hadn't known since that day at the lake. It felt good.

"And then we decided we wanted to fly with the hawk, so we jumped off the barn roof, too, and sailed around the pasture," Jathan was saying.

"Excuse me?"

He chuckled. "I didn't think you were listening."

"Well . . ." How could she explain?

"It doesn't matter." He grinned and shrugged. "You should get some more rest. We still have a few hours before it's light enough to hike out."

"Are you sure?" Sarah scooted closer to the fire and closed her eyes again.

"*Ja*, Sarah. Sweet dreams. I'll wake you at first light."

Sarah nodded and yawned. For some

141

reason she felt more comfortable now than she had for so long. It wasn't that the ground was comfortable. It wasn't. Rather, there was a peace that snuggled deep within. A peace she must have tucked in her memory jar too, but one that had found its way back into her mind, her heart.

And while Sarah knew she'd like to share more memories of Patty, she wondered if she dared tell Jathan about her deepest dream. It was more than just the dream to be a wife and mother — which she wanted most of all. But there was something else she cared about — longed for — too. To have a bakery like Jathan's mother and to bake up all types of fancy things. That word, *fancy,* stuck in her brain like sap on a tree. Sarah couldn't share such nonsense with Jathan.

Her heart ached remembering what her mother had said about that. What *Mem* had tossed in the trash.

Sarah had done many foolish things, including getting lost, but she couldn't risk sharing what mattered most only to have Jathan — have anyone — brush it aside as meaningless.

No, she couldn't do that.

Thirteen-year-old Sarah studied the notes

she'd scribbled down. It was a recipe from one of those baking magazines she'd been reading at the doctor's office in Eureka. Her baby brother, Andy, had become awful sick like. Sarah hadn't liked seeing the worry on *Mem*'s face. She hadn't liked hearing Andy crying as their driver took them all the way down the mountain, but she had liked the waiting room, especially after she'd found the magazine lying on the table for all to look at.

She'd never seen anything like that baking magazine. Unlike *Mem*'s old cookbooks that were put together by Amish friends and photocopied at the office-supply store, the magazines in the doctor's office had color.

Sarah's mouth had dropped open when she'd turned the page and spotted the maple cupcake. It looked so real, she could almost taste it. She'd even lifted up the magazine and smelled the page. Sadly, it only smelled like paper and ink — at least it had then. But now . . .

Now all types of good smells filled the kitchen of the West Kootenai Kraft and Grocery. Sarah had come with *Mem.* Annie, the owner, was on vacation, and *Mem* was supposed to be filling in baking. Sarah thought "supposed to be," because *Mem* really wasn't able to do much. Andy still wasn't feeling well.

Sarah wasn't allowed to help with the bread. *Mem* said she could bake bread at home but not for the restaurant customers. But *Mem had* allowed her to bake cupcakes. Maybe it was because *Mem* had seen that photo in the magazine too.

The kitchen smelled of the maple batter as well as the brown-sugar topping Sarah had made and added to the top. The recipe hadn't called for the topping, but when Sarah looked at the plain beige batter in the pan, she knew exactly what it needed. She couldn't wait to see if the cupcakes tasted as good as she imagined.

Andy slept nearby in a car seat that someone had loaned *Mem.* Sarah's family didn't have a car to use it in. They didn't even use the buggy much, seeing as how both the store and the school were less than a mile from their house. But the car seat had a rounded bottom, and *Mem* was able to keep Andy rocking in it with her foot while she baked.

That only worked for so long though, and just as Sarah was taking her cupcakes out of the oven, Andy's whimpers transformed into wails.

"Sarah," *Mem* breathed out her name with a big sigh. "Will you watch this milk fer my bread? Don't take yer eyes off it. Jest let it scald and then turn it off and remove it from the heat."

"Ja, ja." Sarah set down the cupcake tray on the cooling rack and pressed down on one of the cupcakes ever so gently with her finger. It pushed down just enough, and then bounced back, letting her know it was done.

"Remember, don't let that milk boil over. It'll cause a horrible mess and this isn't our kitchen."

Sarah nodded as an idea struck her. What if, before the cupcakes cooled completely, she plopped a half teaspoon of butter on each cupcake where it would melt? She licked her lips and hurried to the fridge. *Mem* carried Andy on her hip as she passed by.

"Did you hear me, Sarah?"

"Ja, Mem, sorry." She offered a coy smile. "I'll watch yer milk."

Satisfied, *Mem* hurried into the small bathroom to nurse, and Sarah grabbed the butter from the fridge and returned to the kitchen. Before topping the cupcakes, she peeked at the milk. Steam rose, but Sarah knew it needed a minute more.

She'd just plopped the first scoop of butter onto a cupcake when the double jingle of the bell on the front door told Sarah her friend had stopped by. The bell jingled with each customer who entered and exited, but only Patty waited until the door shut to jingle it again.

"I know who's cooking today," Patty's voice called from the restaurant area as she neared. "That smells too sweet to be ordinary bread. I knew from the moment I walked in that it was my friend in the kitchen. 'Sarah's experimenting again,' I told myself."

Sarah narrowed her gaze and placed her free hand on her hip. "Don't you try to be extra nice now. You know you got me in trouble fer copying off my school paper. I'm still mad." Yet even as she said the words, a smile threatened to break out.

"Fine then." Patty took the plastic bag in her hand and tucked it behind her back. "I'm not gonna show you what I got fer you then."

"Fer me?" Sarah jabbed the spoon in the tub of butter and then hurried over to her friend. Instead of opening the bag and showing her what was inside, Patty moved to the closest table in the restaurant area and sat.

"Close yer eyes," Patty demanded as Sarah sat beside her.

Sarah was too excited to argue, and she immediately closed them.

She heard the sounds of shuffling plastic, obviously from the bag, and something else too. Paper maybe?

"*Ja,* open them!"

Sarah opened her eyes to find not one, but three magazines. The array of food on the covers took away her breath. These weren't ordinary magazines, but baking ones.

"Where did you get them?" Sarah asked.

"In Eureka at the old bookstore. My *oma* sent me birthday money . . ."

"*Ne,* you didn't. You spent yer birthday money on me? I can't accept that."

Patty laughed. "I did it fer myself. Purely selfish reasons. When you bake, I get to try yer creations. It's the best present I've ever gotten. I can already taste it." She licked her lips.

Sarah spread her hands over the magazines, and her eyes widened. One cover showed a fancy cake. The other a perfectly made cherry pie, and the third . . .

"Cupcakes!" Sarah grabbed up the magazine and flipped through the pages. Some cupcakes were decorated like monkey faces, others like bumblebees. Sarah stopped on one page that showed a cupcake that looked like a flower. If she hadn't been looking at a baking magazine, she would have been sure the cupcake had just been plucked out of a garden.

Sarah held up the magazine. "Patty, look."

Just then a loud hiss sounded. Sarah turned to see the flames from the gas stove shooting up.

"The milk!" It bubbled over onto the flames, causing the fire to stretch and grow, engulfing everything in its path.

In an instant, *Mem*'s cookbook that had been sitting on the counter next to the stove burst into flames.

Sarah gasped and ran into the kitchen, reaching her hand out, not knowing whether to grab the pan or brush the book to the floor and try to stomp out the fire.

"No! Wait!" A deep voice called from behind. Sarah recognized Edgar's voice. In one smooth motion, he ran to the cabinet under the sink, pulled out a fire extinguisher, and pointed the fire extinguisher's hose at the stove.

"Sarah, move!"

She quickly jumped to the side, but not quickly enough.

148

A white cloud filled the air, covering everything. Sarah too.

Just then, the smoke alarm went off, and everyone in the place rushed to the kitchen to see what was the matter, including *Mem.* She hurried from the bathroom with a wailing Andy in her arms. He didn't seem too happy about having his lunch inter- rupted. *Mem* didn't seem too happy about the mess.

Edgar shook his head and returned to the front register with a "Humph." The restaurant guests returned to their tables, seemingly disappointed the ordeal was over so soon.

Without a word, *Mem* took the baby back to the bathroom to finish feeding, and Sarah set to work cleaning up the mess. White powder covered everything. Sarah would have to throw out all the ingredients *Mem* had out for the bread. She looked at her cupcakes on the cooling tray. She'd have to throw them out, too, as well as the tub of butter she'd had sitting out on the kitchen countertop. All the pots and pans were coated with the dust, as were the cooking utensils, walls, and floors. Sarah guessed what she'd be doing for the next week.

With a heavy sigh, she picked up the

cupcake tray and dumped her creations in the trash one by one.

Footsteps shuffled behind her, and Sarah didn't have to turn to know Patty stood there.

Just when Sarah thought things couldn't get worse, she heard what sounded like a soft snickering behind her. The snickering grew until it turned into a laugh that radiated from Patty's gut.

"I don't know what yer laughing at," Sarah hissed, brushing white powder from her *kapp.* She crossed her arms over her chest. She held a cupcake in her hand and seriously considered throwing it as hard as she could at her friend. Or who she used to call a friend. No friend of Sarah's would ever think something as horrible as this was funny.

Between gasps, Patty held up the cupcake magazine. "I'm so sorry, Sarah." She gasped for air. "But you look like this." She pointed. On the page was a white bunny cupcake with large, blue-gumdrop eyes.

Sarah touched her face and arm, knowing she was covered with the white powder. What a sight she must be! She would have laughed along with Patty if her mother hadn't walked into the kitchen at just that moment.

Mem didn't scold Sarah. She didn't need to. Sarah glanced at *Mem.* Anger flashed in her eyes. Then, seeing Patty and the magazines, *Mem*'s brow furrowed. She no doubt figured out what had distracted Sarah from the pan of milk.

Mem marched over to Patty and pointed. "These yer magazines?"

Patty shook her head. "Ne."

"Whose are they then?"

"I bought them fer Sarah."

Mem picked them up, turned toward her daughter, and then stalked over to the trash, tossing them in.

"You need to keep yer mind on the task you've been called to." *Mem*'s voice was low with the slightest quiver. "Sarah Shelter, you don't need to get yer mind filled with fancy things, do ya hear? You don't need to let what's pretty fill yer heart, pushing out all that's obedient and *gut.*"

Sarah nodded. She didn't have the heart to look at her friend. Patty had given her the best gift ever. And now those beautiful, colorful magazines sat in the trash.

Sarah's heart felt as if it had cracked in two, like an eggshell, with all her hopes spilling out. It wasn't just the magazines — no, it was more than that. *Mem* thought the very things Sarah wanted to make

were rubbish.
No fancy cupcakes for Sarah.
Not now.
Not ever.

CHAPTER 12

It seemed like she'd just lain down when she was stirred to wakefulness again. Sarah opened her eyes to muted light. It was morning. They'd made it! She was cold, stiff, and sore, but they'd be out of these woods soon and home. She smiled, imagining *Mem*'s sigh of relief and *Dat*'s warm hug.

Jathan scooped snow from the base of the trees, dumping it on the campfire. Sarah sat up and straightened her *kapp,* guessing she looked a mess. It didn't matter though. Not really. They'd been protected through the night. More than that, she felt freer than when she'd entered these woods yesterday. She'd cried about Patty. She'd laughed with Jathan about silly things, and he'd helped her finally allow the truth to sink into her heart — she couldn't have done anything to save Patty if she'd tried.

God had given Patty twenty-two years, and Sarah was blessed to have been a part of her life for over half of them. As much as it knotted up her heart to think about her friend, she saw life differently because of Patty. She also knew that Patty would be quite upset by the way Sarah had held everyone else at arm's length as she'd mourned. That's the last thing her friend would have wanted.

Sarah attempted to tuck strands of hair back into her *kapp,* and then she glanced over at Jathan. He was being strangely quiet as he finished putting out the fire. She sat up, slid on her hiking boot and began to tie the shoe strings. Her ankle didn't feel as sore today . . . which was a good thing.

"So tell me. What are you thinking about?"

"Breakfast." Jathan rubbed his stomach. "When we get down to town, I'm heading over to the restaurant."

Laughter burst from Sarah's mouth. "Yer not thinking about wrapping up in a quilt and sitting before a warm fire? That's what I am looking forward to the most."

"Sarah, do you really think I'd be considering heat more than food?" He smiled. "You have a *dat* and *brieder.* Don't you know how much earnest thinking men put into their meals? In fact, one of my *brieder* told me food was one of the reasons he stayed Amish after *Rumspringa.* Because

154

most *Englisch* women don't know how to cook. It's a joke, of course . . . but there's a ring of truth."

Sarah laughed. "*Ach,* I can see that. Maybe he's not the only one. I have a feeling many an Amish man was corralled by the scents drifting out of an Amish woman's kitchen."

She shook the pine needles off Jathan's shirt and then handed it to him. "You better put this on, or it's not gonna look right when we're rescued."

"Rescued? What do you mean rescued? I've already rescued you." He jutted out his chin. "You watch. We're going to make it to the gate before they even get a chance to send anyone up the trail."

Sarah looked up the hill. She stood clumsily to her feet. "I'm not so sure about that. I'm gonna have to take it easy like. I'll do the best I can, but I'll most likely need to lean on you for support."

"Wait now." He stepped closer to her. "That's not going to work." Jathan opened his arms, and before she knew what was happening, he scooped up Sarah like a father scooping up a five-year-old.

Instinctively, Sarah's arms went around Jathan's neck. Her cheek was just slightly lower than his chin, and she felt his warm breath on her face. She couldn't remember the last time she'd been carried. Maybe when she was a toddler in *Dat*'s arms. This was completely different.

Because of Jathan's muscled arms around her, Sarah's skin smoldered like the dying campfire embers. He felt warm. Safe. At that moment, Sarah knew something else too. They'd entered these woods as almost strangers, but now they were leaving as friends . . . and maybe something more.

She dared to glance up into his smiling face. He was looking at her. Studying her. There was the same care and attention in his gaze that she'd seen yesterday, but now she understood it, understood him.

Jathan wasn't awkward; he was timid, yet caring. He had humor in his gaze when he looked at her not because he was making fun of her, but because she made him smile.

"I'll get you out of here. I know the way."

She didn't argue. Instead she hung on tightly as he climbed the path that would take them to the rock slide trail.

"If that's true, if you know the way, then why didn't we head out last night?" she teased.

"I wasn't sure in the dark, but now that I can see the mountains, I'm sure I can find the trail."

"Just as long as you don't get us lo—"

"Lost?" He finished for her. "We're already lost, Sarah." Instead of getting angry, he smiled. "But I have no plans to stay that way."

Something in Jathan's eyes made her want to believe him. She looked deeper. No, it was more than that. He wanted to succeed. He *needed* to succeed.

Instead of looking around to make sure he was going the right way, she relaxed in his arms. Her legs dangled. The pain in her ankle hadn't lessened after all — not really. Even the movement of its swaying hurt. She never would have been able to walk out of these woods. Jathan had realized that.

He moved with steady steps and watched his footing closely.

"I'm not a glass vase," she said, not much louder than a whisper, after they made it a little way up the trail.

"Excuse me?"

"If you drop me, I won't break, I promise."

"Is that what you thought before you hurt yer ankle?" He stepped upward with deliberate steps and sucked in deep breaths.

"That's not funny."

"I know. That's why I'm going to make sure you don't get hurt any worse."

"Thank you."

157

He walked for a while, and she tried not to stare at his face, but she couldn't help but notice his strong jaw, the stubble on his chin, and the small scar over his eye.

"How did you get your scar?" She lifted her hand, instinctively wanting to touch the scar, before lowering it again.

He pulled back his head and winced. "It happened a long time ago."

"Did that happen when you fell out of one of those trees?"

"No." He shook his head. "After that. I don't mean to be vague, but it isn't one of my favorite memories. I would like to tell you sometime, but . . ." His breathing grew labored as the path rose up the hill. "Another time would be better."

"*Ja,* of course, I understand." And she did.

There were stories about Patty Sarah hadn't shared with anyone, like the day they'd worked on Patty's quilt. Sarah hoped she could share someday. In a strange way, it was the happiest moments with her friend that would be the hardest to share. But things would get better. Sarah had a feeling the more she shared, the easier it would be.

And what if instead of holding back, Sarah stepped out and started becoming the person Patty had seen her as? What would it be like to allow herself to be creative in the kitchen and open-hearted to those she served — the Amish and *Englisch* alike?

Patty always told Sarah she should own her own bakery because she had both cooking skills and a love for people, but what would that really mean? Would her Amish community accuse her of being too independent? It just wasn't something a young Amish woman did. More than that, the West Kootenai was a small place. There wasn't a need for two bakeries, let alone one that specialized in *fancy.*

And what about Jathan? How did he fit into everything? Sarah couldn't imagine leaving these woods and not having him in her life.

As Sarah rested in his arms as he walked up the hill, she knew one thing. Jathan wouldn't shrink away from carrying her through the rough patches.

She leaned her cheek into his neck. She had a feeling her question from now on would continue to be, *What about Jathan?*

The only time Jathan set Sarah down was when they stopped at the spring by Lake Geneva and filled their water bottles. He'd found the trail easily enough and had insisted on taking her to the bottom of the hill. That included carrying her as he walked down the rock slide.

Not wanting to look, Sarah had clung to his shirt and pressed her forehead into his neck. He was steady on his feet, and she never truly feared falling . . . but she didn't want him to know that. She enjoyed the closeness. She had a hunch he did too.

Just as Jathan had predicted, the search-and-rescue team in their bright orange vests — along with members of their community, both Amish and *Englisch* — were gathering in the parking area behind the gate when Amos spotted Jathan carrying Sarah down the road.

"There they are!" Amos shouted.

Sarah studied the faces as they approached — her parents, Edgar, Jenny, Annie, the Carashes, the Peachy family, and numerous other friends. Sarah hadn't seen so many Amish and *Englisch* gathered together in one place since . . . she swallowed hard. Since Patty's funeral.

Her parents rushed toward them, closely followed by their friends. Sarah softly sighed and then patted Jathan's chest. "You did it. You rescued me."

A grin filled his face, and she could feel his chest puff up. No Amish man would ever admit pride, but she had a feeling Jathan

160

would be retelling the story often. And even though many would know how foolish Sarah had been for veering from the main trail, Sarah was fine with it. They could gossip about her. She didn't mind, so long as everyone also knew what a brave and kind man Jathan was. So long as her parents knew too.

She patted his chest with the palm of her hand. "*Ach,* you can let me down now. My *mem* was quite concerned when she heard that some of the bachelors had seen me without my *kapp.* I bet she's even more worried now. To see this with her own eyes and to know that word will get out that we walked out of the woods with me in yer arms. Who's going to want to be caught by me now?"

"Do you want to catch a bachelor?" Jathan asked as he gently set her down.

The question caught her off guard, and her ankle ached as soon as her foot touched down. She stumbled slightly. Sarah grabbed Jathan's arm to steady herself.

"Uh, *ne,*" she answered. "I'm not wanting to catch anyone . . . else." She swallowed hard and squeezed his arm. She couldn't believe she'd added that last word, but seeing his face brighten, she continued, "What is the *Englisch* saying, 'A bird in the hand is

161

worth two in the bush'?"

Jathan chuckled, his laugher causing her heart to dance. "Well, Sarah, if I'm a bird, I'm a big one. But I don't mind being caught, not one bit."

"Sarah!" Her mother reached her first, wrapping her arms around Sarah's shoulders. "Are you cold, hungry? We need to get you home."

Dat hugged her next, pulling her close. "Sarah, yer well. Look at you, yer safe. W-we . . ." *Dat*'s voice trailed off. "We were so worried."

"*Ja,* me too, at least for a while, but then . . . God sent help. *Mem, Dat,* I want you to meet Jathan."

They barely had time to greet him before the rest of the rescue party approached.

A tall man in an orange vest waited patiently while everyone offered Sarah hugs and Jathan handshakes, and then he stepped forward.

"Are both of you okay?"

"*Ja,* I am." Sarah looked up at Jathan. "Are you? What about yer foot?"

"What about *your* foot?" Jathan looked down at Sarah's ankle. "Yer the one who can't walk more than ten steps."

"I can too." She scowled at him. "I'm sure I can walk eleven." She laughed.

Dat cleared his throat and only then did Sarah realize how things must look. Jathan had just been carrying her and now — after a night spent together in the woods — they were harassing each other like an old married couple. Sarah bit her lip and attempted to be serious.

"*Ja*, my ankle hurts very much. My friend is right. I can't walk on it much at all." She emphasized the word *friend*.

"Well, Miss —" The *Englisch* man put a hand on her shoulders — "we're so glad you're out of those woods. We also like happy endings like this. Can you do us a favor?"

"What's that?"

"Can you let these kind paramedics take a look at your ankle? I don't want them to leave disappointed that they didn't get to offer any help." He turned to Jathan. "And you, too, sir. Even if there's not much we can do, it'll make us feel good after having come all this way."

Jathan nodded, even though she could tell he felt foolish for having a bruise and slight burn checked out.

Sarah tried to show more enthusiasm. "*Ja*, yes, of course. I appreciate you coming, but I want to assure everyone that I was in very good hands. Jathan protected me completely. Honored me as any noble man should."

Sarah didn't have to look up into Jathan's face to know he was smiling. She saw his smile reflected in her father's gaze and knew that Jathan would be a welcome visitor to their home, whenever he had that chance.

And as Sarah limped over to the paramedics, she prayed a secret prayer that the chances would be often.

She felt God had brought her Jathan to be a balm, to help heal the pain of her loss. And she was glad for that, because when she did decide to marry, she wanted to offer a whole and healed heart to her husband.

And maybe, just maybe, the man who helped heal her heart would be the one to benefit from it, to claim it for himself. Even though it was too soon to think about such things, Sarah smiled more broadly. It seemed just the way God would work.

At least they had months for time to tell. Months to get to know each other better and come to the place where they could share their hardest stories while also creating memories of their own.

CHAPTER 13

Sarah plopped herself down on a chair and elevated her foot on a stepping stool. The bell on the front door jingled, and she considered getting up to see who it was, but then she changed her mind. Anyone coming into the West Kootenai Kraft and Grocery this early in the morning was no doubt a regular. And if they'd been around the store more than a few times, they'd know where to find her.

She held the measuring cup in her hand and watched the doorway. A tall figure moved her direction and her heart leaped in her chest. It still surprised her how Jathan walked so gracefully for a man his size.

Seeing her, he paused in the doorway and crossed his arms over his chest. "I cannot believe that yer here, working, jest one day after you've been rescued from the perilous woods."

"Of course you can. That's why you came,

because you *hoped* I would be. Isn't that the truth?"

His neck grew red, and he rubbed it. "*Ja,* you caught me. I suppose that's the truth. But even though I expected you would be here, I also hoped you'd rest a while. It was a hard couple of days."

Sarah picked up a cookbook on the counter and flipped through it, but she wasn't sure why. She already knew what she was going to make. She also knew the recipe by heart. Maybe she diverted her attention because she was fearful of looking too closely into Jathan's gaze. Not because she didn't want to look at him; she did. Mostly because she feared that the connection they'd experienced yesterday wouldn't be there. Or perhaps wouldn't be as strong now that they were safe and had returned to their normal routines.

"I couldn't stay home. Sitting on my bed doing nothing is the worst type of punishment. 'Idleness is the nest in which mischief lays its eggs,' as my *mem* says," Sarah said. "I thought about staying home, but I knew Annie would need help. I also . . ." She lowered her head. "Well, truth is, I'd hoped to see you here too."

Jathan stepped farther into the bright kitchen, and she dared to glance up. He wasn't smiling. No, his gaze was more tender than that. He seemed to take her words and breathe them in. Her comment had done more than make him happy. Her words seemed to give life to his heart.

He removed his wide-brimmed hat and placed it on the coatrack and then ran a hand through his hair.

"Do you mind if I sit and watch?" he asked. "I've been working with Abe Sommer, but he's back in Indiana fer a spell, and I have the day off."

"Mr. Sommer? Oh *ja*. They're back for a wedding. Of course I don't mind if you sit and watch. Not at all. I'd like the company. And I can use help too. Can you get me the flour and oil? Both are in that large pantry." She pointed.

Jathan rose and moved to the pantry. He returned with the flour and oil, and he'd also grabbed baking soda, baking powder, and salt. Then, without her asking, he moved to the walk-in refrigerator and got the butter and a jar of buttermilk.

"Is this what you use?" he asked, holding up the glass jar.

"*Ja*. I can understand how you figured out I'm making buttermilk biscuits, because I make them every morning I'm here . . . but how did you know the ingredients?"

He shrugged. "A good guess."

Sarah lowered her head and looked at him from under her eyelashes. "Good guess indeed." Then she folded her hands on her apron and watched as he pulled a large mixing bowl off the top shelf and picked a wooden spoon from out of the drawer in the workstation — the exact spoon she would have chosen.

"There's something different about you, Jathan."

The words were just barely out of her mouth when he stiffened. He still smiled, but it seemed forced. He turned his back to her, pretending to be interested in something outside the window.

Did I say something wrong? Sarah measured the buttermilk and then slowly stirred it into the dry ingredients.

A sinking feeling came over her, just like it had when they were in the woods and she'd asked about the scar over his eye.

"I don't mean that in a bad way. Yer different, easy fer me to talk to, and you seem to be comfortable around the kitchen. I like that."

He nodded, but as he glanced back at her there was a distance in his gaze that she hadn't seen before. "I'm glad you do, Sarah, but I have to say there's others who —" He

168

paused. "Never mind."

"Never mind what?"

"I don't want to ruin the day — a beautiful day with a beautiful girl."

"If you say so," she commented, feeling her own heart withdraw. Is that how others felt when she kept to herself? No wonder she hadn't found love. Who would want to fall in love with a wall?

Jathan offered half a smile and then measured a tablespoon of baking soda into the triple batch. *How did he know the right amount?*

He wasn't ordinary, that was for certain. And she liked that. But would the special friendship they both obviously wanted end before it was given a chance?

After all, how could she open her heart to someone who kept himself guarded as if chained up by lock and key? And how could she offer her jumbled mass of emotions to him in return? As with a ball of knitting yarn, she didn't know where pulling one string of thoughts and feelings would lead.

In math, two halves made a whole. But in life — and with relationships — two halves offered up from broken souls seemed a poor way to begin something wonderful.

Being the youngest of eight, with all his

169

siblings married, Jathan thought he understood what to do when one desired to court a lady. Long walks and heartfelt talks were in order. Buggy rides, picnic lunches, and sharing stories by lantern light brought a couple closer.

Some of his brothers had participated in bedroom courtship, bringing their intended home — or to the house of a friend — and sleeping side by side through the night with a bolster between them. Jathan had never liked a woman enough to even consider that . . . until now. Yet as he watched Sarah measure all her ingredients, he realized he didn't need to follow in the footsteps of his siblings. He'd never experienced a more intimate moment than being in the kitchen with Sarah, especially when he saw her bow her head.

"What were ya doin'?" Jathan asked when she lifted it less than a minute later.

"Saying a simple prayer. My *oma* said the surest way to make *gut* food is to bake it with love . . . and to ask the Lord to bless yer kitchen and yer home." She giggled. "This is neither my kitchen nor my home, but I still pray over the food I prepare, that it may turn out well and bring joy and nourishment to those who eat it."

Jathan nodded, not knowing what to say.

Words could not express the respect he had for Sarah, the appreciation he had that God had brought someone into his life as wonderful as Sarah.

Although neither of them had stated anything more than friendship — well, not in clear language at least — he sensed her care for him was growing. He'd noticed it in the way her face had brightened when he walked into the kitchen, as if he was the one she'd been hoping to see most of all.

Sarah pulled her lip between her teeth, concentrating hard as she measured the last items for the recipe. When she'd gotten everything she needed into the mixing bowl, she looked up at him and cleared her throat, as if picking up where their last conversation left off.

"There's something special about making *gut* things and being able to serve them. It makes me feel like I'm part of God's creative process."

He nodded as he washed his hands in the sink. "I agree."

Her words stirred his own desires to open his own business. Some days he considered a retail store for his father's and brother's furniture. Some days, a store and restaurant like the West Kootenai Kraft and Grocery that Annie ran. But most times, he knew he'd like to run a bakery best, one with someone as skilled and caring as Sarah to head things up. What would she think of that?

Jathan shook his head. He wouldn't mention it. Not yet. He didn't want Sarah to think he was more interested in her baking skills than her heart — no, it was her heart he wanted most.

After he dried his hands, he wiped down the counter and spread out flour, making it easier for her to roll out the dough for the biscuits when it was time.

Sarah cocked her head and eyed him. "How did you know to do that? I realize you have been coming in early in the mornings, but you haven't been here early enough to watch me bake."

He cleared his throat. "My *mem* has a bakery, remember? I, uh, have watched her more than once." Jathan rubbed the side of his nose, hoping she didn't question him further. He thought about offering to roll out the dough for her, but then he changed his mind.

He enjoyed spending time with Sarah, and he wanted her to remember him as the one who carried her out of the forest. He didn't want her to see him as weak, as someone who did women's work. So instead of helping, he crossed his arms over his chest and watched.

"Tell me a little about yer *oma,* Sarah," he asked, remembering the smile on Sarah's face when she mentioned her.

She shrugged. "Bcfore her passing, she lived her whole life in Kentucky, and the one thing I remember is that her cookie jar was never empty." She sighed. "Her cookies were like a gift to me. Very yummy gifts, and I felt special every time I ate one."

"Yer customers feel that way too. I've heard the other diners commenting. I've felt the same. When a plate is brought out by the server, well . . . it feels like you made something special jest for me."

"I'm not the only baker and cook. Annie and Marianna also bake and cook. And Jenny is helping and learning too."

"*Ja,* I know." He shrugged. "But I didn't come in here for the last two months to see any of them."

Embarrassed by his words, Jathan took the lid off the jar of buttermilk and then looked at it closer. "Is this still good? There's something floating in it, like little flakes." He sniffed it. "Hmm. It smells good."

Sarah laughed. "Haven't you seen old-fashioned buttermilk before? My *mem* showed me how to make it from churning butter. Those flakes are butter, and you can smell it, but I don't recommend you drink it. It's much sourer than regular buttermilk."

"That's what must make yer biscuits so good."

"And my pancakes, too, if I say so myself." She jutted out her chin slightly and her *kapp* strings danced where they hung. "Although you must promise you never heard me say that. I'm supposed to be *demut,* remember?"

"Sarah, you needn't worry about that. Yer one of the most humble women I know." *And one of the most beautiful,* he wanted to add, but knew he shouldn't.

Sarah was pretty. He'd been attracted to her from the first time he saw her — with her heart-shaped face and light hair and eyebrows. Of course, it was also her joy in the kitchen that had drawn him in from the beginning. She was just the type of woman he'd enjoy spending a lifetime with, and he still had all of summer, fall, and into winter to discover if she could have such feelings for him in return. Feelings that went deeper than playful banter.

Jathan thought about Ohio. If it was up to him, would he return at all? There was nothing drawing him back. There were expectations. Expectations from the woman who'd told him from the age of sixteen that they were to be married. Expectations from his father and brothers, who all believed a stable job, no matter how boring and meaningless, was all one needed to aspire to in life — and they thought that's all *he* needed to aspire to.

"What are you thinking about?" Sarah asked, kneading the biscuit dough into a ball. "You left this kitchen about five minutes ago, or at least that's how it seemed."

"*Ach,* so sorry. It's jest that I'm regretting having to go back home after hunting season."

Sarah nodded and then looked at him, narrowing her gaze. "Regret it? Returning to family and yer *mem*'s bakery? It sounds delightful to me."

He eyed her, his curiosity piqued. "But going back means leaving what I'm growing to care for here."

Sarah pointed to the window. He followed her gaze and noticed the sunrise had transformed the snowy peaks, making them look like they were frosted in pink.

"Oh, the mountains. It will be hard to leave them," she said. "*Ja,* I understand."

Jathan cleared his throat. "Sarah, you know I'm not talking about the moun-

175

tains. . . ." He couldn't come out and say it, but by the light that appeared in her eyes, he sensed she understood.

"Jathan . . . do you read the Bible?" She lowered her voice so it sounded deeper, as if mimicking his words from yesterday.

"*Ja.*"

She stroked her chin and unknowingly left a smudge of flour there. "If I remember right, there is a verse that says, 'Therefore do not worry about tomorrow, for tomorrow will worry about itself. Each day has enough trouble of its own.' Perhaps there will be a way that everything you dream fer will come true."

"That's true. We're not to worry. But it's hard; especially when someone else has yer whole life planned out fer you. Yer ideas and dreams. With my dreams taken from me, sometimes it seems the only feelings I have left fer myself are my worries."

"What do you mean, yer dreams taken away?"

He held in a breath. *How can I explain? How can I let her know that when I do return, I'll have little or no time to enjoy* Mem*'s bakery?*

As much as he'd enjoyed spending time with Sarah yesterday, and as much as he hoped conversations like today could lead to a growing relationship between them, a part of him said to walk away and not get her involved. What he wanted to offer Sarah and what he could offer were two different things. Who he wanted to be and the son and brother he would step back into being when he returned to Ohio were two different men.

"I suppose I should tell you. My life is planned out fer me. Since I finished grade eight, I've been working around the farm and in my *dat*'s workshop, but my family needs more money coming in. My *dat* has already talked with a friend of his who works in a local factory. They have a job fer me when I return. And then there's the farm. *Dat* and *Mem* had already begun to move their things into the *dawdi* house before I left. The big house will be mine . . . and all the responsibilities. They figure when I start my job, they can keep the shop running and keep the farm from going under."

"The shop?" She slowly rolled out the dough.

"My *dat* and oldest *bruder,* Yonnie, are woodworkers. It was Yonnie who came up with the idea of me going to the factory. He and *Dat* have ideas for expanding their wholesale market beyond Holmes County but need some money to invest to do that."

"Money you'll bring in from yer job?"

Jathan nodded.

"But that doesn't seem right. I know we are called to care fer our elders, but I know you — you'd do that anyway."

"I would — in my own time and own way maybe — but all the ways I imagine spending my life can't help them now, with their current needs."

"And how would you like to spend yer life?" She tilted her face up to his. The morning light from the kitchen window sent a beam of radiance across the narrow strip of hair her prayer *kapp* didn't cover. More than anything, Jathan wished he could bend down and kiss that spot.

"Like you, Sarah, I enjoy spending time with people. I appreciate our Amish heritage and faith and know not everyone has that. Day by day, I'd love to interact with customers and remind them it's the simple things in life that matter most — to share a bit of our heritage with *Englischers.* To provide fer their needs and . . ." He looked away.

"What?" She adjusted her stance, keeping the weight off her sore ankle and reached out and touched his arm. "What were you going to say?"

He lifted his head and looked to the ceiling, imagining the sky outside and heaven beyond. "I was going to say, I would like to spend my days doing something closer to this —" he waved his hand around the room — "than being part of an assembly line. But you see, Sarah . . ." He returned his gaze to her. "That's where my struggle is. It's impossible for me to honor my *dat* and follow my dreams at the same time."

He watched closely as she looked away. She focused on the cookbook she'd been holding when he'd first walked in. Sarah brushed her fingers over the cover, curving them to follow the swirl of the cupcake's pink frosting in the photograph. Then she turned back to him.

"I know what yer sayin'." Her eyes pulled him into their blue depths, and then she nodded and crossed her arms over her apron. "It's too easy to think it's wrong to want to spend our days doing what we enjoy. It's easy to give up on that dreaming, isn't it? To let those who've given us life — and who direct us on God's path — draw us away from what our hearts long to do."

Out of all the people he knew, Jathan somehow knew she would be the one to understand.

He thought about the night before he'd left for Montana. How *Dat* and Yonnie had sat him down with their accounting books.

179

They'd asked him not to go. They needed him, needed his income. He told them he'd send what he could once he had a job in Montana, and he'd done that. Working with Abe Sommer had given him some money, but not enough.

He felt selfish for taking this trip, but he needed it. He needed space and time to think and to connect with God. He was thankful he'd met Sarah and felt blessed today more than ever to be with her, but that didn't shake off the burden of guilt he carried for not doing all he could for his family. It was as if he'd packed guilt into two of the largest cedar chests his father made and had brought them with him, carrying one burden on each shoulder.

Jathan picked up the biscuit cutter and started cutting small, round discs from the dough Sarah had already rolled out, placing the circles on a baking sheet in neat, straight lines.

She looked up at him. He could tell from her serious expression that she was pondering their talk of dreaming and of obeying and how the two mixed — or rather how they clashed at times.

"Sometimes I struggle with thinking my dreams are foolish too," she finally said. "I also try to weigh my motives. Am I doing what I'm doing because it's what God desires, or because I'm afraid people will be disappointed if I don't?"

Jathan nodded. "Or because I'm following in the ways I've been taught, respecting those who've gone before me and obeying my father and mother? If I believe that's what God wants — and I know it is — then I know what I have to do."

"So yer parents want you to take over their property and house?" she asked.

"*Ja,* and many expenses go with that, and the farm itself takes much work with little profit. The only way to make it will be to get an outside job."

"I don't know what to say," Sarah finally offered.

"There is nothing to say. I jest wanted you to know — thought it was important."

Sarah tilted her head as if trying to distinguish if there was a deeper meaning behind his last statement. She opened her mouth as if she wanted to say something, then closed it again.

"Were you going to ask me something, Sarah?"

"*Ne.* Well, *ja,* but *ne,* I can't. It would be far too forward." She looked down at the cookbook and flipped through the pages, but he knew her mind wasn't on the recipes.

He knew she was wondering about him — about them — just as he was.

"Then if you are too shy to ask, I will tell you. I know our friendship is jest beginning, but I wanted to tell you everything, because I care about you, Sarah. Yer exactly the type of person I can imagine spending my life with."

She stopped flipping pages and glanced up at him. She smiled and her nose wrinkled, and then she placed a hand to her lips. "A friendship is a wonderful place to start, and I feel the same about you, but there are so many questions. You being from Ohio and my family being here. Your *dat*'s expectations and . . ." Pink rose to her cheeks and she touched them. "Wait, I'm getting ahead of myself, aren't I?"

Joy bubbled up in Jathan and it emerged from his lips as laughter. "I don't mind, really, but I should get to know yer family — talk to yer *dat*. See if he'd consider me someone worthy of his daughter's, uh, friendship."

"*Ja,* that makes sense." Hope and joy warmed her eyes.

"I'd like to plan my whole future the way I want it, but we both know that's not the Amish way. We're taught the ways of our ancestors from the time we're children. We know honoring our parents is most important," he said. "I jest have to trust that my Christian duty is to care fer people as they need and trust that if God has different plans fer me — fer us — he will make a way."

"It's true." She nodded. "It's all we can do. And as Patty used to tell me, we jest need to keep walking in the direction God pointed us last, and if we keep looking fer him and waiting on him, God will let us know when to make a change of direction."

She finished up the biscuits and put them into the oven to bake. She hobbled over to the list of baked goods she still needed to make, and he wished she'd let him help more. But he also knew it would be impossible to keep her still all day.

Returning to her chair, Sarah grimaced and then blew out a breath. When she got her foot situated on the stool once again, she turned her attention back to him and wore a serious expression. "I appreciate you sharing all that. I like knowing more about you. It also tells me how to pray. And, well, Jathan, there's something I need you to know too."

He leaned forward in his chair. "What's that?"

She reached across the counter and pulled

a paper sack toward her. Looking into it, she had a satisfied look on her face, and then she handed the sack to him. It was heavy and rattled slightly in his hands.

Jathan looked inside. *Walnuts?* "Uh, what is this for?"

"I need you to know I'm making banana bread today." Sarah spoke in a serious tone. Then she reached over to the top drawer, pulled out a nut cracker, and handed it to him. "Since yer here to help."

"Sure." He chuckled. "It doesn't look as if I have a choice."

"If you want banana bread you don't." She laughed, and Jathan joined in. He liked seeing her this way. He liked the happy, playful side of Sarah. He wasn't sure if he was just getting to know a different side of her or if something had happened deep in her heart during the night before last. He felt like he carried a different woman out of the woods than the one who'd entered. He'd like to think Sarah opening up to him about Patty had something to do with that.

"If I didn't have so much baking to do, I'd be happy to crack the walnuts," she said. "It's one of my favorite chores, 'cept *Mem* doesn't allow me to lend a hand too often at home. Seems more of the meat makes it into my mouth than into the bowl. Then

Mem always wonders why the banana bread seems sparse. Of course, we don't have walnut trees here in Montana. We have a friend who brings us a large bag whenever he heads out this way."

Over the next thirty minutes, Jathan cracked the nuts. Then he moved to the pantry for wax paper.

"What are you doing?" Sarah paused from kneading dough to watch him.

"I have a trick." He laid out two pieces of wax paper, placed the nuts in between, and then rolled over them with a rolling pin.

Sarah's mouth dropped open. "That's so smart. Out of all my years in the kitchen, I've never seen that before."

Jathan grinned. "All the years in the kitchen? That makes you sound like an old maid."

"To some I am. But hopefully not in the opinion of someone special."

Jathan paused and eyed her. Sarah placed a hand over her mouth as if in disbelief that those words had just spilled out.

"Would this someone be holding a rolling pin in his hand?" Jathan asked.

Sarah nodded.

"Then you don't have anything to worry about, Sarah," he said as he tossed the walnuts into the batter Sarah had prepared.

"You don't have anything to worry about at all."

CHAPTER 14

Sarah eyed Jathan as he moved around the kitchen. He acted much more at ease here than when he'd been in the forest the other night. In the forest, he'd fumbled around as he searched for dry wood. He'd woken her at the cry of a coyote.

Yet here in the kitchen, there was a peace about Jathan she couldn't explain. He'd pulled items from the pantry with confidence. He watched her closely as she worked, as if he were memorizing her recipes. He tried to act like he was just a simple observer, but the way he crushed the walnuts revealed that he was more.

What type of Amish man was this? Did he think he could spend time with her here and think she'd not notice how comfortable he was? And what did he mean by saying he'd rather spend days like this rather than working in a mill? Had he considered helping at his mother's bakery? If so, maybe he wouldn't consider Sarah's own dreams so foolish. Her heart leapt within her at the thought.

He was wiping down the counters and washing up the dirty dishes when Sarah knew she had to get to the bottom of it. She poured the banana bread batter into greased and floured bread pans and then attempted to stand.

She pressed her lips into a thin line, stood, and took one step. A stabbing feeling radiated through her ankle. Sarah moaned and grabbed the counter.

Jathan turned, eyes wide. "What are you doing? I'm standing right here, Sarah. What do you need?"

"I was jest going to turn on the oven. It's only five steps away."

"Jest ask, won't you? I've never known such a stubborn woman." He shook his head and then walked over to the industrial oven and turned it on to 350 degrees. He hadn't needed to ask her how to make it work, and he hadn't asked about the temperature.

"*Ja, gut.* Now can you put these loaves inside?"

He glanced over at her, his eyebrows forming a *V.* "Now?"

"Of course now. I'm moving slowly this

morning and our customers will be here before I know it —"

Jathan held up his hands, refusing her request. "*Ne,* you can't. It'll ruin yer batter. The oven has to prehea—"

"Ah-ha!" She picked up a kitchen towel and flicked it his direction. "Caught you."

He took a step back, surprised. "Excuse me?"

Sarah laughed. "You act as if yer jest a casual observer, but yer far from that. You move around the kitchen like my *dat* moves around his barn. I've never seen an Amish man like you. If I didn't know better . . ." Sarah paused. As she watched, a shadow fell over Jathan's face and an expression flashed through his eyes, breaking her heart. What was that look? Shame.

He lowered his head and turned away, then moved to the farthest corner of the kitchen, like a young child running to the corner, to start wiping down the already clean shelves. His shoulders slumped heavily as if a great, invisible burden settled on them. It was as if the tall man before her had crumbled inside from her words and had a hard time holding himself erect.

Her smiled faded. "What's wrong? Did I say something wrong?"

"*Ne,* it's nothing." He turned and moved

189

toward the coatrack near the door. "I was jest thinking I should get home. Uh, Amos wanted to go shooting today and —"

"Jathan, stop." The words shot from her mouth. Thankfully, he did.

He turned to her slowly. "What is it, Sarah?"

Pain radiated from his gaze, and deep down, Sarah knew exactly what he was feeling. She knew because she'd held the same feelings — tucked them away inside for many years.

She cleared her throat. "There is something I should have told you in the woods. Something I should have confessed."

His eyes widened slightly and he took a step forward.

"I have loved getting to know you, and it crossed my mind that when you return to Berlin next year, I'd like to visit. After all, my aunt lives there . . ." She let her voice trail off. "There's only one problem, you see." She bit her lip and, even as she said the words, a small remnant of shame stirred within. "I'm afraid if I ever met yer *mem,* she wouldn't care much for me."

He took three steps toward her now and kneeled before her. "*Ne,* that wouldn't be. Why would you ever think that?"

She blew out a heavy breath. For many

reasons. "I hate quilting. I've only finished one quilt, and it was fer a, uh, friend. I don't like to sew, and *Mem* gave up trying to teach me how. I enjoy gardening, but I don't like to can. I'm not much fer cooking meals, and I'm afraid when I have children someday, I'd be tempted to serve them pie fer dinner every night. My *mem* calls me a daydreamer too. I spend a lot of time each day with my thoughts — my memories. Jest my experiences with Patty have filled a couple of memory jars. I can spend an hour staring at the clouds or thinking up the perfect ingredients fer a cupcake recipe." She touched her *kapp.* "Truth is, I'm not much of an Amish woman."

"What? *Ne.*" He reached out and touched her hand. "None of those things matter, Sarah. At least they don't matter to me."

"Honestly?" A lightness filled her chest at his words, and she smiled. She placed her other hand on his. "Do you really mean that?"

"*Ja,* of course."

Sarah tilted her head. "Jathan, deep down I had a feeling you'd say that. Out of all the other bachelors in these parts, I wouldn't admit such things to another. But I have to say my confession is only part of what was weighing down my heart. There is more I must tell you too . . . about my faith.

"All my years growing up, I was not so impressed by the people who lived perfect lives, who did everything by the *Ordnung,*" she continued. "The people I've loved are the ones who don't force themselves to be who everyone else expects but who seek God so they can understand who they already are. *Mem* and *Dat* attend *Englisch* prayer meetings. They pray out loud at times. Most of their Amish friends don't know, and their family back in Kentucky would be shocked if they knew."

She thought of another wild spirit and a sad smile filled her face. "Then there was Patty. My dear friend was not quiet. She was not meek. She would rather have tromped through the forest than sit before a fireplace and quilt. I spent nearly every day with her for twelve years, and I'm afraid I picked up her bad habits." Sarah touched her hand to her cheek. The confession hurt her heart more than she expected it would. "The Amish in these parts know I'm different. I've heard them comment when they didn't think I could hear. 'That Sarah Shelter, she'll be an old maid fer sure. Whoever would choose a wife like that . . .'" Tears rimmed her eyes, and she touched her fingers to trembling lips.

"Sarah, *ne.*" He brushed a tear from her cheek with his thumb. "Don't listen to those words. Yer faith inspires me. They don't know what they're talking about."

She could see from his face he wanted to continue. Wanted to tell her he'd like a wife like that. She smiled, realizing it was enough to see it in his gaze.

"That really doesn't bother you then?"

He rose and shook his head. "*Ne,* if anything, it makes me appreciate you even more. That's why I enjoy being with you, Sarah. Yer not like the other women."

"If you believe that, Jathan, and I know you do, then I have something else to say."

He looked down at her and waited.

"Yer unlike any other Amish man, and I like that. I enjoy yer ease in the kitchen, and I have a feeling you enjoy being here too." She ignored the red rising up his neck and continued, "I don't want you to feel as if you have to hide from me — hide the real you. To repeat the words of a very wise person, 'if anything, it makes me appreciate you even more.' That's why I enjoy being with you, Jathan. Yer not like other men."

He nodded. He was listening, but did he truly hear her?

Who hurt yer heart, Jathan? she wanted to ask. *Who made you feel unworthy?* They were questions she wanted answered, but not now. They had plenty of days ahead for that. For now, she just wanted to give him something to think about. She wanted for him to know she saw a glimpse of the real him.

He turned to the window and stood quietly. She could see the battle that raged within. Things like this took time. They had with her. And for some broken pieces of her heart, more time was required still.

The jingle of the front door caught her attention. The day had begun, and she had a lot yet to prepare. Many words were yet unspoken, she knew, but Sarah was thankful they'd started this journey.

CHAPTER 15

Even though Jathan couldn't spend every day of the next two weeks in the kitchen with Sarah, he often visited with her early in the morning before he headed over to his construction job. Only today, he was headed there after work too. The evening breeze stirred the scent of pine as Jathan returned to the West Kootenai Kraft and Grocery. He'd talked to Annie a few times in the past, but today an urgency pressed, and he wondered if she'd be willing to talk to him — really talk to him — about what it was like to run a business.

He entered the front door, and the small bell jingled, announcing his presence. He noticed right away that Edgar, the front store clerk, had already gone home. The store was in the lull that occurred before the dinner rush. Annie sat behind the front counter at a small desk. She was writing something down in a ledger. She looked up as he entered.

"Jathan, hello!" She smiled. "I appreciated you helping Sarah this morning, but I'm surprised to see you back. Would have thought you'd have had enough of this place."

Annie rose, and her long, blonde ponytail swished back and forth as she stood. She wore a red plaid shirt and jeans and looked as if she were more prepared to work at the Log Works next door.

"I've actually come to talk to you about running a business. I've been thinking about the future and . . . well . . . trying to start some plans that would allow me to care fer a family someday. Care for them in a way that will benefit my parents — and my *brieder* — and be a *gut* start fer my own dreams too."

Annie nodded. "Yes, I'm listening."

"My *mem* has a bakery back in Ohio, and *Dat* makes furniture that we ship all over the county, and I just want your advice."

Annie motioned to a stool next to her. Jathan walked around the counter and sat.

"I'd love to help," she said. "What do you need to know?"

"Well, mostly if my idea makes good business sense. I'd like to spruce up my *mem*'s bakery. She has mostly Amish clients, but millions of *Englisch* tourists come through Berlin every year, and I know we can draw their business. If we expand, we could include some of *Dat*'s furniture. He sells it wholesale now, but we could make much morc selling retail." Jathan reached into his pocket and pulled out two pieces of paper. "I've estimated the costs of change, including some remodeling work and hiring another baker. It will take some investment, but considering where we live and the high-peak tourist season, I think we could grow our revenue in jest a year's time."

He continued on, telling Annie his ideas for advertising and display. He asked questions, too, about ordering, invoices, and customer loyalty. Annie seemed supportive of his ideas and answered all his questions with enthusiasm.

As they talked, the scents of the roast bccf and fried chicken being preparcd by the cooks in the kitchen caused Jathan's stomach to rumble, and he realized he only had a few minutes before the dinner rush would be upon them.

"I have one last thought," he said. "I'd like to offer custom cupcakes. It's different from what Amish bakeries typically offer, but I believe it would delight regular customers who could continually return to discover new flavors."

Annie nodded and her eyes sparkled. "Your idea doesn't involve *my* baker does it? Sarah's cupcakes are the best."

Jathan squirmed in his seat. "Actually, uh . . ." He let his words trail off.

Annie reached over and patted his hand. "I sure hope so. Because from what I can see, Sarah thinks you're pretty special."

A smile spread over Jathan's face and he stood.

"There's one more thing." Annie stood, too, and crossed her arms over her chest. "I don't think you came to me for help, young man." She wagged her finger at him.

He scratched his forehead. "I didn't?"

"No." She softened her gaze. "You already know all you need, son. You've done your homework." She placed a soft hand on his arm. "What you really came to me for was *permission.* And I want to give you that. You'll make a fine businessman. You should follow your dream. It's one that will not only benefit you, but your future wife too."

Warmth filled Jathan's chest, and his shoulders rose slightly.

"And Jathan, remember this —" Annie's tone was urgent — "God created you with special talents for a purpose, and sometimes those we love most don't understand that.

Don't let the doubts of others ring louder than God's whispers to your spirit. Sometimes God's whispers are harder to hear, but they're to be trusted the most. Understand?"

Jathan nodded and then stepped back. "*Ja,* I do, and knowing that, I wonder if it would be too much to drop in on Sarah's family? That day on the mountain, her *dat* told me I could stop by anytime."

"Go for it. Especially if you show up with this." She walked to the bakery rack and pulled out a cherry pie.

"*Ja.* I would say so." He reached for money in his pocket, but Annie waved it away.

"After all your help lately, consider this your payment. Just enjoy tonight. And have fun getting to know Sarah's family. There's a reason she's so special — she has wonderful parents."

Jathan nodded and offered a wave as he left. He had no doubt about Sarah's parents. But he also knew there was someone else who'd helped Sarah grow into the wonderful woman she was. He just felt bad that he didn't have a way to thank Patty — to honor her — for that.

It was something he'd have to think about, but for now his eager steps took him toward the place he wanted to be most — right by Sarah's side.

Sarah held her memory jar on her lap and pushed her good foot against the porch floor ever so gently, causing the porch swing to rock. Her body ached from working, even though Annie had sent her home early. Her ankle throbbed, and she had it propped up on the swing. A handkerchief of ice rested on it.

Yet even with the aches and pains, her heart felt lighter than it had in a long time. She picked a small thimble out of the memory jar and turned it over in her hands. She'd used it the first time she'd gone to a sewing circle. Patty hadn't been there, and at first Sarah had felt out of place. Yet the more she sat and chatted with the other ladies, the more she realized she enjoyed their company too. The sewing hadn't been her favorite part; it was the interaction with other women she'd enjoyed. She'd forgotten that memory until now.

Sarah put the thimble back into the jar. She pulled out a purple plastic toy ring she'd gotten during a shopping trip to Kalispell. She'd watched a boy put fifty cents into a machine and his smile had turned into a frown when he realized he'd gotten a ring. The boy had turned and handed it to Sarah. Knowing Amish people didn't wear jewelry, Sarah had worn it, but only to bed, each night for a week until she finally tucked it away in the jar. More memories. More smiles. As she looked at the items, it was as if she was allowing her heart to wake up and celebrate what she'd experienced, not only what she'd lost.

She held up two other objects. The first was the piece of quartz rock that Jathan had given to her on the mountain. And the second was the metal nut cracker Jathan had used in the kitchen. She'd already bought another nut cracker from Annie's store shelf to replace the one she took. And as she replaced both items in the jar, she hoped these would be just the first of many with Jathan's name attached to them.

It had been good to spend time with him over the past two weeks — almost as if it were the most natural thing in the world. And that made sense. Despite her mother's insistence that love was more about function than fancy romance, Sarah had gone against the Amish way and had let her mind and imagination run off with elaborate notions there too.

Her whole life she always pictured falling in love being full of nervous emotion, peaks

201

of romance, and the excitement of wondering if he loved her as much as she loved him. But maybe love was simpler. Maybe true love was finding someone you could talk to with ease, whose heart cared for the same things, and whose dreams could meld with your own.

As Sarah pondered these thoughts again, she spotted Jathan coming down the dirt road from the direction of the store. He held a very familiar-looking cherry pie in one hand and waved with the other as he walked into the yard and approached the porch steps.

She waved back. "How did you know I was thinking of you jest now?" she asked as he stepped up onto the porch and sat on the chair next to the swing.

He shrugged. "I was thinking about you . . . so it makes sense."

"Really?" She paused her swinging and leaned forward. "What were you thinking?"

"Oh, I jest got done talking to Annie, telling her how much I want to steal you away."

"You do, huh?" She tapped her finger on her chin. "Where to?"

"Well, I really don't want to steal you — not jest yet — but I was talking to her about how I could help grow my *mem*'s bakery . . ."

Sarah felt her lower lip rise up in a slight pout, but she hoped he didn't notice.

"What, Sarah? What's wrong?"

"Oh, I was jest hoping you were going to say *our* bakery."

"Well . . ." He leaned forward and took her hand. "That is something I haven't dared to dream about — and didn't want to press. *Mem*'s bakery seemed like a good start. And then . . . I couldn't think of anything more wonderful than having a bakery with you."

Her heart fluttered as if it were going to lift from her chest and fly away, but even though they were the very words she wanted to hear, she could see in his gaze that it cost him something to speak them. They cost a sense of pride, although she wasn't sure why. She'd ask him — bring it up another time — but she couldn't squelch the joy that bubbled over in this moment.

Laughter burst from Sarah's lips. "You know, working with *Englischers,* I hear all types of romantic proposals, but Mr. Schrock, I do believe that's the most romantic yet."

He smiled, too, but then, as he set the pie on the empty chair and leaned forward, the smile faded. He looked upon her with seriousness. "I'm enjoying this banter jest as

203

much as you, Sarah, but I hope you know I'm not taking this conversation lightly. I'd like to spend time together and . . . dream. I jest don't know if you've ever thought about running yer own bakery."

Laughter burst from Sarah's lips. "Only for as long as I can remember."

"Then it's something we should talk about, plan for . . ." He smiled. "As we get to know each other, that is." Then Jathan tilted his head. "It's amazing, don't you think, that it's something we could do together?"

"*Ja*. It reminds me of an Amish proverb my *oma* had written in a letter once before she passed: 'The grand essentials of happiness in this life are something to do, something to love, and something to hope for.' Having a bakery together would be a great thing to do. It fills me with hope jest thinking about it." She paused and fiddled with her *kapp* string, wondering if she should say more.

"And love?" Jathan dared to ask.

Sarah wrinkled her nose. "I'm unfamiliar with knowing how that feels — the love fer a man that is — but if my emotions are not leading me astray, something like I'd expect love to be is growing in me more each day."

He exhaled a deep breath and opened his

mouth, but just then the front door opened.

"Jathan!" *Mem*'s voice exclaimed. "I thought I heard yer voice. I told Evelyn to set another plate jest in case. Please tell us you can stay."

Jathan released Sarah's hand, like a child who'd been caught in the cookie tin. Then he rose. "I'd love to. I hope you do not mind." He lifted the pie out of the chair and held it out as an offering. "We, uh, Sarah made it today."

"Ja, gut, gut," *Mem* stepped forward and accepted it. "It's a lovely pie and the perfect addition to our meal." She turned to Sarah and winked. "And I'm sure Sarah — all of us — couldn't be happier about our dinner guest. May this be only one of many, many meals together."

Jathan had just sat down at the Shelters' table, and was breathing in the smell of Mrs. Shelter's pot roast, when a sharp ringing interrupted their silent prayer. It sounded like a telephone, and Jathan's head shot up. He looked around but the others still had their heads lowered. A moment later, Sarah's father lifted his head and soon the other family members did the same.

"The phone is in the shed, right next to the house," Mrs. Shelter explained. Her

205

voice wobbled slightly, and Jathan could tell she was embarrassed. "My husband uses it fer his business some, and . . ." She let her voice trail off.

Sarah cleared her throat, and Jathan turned to her. She was seated beside him and fidgeted slightly in her chair. "After Patty's accident, many Amish people put one in their sheds. We live in a dangerous community. With the logging, the forests, and the wild animals, we're learning to be prepared. It's not as if we're going against the *Ordnung* . . ."

"I understand. Things are different here." Jathan reached out and accepted the green beans Mrs. Shelter offered. "It makes sense."

"I know how to check the messages." Twelve-year-old Andy's chest puffed out with pride.

"I phone!" Little Evelyn chattered, practicing her English. She sat on the bench seat next to him and Jathan noticed every few minutes she'd scoot an inch closer.

"Shh . . ." Sarah placed a finger over her lips. "Evie, you don't want to share that with any visiting family from back east."

Jathan laughed and then he turned to Mrs. Shelter. "So Sarah tells me you have a sister in Berlin?"

"Oh, *ja,* and I've visited Holmes County a few times. It's a lovely place with all the rolling hills. I'm sad to say our children have not been there yet. I'm sure they'd love it." Mrs. Shelter glanced at Sarah.

"I hope that Sarah can come visit sometime." Jathan cut a piece of pot roast with his fork and knife, but his thoughts were more on the pink of Sarah's cheeks than on his meal. "I was telling her my *mem* has a bakery. They would be best friends, I'm sure of it. I wrote *Mem* —" Evelyn tugged on his shirt sleeve. "I wrote *Mem* last month telling her about —" Evelyn tugged harder and he paused, turning his attention to her.

"You marry Sarah?" Evelyn asked.

"Marry, uh . . ." Jathan looked from Evelyn to Sarah, unsure how to answer that.

Laughter burst from Andy's lips. "You saved her. Now you've got to live with her."

"Andy . . ." Mr. Shelter's voice was firm, but Jathan noticed humor in his gaze.

"Bensel." Mrs. Shelter shook her head.

"I'm not a silly child, *Mem."* Andy pouted. "You said yerself that Jathan would make a fine husband for Sarah."

Now it was Mrs. Shelter's turn to flush pink.

Jathan glanced over at Sarah, who was busy buttering her biscuit, ensuring every inch was slathered in butter, afraid to make eye contact.

"The truth is," Jathan finally said, "I was hoping to bring up this conversation with Mr. Shelter." He turned to the older man. "I'd like to spend more time with her, sir. To court her with hopes of a future together." Even as he said the words, he felt as if it was a dream. He'd never have believed a month ago that this could be happening. He'd cared for Sarah from afar and now she was right here at his side. And her family seemed not only welcoming — but also hopeful of their possible future together.

"That is my desire, at least . . . if that's all right with you, Sarah."

She looked at him, her blue eyes shining. *"Ja."*

It was one simple word, but Jathan's heart doubled in size within him.

Mr. Shelter nodded and then opened his mouth to speak. But before words could emerge, his eyes moved beyond Jathan, as if he were studying something out the window beyond Jathan's shoulder. Then, his eyes fixed in fear, he jumped from the table and hurried to the door.

What? Jathan turned, but his question

changed upon seeing the figure in motion. *Who?*

CHAPTER 16

It was only as she neared that Jathan recognized Sarah's boss, Annie, running across the Shelters' front lawn with long strides. Within moments she was up the porch steps and through the front door Mr. Shelter had opened for her.

Annie's breathing came fast, as if she'd run all the way to the Shelter home from her store.

She looked to Sarah first. "Did you hear the phone ringing?"

"*Ja* . . . but we were eating dinner. We usually let it go to message first —"

"Never mind." Annie looked to Jathan. Her eyes bore into him, and his head jerked back. Concern folded her eyebrows and her lips were pressed together. Seeing that, fear pinched down on his gut like a vice.

"It was your mother calling." Annie swallowed hard. "She's been trying to find a way to get ahold of you. She wouldn't tell me what the problem was, but —" Annie's voice quivered. "She seemed pretty shaken up. She wants you to call her right away."

Annie handed him a piece of paper with a phone number on it.

"Come with me." Sarah placed her hand on his arm. "I'll show you where our phone is."

In the space of one heartbeat, Jathan's knees grew weak. He looked down at the paper and the numbers blurred.

Had something happened to one of his brothers?

The faces of his nieces and nephews flashed through his mind next. Accidents happened every year.

Jathan tried to remember if one of his sisters or sisters-in-law had a baby due. It seemed like one of them always did. Could there be a problem there?

His family had been spared from great tragedy thus far. But now?

He brushed her hand aside, feeling as if he were going to be sick. "Thank you, but I need to do this alone. If you can jest point me in the right direction . . ." He moved toward the front door. Sarah stepped back. Hurt flashed over her face, but he couldn't worry about that now.

"It's in the shed right next to the house,"

Mr. Shelter commented. "There should be enough light yet that you won't need to light the lantern."

Jathan took long strides out the door and into the small shed. Mr. Shelter's tools hung on the wall, and the simple telephone sat on a worktable. As Jathan lifted the phone's receiver he suddenly knew. It had to be *Dat.* If the problem was with one of the other family members, *Mem* would have asked Yonnie to make the call, but not for his father. *Mem* would have wanted to break the news herself.

He dialed the number on the paper. Someone picked up the phone on the first ring.

"Hello, Jathan? Is it you?" His mother sounded a million miles away.

"*Ja, Mem.* It's me. Is something —" He couldn't get his words out before a wail sounded in his ear.

"Jathan, it's yer *dat.* He — he . . ." More sobs.

"Let me tell him, *Mem,*" Yonnie's voice said in the background. There was a shuffling sound and then his oldest brother cleared his throat.

"*Ja,* Jathan?"

"Yes, it's me. What happened? What's wrong with *Dat*?"

"They say it's a stroke, Jathan. I found him inside the workshop, collapsed. You need to come home now, ya hear?" Yonnie's voice was loud, and Jathan pulled the phone from his ear.

"See if you can make the next train," Yonnie continued. "We need you now more than ever. All right?"

"*Ja,* but how is *Dat*? Is he going to be all right? How serious is it?"

More voices filtered through the phone, noises. Hospital sounds. Yonnie's voice was distant, as if he'd pulled the phone back from his mouth and was talking to somebody else.

"Yonnie! Are you there?" Jathan raised his voice. "How is our father? Will he be all right?"

There was a slight buzzing, and then Yonnie clearing his throat again. "The doctor is here now. I must go. We'll see you soon now?" Then there was only the click of Yonnie's phone hanging up, followed by silence.

Jathan stood for a minute, trying to comprehend what he'd just heard. He'd spent the last few weeks thinking of how he'd write home and tell *Mem* about spending the night in the woods without worrying her much. That didn't matter now. Nothing seemed to matter.

He rose and moved back to the house. Both Sarah and Annie stood there, watching him walk in. The food was still on the table but everyone else was gone. Jathan guessed they'd all gone out to the barn to do evening chores together to give him privacy.

Jathan shrugged. "It's my *dat.* My *bruder* Yonnie said he had a stroke. That's all I could get out of them. They're not used to talking on the phone. There was a lot of commotion."

"Is he in the hospital?" Annie stepped forward and took Jathan's hand and squeezed. She sometimes acted like a mom to many of the bachelors and Jathan appreciated her in that role now more than ever.

He nodded. "*Ja,* but I don't know fer how long. I don't even know if he'll —" His throat tightened as if someone were wrapping it with a thick rope. "They didn't even tell me if he was going to make it. They want me to come home."

He glanced at Sarah. Tears filled her eyes. "Yer leaving? When?"

"As soon as possible."

Annie squeezed his hand harder. "Let me help you with that. I'll make some calls and get you a driver. We can check the train schedule too." She straightened her shoulders and looked all business again. "Why don't we head back to the store? We can check on my computer." She moved to the doorway.

Jathan followed Annie, and in fifteen minutes' time, he had a driver committed to taking him to the train station in Whitefish the following morning and a train ticket to Ohio in hand.

He was leaving — really leaving — just like that.

It was dark when Jathan returned to the Shelter house. He thought he'd just walk by in case there was a light on. There was, and as he peered into the brightness through the kitchen window, he wasn't surprised to find Sarah baking. His mother always baked when the world around her felt out of control, as if the measurements and steps put a sense of order in the world.

He knocked once and Sarah answered the door. When he entered, he noticed Mrs. Shelter was still awake, too, scooping peanut-butter filling into pie shells. She glanced up at him and then quickly looked down at her pie. He knew then that Sarah had told her. He could tell from Mrs. Shelter's slumped shoulders that her heart ached for him. With a sad smile, she placed the spoon on the counter and hurried out of the kitchen, heading upstairs, giving them space.

Jathan watched as Sarah put two loaves of banana bread into the oven. "I'm baking some things — some treats fer yer ride home."

He reached out a hand and placed it on Sarah's shoulder. She looked disappointed. To her, he was leaving because of a family matter. To him, his father's illness changed everything. Jathan had no choice now. He had to stay in Ohio. He had to work. He would need money right away to help. Their community, he knew, would pitch together to help cover the hospital bills, but caring for his mother and his father — in whatever condition *Dat* would be — would be up to Jathan. The factory job was the only thing that would bring in sufficient funds right away, which meant all those dreams he'd shared with Sarah . . . well, now none of them would ever come to be.

"I'll write to let you know how my father is. I'm not sure when I'll see you again . . ."

She nodded but said nothing, as if waiting for him to go on, to offer an invitation to follow him to Ohio. The thing was, he didn't want her to see him like that, working in a factory. He should appreciate the fact that he could work, but to him the idea of working on machines — well, anyone could do that. Now he had to give up on his dreams before he even had a chance to get started.

"Maybe I could come for a visit?" she finally asked.

How could he tell her no — that he didn't want to see her? He couldn't say it, but he had no doubt the distance between them would offer the space he needed to let their relationship die.

"*Ja,* but I'll understand if you can't. It is a long way. It was nice meeting you though." As soon as the words were out of his mouth, he felt coarse, guilty.

Sarah stiffened and raised one eyebrow. Then with a frustrated squeak, she threw the wooden spoon into the sink and flung up her hands. Jathan jumped back, surprised.

"Jest tell me the truth. You don't want to see me. You don't want me to visit. Maybe there's someone there? Perhaps you forgot that part of the story?"

"*Ne!*" The word burst from Jathan's lips, and then he said the only thing he could. "I'm jest in shock, that's all. When I left, my *dat* seemed strong, healthy. I —" His words caught in his throat. "I never expected this."

Sarah's shoulders slumped. "I'm so sorry." She covered her face with her hands. "I don't know what's come over me. This isn't about me and my loss. It's about you. It's about yer family." She leaned forward and placed a hand on his arm. "We were jest getting to know each other. We were jest starting to dream."

"You don't understand, do you? I have to go back. I have to start that job. There will be no chance fer our dreams to come true."

She gazed up at him, eyes wide. Her shoulders trembled, and she looked like a scared and frightened lamb.

Hug her, Jathan. Tell her you do care. It's only been a short time, but you care even if you can't see how things will ever work out.

Instead, he stood there silent and motionless, holding himself back from all his heart was telling him to do.

"Please write and tell me how he is," she said.

Jathan nodded. "*Ja,* I can do that."

"Is this good-bye?" Sarah asked.

Jathan nodded again and then glanced at the clock on the wall. "I'm afraid so. I need to hurry to my cabin and pack. My driver's picking me up at dawn."

She puckered her lip and her chin quivered.

"None of that now. And no long good-byes." Jathan patted Sarah's shoulder. She stiffened under his touch.

Then, with a heavy sigh, Jathan cast Sarah one parting look and turned toward the door.

Long good-byes never do anyone any good, he told himself. Especially when all hope of seeing Sarah again had crashed to the floor like one of *Mem*'s flowerpots, splintering into a million shards.

Any hope of romance sprouting out of the seeds of friendship they'd planted was gone. And as he walked out the front door of the Shelter home, Jathan's heart ached for what he was leaving behind. His heart also ached for what he was sure to find at the end of a very long train ride.

CHAPTER 17

Sarah watched him leave, unsure of what had just happened. He was gone, just like that. She placed a palm on her forehead, chiding herself.

He was here for months. He sat at the first table nearly every day since he arrived, yet I didn't talk to him, at least not more than a few sentences and not about anything that truly mattered. Not until I was lost, did I find what I'd been looking for.

Why? She'd been foolish, paying more attention to Amos. Amos was loud and playful, yet because he'd captured her attention, she'd missed the opportunity to get to know Jathan's heart.

Her ankle began to ache. She moved to the stool and sat, not realizing until that moment how long she'd been standing. Maybe it had been aching all along but she hadn't noticed until now. Maybe because the pain in her heart matched.

The oven timer buzzed for her banana bread, but Sarah didn't move.

After a minute, *Mem* hurried into the kitchen. "I'll get that." She pulled out the loaves of banana bread, placing them on a cooling rack.

"I feel so bad about his family — his father. Yer *dat* and I will pray. Poor Jathan, to have to hear the news from so far away."

"Ja." Sarah felt bad for Jathan, but she felt horrible for herself too. Robbed. Just like when Patty was taken. Jathan still lived, yes, but Sarah felt the glimmer of hope inside go black, as if someone had blown it out.

"I hope his *dat* will be okay," Sarah whispered. "I'll miss him."

Tears filled her eyes. How could this happen so quickly? A month ago she hardly knew Jathan existed and now . . .

She swallowed and felt a flash of dread. She was going to have to work tomorrow knowing Jathan wouldn't be there, and the next day, and the next. She'd also be waiting not-so-patiently for the mailman, wondering every time he showed up if he brought a letter from Ohio.

Lord, why did you bring someone into my life jest to have that person snatched away? Once again . . .

Thinking that made things seem even worse.

When did this become about you, Sarah? She could hear the voice in her head. *When did a man's serious injury — and his son's suffering — become all about you?*

Fourteen-year-old Sarah looked at the quilt pieces spread before them. The Amish auction was coming up and for some reason Patty had volunteered them to make a quilt.

She blew out a puff of air and looked at the colors before her. Red, blue, yellow. Boring.

A few of the older ladies had raised an eyebrow when Patty announced they'd donate a quilt too. They were going to be watched. Watched closely. One woman had chuckled, and Sarah had overheard her whispering to her friend, "Do those girls even know how to sew?"

This upset Sarah. They weren't girls, for one. Both Sarah and Patty had finished school and both had jobs helping mothers with their children. Patty helped care for a family with five young boys, which suited her just fine. Sarah's job was working for a mother with twins. Thankfully, the mother enjoyed tending to the children and asked

Sarah to focus on the kitchen duties.

Sarah frowned at the spools of thread. She would rather peel potatoes than quilt. Not only were the women in the community going to be eyeing their work, having it at an auction meant it would be displayed for all the world to see.

"Maybe we should jest choose one color," Patty suggested, "and make a subtle pattern with the different shades."

Sarah shook her head and tossed the squares she was holding back onto the table. "Yer acting like you know what yer talking about. It's going to look drab, and I'm gonna look like a fool."

Patty stood there silently. Sarah expected her to answer with a smart remark. Or stomp out. Patty did neither.

"Sarah, when did this become about you?" Patty's voice was calm.

"Excuse me?"

"We're making a quilt for the benefit auction. The money's going to help the school. This quilt will cover someone's bed." Patty closed her eyes. "I can imagine two little girls — friends — lying under it and sharing whispers jest like we did when we were ten." She opened her eyes again and looked at Sarah.

Sarah jutted out her chin. "Are you

reprimanding me? Trying to make me feel bad?"

"*Ne.* Not that." Patty shrugged. "Jest making an observation."

Sarah crossed her arms. Anger bubbled inside like oatmeal at full boil. How could Patty act so calm? It made her mad that her friend's motives were so pure.

Patty placed two squares side by side. "I think blue and yellow will look pretty. It won't be the best quilt but —"

"Don't you care that yer name will be on it?" Sarah interrupted. "Everyone will judge you."

Patty placed a hand over her chest. "I know I'm not the best quilter. Everyone else must guess that, too, since I don't sit here all day with a needle in my hand."

Patty rose and moved to the window, looking out at the larch trees that had turned brilliant yellow. "Do you ever consider it odd how we live our life? We know what pins and snaps to use fer our garments. We count the pleats in each other's *kapps.* Our dress, our humility, everyone judging each other all the day long — fer what you do and you don't. They've already judged me before they've seen anything I've sewn. Some might see my attempt as weak, but fer one person —

the buyer — the quilt will be a true gift, and I choose to focus on that."

Sarah understood what Patty was saying, but tension mounted inside. *Why am I always so worried about others' approval?*

As if reading her thoughts, Patty placed her hand over Sarah's. "You don't have to do this with me. I won't be mad if you don't." Patty wrinkled her nose. "I doubt I'll get it done, but I won't be mad."

Patty's words eased the tension building inside.

"I wish you would have jest talked to me about it first," Sarah muttered.

"Yer right. I'm sorry, Sarah. Since I've known you, I've been bossing you around. It's a hard habit to break, mostly because you usually go along with my ideas jest fine."

Patty picked up the photocopy of the sign-up sheet and ran her finger down the list of volunteers until she came to their names. Then with a pen she crossed out their names. And over them she wrote "Patty's Quilt."

Sarah frowned. Had she just been . . . fired?

Patty turned to her and smiled. "Sarah, I volunteered to make a quilt fer the auction. Everyone knows I don't sew well, and it's a project I can't finish in time. I was wondering if you — as my loving best friend who I appreciate — would be willing to help me."

Sarah looked from Patty's gaze to the scattered colored squares before her. Red. Blue. Yellow. Bold colors just like Patty. She rushed over and swept her friend in a hug.

"*Ja,* Patty. I would love to help you with yer quilt." Sarah released a long sigh, and then followed it with a smile. "Thank you for asking."

Thirty hours had passed since Jathan's train had left Montana. Thirty hours and thoughts of Sarah had only been halted for a time by a few hours of sleep and by worries about *Dat.*

If there was ever a moment Jathan had wished he could turn back time, it was now. He'd go back to the day he left home. *Dat* had been out in the barn and Jathan had waved a quick good-bye. If he could do it again, instead of waving, he would give *Dat* a handshake. He would tell *Dat* that even though they hadn't always seen eye-to-eye, he cared.

But Jathan couldn't turn back time. Would he even see his father alive? He couldn't imagine life without him. The thought made his burden even heavier. Heavier because there'd be more to care for, but also because it made him think about something he'd given up considering . . .

Without *Dat*'s opposition, would it be possible to approach *Mem* about helping her with the bakery? Would she listen to Jathan's ideas? He'd always known she'd never go against *Dat*'s wishes. Still, for a season, she'd enjoyed having Jathan in the kitchen as much as she enjoyed being there herself.

Another thought struck. If he could talk *Mem* into it, would Sarah come and help in the bakery? Jathan clung to the thought like a lifeline. Would that be too much to hope for, dream about — especially after the way he'd left things?

If ever there was a second moment he could also return to, he'd go back and give Sarah a good-bye hug and tell her that maybe, with God's help, their dreams could work out someday.

The train rocked gently as it moved down the tracks, and the bright daylight cast shadows across the expansive fields and hardwood forests. He recognized the area. He was in Ohio again.

Yet Jathan wasn't as interested in the view as he was in the newspaper sitting on the seat next to the businessman nearby. The older man had set it down ten minutes ago and hadn't picked it back up.

Jathan leaned forward. "Sir, are you done with that newspaper?"

The man lifted his eyebrows, surprised. "Uh, yes." He handed it over.

Jathan flipped through it to the article he'd been trying to read from across the aisle. It was an article about the growth of small businesses and how to determine if one would succeed.

He'd just neared the end of the article when the man cleared his throat. Jathan glanced up.

"Do you have a business?" the man asked. Then he leaned forward and offered his hand. "I'm Bob, by the way."

"I'm Jathan. It's nice to know you. To answer yer question, well, my family has two businesses. *Dat* — uh, my brother makes log furniture and my *Mem* runs a bakery. She makes the best bread I've ever had. Have you been to Holmes County, Ohio, before?"

"I haven't, but my sister goes there with her friend. She likes to buy quilts and other such things."

"You should tell her about the bakery. It's in Berlin. Our Daily Bread is the name of

228

it, right on Main Street." Jathan smiled. "The tourists come year round, but more come in the summer. I've seen the line go out the door."

"I imagine it would. Do you have other baked goods, too, like cakes and pies and such?" There was an interest in the man's eyes Jathan didn't understand.

Jathan nodded. "*Ja,* but they're not *Mem*'s specialty." They were good, but not like what Sarah made. He smiled, thinking of her again, of how she'd taken his breath away the first time he'd seen her. How much he liked her smile . . . and her cupcakes.

Jathan pushed away those thoughts and instead launched into talking about his mother's cinnamon rolls and fall pumpkin bread, which always brought big orders. Talking about those things was easier than accepting that the train was taking him farther away from Sarah with each passing minute.

The man listened with interest. He asked about their baking methods and focused on Jathan's words. When the train slowed, Jathan rose to get off.

The man stood and took a step closer. "Listen, I know we don't have time to talk about it fully now, but I'd like to talk to you about some sandwich shops I have in New York State. If you think you could find a way to service some orders of bread and pastries, I'd love to talk to you more about your business." He pulled out his wallet and handed his business card to Jathan.

"It's not my business. My *mem* —"

The man interrupted. "If you haven't talked your mother into hiring you, son, you should. I listen to business presentations all the time, and if they were half as informative or interesting as what you just talked about, I'd love my job much more than I do. I won't keep you, but email me . . ." The man paused as if remembering to whom he was speaking. "I mean —" He looked at the floor as if wishing it would open up and swallow him.

Jathan chuckled deep from his gut. "There is a phone down the street. I can borrow it." Excitement caused his heart to pound, and he felt his heartbeat in his throat. He'd just thought about the idea of helping *Mem* when he returned and here he was meeting a possible future client.

Even though his Amish community believed in the importance of prayer, *Mem* had taught him something else too: True followers of Christ took time to listen. Not only to listen to the still, small voice of God the

230

Bible talks about, but to also listen to the people and circumstances God brings into their lives, to consider where God is at work.

Lord, are you telling me something?

Jathan felt a stirring inside, something that told him to wait and pray about it. But was there really a need to pray when the answer had been placed right in front of him?

With enthusiasm Jathan stretched out his hand, accepting the man's handshake. "Thank you, sir. You'll be hearing from me. I'm not sure how we'll work it out, but I have a feeling we will."

Jathan grabbed his small suitcase and exited the train. Two men in Amish dress stood by the curb next to an *Englisch* driver.

Seeing their solemn faces, guilt rushed over him. How could he think about the bakery when the only reason it was a possibility was because his father had a stroke?

He hurried to Yonnie and Otto and stopped before them. Tears rimmed Yonnie's eyes and Otto's eyes were red. Neither looked as if they'd slept at all in the past week.

"*Dat,* is he . . ."

Otto placed a hand on Jathan's shoulder. "He's home. He's resting."

Jathan let out the breath he'd been holding.

"Yet *Mem* says not to tarry in heading home. With *Dat*'s condition, you never know." Yonnie shook his head. "You jest never know."

CHAPTER 18

Jathan walked into the *dawdi* house and hung his hat on the hook. The last time he'd been there was when his *oma* was still around. His parents had cared for her then. Now they were the ones being cared for.

The kerosene lantern hung in the middle of the room. The walls were white. The furniture simple. The only color came from the quilt folded over the back of the sofa and the green potted plants his mother managed to nurture even in the midst of caring for her children and grandchildren and running a bakery.

Mem slept in the recliner, her stockinged feet sticking up in the air, her prayer *kapp* still on and her mouth hanging open like it always did when she was exhausted. She had no doubt been waiting up for Jathan to arrive. Unfortunately, their driver's car had gotten a flat tire, making Jathan later than he'd expected.

Talking to Yonnie and Otto on the drive home had made everything more real. His heart ached considering what they'd all gone through.

"I found him in the workshop," Yonnie'd said. "*Dat* had been up late working on a dining room table fer a client. He said he was following me out and would be heading fer bed. I went and hitched up the horse to my buggy to head fer home, and then I glanced back at the shop. The kerosene lantern was still burning. Something told me to go back and check on him, and there he was, collapsed by the door. I think he musta been coming fer me . . . coming fer help when he started feeling not right."

It had only been two months, but Yonnie's hair was far more gray than when Jathan had left, and Jathan guessed working in the shop had done that. All the orders, all the competition, the intricate woodwork they took pride in. Maybe these things had even caused *Dat*'s stroke. Jathan shook his head.

Ne, *I'm not going to take on that burden too.*

Jathan took two steps toward the bedroom where his father rested and then paused, trying to control his emotions before he went in.

Rested was the word his brother Otto had

used. Otto had always been optimistic. But on the drive to Berlin, Yonnie had explained the facts.

"It was a severe stroke. He's paralyzed on one side. He can't talk. We aren't sure if he recognizes us. Our sisters asked if physical therapy would help, but the doctor didn't think it would. They told us to take him home and make him as comfortable as possible. The good news is, when *Mem* puts soft foods to his lips he opens his mouth and swallows. *Dat* never did have a problem eating." Yonnie had offered a sad laugh.

Jathan took a few more steps toward the bedroom to see his father — to touch him and pray. As he quietly moved past *Mem* in the recliner, her eyes popped open. She rose from the chair and rushed to him. "Yer home. Yer home."

"*Ja, Mem.* I made it. How's —" He started to ask how *Dat* was, but he knew the answer. Instead, he kissed the top of her forehead. "Can I see him?"

Mem nodded. "*Dat* was watching me tonight as I moved around the room. I was unpacking my things, and I could almost hear him in my mind. 'Maggie, can't you sit fer a spell?' " She chuckled.

She took Jathan's hand. "Come." She led the way.

He walked with quiet steps into the room. A hospital bed had been set up next to his parents' bed. *Dat* lay it in peacefully, eyes closed.

"Yer *dat*'s eyes fluttered open at four o'clock, as if he was going to wake up and do the chores." *Mem* smiled. "He didn't wake up fer long, and he can't speak, but he moved his head from side to side as if he wanted to tell me somethi—" She covered her mouth with her hand. "I've jest never known him to be so quiet. You know yer *dat*. He has an opinion about everything."

"*Ja,* I know him." Jathan approached his father's bedside. He considered taking his hand, but stopped short. His father had many good qualities, but he was stubborn. And his temper . . . Jathan swallowed hard, wishing he could erase all the memories he had stored up. Wishing he could peer down at his father with the same look of adoration that *Mem* wore.

Mem motioned to her bed and Jathan sat. She sat beside him.

"I'm so glad you've come. Yer *bruder* Clyde wants to talk to you tomorrow. He called Chuck from the factory, and Chuck said you'll be able to start Monday."

"*Ne.*" The word blurted from Jathan's mouth. "I know *Dat* thought that would be the best — would help everyone out, but I don't want to do that."

I have to fight for this. Fight for Sarah. Fight for our dream.

He only wished he'd realized that before he'd left — had been able to tell her.

Mem's eyes widened, and her mouth dropped open. Her fingers fiddled with her apron and then she looked at her husband. Jathan read the expression on her face. *If yer dat were able to talk, he'd have something to say about that.*

"I had a long train ride home from Montana, and I've been doing a lot of thinking. You know me, *Mem*. You — more than anyone — know what I truly enjoy."

She narrowed her gaze, as if worried about what he was going to say next. Jathan didn't let that stop him.

"What I'd really like to do is help at the bakery. Some things need to be fixed on the building. I can help with the orders and make deliveries around town. I'd thought about selling furniture in the bakery, too, but something even better came up. When I was on the train, there was a man who asked if we'd be able to ship orders to stores in New York."

Mem raised her hands and waved away Jathan's words. Then she shook her head

237

back and forth. "And how are we going to do that yet? We can hardly keep up with the orders we have. I'm not a spring chicken anymore, you know."

Jathan scooted closer. "*Ja,* I was thinking of that too. If you and Aunt Kay are freed from the business duties, you'll have more time to bake. And instead of working at the factory, I can help you with that part."

There was movement in the bedroom doorway, and for the first time, Jathan realized Yonnie had walked in. A scowl crossed Yonnie's face, showing he'd overheard.

"And what would *Dat* think of that?" Yonnie asked.

"What would he think of me providing for his wife and other members of the family? I think he would like that idea.

"Wait, let me rephrase that," Jathan continued. "*Dat* wouldn't like that I didn't obey his directive, but he'd change his mind once he saw the bills being paid." Jathan stood and approached his brother. Though Jathan was younger, he stood at least four inches taller than Yonnie. "Isn't that the point of the factory job? Fer me to bring in money, income? Is the source as important as the result?"

"You have high hopes, Jathan, foolish dreams. They are but two women," Yonnie muttered. "They surely cannot make enough . . ."

"I have an idea." Jathan glanced at *Mem.* He straightened his shoulders, determined to speak his mind, even though he noted how pale she was.

"I met a young woman back in Montana. She's a *gut* baker, and she mentioned that she'd love to come to Berlin. Maybe she'd like to come and help us pick up our business?"

"Sarah Shelter?" *Mem* asked.

"Ja." His eyes widened. "How did you know?"

"Son, a letter arrived today. It beat you home. It must be important if she paid to have it delivered in one day. You should have known that yer mother would pay attention to the name on the return label, especially one written in a pretty script."

Heat rose to his cheeks. Yes, he should have known better. Not much got past *Mem.*

"A woman?" Yonnie spit the words out as if they were poison in his mouth. "You have a woman writing you? Is that what you were doing while I've been here trying to keep the shop going? Trying to provide?" Yonnie balled his hands into fists. "Jest what did you do in Montana? Wait, don't tell me. I don't want to know. And I wouldn't let word get out none either. Not when yer intended is here —"

"My intended?" Jathan was used to letting his older brother rant. Yonnie liked to put his youngest brother in his place often, but this . . . "I have no intended. Do you honestly think I'd have one woman here while I'm spending time with another in Montana?"

"*Ja,* there *is* a woman. Don't be lying to my face, Jathan." Yonnie pointed a finger at Jathan's chest. "Anna Troyer is in the same quilting circle as my Leah."

"Anna Troyer?" Jathan shook his head and turned to *Mem.* "See what you started, *Mem*? She honestly does not still believe that, does she?"

Mem twirled one of her *kapp* strings around her finger, as she always did when she was nervous. "If she does, it's none of my doing. I haven't spoken of such a thing with her mother recently."

"Recently?" Jathan cocked an eyebrow.

Mem crossed her arms over her ample chest. "Well, not since you left for Montana."

Jathan released a sigh. "And what did you say then?"

"I jest told her mother that my guess was you *were* going for the hunting since I doubted there could be anyone as lovely as Anna in those parts."

Jathan rubbed his eyes with the palms of his hands, wishing he could wipe away her words.

Yonnie rubbed the back of his neck. "So yer not marrying Anna now?"

Jathan lowered his hands and shook his head. The room around him blurred slightly, then cleared. Frustration tightened the veins of his neck, but he told himself not to take it out on *Mem.* She was just an old woman who wished to see her youngest son happy.

"*Ne.* I've never thought of marrying Anna," Jathan answered. "Ever since Anna and I were babies, *Mem* and Mrs. Troyer have joked that we'd get married someday. I got used to the teasing, but obviously someone took it more serious like."

Mem fanned her face with her hand. "*Ja,* but you have to admit Anna Troyer is a lovely girl."

"Some may consider her lovely, but she's not the type of woman I'd consider spending my life with." Instead, Sarah's face filled Jathan's mind. Sarah was lovely as well, to be sure, with her blonde hair and light eyes, but there was more to her than that. She had a playful side and didn't take herself too seriously. She also followed their Amish traditions without taking *those* none too serious either, if that were possible. She followed their directives without focusing more on the rules than the intent behind them.

Mostly, it was her love of God that drew Jathan in. To Sarah, following God wasn't just something she did because it's what the community did. She loved God and spoke of him through her love. Jathan knew he wanted his children raised by a mother like that. He, too, wanted to walk through life with a woman such as her.

"Where's Sarah's letter?" he asked *Mem.*

"On the kitchen counter in the big house — in yer house."

Jathan nodded and glanced out the window. Moonlight illuminated the two-story white home. It filled his vision, and he pictured the empty rooms inside and the expansive living and dining room that had hosted many church services. He knew about the windows that needed to be fixed. The floorboards that creaked. And that was only the start. It was the only home he'd ever known. And caring for it — for his family too — was his responsibility now.

"Do you think it will work, Sarah coming?" *Mem* asked.

Jathan looked back at her and prepared to answer, but then he saw she was focused on

242

Dat. Talking to him instead.

No answer came, of course, but a smile curled on *Mem*'s lips. She turned her attention back to Jathan.

"If you think this Sarah Shelter would come, I'd love to meet her. I sure could use some *gut* help in the bakery. I've been saying that to *Dat* for a while. I think yer business sense could help much too."

Jathan's heart pounded from her words. His stomach flipped and danced. Did she just say what he thought she said? Did she approve? Would he really be able to run the business side of the bakery and also invite Sarah to come?

Yonnie grunted his disapproval. He shook his head and then stomped out of the room.

Jathan had figured on this reaction. Yonnie would never be happy about letting Jathan work at the bakery instead of getting a factory job, but even as Jathan had thought about it on the train, he'd hoped *Mem* would be swayed if she knew a beautiful woman would be involved, one he was clearly interested in.

"So what is this Sarah Shelter like?" *Mem* asked, no louder than a whisper.

"Let me see." He stroked his chin. "She loves God. She cares fer people. She's beautiful . . . and she's a fine baker."

Mem tilted her head. "And she cares for you?"

Jathan smiled. *"Ja."*

"And you think she'd come?"

He answered her with his widening smile. "I believe so, although I should go see what the letter has to say."

Mem stretched out her hand. He grasped it. "Then, son, I believe we're in business together. I trust you, I really do, and if you think this will work —"

"I think this will work, *Mem.*"

"Then you better go read that letter and then get some rest. We have plans to make tomorrow. Big plans."

Dear Jathan,

You left today. Just writing those words brings tears to my eyes. After you left, I thought of one hundred things I wanted to say. Edgar's the one who urged me to write some of them down and get this note sent before the two o'clock mail pickup. He said he'd personally make sure the letter got to you in a timely manner.

I know why you didn't offer me any hope of us seeing each other. You didn't have hope for yourself and what you're returning to. I understand. I also want you to know that things aren't always as helpless as they seem. Let me explain by telling you a story.

You've seen my memory jar . . . but I never intended to start my collection. It was a small canning jar I started with first. You know, the kind our mems can jelly in. I was in the backyard looking at pinecones. I hadn't ever seen small ones like I found in the West Kootenai before. I searched the ground for the perfect one. One as small as my pinky finger without a blemish. That's when everything changed. My world flipped upside down in the span of a breath, and I didn't even know it was coming.

I'd just found the perfect pinecone when I glanced up. I couldn't see our home anymore. I'd wandered off without knowing it. I'm smiling as I write these words considering our time in the woods. Maybe I'm more prone to wandering than I thought.

That day, nothing seemed out of the ordinary; then, in a moment's time, I found myself lost. Just when I didn't think things could get any worse, I heard a crashing through the trees. I thought for sure I was dead. Just the day before, I'd overheard Edgar from the store talking about a black bear in the trash. That's when Patty came running in my direction. Her kapp hung down her back and her face was smudged with dirt. I knew that if I invited her home, Mem would pack us up and take us back to Kentucky. She'd told Dat she was raising no wild children even if we did live in the woods.

I kept that pinecone in the jelly jar because I wanted to remember the day when what had seemed like my worst moment — being lost, being attacked — turned into the best moment, when I met my best friend.

You may wonder, Jathan, why I told you that story. Mostly because I want you to have hope. Everything can change in the blink of an eye. Ja, I've had great tragedy heaped upon me, but I've had unexpected blessings come just the same. Patty was a blessing I didn't know was coming. You are too. I wanted you to know that. I just wanted to tell you not to give up hope. What's impossible today might be birthed tomorrow. And when it happens, I want to be the first to know, for as your friend, I'll be cheer-

ing the loudest.
With much appreciation for you saving
my life,
Sarah Shelter

CHAPTER 19

These days, two weeks after Jathan left, morning always seemed to come too early. Sarah rolled over in bed and listened as *Dat* and Andy shoed up and headed out to the barn. Even though their spread in Montana was much smaller than the one in Kentucky had been, there were still cows to milk, horses and pigs to feed, and eggs to gather.

Once, when she was working at the store, someone had asked Sarah if they sold alarm clocks. The customer had been surprised to hear Sarah didn't own one and hadn't seen one either. *Mem*'s rattling of the cookstove as she lit it and started breakfast was the only clock that ever woke Sarah. And that "alarm" was happening right now as she stretched. Sarah needed to get down there to help. She wasn't usually this slow about things, but maybe today was different because her mind carried so many thoughts.

Had Jathan received her letter? Had she

been foolish to send it?

No. She guessed he would be happy to have heard from her so soon. Even though that last evening he'd acted as if nothing special had happened between them, a hundred other looks and smiles before that moment told her something had.

It wasn't as if she'd been trying to force anything through her letter either. What had been heaviest on her heart was just to let Jathan know that she cared and that she hoped things were going to change for the better. It wasn't anything she could put her finger on, just something that came to mind as she prayed for Jathan. It was as if God was speaking to her heart. "I have something in store for him, Sarah. Just you wait."

Sarah lay there just a moment longer, offering up prayers for Jathan's father. She pictured Jathan's face as he stood by his father's bedside. She pictured weariness from the journey mixed with a pained acceptance of what he'd have to do to provide for his family. She pictured him lost — not stuck in the cold, dark woods but lost in his own search for fulfillment. To the outside world, the Amish were plain, simple people. But wasn't it the quest of every man and woman — Amish and *Englisch* alike — to find one's purpose? To discover a way one's work could brighten one's heart so it didn't feel like work at all?

"Sarah, yer not ill, are you?" *Mem*'s voice traveled across the living room and slipped under her closed door.

"No, *Mem.* Sorry. I'll be out in a minute yet. Annie told me to come in late today. She said I was looking weary and in need of rest."

She rose, scolding herself for not getting up. Not only must she help *Mem* with morning chores, but she had to go to work.

Maybe that's what truly caused her to linger. Once she got to the restaurant, she'd see that empty booth and remember again so clearly that Jathan was gone.

Forty-five minutes later, when she was on her way to work, Sarah's brother Andy and her sister Evelyn were finishing chores. Andy strode toward the house with quickened steps, and Evelyn skipped at his side. Only today, their walk was joined by a third.

Last night, *Dat* had shown up with a new puppy — a sheepdog. They'd named him Moe. This morning, Moe ran circles around Sarah's siblings, barking as if herding them was his chore.

The air around them was fresh with the scent of spring. Their pasture had turned a brilliant shade of green seemingly overnight. Sarah took the pressure off her sore ankle and reached down to pluck a small white flower from the ground before twirling it in her fingers. The place was just as pretty as it had always been, but it seemed emptier now. Who knew how a bachelor who'd been here for such a short time could make it feel so?

Just before she got to the house, Evelyn plopped to the ground, much to Moe's liking. He placed two of his paws on Evelyn's shoulders and licked her cheeks until they shone. Sarah laughed and then turned the corner of the road, not realizing how long the last stretch was to the store.

A month ago, the search-and-rescue paramedics had confirmed she'd sprained her ankle and had told her to keep off it as much as possible. She'd been a poor patient. She walked everywhere in these parts. Walking a mile to the store or to her friend Jenny's house or two miles to the lake — that always seemed like less work than hooking up the buggy.

Even after all this time, her walk was more like a limp.

If only Jathan were here to carry me again, she thought as she cut across the school-yard in front of the one-room Amish school.

A soft smile formed on her lips as she remembered how safe, protected, and cared for she'd felt in his arms.

She was just exiting the schoolyard when Sarah saw someone running her direction.

"It's Edgar," she whispered. He was calling her name. Sarah picked up her pace, limping with each step.

"Sarah, come quick. You have a phone call," Edgar said as she neared.

Fear hammered against her heart until she heard something else. Edgar's laughter. She'd only seen him laugh maybe a dozen times during the two years she'd worked at the store. What could be so funny now?

"I headed in early this morning and walked in to find the phone ringing." Edgar panted as he approached. "It was a storekeeper in Ohio calling for his friend. Seems Jathan wants to talk to you. I told him you'd be in soon. He said he'd wait." Edgar shook his head, chuckled again, and pointed to the store. "Can you believe that? He's sitting there, paying for that long-distance phone call, waiting until you come in instead of calling back. I tried to give him the number to yer phone, but he said he'd wait. Hurry now, won't you?"

"*Ja,* of course."

Edgar turned. "And that's why these

Amish folks need to just get phones and use them," Edgar mumbled as he hurried away. "They need to know they can use a phone just to talk, and that it doesn't mean it's an emergency every time it rings. They need to know they can hang up and call someone back."

Sarah picked up her pace again. When she got to the store a few minutes later, she worked hard to keep her voice steady as she picked up the phone.

"*Ja*, hello?"

"Sarah, is that you?"

Sarah nodded and smiled before she remembered he couldn't see her. "*Ja*, this is Sarah."

"I got yer letter a couple weeks back." It was a simple statement.

Laughter filled the space between her mouth and the receiver. "You called me on the telephone to tell me that?"

"*Ja*, and to tell you something else too."

Sarah twirled the cord around her finger as she waited. "Well?"

"It's happened already."

She furrowed her brow. "What's happened?"

"What you said in the letter. The unexpected. I talked to my *mem*. She agreed. She said I could help run the bakery. I've been working on a business plan and talking to suppliers."

"But you said that wasn't possible," she interrupted.

"I was wrong. My *mem* also agrees we need more help. Sarah, will you come?"

"Come?"

"To Ohio? To Berlin? Do ya think yer aunt would let you stay with her?"

Even over the miles, the emotions in Jathan's voice were clear. She knew what he was asking, and the truth was, it had nothing to do with Ohio or Berlin. He was asking, "Will you come to me?" He'd only been gone two weeks, but he was saying, "I don't want to be apart."

Sarah smiled. "Well, that depends. What are yer plans for the bakery? My boss here, Annie, needs me. Also, I jest need to know what yer thinking about. It's a big step, and I need to make sure yer ideas are in line with what I've been carrying on my heart."

"Sarah, I want yer help to make the bakery as *gut* as we can. We can add some of yer items to the menu. There's a chance we can put our baked goods into restaurants and cafes too."

She turned her back to the door and cupped her hand over the phone receiver so no one else could hear. "Jathan, I wasn't talking about the bakery. I was talking about our, uh, friendship. I wanted to know what yer thinking."

"What I'm thinking?" She heard Jathan's heavy sigh. "I wouldn't have asked you to come to Ohio if I didn't want to see you more, to know you better. Sarah, fer the first time in a long time, I have hope, not just fer the bakery, but fer so much more than that."

Sarah wiped a tear from the corner of her eye. She'd heard of people crying tears of happiness before, but she'd never done it herself. Not until now. She picked up a penny from the coin cup on the counter and tucked it into her pocket for her memory jar. And then a new thought crossed her mind.

"I imagine we'll be making a whole new set of memories, won't we? And from all you've said, it seems like Ohio will be a nice place. A real nice place."

Sarah set the apple pie on the table, and *Dat*'s eyes widened in surprise. "Did you make that fer us?" He ran a hand down his beard and then leaned forward and took a deep sniff. "Nobody makes pies like my dear daughter — or at least that's what all the neighbors say. I wouldn't know. The baker's *dat* is usually the last one to get pie."

She chuckled and grabbed his hand. Her heart was so full she was certain nothing could take away her smile. Not even the aching of her ankle. It throbbed, hard and deep, but it didn't matter. All that mattered was the phone call she'd received today. All that mattered were the smiling faces of her family. How had she not paid more attention over the last months and years to the gift they were to her? Emotion filled her throat over the heaviness of Patty's death. That one act had been like a wide brush, painting a layer of gray over the landscape of her life. And then it was as if Jathan had stepped in, taken off his over-shirt, and wiped away the gray like one would wipe mud off a window. If not all of the gray had come off . . . at least most had.

Mem placed her crock of homemade ham-and-bean soup on the table, and Sarah took a deep breath and watched as she hurried back into the kitchen for their bread and fresh vegetables.

"I talked to Annie at the store, and Arlene has some flats of strawberries from her greenhouse. Would you like some fer canning?"

"Can you get them tomorrow after work?" *Mem* asked.

"*Ja,* I'm sure I can. Or I can head back

256

over there tonight. It's not too far out of the way."

Mem shook her head. "Tomorrow's fine, but *danki.*"

"No problem." Sarah's smile widened. She stood and served soup to Andy and Evelyn. Then she passed them the fresh bread she'd brought home. They both stared at her as if they didn't know the person who sat at the table with them. Had she been that different? Had she tucked away her smile within the memory jar, too, after Patty's death?

Sarah ignored their stares and looked at her mother. "You sittin' tomorrow, *Mem*?"

"*Ja,* Jenny works at the store fer jest four hours. Kenzie is learning to knead bread as well as you did when you were that age."

"Are you off, Sarah? I'm heading down to Eureka after breakfast," *Dat* offered. "A couple of us hired a driver. There's an open seat if you want a ride. I'm sure we can drop you by that kitchen store you like so well."

"*Ne,* that won't work tomorrow," she blurted out. "I already have plans."

"Working at the store later? I thought it was yer day off."

"Not plans like that. Other plans. Bigger plans. I was thinking of moving to Ohio, and I wanted to hear your thoughts."

Dat hurriedly swallowed the drink he'd just taken and set down his cup. "Ohio? To spend more time with Jathan, I suppose." His eyes widened. "But it's only been a few weeks, Sarah. And you've jest started to get to know him. Do you think it's wise to travel so far when he's made no clear intentions of marriage?"

"*Dat,* he did ask if we could court . . . but even more than that, I jest know he's the one. We complement each other. We already share dreams."

Mem pushed away her dinner plate as if she were no longer hungry. She sighed. "Out of the thirty bachelors that visit each year, why does the one Sarah becomes especially close to have to leave early?" she asked *Dat.* Then she turned back to Sarah. "Are you sure it's wise?"

"It won't be as if yer sending me to strangers." She hoped her words sounded convincing. "Aunt Lynnette has been begging me to come and stay fer years. And she lives less than one mile from the bakery that Jathan's running with his *mem.* I've been praying about my care for him, and I have peace. Don't you think that God must have a hand in all this? To think that we didn't know of Jathan more than two months ago and here he lives so close to my aunt."

Evelyn shuffled in her seat and looked down at her plate, as if reminding everyone of why they'd gathered around the table.

Dat looked to his plate and then bowed his head. All the heads around the table followed suit, and Sarah offered a silent prayer to God, just as she'd learned to do when she was a child. Being more progressive, her parents weren't shy about praying out loud at times, but silent prayer at meals was one tradition they continued to follow.

"Tell me about this shop." *Dat* took a large bite of his biscuit. Beside him, Andy shoveled food into his mouth, acting as if he wasn't hearing a word being said. Or at least if he heard, not caring.

"It's a bakery. Jathan's *mem* and aunt run it. They want to expand, and Jathan wants to help. Wants me to help too."

"And you'll get paid?" *Dat* asked between bites.

"*Ja.*" Sarah nodded, even though thinking of it now she didn't remember anything in the conversation being about money. But surely he was going to pay her. "And I'll get to learn more about running my own bakery. I never thought before that it could really happen. In the West Kootenai, there really isn't a need for another one, but now, perhaps . . ."

Dat focused on her face and then set his fork on the table. She'd never seen him stop eating in the middle of a meal before. "This is not jest talk? This is happening . . . tomorrow?"

"*Ach,* well, I'm not leaving tomorrow, but I need to get things done fer it. Talk to Annie, get train tickets, pack my things. Help train someone at the bakery."

Mem released a long breath and nodded. Although *Dat*'s face was pale from shock and concern, *Mem*'s lips held a hint of a contented smile. If anyone had seen Sarah's tears over losing her friend, it had been *Mem* most. If anyone knew the worries and questions of the years passing without an acceptable suitor, it was her mother who understood that too.

Mem reached out and placed her hand over Sarah's. "I knew the day would arrive when we saw this happening. While a son stays close, digs his roots deep, and works the land of his *dat,* a daughter's role is to start a new life and carry on her husband's lineage. To strengthen his family and home."

Dat shook his head to hear such talk. He leaned back in his chair and stroked his long, dark beard. "*Ach,* who is this boy, really?" He spread his hands on the table, as if trying to get a grasp of the situation.

"*Dat,* I wish you would have had a chance to know him, to have heard Jathan's heart. He's like us in his beliefs. Being Amish and following God isn't jest tradition to him. His faith in God is strong. He believes in serving God and in discovering who God designed each of us to be."

"Has he eaten one of yer cupcakes?" Andy interrupted.

She paused, turned, and looked at him. "*Ja,* I suppose he has."

Andy nodded, knowingly. He crossed his arms over his chest. "That's what this is all about," he said with all the wisdom of a twelve-year-old. "Yep, it's all about the cupcakes."

CHAPTER 20

It only took five days for Sarah to completely change the direction of her life. Five days to train a new baker at the West Kootenai Kraft and Grocery. Five days to visit friends. Five days to sort through her things. She packed two boxes, knowing that she could always send for more later, if need be.

After she finished sorting through her books — choosing only a few cookbooks to add to the box — Sarah paused and looked out the sitting room window. The small room was upstairs, and the window sat in the peak of the roof. She enjoyed this room for the view it gave of their front yard, the forest, and the peak of Robinson Mountain in the distance. It was a good place to get away, to think, and Sarah had a lot of thinking that needed to be done today.

She would miss this view some, but inside was an eagerness of what was to come. She looked forward to living in a large Amish community again, to making new friends, to discovering a new place. She'd read some about Holmes County in the Amish newspaper, *The Budget.* Berlin was just one small town in the largest Amish community in the world. Not only that, there were Old Order, New Order, Swartzentruber Amish, Troyer Amish, Mennonites, and more all in one place.

She thought of all the people up in the West Kootenai — so many different personalities in such a small place. What would it be like in a bigger community? She couldn't even imagine. Young, old, strict, joyful, outgoing, quiet, eager, reserved. Hopefully, working in the bakery, Sarah would be able to interact with them all.

Footsteps sounded on the stairs leading up to the sitting room, and Sarah turned. It was *Mem* who walked up with such slow steps. She wore a tender smile and carried something in her arms. It looked to be a jar. Sarah wrinkled her brow. It wasn't one of Sarah's memory jars; those had already been packed away.

Mem neared, sat in the chair next to Sarah, and placed the jar on her own lap. Her face was blotchy as if she'd been crying, or at least holding back tears.

Sarah leaned forward to get a better look.

The jar was filled with things she recognized. A matchbook, a pinecone, a yellow quilt square. Her heart pounded and the room seemed to spin. Her eyes widened and she looked at *Mem*'s face. The sadness in *Mem*'s eyes confirmed what it was. It wasn't one of Sarah's memory jars. It was Patty's.

The wrinkles on *Mem*'s face deepened as she tried to hold back her emotion. After Patty's death, *Mem* had cried with Sarah more times than she could count. "I've been holding this fer you for a while." *Mem*'s lower lip quivered slightly as she spoke. "I've been waiting fer the right time, a *gut* time, and I knew it was today."

Questions tossed in Sarah's mind, fighting to be first on her lips. "How? When? When did you get it?"

"About three weeks after Patty's death, I saw someone walking down the road to our house. It was Patty's *bruder* Michael. He said they were packing up and moving back to Pennsylvania. Some people grieve differently, he told me, and his *mem* needed to be surrounded by her family — her parents, *brieder,* and sisters.

"He said his *mem* was cleaning out Patty's room and was going to throw the jar out. But Michael knew you'd want it. Yet he also knew you weren't ready fer it. That yer heart was jest as broken as anyone's in their family. He asked me to save it fer you. To hold it and give it to you when the time was right."

Sarah struggled to swallow. Tried to take in *Mem*'s words, but her eyes were too busy focusing on the items. The empty spool from Patty's finished quilt. The handkerchief Patty'd paid Sarah to embroider for her, just so she didn't have to do it. There were other items too, ones Sarah didn't know the story behind. A paper clip, a small mirror, a letter opener. Sarah puckered her lips, realizing no one would ever know now. The only thing she knew was that everything in this jar was important enough for Patty to keep, so Sarah would keep it too. Always.

Sarah reached for the jar. The glass was cool under her fingers. The tears came, and Sarah's throat grew tight. She wanted to thank *Mem,* to tell her how much she appreciated this, but from the look on her face, *Mem* already knew.

Sarah picked out a few items, fingering them, and then focused her gaze on *Mem.* "How did you know?" she asked. "How did you realize the right time was now?"

Mem wiped a tear from her own cheek, and Sarah's lips pressed tight. *Mem* had loved Patty too.

"I knew there would be a day when yer gaze would be more focused on the future than the past. I never wanted this jar to be a weight that held you back, but a warm breeze that would carry you forward with Patty's unique way of looking at life. Carry you forward with her sweet memories."

"I'm so thankful," Sarah finally managed to say. Her own tears weren't tears of sorrow, but rather of joy. It was the second time it had happened in a week.

"I'm so thankful I can look at this jar and remember the times we spent together. I'd almost forgotten some memories until I saw this again." She sighed deeply. "But now those memories will forever live in my thoughts."

She recognized more of the items lying on top. The piece of green glass they'd found on the shore of Lake Koocanusa. Patty had claimed it was her favorite shade of green. A red bead Patty had found on the forest floor. She'd been so sure it was from a Native American moccasin. A piece of yarn tied into a bow. Patty had worn it on her finger to remind herself to pick up her younger brother from school after she'd forgotten him three days in a row.

"She'll never be far away, will she?" *Mem* asked.

Sarah shook her head. She pressed the jar against her chest, close to her heart. "*Ne, Mem,* not very far at all."

Sarah reached into Patty's memory jar and pulled out the stub of a candle. *"Mem,"* she said.

"Ja?"

"Thank you fer giving me this. Thank you fer waiting fer the right time." She folded both hands around the candle stub and held it tight. "I needed the reminder that one person makes a difference. Just like Patty was a light fer me, I have a new hope. I want to support Jathan, *ja,* and discover if our dreams fer the future include each other. But for some reason, I also want to make a difference in the community. I have a feeling I might be there not only to shine God's love, but maybe to spread that love to others in unexpected ways."

"I have no doubt about that, Sarah." *Mem* kissed her cheek. "I have no doubt about that at all."

Fifteen-year-old Sarah stretched her legs across the sofa and looked around the living room. She and Patty had left a mess, if she said so herself. Patty had gotten the wild idea that they could make Christmas wreaths and sell them at the store.

"The materials are free. We can walk ten feet behind our house and cut down all the branches we want."

With Patty's parents and other family members out of town visiting relatives in Pennsylvania, they'd turned the living room into a work station with pine branches, wires, and red ribbon. What they hadn't counted on was how quickly the wood stove dried out the branches. Or that everyone else in the West Kootenai could step outside to the backs of their homes and cut down branches for their own use. Why would they pay for wreaths when they could make them for free?

So after a day of selling only one wreath to a tourist who seemed more impressed that they were Amish than by their handiwork, they'd found Patty's father's hammer and nails and hammered their creations onto the trees along the road. If they couldn't make money, at least they could pretend that the forest was holding the biggest Christmas celebration and all were invited.

"We should have made cupcakes," Patty said as she rose and took another turn at sweeping up the needles.

"I think that's the fifth time you've said that."

"I pay for yer cupcakes. I buy them all the time at the store. I'm not sure why I didn't think of that. Why did we spend time making something people don't need, rather than something they want? Two hours and yer cupcakes are always sold out."

Sarah took a deep breath. "*Ja,* well, at least the pine needles smell good."

Patty laughed. "It smells exactly like it does outside!"

Night was lengthening its shadows, but instead of lighting the kerosene lamp, Patty lit a candle and the small flame flickered and danced, brightening the room. She cupped her hand and placed it near the flame.

"What are you doing, trying to burn yerself?"

Patty pointed to the wall with her free hand. "An alligator, look."

Sarah glanced over and saw that the shadow did look like an alligator chomping its way along the log walls.

"I'm still not sure this is a good idea." Sarah sighed. "I know yer *dat* asked you to keep the fire going, but didn't they ban you from candles?"

Laughter shook Patty's shoulders. "*Ja,* when I was ten, and I don't remember them lifting that ban. But it's been five years, and I think it'll be fine as long as I'm careful," Patty announced with authority and then winked.

Patty showed her a shadow rabbit next, then an eagle. Sarah was enjoying the game until Patty's face grew serious.

"Isn't it strange, Sarah, that one little light can make such a big difference?" She glanced around the room.

"*Ja,* in a way, but I understand it too." Sarah sighed. "Yer sort of a candle to me, Patty." Sarah tilted her head as she gazed at her friend. "I don't want to imagine how boring my life would be if you hadn't come into it. To think I would have spent the days making Christmas cookies instead of decorating the forest."

Sarah watched the flame dance and leap, and she thought of a Scripture her father had read from their Bible earlier that morning. He'd been doing that more often — reading God's Word to her and her siblings after dinner instead of them just hearing it at church. It made such a difference and Sarah often thought about those words throughout the day.

"You are the light of the world. A town built on a hill cannot be hidden," he'd read this morning. As he read that, Sarah had pictured how *Mem* and *Dat*'s home looked when she walked down the road after babysitting. The lanterns in the kitchen and living room could be seen from quite a distance away.

Like their lighted windows on the dark country road, this candle made such a difference because the room around it was dark. During the day, if the same candle were lit, it wouldn't get much notice, but at night, it made all the difference.

Sarah and Patty sat for a while, settling down and allowing thoughts of sleep to cause their eyelids to grow heavy. Sarah saw Patty point to the candle. It had burned down and only a few inches were left. Had they really sat there that long?

That was a sign of good friends, she knew. That each could be perfectly content together, though lost in her own thoughts.

Patty left the room and returned with a tall candle, using the shorter one to light it. She placed the taller one in the candle holder, and then blew out the shorter one. "A candle loses nothing by lighting another candle." She looked over at Sarah. "Or so I've heard it said."

"I like that." Sarah replayed Patty's words in her mind. "*Ja,* I really do."

Then she watched as Patty carried the

smaller candle to her room.

"Where you going?" Sarah asked, not wanting to submit to sleep yet.

Patty returned seconds later with empty hands. "Do you really have to ask?"

The memory jar. Of course. If Sarah had thought of it sooner, she would have taken the candle first. She released a sigh. Then again, she had a feeling she'd remember this night for a while.

"Spreading our light, that's what it's all about," Patty said. And then she finally submitted to a yawn.

Sarah covered her mouth with her hand and did the same. "*Ja,* the world needs more of it, don't you think?"

"Not only the world but our neighbors." Patty stretched. "Sometimes it seems the ones who have the light are the worst at realizing all they hold within. With sharing it."

Dear Jathan,

It was wonderful hearing your voice on the phone the other morning. What a surprise! I never thought I'd hear from you so soon, and for certain didn't think I'd hear your voice through a phone call. You should have seen Edgar running down the road to come and tell me. He bounced as he ran, and his white hair was tousled in all directions by the wind. He looked like a fawn frolicking in a high meadow.

What surprised me even more than hearing from you was you asking me to come work with your mem and aunt. That means a lot. I'm thankful you trust my work and trust me to work well with them. I'm sure I can learn much working in their kitchen. Just like you learned to roll nuts within waxed paper!

I also hope they'll be interested in some of my recipes and ideas. I've been thinking of some things I'd like to bake first. I am also bringing some of my favorite cookbooks.

Enclosed is a slip of paper with my time of arrival and location. Annie, from the store, said it's a bit of a drive to come get me, and I thank you for hiring a driver to do that.

One of the things I'm also excited about is making new friends and getting to know members of the community and tourists. My aunt has told us before that millions of people come every year to Holmes County to enjoy the countryside and to buy Amish products. She said they like stepping out of their busy lives for a time to enjoy our quiet existence. I had to laugh about that!

Yes, things might be quieter without the radio and television and the noise from all their machines, but it seems like I'm always busy. Do they not know we make our own clothes, grow and raise our food, bake our own bread? It seems going into their world for a time with machines that do all those things might be a vacation for me.

But enough about that. I really didn't mean to share so much. What I do hope is that in addition to the things I bake, God will use my smile — and his love within me — to brighten a person's day.

I have so much to do (in my quiet and simple life) before I leave. I'll say hello to Amos and Edgar for you. I'll also give Robinson Mountain a wave from both of us.

Looking forward to seeing you soon!

With care,
Sarah

CHAPTER 21

In both directions, the tracks stretched as far as his eyes could see, and goose bumps rose on Jathan's arms. How many people did the trains carry on these pieces of steel? Millions, he supposed. Yet although the train would be carrying hundreds tonight, he cared about only one. He knew what he hoped for, but he also knew life rarely turned out how one hoped. His brothers believed he was making a big mistake, and Jathan's thoughts flipped between confidence he'd prove them wrong and worry they'd seen the facts all along.

Sarah was coming and Jathan didn't know if he was setting up his own ideas of what could come of it — come of them. While he wanted them to spend more time together and wished their relationship would grow, he also hoped he could prove his brothers' expectations wrong. His father's expectations wrong.

Jathan had never known a time when he didn't understand expectations. As a small child, he knew he must be quiet and behave during their church services. From the time he could grasp the handle of a pitchfork, he knew he was expected to muck stalls. As soon as he could sit on a stool, he watched his father in the workshop and knew he would soon begin to help. He supplied *Dat* with nails and helped choose the best pieces of lumber at the lumberyard. He knew what he had to do and was good at it, but just because he could find a fine piece of maple didn't mean it brought joy to his heart.

Of all the siblings, Jathan was the only one who never went wild during *Rumspringa.* What good would it have done?

He knew what people expected from him as an Amish man too. As the youngest son, his role was to care for his parents. To see they lived their last years on earth well. His father had reminded Jathan of that often. And when Jathan's woodworking proved to be too slow, *Dat* had come up with the idea of working at the factory. It was a good job and Jathan knew many Amish men worked there and were thankful for the job. The fact was, it just wasn't right for Jathan. He knew it as clearly as he knew his own name.

The breeze picked up and he flipped up

his collar, protecting himself from the nip of the wind. Was he making a mistake asking Sarah to come? She came to experience a new culture. Her letter had said she looked forward to baking and trying out new recipes. His heart ached at the thought of that — of her playful side and her joy in the kitchen. Those were two things he enjoyed about her most, but he also guessed they were the very things that would cause his mother and aunt to raise their eyebrows. He'd worried about that before he'd called. He'd worried that asking her to come would be like taking a racing stallion and penning it up in a barn for the rest of its life.

Yet it was longing to see her smile that convinced him to drive his buggy to the grocery store at the end of the lane and use the telephone. That and the small hope that things would be different. A hope that the rest of the family would fall under Sarah's trance as he had.

The train approached, and Jathan straightened. He searched the windows for any sign of Sarah, but he could only see the moonlight reflecting off the glass.

"Sarah." His lips whispered her name onto the breeze. His finding her in those dark woods had led to this moment now. He just hoped that tomorrow, when light dawned, she'd be as excited about this new adventure as he was. If only the morning light would also push his concerns — his fears — into the shadows.

Sarah rubbed her eyes as she looked out the train window, waiting to see the train station in the distance. The train slowed, but there was no station. Rather than a beautiful train station with flower baskets decorating the platform like the one in Whitefish, Montana, this small Ohio town had no fine building — no building at all — only a small shelter to keep waiting travelers out of the rain.

By car, the train station was an hour from Berlin, and Jathan said he'd have a driver there waiting for her. It was the silhouette of an Amish man, however, that caught her attention. Sarah's heart leaped in her chest. It wasn't only the driver who was waiting for her. Even though his wide-brimmed hat shadowed his face, Sarah recognized Jathan's wide shoulders and stance. She placed a hand to her neck, telling herself to breathe. He'd come. He hadn't just sent a driver; he'd come for her.

She tucked a stray hair under her *kapp* and grabbed the small basket *Mem* had used to pack food for the long journey. She was still limping, but not nearly as badly. When the train stopped, she walked cautiously down the aisle and down the steps of the train. A moment later, she stood on the platform where the cool Ohio breeze caused her *kapp* strings to dance. Her heart did a dance of its own.

She looked at Jathan and waited for him to see her. Jathan's eyes scanned the train's doorways until finally he saw her. He waved and strode over to her with quick steps. During the passing miles, Sarah had worried whether there would be any awkwardness between them. She didn't have to worry for long. Jathan rushed forward and paused before her, smiling. Sarah's knees softened to see his smile once again.

"You made it."

"*Ja,* jest a little late."

He smiled, studying her face. "Not bad. Jest an hour or so." He blew out a breath as if not believing she was really here. "Yer worth the wait."

She grinned. How had everything changed so quickly? Just last month, she'd hardly spoken to him. Now there was no place she'd rather be than here, and no one she'd prefer to be with than him.

"Do you have a suitcase?"

"Not a suitcase, but two boxes taped up

real *gut.* I hope that won't be a problem. *Mem* helped me pack. Since I'm staying a while, she wanted to make sure I had what I needed."

"Staying a while." Jathan motioned to a van parked near the road. "I like that."

The driver helped them load her things, and soon they were off.

Jathan sat beside her on the bench seat behind the driver. She tilted her head slightly, studying him in the dim light. He looked the same as when he'd left, but there was a heaviness about him she hadn't noticed before. He look tired, worried.

"How's yer *dat*?" She studied Jathan's profile as the driver pulled out.

He shrugged. "The same. A home health nurse came by earlier today. She says he's being cared fer well, but there's no real improvement. I overheard her talking to *Mem.* She said some people never change and jest get weaker and weaker . . ." He let his voice trail off. "But others, well . . . The nurse said some of her patients sit up and start talking eventually. *Mem* hopes that'll be the case."

Sarah bit her bottom lip and nodded.

Jathan settled back against the seat. He folded his arms over his chest and stretched out his legs between the driver and passenger seats and crossed his ankles.

"You know, I was thinking about it. I learned a lot about yer *mem,* yer *brieder,* Berlin, and the community during our talk in the forest, but you didn't talk much about your *dat.*"

"I didn't? Maybe you drifted off during that part," he mumbled.

She wrinkled her nose. "Did I? That's possible. Or maybe it was because you didn't talk about him much fer some reason . . ."

He looked at her as if he were assessing her. Was he wondering what he should tell? She glanced at the driver. Was having him here limiting Jathan's words?

In Montana, they had only a few drivers, and Sarah considered them friends, but this driver — he hadn't said more than hello to her after she'd gotten into the van and he hadn't said much to Jathan either. Maybe Jathan was trying to figure out what he could say in front of the driver without having it spread around the community.

He cleared his throat. "*Dat* was a hard-working man, respected in the community. We have a small farm and a woodworking workshop behind our house. My oldest *bruder,* Yonnie, works with *Dat.* Many stores in the area sell his furniture. They take special orders . . . or at least *used* to take

281

special orders."

"That sounds wonderful. Do you do woodwork —"

"Some." The word was out before she even finished asking her question. "But I was never any good at that. Let's not bring it up." He looked at her and offered a smile. "Don't you want to look around and see Ohio, Sarah?" He pointed out the window. "It's very different from Montana, but jest as beautiful."

"*Ja.*" She nodded and turned her attention out the window. They drove through countryside and even though there were no buggies out at this hour, she could imagine the clip-clop of slow horses and the rasp of buggy wheels on the gravel lane.

She was thankful for the round, full moon, which cast a warm glow over the countryside, giving her a view of the place she'd be calling home — at least for a time. Maybe . . . maybe for a lifetime.

"Are the farms here in Ohio quite large?"

"Not as large as they used to be. Many family farms have given way to new houses on small tracts of land. It's not busy like you'd suspect though. It's still tranquil there. Not as quiet as the West Kootenai, of course, but many people come back every year to visit Holmes County. It's because of the visitors that I think our bakery will do well."

"*Ja,* I remember." She wrinkled her nose. "I didn't come all this way jest to bake, Jathan. I've come to help you fulfill yer dream."

He reached over and took her hand, and she scooted closer to him so their shoulders touched. Neither said a word for a while, but they didn't need to. She'd entered his world, and they were both content to just be together and soak it in.

After fifteen minutes, Jathan leaned forward and peered out the window. "This is the edge of our community here."

Sarah nodded but didn't see a difference. She saw the same types of farms, similar layouts of the property with houses and barns and shops surrounded by fields and pastures. Yet while she didn't see the difference, she felt it. It was as if an electric charge now radiated from Jathan, causing Sarah's heart to beat extra fast.

Outside the van window, windmills stretched their arms into the night air, some still slowly turning, and Sarah knew from what *Dat* had told her that they powered water pumps. What did Jathan's house look like? Was it as large as the ones on these farms?

In Montana, their log homes were small, their barns were small, and their farms were small. Here, they were driving past houses that seemed big enough to fit the West Kootenai Kraft and Grocery, the West Kootenai school, and Sarah's house inside all at once.

"What are all those little white boxes next to the houses?" she asked Jathan.

"They're birdhouses for purple martins. In the daytime, they look like small apartment buildings on poles." Jathan chuckled. "Of course, I didn't see many apartment buildings in the West Kootenai."

"*Ne, ne,* but I know what yer talking about. I have seen some apartments in Kalispell. And on the train . . ." Her eyes widened. "I saw things from the train I'd only read about in books. In Chicago, I saw a skyscraper. It was cloudy out and the top of it really reached into the clouds — jest like my little sister's favorite book, *Jack and the Beanstalk.*"

"Do you miss them, Evelyn and Andy?"

"*Ja.* How could I not? But with all the hours I used to work at the store, well . . . I haven't spent as much time with them as I wish I could have. Even though I jest got here, I can see that things are different here than in Montana. In Montana, we all had to pull together, work together to make enough money to survive the long winters."

"*Ach,* there are wealthy Amish here, to be sure, but the people care fer each other too. They're generous. Living here, you'll discover that relief auctions are common. Last year, we raised over a million dollars to help needy causes, including sending money to Haiti. My *mem* and sisters made three quilts each through the year and donated them."

Heat rose to Sarah's face as she remembered her and Patty's quilt. They'd created a yellow and blue design, and it had turned out beautiful, much to their surprise. Where was that quilt now?

Sarah forced a sad smile, turning her attention back to the conversation at hand. "A million dollars of relief raised, imagine that," she said. "Maybe fer the next auction, I'll donate some cupcakes. It'll be a *gut* excuse to bake some of my favorites."

"*Ach,* believe me, Sarah. You'll have plenty of excuses to bake. I have a feeling that after people take a single bite of one of yer cupcakes, the line will be out the door."

"Please, Jathan, are you trying to make me a prideful woman? I do what I do because God gifted me with this ability. If I can bring joy to customers, well, it's my way of pointing them to God."

Like a light, she thought. No matter where she was, she could find a way to brighten someone's day. Holmes County was filled with good, Amish folks, but surely there had to be at least one person who needed some brightness, who needed a bit of joy. Sarah would pray for God to lead her to them. To use her in such a way.

As Sarah considered that, she glanced at Jathan. There was a tightness in his jaw she hadn't seen in Montana. She knew he was carrying both the burden of caring for his family and worry about his father's health, and they had to be a heavy load.

We'll start with him, Lord, she thought. *We'll start with him.*

CHAPTER 22

Sarah removed her *kapp* and apron and moved around the bedroom. Her aunt, uncle, and cousins were already in bed when she'd arrived, but they'd left her a plate of food on the table and a note telling her which room they'd prepared for her. Sarah didn't need the note though. There was only one door down the hall that was open and a lantern burned inside the room.

Aunt Lynette had been excited when Sarah asked if she could come. Her aunt had always complained that because her sisters lived in different states, her nieces and nephews were like strangers. She'd been thrilled at the chance to get to know her niece better.

Her aunt and uncle's house was small and had seen better years, but it was clean. Uncle Ivan worked at an organic farm down the road and Aunt Lynette cared for their seven children.

Even though Sarah's heart felt light and full, her eyelids were heavy. By pushing down with two hands, she tested the mattress and then moved her boxes from where they sat by the door onto a trunk by the bed. She knew better than to consider unpacking her things into the trunk. Even though Aunt Lynette's oldest daughter was only six — with three older brothers — Sarah guessed the trunk was already starting to fill with blankets, linens, and other various things a young woman would need upon marriage. Sara had a similar trunk at home. But much to her mother's dismay, Sarah had often spent more time exploring the hills with Patty than sitting home with embroidery.

Patty.

What would Patty think of Sarah being here? Patty no doubt would have cheered on the move, especially with Sarah's hopes of finding love with Jathan. She probably would have mourned the fact they were so far apart, but then again, if Patty were still alive, at least they could have exchanged letters.

A new thought hit Sarah as she considered her friend. What had happened to Patty's hope chest? Her lower lip quivered as Sarah considered that perhaps the towels still sat neatly folded in the trunk rather than drying dishes after a family meal.

Then again, the chest had been far from full. Patty had often complained about having to sit on the porch and sew tiny stitches with thread and needle when she was more interested in visiting the beavers in the pond behind her house.

Sarah attempted to open her boxes as quietly as she could, but the packing tape still sounded like a roaring river as it ripped away from the cardboard. She knew what box she wanted to check first. Sarah took out two objects wrapped in paper. She was careful as she unwrapped them, and she released a sigh of relief when she saw that neither of the jars were broken. One jar was hers, the other Patty's. After she'd received Patty's jar from *Mem,* Sarah had repacked her boxes, bringing Patty's jar with her instead of one of her own. Now she set both jars on top of the dresser. Then she opened the other box and found her nightgown and sleeping kerchief.

Preparing to climb into bed, Sarah planned on turning down the lantern, but then she changed her mind. Not yet. She had one more thing she wanted to do.

Sarah went to the living room and found the matches. When she returned, she dug the small candle out of Patty's jar and set it in the candle stand. She lit it and only then did she dim the lantern's light. The candle's flame flickered and danced, and Sarah smiled, knowing that the last time it had been lit, she'd been with Patty and the room had smelled of pine needles. It made Sarah feel closer to her friend. It made her feel as if she were sharing this moment with her.

And it was at this exact moment that Sarah knew Jathan was a man she could marry, and Holmes County, Ohio, was a community she could plant herself in for life. Seeing him again tonight and the way he'd brushed his fingers down her cheek and told her to have sweet dreams told her it was so.

Jathan sat on the sofa in the living room of his parents' farmhouse and tried to let it sink in that Sarah was really here. If he had a choice, both of them would still be in Montana where he'd have more time to get to know her without the pressures of business and family needs weighing him down. Of course, Jathan didn't have a choice.

He lowered his face into his hands. Tomorrow was the day both he and Sarah were to start at the bakery, but every time he considered the joy of them working together, a heavier burden weighed him down.

"I can't ignore this anymore. I have to face it," Jathan said out loud.

Honor your father and your mother. The words played through his thoughts. They were a foundation to all that the Amish believed. He'd never followed *Englisch* ways, yet was that any worse than Jathan purposefully setting into action what he knew his father would despise?

But to honor them . . . Did that mean he should tell *Mem* he'd go to the factory after all? Tell Sarah he'd changed his mind and he wouldn't be working with her?

He rose and headed out the back door, knowing what he had to do.

Jathan stood on the walk that led to the back of the *dawdi* house. The light from the lantern in his parents' room lit the shrubs that bordered the back of the house, and Jathan pictured *Mem* there with *Dat.* Sitting by him, sharing her day. Were *Dat*'s eyes open? Did he look at her? Did he understand her words? That's what bothered Jathan most. It was bad enough that his father was only a shell of who he used to be, but . . . was his mind still active while trapped in an unresponsive body?

Before the stroke, his father couldn't sit still for five minutes. Now was he lying there worrying about the shop? About the orders? Did he wonder if the tourists were in a buying mood this year? Did he long to head out back, take in the woody scents of his shop, and get lost in a piece of maple?

Jathan walked with slow steps, thinking about how often he'd wished his father would talk less and just listen for a while. His father always had his plans figured out without taking time to hear what others thought about those ideas.

Now all he could do was listen.

The roofline loomed overhead, blocking out the moonlight. Jathan paused, then moved into the shadows, taking the back porch steps one at a time.

He stuck his hands deep into his pockets.

He entered as quietly as he could, but didn't have to worry about waking *Mem.* She sat at the kitchen table with books spread open before her. She had dark circles under her eyes, but she was also smiling. It was the first time he'd seen her smile since he'd been back. During his growing-up years, *Mem* was the last to go to bed, the first to rise. It was nearly one o'clock. Was it hard for her to go to bed without *Dat* sleeping in the bed beside her? He imagined it would be.

Mem eyed him, and then she nodded and

smiled. "*Ja,* she's here."

Jathan removed his hat and put it on the coatrack. Then he ran a hand down his face, trying to hide the smile that had sprouted at *Mem*'s words. "How can you tell?"

"I can read it all over ycr face."

He lowered his head and scuffed his foot against the wooden floor.

Mem chuckled. "She's a *gut* baker now, is she? Is that why you wanted her here?"

He sat down at the table, next to *Mem.* "*Ja,* Sarah is a *gut* baker. I know you'll approve, but I've never been able to hide anything from you. Even as a little boy." He forced a smile, and he hoped *Mem* couldn't see what else he was thinking about. The truth was, there were some things he'd hidden from her. He'd been surprised she never asked why one day — as a child — he'd changed from sitting in the kitchen with her to staying outside all day with his brothers. Did she think the change had come of his own accord?

"Well, I'm excited to meet her. Will she be in the bakery in the morn?" Mem asked.

"*Ja,* but not at five o'clock. I told her to sleep in, to rest, and come in at eight."

"Eight o'clock?" *Mem* gasped the same as if he'd have told her Sarah would be driving a car to work.

"It's all *gut*." He covered *Mem*'s hand with his. "I jest thought she'd like a little time to visit with her aunt and cousins, that's all. She's a hard worker, I promise. If anything, we'll have to tell her to slow down."

"I figured that. I can't imagine you with any other type of woman, and I find it exciting to see what recipes she brings. I've been looking through my books to find some of the favorites I've written down over time. If we're going to work together and build our business, I thought it would be nice to add a few more treats to what we're already selling." *Mem*'s brow furrowed. "Jest as long as we don't change things too much."

"*Ne,* of course not. There have been enough changes around here." Wasn't that just like life, to always be changing? And as sad as the fact was, life never seemed to offer up too much good all at once without having to add in bad too.

"Sunlight and shade," his *oma* had commented once. Jathan liked that, mostly because shade meant that even though things were dim for a time, the sun was still there, just on the other side of the barrier.

As if seeing his sinking spirits, *Mem* opened the cookbook wider and pointed to a page with sticky rolls. "Did ya see these?

Don't they look *gut*?"

"I suppose they do." His eyes darted from the cookbook to the door of his parents' bedroom — the real reason he'd come — and then he looked back at the page. As much as he'd like to sit here and discuss recipes, it was getting late. He wouldn't be able to sleep unless he said his piece.

Jathan pushed back from the table and turned in the direction of his parents' room.

Mem swallowed hard and closed the cookbook. "Do you want to see *Dat*?"

Jathan nodded. "I'd like to talk to him, if that's okay — even if I know he can't say anything back."

"I wish he could talk. I don't mind that he's not physically strong, but I have so many questions." *Mem* sighed. "Is he in pain? Does he know what's going on? One of the nurses thought seeing a physical therapist might help him, but the doctor —" *Mem* gazed up at Jathan, and he could see the emotion building. Her face grew red and blotchy, her lips pinched closed, and without warning, a shuddering sob emerged. "The doctor said it's no use. We'd jest be wasting our money. He said to think of *Dat* as already gone."

Jathan scooted closer and wrapped one arm around his mother. "Don't listen to

295

that." He thought of Sarah and her friend Patty. He thought of their conversation in the woods. "You know what the Bible says. God knows all of our days before one of them came to be. *Dat*'s jest as much alive today as he was weeks ago when he was out in the fields planting. We jest need to appreciate the time we have together until he's called to his heavenly home."

Mem nodded, but Jathan wasn't sure his words helped. It meant loss either way. Continued loss as *Dat*'s body slipped away or final loss when his spirit was called home.

"I-I don't know what I'd do without him. We've been together over forty years. I know his thoughts as well as my own." She paused and looked around the room as if fully taking in where she was and why she was here. "I spent time with my mother-in-law here. I came to keep her company after yer *opa*'s passing. Who knew that someday I'd be the old woman out back? Who would have guessed it would come so soon?" She rose and approached him, offering a hug. Her shoulders quivered but no words came out.

"I usually know what he's thinking too," Jathan finally said. "And I have a feeling if he could talk, we'd get quite an earful about our plan concerning the bakery."

"You better go in and discuss this with

him." She looked up at him with a knowing look. "Even if he can't answer, you'll feel better, son. And maybe tomorrow you can start — we can start — with peace in yer heart."

Jathan entered the bedroom and closed the door behind him. *Dat* lay in the hospital bed, eyes closed. He was thinner than the last time Jathan had seen him and somehow, lying on the bed, he seemed smaller too. Jathan looked at the chair next to the bed and thought about sitting but decided against it. This wouldn't take long.

He cleared his throat and then looked down.

"It seems to me that if this were a game of baseball like we used to play on the Fourth of July, I'd be standing before you now with one strike behind me already, but with a good swing too."

He reached out and grasped his father's foot through the quilt. "The strike? I went to the factory today and turned down the job. You'd have something to say about that, I know. The most important thing to you has always been hard work and a good attitude. But even though I didn't stay in Montana as long as I'd hoped, I learned a few things . . ."

Jathan grinned, remembering his time with Amos. "I learned I'm a pretty *gut* shot. I learned there is a woman I hope to get to know better over the days to come. I also learned something else." He lowered his head and returned his hand to his pocket.

"I'll never be the Amish man you've always wanted me to be. Instead, I have a mind fixed on business and cooking. No matter how many days I spent out in the workshop with you, I was still more inter- ested in how to make a recipe better and how to run a better business. I was never interested in how to craft a fine piece of furniture, and I jest have to say . . ." Jathan sucked in a deep breath and then released it slowly. He opened his mouth and then closed it again. His heart pounded. He felt his face flush. How could what he have to say be so hard? It's not like his father could argue.

Still it was difficult, because the ache behind the words wasn't just something that had stung in the last few months or years. The words he planned had run through a script in his mind ever since he'd been old enough to know how different he was. Since he'd been old enough to hurry through his chores so he could help with dinner.

"I'm sorry I've disappointed you. It was

never my intention, but I promise you I will do what I can to provide fer *Mem.* And fer you. And maybe . . .” Jathan paused and looked out the window in the direction of Sarah's aunt's farm. “And maybe if God blesses me, I'll have a wife to care fer soon. A wife who asks about my dreams and wants to share them. Maybe it's too early to start thinking about that, but you yerself always told me a *gut* woman is worth her weight in gold. I also like to ponder something I heard said in Montana: 'There is not a pot so crooked there isn't a lid to fit it.' ” He let his voice trail off.

Years ago, Jathan knew, he would have tried to pound himself into shape — or face his father's wrath. But now? Things had changed. He had changed. He needed Sarah's love, that was certain, but he also appreciated someone outside of his family who didn't have a mind so full of expectations there was no room for dreams.

“But *Dat,*” he continued, “maybe it wasn't so much becoming the right shape, as it was finding someone who complements you, who fits who you are.”

He hoped that was the case with him and Sarah.

Jathan looked down and thought he saw the slightest flutter of his father's eyelids.

His heart leaped, and he rushed forward, grabbing his father's hand.

"*Dat?*" Jathan leaned in to touch his father's face. "*Dat,* can you hear me?"

There it was, the flutter again. Jathan didn't know if he should rejoice or cry. Maybe *Dat* had heard. Jathan swallowed hard.

And maybe he had just broken his father's heart, yet again.

CHAPTER 23

Sarah looked down at her dark blue dress and full, white apron. *Will I fit in?* She touched her prayer *kapp*. Aunt Lynette had come to her room this morning with the gift. The *kapp* she wore in Montana was similar to what the Amish wore in Indiana, with thick fabric and precise folds. The Ohio *kapp* had a different pattern, and women wore it in both black and white. Aunt Lynette had made a white one for Sarah. Even though the style was different, it was close enough for Sarah to still feel like herself as she wore it.

She glanced at the mirror hanging on Aunt Lynette's wall, most of it covered by a piece of fabric so no one would be tempted to look too long at his or her image. She lifted the fabric just enough — looked just long enough — to gain an ounce of confidence that Jathan would like what he saw. She'd come for work, that was true, but she trusted Jathan had more in mind.

A knock sounded on the front door, and she hurried in that direction. It was six-thirty in the morning. Who could it be at this hour? She glanced at the clock, knowing Uncle Ivan wouldn't leave for work for another twenty minutes and was still in the barn finishing chores.

Opening the front door and screen, a familiar, smiling face greeted her. Jathan's curly, blond hair glimmered in the morning sun. "Mornin'."

"Jathan."

She stepped forward, and he reached out and took her hands.

"What are you doing here?" she asked.

"I couldn't wait. I know I told you not to come in until later, but . . ." He stood for a long moment, still holding both her hands. His eyes moved from her face to her hair. He smiled and her cheeks grew warm.

"I like yer *kapp*," he finally said.

"*Ja.* Aunt Lynette thought I should wear an Ohio *kapp*."

"Looks nice."

They stood two feet apart. Her heartbeat pounded like a hammer. She looked at his strong jaw, remembering how she had rested her head there when he'd carried her down the mountain.

He didn't move and she didn't either. She wanted to hold on to this moment before the busyness of the day took over. She would never get used to the look in his gaze. The touch of adoration, appreciation it held. She didn't understand it but liked it all the same.

Footsteps sounded behind her. Aunt Lynette approached. Jathan released her hands and his eyes dropped shyly to his boots for just a moment.

"What are you doing here?" Sarah asked again with a shy smile.

"I thought you'd like a ride to the bakery."

"It's a little out of yer way."

"An extra mile, not too much. Are you saying you'd rather walk?" He winked.

"*Ach, ne,* but I'm not ready quite yet." She glanced down at her stockinged feet. "Won't you come in?"

Aunt Lynette was already adding another plate to the breakfast table as Jathan entered. She approached him with an outstretched hand. "You must be Jathan Schrock. My husband, Ivan, went to school with yer *bruder* Joe. They were in the same grade."

"Ivan, *ja.* I've met him around town."

"Aren't you in the same church?" Sarah

asked. "How far away did you say you lived?"

"Three miles perhaps. But even though I've met Ivan around town, we're in different districts. The churches grow and new ones form."

"I've visited yer *mem*'s bakery," Aunt Lynette said. "It's the favorite in town for authentic Amish bread and such. None of that fancy stuff like you find in other bakeries in nearby towns."

Uncle Ivan came in from the barn, called a greeting, and began washing his hands at the sink. Three older boys followed him, and Sarah tried to remember their names. Three younger girls had already found their seats at the table, and the youngest child — a boy — peeked around the corner, staring at Jathan with large brown eyes. With big families on both of her parents' sides, keeping track of everyone's names was always a challenge for Sarah.

"Fancy stuff in bakeries?" Sarah rubbed her hands up and down her arms. "Like what?" Sarah finally had the nerve to ask.

"*Ja.*" Aunt Lynette's eyes widened. "One bakery in Walnut Creek makes fancy chocolates." Her words were released in a whisper. "Imagine that. I'd hate to see what folks think up next." Aunt Lynette clicked her tongue. "They're acting so much like the *Englisch*, I wouldn't be surprised if they jest become *Englisch* themselves."

Did others feel the same? Would they have a problem if she tried new things too? Sarah glanced at Jathan, hoping to read his expression. Instead, he was kneeling down and playing with her youngest cousin. He didn't seem bothered by Aunt Lynette's words. She supposed she shouldn't be either.

The clopping of the horse's hooves accompanied them down the street, and Sarah's heart seemed to clop within as the farmland gave way to the downtown area, which was filled with small shops and various businesses. Even though it was barely 7:30 yet, cars and buggies clogged the roadway. Men and women walked the hilly streets of Berlin, entering shops, watering flowers in front porch planters, and visiting with each other as if it were the most important part of their day.

The area couldn't be more different than the West Kootenai. In the small community back home, there wasn't a main street, only dirt roads that traveled in various directions and tall posts with arrows that pointed to family homes. Sure there was the West Kootenai store, Montana Log Works, and the school all within a half mile of each other, but that was "downtown" in the same way Evelyn's dog, Moe, was a "fine breed."

Sarah glanced from one side of the paved road to the other, not wanting to miss anything. Unlike the Amish in the West Kootenai, who wore plain garb, the women here seemed partial to beautifully colored dresses. The greens, purples, and blues of their dresses appeared as vibrant as a king's jewels.

This county seemed more prosperous than the one she'd moved from. In Montana, women carried in armloads of firewood and could often be seen walking down muddy roads toward the store. In the West Kootenai, colors faded from the hard lifestyle, and folks didn't have extra money or time to replace their dresses. In the West Kootenai, the women's dresses were faded from washing and use. In Berlin, the garments seemed so bright and the aprons and bonnets were just so. The dress colors were only slightly subdued by the black aprons, capes, and bonnets some of the women wore here. The only thing plain about these clothes was that they were plainly made.

She glanced at Jathan, who sat beside her in his broad-brimmed hat with low crown. She let her imagination wander to an image of a little boy sitting between them wearing long trousers, a jacket, and a low-crowned hat over his blocked hair. A smile filled her face. She liked the idea of raising children in this community, raising children with Jathan.

"Where are you letting yer mind wander so?" Jathan asked.

"Ach." She readjusted herself in her seat. "Just thinking of the days ahead and lookin' forward to, uh, spending time in this community. Getting to know the people better."

"I like that, Sarah. I was worried you'd miss home too much . . ."

"Ne, not so much. At least not yet. I know I will, but I also know the missing's not enough to make me want to return." She watched the strong muscles of the horse's back flexing as it pulled them. She knew what Jathan was going to ask next.

"Really? Why's that?"

Sarah smiled. "I'm ready for this. I've had a good life in Montana, *ja,* but being there keeps me fixed on all that's in the past. I didn't know I was ready for new scenery and a different challenge with my baking until I was on my way here. I didn't know my heart had only been beating a half beat until . . ." She let her voice trail off and studied her hands on her lap.

"Until what, Sarah?"

She blinked quickly, then dared to look at him. "Until I met you."

He nodded and his face brightened, as if lit by a kerosene lantern from within. Then he pulled the buggy up in front of a building, parking it. "Is this the type of place you'd imagine working in?"

Sarah followed his gaze. It was a small log building on a side street. It looked a bit tired, and as if it had been there for years, but she smiled. Amos had been right. It did look like a smaller version of the West Kootenai Kraft and Grocery.

"Imagine that." She allowed him to help her down. "To think there's two peas in a pod, but they're halfway across the country apart."

"I wish our place was half as nice inside as the West Kootenai store. It's been in the family for years. One of my uncles used to sell farm supplies and feed here. Maybe I should have warned you about its condition before you came. But one of the first things I'll be doing is fixing it up — not the equipment, not jest yet — but jest things to make the place look newer and more welcoming. I want yer advice and help too. You've worked fer Annie fer years. Please don't be shy in telling us what changes need to be made. I want this business to succeed. I need it to succeed."

Sarah nodded. She understood. This was the first step of their dream. To fail here would be to shut the door on having their own place someday, on their future.

Sarah leaned forward and looked closer. "Is it open? It looks dark inside."

"*Ja,* my aunt should be there, and *Mem* is coming over once my sister Connie arrives to care for *Dat.* If she doesn't make it today, she said to count on her tomorrow fer certain.

"From what *Mem* told me last night, because of *Dat*'s stroke, the bakery has been shut down more than it's been open the last few weeks," he continued, "but folks around town have been understanding. Some customers paid fer orders they knew they wouldn't receive, jest to help out *Mem* . . . but with Connie caring for *Dat* during the day, *Mem*'s hoping to be completely back in business by the end of the week."

"Maybe I can help with that," Sarah said as she followed Jathan inside.

The wood floor was clean but worn. Three small wooden tables with chairs were set up for customers. Lanterns hung overhead, but were dimmed down. The best part was the beautiful wood and glass display case. It was only filled a quarter of the way with baked items, but seeing how little was in it made Sarah want to roll up her sleeves.

She pointed. "Did yer *dat* make that display case?"

"*Ja,* five years ago, I'd guess."

"It's lovely, jest lovely."

Hearing the sound of their voices, an older woman exited the kitchen wearing a cooking apron.

"Sarah, this is Aunt Kay, one of *Mem*'s sisters."

"Hello. I —" Sarah stepped forward to shake the woman's hand and was pulled into a quick embrace.

"Sarah, dear, you've come. I've been praying fer *gut* help. And look what God has done. Both you and Jathan here are answered prayers indeed." Kay wagged her finger in the air. She looked to be about fifty and was rail thin. The only family resemblance to Jathan were the two dimples that highlighted her face when she smiled. "Don't let this tall, handsome boy fool you." Kay patted Jathan's cheek. "He can do any work around the farm, but unlike most men, he also knows how to bake and cook. In fact, I don't know if he told you about his cornbread yet, but mine never turns out half as *gut* as his."

"Cornbread? No, he hasn't shared that." Sarah glanced at Jathan out of the corner of her eye and noticed his cheeks flushing pink. "In fact, there's much I'm lookin' forward to hearing."

Customers entered, and Kay hustled behind the counter to wait on them, but not before offering Sarah a wink. With Kay busy with the two older Amish women at the counter, Sarah turned fully to Jathan. His neck was bright red and he wore a troubled frown.

"Don't worry." She placed a hand on his arm. "Whenever you meet my aunts, I'm sure they'll give you an earful too."

"You'll learn everything in time, I suppose." He turned to the kitchen and cleared his throat. Then he took out a red handkerchief from his pocket and wiped away the sweat beading on his brow. "But for now, let's talk about what we can do to fix up this place."

"*Ja* . . . I'd like that." She placed her hand under the crook of his elbow and walked with him through the wide doorway to the kitchen. "I can't wait to get started."

Sarah glanced around. The kitchen walls were a dingy yellow. The floor was white-and-green checked. Sarah placed a hand on her hip. She supposed the floors were good

311

enough.

"The first thing this kitchen needs is a gallon of white paint. And we need new aprons. Blue, I think." She stroked her chin. "*Ja,* a nice blue."

"I don't understand. When I spoke of spiffing things up, I meant the front area. Painting the kitchen? Sarah . . . is that necessary?" Jathan asked.

Kay entered as Jathan said those words, and Sarah could read the same questions on her face as well.

"*Ja,* because these dingy walls give the impression that the food will be dull too. And once we cut down the wall . . ."

"Cut down the wall?" Jathan raised a hand. "I know I asked for your advice, but —"

"*Ja!* Of course. How else are we going to interact with our customers? Half the draw to the bakery will be our *appeditlich* food. The other half, our smiles." She turned to Kay, who was standing next to her.

"I — I do not understand," Kay said.

"Consider this. Imagine you are a customer. If there are two bakeries in town and one's food is jest as *gut* as the other's, whose cookies do you think you'll buy — ones set up in a nice display case . . . or ones offered to you fresh from the oven by yer friends

312

Sarah and Kay? We want them to feel as if they're stepping into our kitchen. As if we're friends."

"*Ja,* but many of the customers are *Englisch.*" Kay placed a finger over her lips and her brows furrowed.

Sarah nodded. She closed her eyes briefly and thought of her friends back in Montana, of Annie, Jenny, and Edgar, and the customers at the store. She considered telling Kay about these friendships and how she'd found through the years she had more similarities than differences with the *Englisch,* but she knew now was not the time. Letting her — someone new — into their business would be a challenge, and change was hard to face. Maybe she should take things more slowly. One thing at a time.

"Don't you think our *Englisch* friends could use a kind word and a smile too?" Sarah finally said with a soft smile.

Kay nodded, but she did not smile. Instead she turned to Jathan. "I trust you and I trust yer business sense. I know you'll do right by us." She released a sigh. "I'll let you take care of yer mother though. If my sister Maggie likes anything, she likes things to stay the same."

"No need to worry, Aunt. I've already talked to *Mem,* and she told me she's

313

excited about some of Sarah's new recipes and that she's excited to add them to the menu."

"Really now?" Kay's eyebrows rose as if trying to stretch and reach her forehead. Then she turned to Sarah and forced a smile. "She must be excited about you coming. Excited that Jathan cares for one such as you."

"I appreciate that." Sarah walked to the sink and washed her hands, reminding herself to be as gentle as a fawn. "Why don't we start by you telling me what I can help with."

Kay pointed back the direction they'd just come. "Why don't you clean the front area and wait on customers? The chalkboard lists the prices of the items, and I assume you know how to use a cash register."

"*Ja,* of course," Sarah answered. Then she glanced at Jathan. Did he think that was the best use of her time? Jathan wasn't focused on her or their conversation though. Instead his eyes studied the wall between the kitchen and the front area. He stood quietly, most likely estimating how much paint he'd need. What tools would be needed to take down that wall.

"I'll be back." He hurried out the front door without a wave.

314

Sarah forced a smile as she picked up the broom. *This is jest the first day. It'll take time to find the right rhythm.*

As much as she wanted to get into that kitchen and start baking, Sarah realized she didn't want to push. She wanted to be a welcome employee rather than a demanding stranger.

CHAPTER 24

Sarah had just finished cleaning up the front area when Jathan returned with his arms full. Kay had already gone home for the day, and Sarah raced forward to help Jathan as he set down the paint, brushes, and drop cloths and then went back to the buggy for more supplies. He returned with a saw, a hammer, nails, and wood.

"I've been thinking about yer suggestion, and I like it. The kitchen does need paint, but I don't think the whole wall between the front area and kitchen needs to come down." He eyed her, obviously concerned about her response. "Since there's no electricity in this place or any wiring, and since it's not a load-bearing wall, it'll be easy to put in a large window."

Sarah eyed the wall. "*Ja,* I like that. What a perfect solution!"

The tension in Jathan's face eased.

"Yer going to do it yerself?" she asked.

"*Ja,* of course. Just because I don't enjoy woodworking doesn't mean I don't know how to do it. I'm going to cut the window, build a box to place it in, and then frame it all in."

"I have no doubt it'll be amazing, Jathan. I can see it now."

His nostrils flared slightly and his eyes blinked closed for a moment. He tried to hide his smile, but didn't do a very good job. He reminded her of a small boy who'd been called out by his teacher for a job well done.

"I'll do my best, at least. My *bruder* Yonnie's heading over soon to help. I figured I should be able to work through the afternoon and evening and have it finished up before you and *Mem* come in to work tomorrow."

"Oh." Sarah clasped her hands to her chest. "I'm not sure what I'm more excited about, finally meeting yer *mem* or seeing this place fixed up. And I'm eager to meet Yonnie too."

He nodded. "Our bakery will look nice, if I say so myself."

Sarah noticed he didn't comment about Yonnie. She also noted tension on Jathan's face. She remembered Jathan talking about how Yonnie agreed that he needed to work

317

at the factory. What did his oldest brother think now that Jathan was helping with the bakery instead? He must not be too angry. If he was, surely he wouldn't be coming to help.

Before Sarah had a chance to ask, Jathan turned back to her. "Our customers will like the way we fix things up, but I also think folks will be excited about yer bakery items too."

"I hope so. I had some ideas for things I wanted to bake today, but it really didn't work out that way." Sarah crossed her arms over her chest and then hooked her sore ankle over the other, leaning forward so her arms rested on the top of the display case. She looked down into it. She hadn't had a chance to bake yet, and she wondered how much freedom she would have when she was given a chance. The display case was filled with bread, muffins, rolls — things she'd known how to make since she was eight. She hadn't thought about asking Jathan how much variety his mother and aunt would allow. Her stomach ached at the thought of spending all her days just making the same things over and over.

"*Ja,* I know. Sorry about that," Jathan said. "My aunt is still getting used to the idea that things will be changing. She and

Mem have run this little bakery fer fifteen years. I'm afraid they've settled into how things are, jest like buggy ruts in a dirt road."

"Well, a little at a time. Speaking of such, I can paint while you work on the window."

"I don't think that's a *gut* idea."

"What?" She looked at him. "I'll do a good job. I promise."

He neared her and reached over to tilt up her chin. "Oh, Sarah, I have no doubt about that. I jest think you should head home and spend some time with yer aunt. You got in late last night. I stole you away early this morning . . ."

She wrinkled her nose. "Do I have to?" And then, as she looked into his face, her stomach did a flip.

They'd been alone in the bakery for fifteen minutes at least, but Sarah hadn't noticed until this moment. Suddenly, she was aware of his shirt sleeves, which he'd rolled up so he could get to work. His arms appeared so strong, and his strength made him even more handsome. Not just his strength and ability to remodel the bakery, but the strength to stand up to his family for what he wanted for his life.

"I won't make you, but you should." Even as he said the words, she could tell from his dancing eyes that he didn't want her to go. She didn't want to go either, but it would be rude of her not to return home to see her aunt.

"Ja." Sarah blew out a long breath. "You are right." She moved to the door with slow steps.

"Do you need me to give you a ride?" He hurried over and reached around her to push open the heavy plateglass door for her to pass.

She shook her head, feeling his breath on her cheek. *"Ne.* It's only a mile. I'd love to stretch my legs and maybe I'll make a friend or two on the way home."

Jathan eyed her and nodded. "I have no doubt about that, Sarah. I've never met anyone who cared fer people as much as you. Somewhere along the way, you've learned to be a great friend."

"Why, thank you." She patted his chest as she strode out the door, fighting off the urge to linger. Jathan followed her out.

Outside in the parking lot, she turned back, taking an extra moment to gaze at him in front of the bakery, telling herself not to forget this moment when something they'd talked about only a little over a month ago had become real. They'd both had dreams and it amazed her how God had used each other to help fulfill them.

As Sarah resumed her walk down the sidewalk, she remembered something *Dat* always told her: "Many things I have tried to grasp and have lost. That which I have placed in God's hands I still have." She needed to trust those words for this situation too. As easily as she and Jathan were coming together, he wasn't something to grasp and claim. Rather she needed to continue to place him — place their budding relationship — in God's hands and take each day, each moment, as it came.

Sarah thought of this as she strode down Main Street, strolling among both Amish and *Englisch.* On the outside, she looked like any of the other Amish women who walked down the sidewalk — her dress, apron, and prayer *kapp* matched — but on the inside, she felt as different as if she were walking down the streets of New York City. Tourists walking by seemed surprised when she made eye contact and offered a hello.

Can they tell I'm not from around here? she wondered.

Angst stirred in her gut where peace had been a moment before. And she realized why. Had she not fifty steps ago given her relationship with Jathan to God? She'd thought about, prayed for, and talked to

Patty about her future husband from the time she was thirteen and started taking note of the Amish bachelors coming to town. And if she'd been able to give something as important as that to God, why couldn't she release the tension she felt about walking among these people? Didn't God care about her fitting in in these parts too? Would he bring her all this way only for her to feel out of place and rejected? Was it too much to hope that she'd be loved by Jathan *and* this community?

Sarah continued on, and when she walked up the small hill that led to Uncle Ivan and Aunt Lynette's house, something inside told her to pause and to turn. She did, gazing at the town behind her — the cars and the buggies, the people and the businesses, the trees and the sky that stretched down to the horizon.

Something inside her told her she was home. Tingles danced up her arms, and she wasn't sure why. Maybe because home meant love, belonging, acceptance . . . didn't it?

Sarah approached her aunt's house. The scent of violets filled the air and, for the first time, Sarah got a good look at the place. The walkway was lined with small purple flowers. They even peeked out of the flower box by the kitchen window. Sarah did not have to guess her aunt's favorite flower.

The front door was open, and Sarah took another deep breath before hurrying in.

"There she is now," Aunt Lynette's voice carried to Sarah. Her aunt hurried from the kitchen and opened her arms wide. "Did you have a *gut* day at the bakery?"

"It was a wonderful start. Jathan's Aunt Kay was there. She's very nice, but I didn't get to bake —"

"Sarah, we have company," Aunt Lynette interrupted. She placed her finger over her lips and then motioned to the kitchen.

Sarah followed her inside. An older woman was standing in the kitchen. She was just a hair taller than Aunt Lynette, plump with gray hair perfectly arranged under her *kapp.* She was slightly stooped, but Sarah would have recognized Jathan's mother anywhere. He had her eyes, her smile.

"Mrs. Schrock, correct?" Sarah turned to her aunt. "I did not know you knew Jathan's *mem.*"

Aunt Lynette grinned. "We have mutual friends, but we jest met ten minutes ago when there was a knock on the door."

"Yonnie told me where you were staying." Mrs. Schrock studied Sarah from head to toe as she spoke. "His wife, Leah, brought me by. She's dropping Yonnie off at the bakery and then returning for me. I couldn't go to bed another night without meeting the young woman who has added the bounce to Jathan's step and the smile to a face that has been solemn fer far too long."

From upstairs came the reverberations of her younger cousins' antics. It sounded like they had started an impromptu game of tag when they were supposed to be changing out of their school clothes.

One set of footsteps pounded above their heads, then two, then three. Aunt Lynette moved to the stairway as if to call up to tell them all to calm down. Laughter spilled from Mrs. Schrock. "Please, don't shush them on my account. I raised eight children, five of them boys. I have ten grandchildren and some of my children have yet to get started with children of their own. But enough about me." She stretched out her arms to Sarah. "Come, I have to meet you. What a beautiful girl! No wonder my Jathan is smitten."

"Smitten?" Sarah felt herself blushing. Blushing! What a first impression for someone from whom she wanted so much to gain approval.

She didn't have to worry. Mrs. Schrock

noticed her pink cheeks and a smile caused her round eyes to squint. "*Ja,* and I see, my dear, that you have come fer more than jest baking. More than jest to explore beautiful Holmes County. Every time I mention my son's name, you turn a new shade of pink."

Sarah stepped into the old woman's embrace. "*Ja,* you caught me. It's so *gut* to meet you. Jathan, well, he has yer smile and yer eyes."

"He does. And his *dat*'s stubborn nature. If he has something on his mind, you can be sure he's not gonna let it go. Not ever."

"Like the bakery?" Sarah asked as she noticed her youngest cousin waddling into the room. Little Elmer had a shock of blond hair that stuck up from his head like a feather duster. She bent down and opened her arms, and he gladly let her sweep him up.

"Like the bakery and other things. My husband, Will, had his mind set on Jathan landing a stable job. With both him and Yonnie at the woodshop . . . well, they have to make — sell — a lot of furniture to provide fer two families." She waved her hand in the air. "But enough about that. Tell me about yerself."

They sat around the kitchen table and Aunt Lynette poured them coffee. Sarah

325

told them about her family, living in Montana, and her former job at the West Kootenai Kraft and Grocery. Yet even as she shared everything else, she couldn't bring herself to talk about Patty. Patty had been Sarah's dearest friend and her influence couldn't be denied, but how could she explain that to these two women?

Maybe I don't need to share — not yet anyway. Maybe it's a sign that I'm changing and growing. That I'm looking forward instead of getting stuck in the past.

Instead, she talked about Jathan, about how he rescued her in the woods, and about how much she enjoyed getting to know him. She also mentioned her ideas for the bakery.

"Oh, dear, sweet girl." Mrs. Schrock patted Sarah's hand. "I've been asking my sons to help fix up that place fer years now. God knew the desires of my heart and brought someone young and pretty — someone who's captured my Jathan's attention — to light a fire under him."

Sarah took a sip from her coffee. "So you aren't upset at my ideas for changes?"

"Upset?" Mrs. Schrock chuckled. "Oh *ne*. I'm looking forward to the help, and I believe my customers will be excited too. We like things simple and plain, but we enjoy a bit of surprise now and then too.

You jest being here has already done that. As I was telling my dear Will this morning, 'That Sarah Shelter has got all of Berlin in a stir, capturing the heart of the most eligible bachelor in town.' "

Chapter 25

Aunt Lynette set the leg of lamb on the table. She met Sarah's eyes and smiled. Her smile said she was thankful Sarah was there with them. Sarah felt the same.

Uncle Ivan cut the lamb into razor-thin slices and served some onto each person's plate, including his, yet he served no more to himself than he did to the children. The potatoes and vegetables were plentiful on the table, but she could tell that the meat was a treat, and she guessed they hoped to serve it over more than one day.

Soon everyone finished eating, and by the looks on their faces, they all wished for seconds, yet no one asked.

"Sarah, would you like more lamb?" Uncle Ivan lifted the platter of meat in her direction.

She patted her stomach. "*Ach, ne,* I'm *gut.* But those carrots were *appeditlich.* You must be an excellent gardener. May I have more

of those?"

Aunt Lynette smiled and handed over the platter of cooked carrots. Sarah scooped a few carrots onto her plate.

"Children, lamb?" Uncle Ivan held up the plate again. Even though their eyes were bright, shakes of head declined the offer. Sarah smiled, picturing the coming week. Lamb for tomorrow's supper. Lamb sandwiches for school. Perhaps lamb stew later in the week. She glanced at her aunt and uncle's dog, Shep, and guessed he'd get the lamb bone for breakfast soon.

With dinner finished, Sarah took the plate of lamb to the kitchen. "Would you like me to wrap it and put it in the icebox?"

"*Ach, ne.* I'm going to wrap it and send it over to the young widow who lives four houses down," Aunt Lynette said. "You haven't met her yet, but Esther is delightful. Poor dear lost her husband. He was an only son and his parents are in the *dawdi* house. That's not counting the twin boys who are near three."

A cold wave washed over Sarah. "How did her husband die?"

"Cancer. He was having headaches and finally went to a doctor in Columbus. There was a tumor — nothing they could do. He was gone jest like that."

"Gone jest like that." Sarah's heart ached, but the sadness didn't overwhelm her like it used to. "It's very sad. I can go with you if you'd like, to offer some encouragement."

"No, you should rest. It's been a long day. You must be so tired." Her aunt patted her hand. "Why don't you head to bed? The girls and I will finish this up."

Normally Sarah would refuse the offer, but she found herself nodding. After giving her aunt a quick hug, she hurried to her room.

She lifted her fingers to her *kapp,* lifting it from her head.

Death.

She hadn't thought much if it before losing Patty.

Old people died.

Englisch people died in automobile accidents. In Montana, the white crosses that dotted the side of the highways proved that. She'd counted them whenever she rode along with an *Englisch* driver on their way to Eureka or Kalispell.

But there was no white cross at the edge of Lake Koocanusa. Sarah didn't need one to remember. Months after Patty's death, people had still been talking about it, but then, after that, it was as if no one remembered except Sarah. Others had gone on

with their normal lives, and Sarah had gone on with her life, too, even though it pained her to do so.

Death.

Sarah looked at her memory jar. It sat on the unfamiliar dresser, and she hadn't had time to look at its contents since she'd arrived. So certain the jars would get broken on the trip, she'd transferred one of her jars and Patty's into plastic peanut butter jars. She'd scraped most of the labels off, but bits of paper still stuck to where they had been glued.

Sarah pulled out a few items that were sitting on top of the pile in Patty's plastic jar. An acorn, a feather, a chunk of wood. They were all dead. The fact shocked Sarah in a way she couldn't explain. What she carried around were symbols of the life they used to have — the growth and beauty.

Is that what I've been doing? Looking back at the life that used to be, rather than looking ahead to the life that could *be?*

Too often she'd focused on what she'd lost, rather than what Patty had found. Patty had loved God, had had faith in him. And the more Sarah thought about the word *faith,* the more she realized it was all about looking ahead.

I am Lord over the beginning and Lord over

the end. Trust me, child.

The words came as a gentle whisper to her heart. She grasped the chair for support. *The end.*

Years ago, when Sarah had started reading her Bible, she discovered that to have a new life in Christ, she had to accept his death.

Now she had a feeling that to live the life Jesus was calling her to, she had to accept that death would come — to her and those she loved — but it was life she needed to focus on.

She had to be willing to trust that God protected her heart and had a good plan for her, for Jathan, and maybe for them together.

Sixteen-year-old Sarah sat up with a start. The first things she noticed were the light all around her and the scent of wildflowers on the breeze. Her cheek felt damp, and she touched it. Only then did she remember. When her eyes adjusted, she noticed Patty sitting on the grass beside her. They'd been sitting in the meadow under the shade of a tall pine, and she must have drifted off to sleep.

Patty pointed to her face. "You drooled."

Sarah wiped at it. "*Ja,* I suppose I did."

Then she closed her eyes and smiled.

"Tell me about it." Patty scooted closer.

"About what?"

"The dream. It was a good one, and I want to hear all the details."

Sarah plucked a blade of grass from the soft earth and twirled it between her fingers. "How do you know it was good?"

"Uh, maybe because it looks as if you've swallowed a bag of sugar and it's sweetened you up. Sweet smile and sweet lashes that are fluttering as if you've jest seen the most handsome Amish man ever."

Sarah leaned back again and folded her arms behind her head. "I did." Then she stretched her arms as far above her as she could reach and her toes as far as she could stretch as if it would take every inch of her to fully absorb the beauty of the dream she'd just had. "Well, I didn't see him, not fully, but he was handsome all the same."

"Really?" Patty scooted so close her knee jabbed into Sarah's ribs.

A pain shot up Sarah's side, and she pushed against Patty's knee. "*Ach,* watch yerself. Behave or I won't tell you."

"*Ja,* you'll tell me, Sarah Shelter, for you haven't been able to keep a secret from me yet."

Sarah pressed her lips together and closed her eyes. She waited for Patty to beg, but instead her friend just sat there, staring. Sarah couldn't see her gaze, because her own eyes were closed, but she could feel it. Patty's stare was so intense, Sarah was sure she'd be able to feel it if Patty were halfway across the state.

"*Ja,* okay, I'll tell." She opened her eyes and sat up, unable to take the tension any longer.

"There was a gate."

"*Ja.*"

"And a white picket fence."

"*Ja.*"

"And a man by my side who was leading me through it."

"What was inside the gate?" Patty's eyes focused intently on Sarah's, as if she were trying to look into her brain and see for herself.

Sarah furrowed her brow, attempting to remember. "I'm not sure, a flower garden maybe? Something beautiful fer sure, but that's not the part I remember most. I jest remember he was an Amish man — my Amish man — and he loved me more than anyone ever has. And he walked with pride when I was at his side, like I was more valuable than the gate or the garden beyond or anything in the world."

"Is he yer future husband?"

Sarah nodded. "I think he is."

"Are you sure you didn't get a good look at him? 'Cause, if so, that will save you a heap of trouble trying to figure out jest who is the one."

"No. I'm not sure I looked at him, saw him much at all. It was jest a feeling I had. A sense deep inside."

"I wish you could have at least seen if his hair was dark or light."

Sarah shrugged. "Would it matter? Would his looks matter at all if he treats me like that? Cares for me like that? Like I was more important than anything else — anything but God, of course."

She turned over onto her side and looked full into Patty's face. "I think that's how I'll know my future husband when the time is right. There will be this sense that he knows me — really knows who I am inside — and he'll love me fer myself, because of who I am."

"I think that's something *gut* to hang onto," Patty grinned. " 'Cause you wouldn't want a husband who jest loved you for yer baking . . . and with those pies you've

335

been making lately, I can see that happening."

Sarah chuckled. "*Ne,* he must love me fer much more than that. Much, much more."

CHAPTER 26

Over the next week, Our Daily Bread picked up in business, but Sarah wasn't sure if it was because of the remodeling in the bakery, the new bakery items, or if they'd all come to see the young woman who'd caught Jathan Schrock's interest.

"Where are you from, dear?" one older Amish woman asked. She'd been in the bakery the last two mornings, ordering a buttermilk pie and two maple cupcakes each day. From the slight smile on the woman's face, Sarah had a feeling only the pie made it to the dinner table each evening.

"West Kootenai, Montana, ma'am."

The woman picked up her items as gingerly as if she carried fine china. "I've read about the Rexford community in *The Budget*. Is West Kootenai near there?"

"Oh, *ja,* the West Kootenai is right across the lake from Rexford. In fact, we have a Rexford address."

"Oh, my, then you must have heard. There was an Amish woman who was lost in those mountains jest last month. Did you hear about that?"

"*Ja,* uh . . ."

Two hands grasped her shoulders. "Did you not know? This is the young woman, and it was my Jathan who rescued her from the forest. She could have died up there." Mrs. Schrock spoke loud enough for everyone in the store to hear.

The older woman's mouth circled in an *O.* "Oh, my. Were you scared, dear?"

"*Ja.*"

The woman's unblinking eyes grew round. "Were you hurt?"

"Well, my ankle —"

"How wonderful for a man like that to be there at the right time."

"I had a friend whose niece got lost once. She'd been on her way to school and a squirrel running through the trees caught her attention," another Amish woman, no taller than Sarah's shoulder, declared.

"Did they find her again?" The first woman reached out and grasped Sarah's arm. "We know how dangerous getting lost can be, even if yer not a *kind.*"

"Oh, *ja,* but it was late at night when they found her, and she was frightfully cold."

The second woman turned to Sarah, lifting her head to meet her gaze. "Were you frightfully cold, dear?"

"For a time I was," Sarah said with forced patience. "Until Jathan lit the fire."

The women gasped and nodded their approval as if that was the most wonderful thing they'd ever heard.

"I'm sure the fire did much to help them both," the taller woman said to her friend. "Not only to warm their bodies but to lift their spirits too. Don't you think?"

Sarah nodded as the women continued, not that they noticed. They spoke about Jathan and the situation as if she weren't there.

As the customers talked with each other, they also ordered bread and rolls and bought the last of Sarah's cupcakes. Without a pause, Mrs. Schrock bagged up the items and handed them over. The women paid and stepped away from the counter, continuing to talk with each other as they did.

Sarah chuckled, watching the way the women's stories jumped from subject to subject with everyone being able to follow along. The Amish in Montana didn't buy as many baked goods — instead making the items themselves — but she heard the same type of talk at ice-cream socials and quilting circles. One spark of an idea led to another thought, and soon each woman was carrying on a conversation with a dozen people at once, but mostly with herself.

Sarah walked into the kitchen and the voices followed her through the large, open window that Jathan and Yonnie had made. She smiled, reminding herself she'd asked for it. Reminding herself she was the only one to blame if she had no relief from the constant chatter.

"Sarah, dear, will you be making any more cupcakes today?" a voice called from behind her. She glanced back, not knowing which woman asked, but all looked to her with eager faces.

"Well, I've never heard of Amish cupcakes being so popular," Mrs. Schrock said with a forced smile. "But I suppose Sarah can make more of those instead of the cinnamon rolls."

A murmur of approval rose up, followed by declarations that the women would be back later that afternoon. Sarah went back to wash the cupcake pans she'd used, but out of the corner of her eye, she watched Jathan's mother. Her smile faded as soon as the women moved to the door.

When the last woman left, Aunt Kay walked up and placed a hand on Mrs.

Schrock's shoulder. "I've never heard of Amish cupcakes. Cupcakes in the *Englisch* bakery in town, *ja,* but here?"

A twinge of anxiety struck Sarah's heart. They had no idea she could hear them. Her embarrassment was tinged with a distant shame. She thought back to that day years ago when Patty had brought her those magazines with fancy cupcakes, the very magazines that ended up in the trash.

"I don't know what's wrong with cupcakes," she mumbled to herself. They had the same ingredients as the other items she made. The only difference was the flavorings and the thin layer of vanilla bean frosting on top.

Jest as long as I don't do any fancy decorating — at least not fer sale. Aunt Lynette's birthday was coming later in the month, and Sarah planned on decorating one cupcake to match the violets her aunt liked so. Tomorrow, she had the afternoon off. Maybe she could visit the cooking store down the street for ideas.

She'd just begun to gather the items for another batch of chocolate cupcakes when the back door opened. She turned just in time to see Jathan enter with a young woman by his side. She looked to be about fifteen years old, and Sarah guessed she was already done with school.

"Sarah!" Excitement filled Jathan's face and he rushed over. "I was doing the books last night and business has already picked up fifty percent in a week."

"You don't have to tell me." She wiped her forehead with the back of her hand. "I'm already working on another large batch of cupcakes and it's only ten o'clock."

She turned to the young woman. "I'm sorry that Jathan forgot an introduction." She winked. "I'm Sarah, and I'm guessing yer related, because I see a hint of dimples on yer face too."

"*Ja*, I'm his niece Catherine. I'll be yer dishwasher."

"Dishwasher? Jathan, are you sure? That's taking away half my job —"

He laughed. "*Ach*, which means more time for cupcakes . . . if our town can handle such a thing." He nodded to his niece. "Sorry I forgot the introduction. Catherine is my brother Otto's oldest girl."

"Girl? She's a woman yet." Sarah pointed to the pile of dishes in the sink. "And that's a woman's work fer sure."

Catherine smiled and stood straighter. In a way, she reminded Sarah of her friend Jenny, and she liked her immediately.

"*Gut*, keep Catherine busy. And speaking

of busy, do you mind if I take away *Mem* and Aunt Kay for just fifteen minutes? Mr. Bell at the print shop wants to talk to them both about writing a cookbook."

Hearing their names, the older women hurried into the kitchen.

"A cookbook? Did I overhear that?" Aunt Kay pressed a hand to her chest. "Aren't we getting fancy now?"

"Not fancy, jest smart. Baked goods you produce every day, but a book is written once and sold over and over."

"But if we give out our recipes, won't people stop coming?" Aunt Kay asked.

"Jest the opposite. They'll hear about you, want to meet you, and come from farther away, don't you think, Sarah?"

"Oh, *ja*. I love the idea." She did love the idea, but she couldn't help but think about Patty's cookbook. She'd tucked it away in her trunk back in Montana. "A cookbook is a treasure . . . and I'd be happy to watch over the store. Catherine's here too, of course."

"Fine then." Jathan led the older women to the back door. "We'll head to the printer and you get more cupcakes out, Sarah Shelter." Her name rolled off his tongue as if he'd said it a hundred times. "And be thinking about yer own recipes too. I have a

343

feeling they're going to be some of our most popular items."

Jathan and the older women hadn't been gone more than five minutes when the front door opened and a woman who looked to be Sarah's age entered. The woman was a dark-haired beauty with skin as perfectly flawless as a white pearl. She wore Amish dress and *kapp* but carried herself like a queen. Not that Sarah'd ever seen a queen, but the woman walked as Sarah expected a queen to walk.

Instead of gazing at the items in the display case, as most customers did, the woman focused on Sarah. She cocked one eyebrow and moved her gaze over Sarah's dress and *kapp.* Sarah couldn't help but touch her *kapp* in response, certain it was askew from the look the woman gave her.

"Can I help you?"

"I'm Anna." She stretched out her hand. "I have heard yer in town. Heard yer a friend of Jathan's."

"*Ja.*" Sarah's skin felt pricked by a thousand pine needles. "We met in Montana."

"I heard that too." Anna glanced at the display case and then tossed her head as if bothered by the presence of the bakery items. "Is Jathan here?" She peeked behind

Sarah to the kitchen.

"Uh, *ne.* He's . . . gone. Can I give him a message?"

Anna nodded. "I'm certain he stopped by my place, but I've been out of town. My sister had twins just two weeks ago. A boy and a girl. The most beautiful *kinner* I've ever laid eyes on."

Sarah nodded, believing that. "So have you known Jathan long?" She forced a smile, reminding herself she planned on being in this community a while. Reminding herself to be polite.

"Know him? Is that what you asked?" Anna placed a hand on her dress collar. "Didn't you know? Jathan and I have been planning on marrying fer as long as I can remember. But we put off our decision fer a year — with him going to Montana to hunt and all." Anna's eyes shimmered.

Sarah stood there for a long moment. Her knees trembled and a sharp pain landed between her shoulder blades. "*Ne.* I didn't know." She tried to sound casual, but her hands reached for the cleaning rag behind the counter and proceeded to wipe down the already-clean surface. Anna took a step closer to the counter, but Sarah found herself hesitant to look at her, lest Anna see the pain in her eyes.

"*Ja,* well, no one really knows these things — not until the invitations are sent — but one can guess, can't they? If you look in our garden, you'll see my *mem* has already planted the celery — hundreds of stalks. Their green leaves have jest begun pushing up from the ground, but I can already imagine what they'll look like by fall."

While the custom wasn't done in Montana, Sarah remembered the tradition from growing up in Kentucky. Brides used stalks of celery to decorate the tables at their wedding dinner and observant folks always knew who would be marrying next just by glancing at their neighbors' gardens.

"*Ja,* well, I'll tell him you stopped by. I'm sure he'll be happy to see yer in town. He shouldn't be gone long." An image flashed in Sarah's mind of Jathan and this woman sitting side by side on a front porch swing, similar to the one at Aunt Lynette's house. Jealousy caused her neck to grow warm. Anger tightened her shoulders. Why hadn't he told her? She'd even asked him if there was someone special back in the West Kootenai. He'd denied it, but this woman seemed very real.

"*Danki,* I'm looking forward to seeing him." Anna offered a soft smile. "Yer baked goods do look nice, but I like to bake myself." And with a wave she turned to the door. "Have a nice day . . ."

A nice day? Sarah moved toward the cash register and sank down onto the stool behind it. An ache pounded at her temples. *What am I doing here?*

Had she been a fool for coming so far hoping for a relationship with someone she hardly knew?

Ja, a fool indeed.

CHAPTER 27

It was Jathan's footsteps that approached the bakery's kitchen. Sarah could tell from his quickened, eager steps on the wood floor. The other women had gone home, though Catherine was still outside shaking out the rugs and sweeping the porches. Sarah didn't turn. Refused to turn to see his smile. To do so would only bring her pain. Instead she hurried toward the sink. Dishes had piled up.

Sarah knew she could head home, but her arms seemed too weary to pull off her apron. Her feet too weary to walk the distance home. Maybe it was her heart that was too heavy. Too heavy to be carried by her trembling legs. Instead she ran hot water for the dishes, adding in a stream of dish soap.

"Sarah, what are you doing? Leave those dishes there. That's what my niece is for."

Sarah wiped her cheek with the back of

her hand, hoping no tears had broken forth. She sucked in a deep breath and forced a smile. *I shouldn't have assumed so much. I should have asked more questions. I should have known a man like Jathan would have attachments in Holmes County.*

"*Ach, ne.* I am *gut.*" She cast a forced smile his way, hoping it was convincing. "I enjoy dishes, really I do. In fact, *Mem* always said a woman should never say she has no quiet time to talk to God. She can always get some time alone by doing the dishes."

Jathan chuckled and the sight of the brightness of his eyes lightened her heart.

Stop it. Stop caring fer him so, she urged herself. She had no right. No right at all.

He moved behind her and placed his hands on her shoulders. She knew he wanted her to turn. She was afraid to. Afraid to look into his face.

Her mind tried to think back, searching for any memory of words of affection toward her. It was clear he was glad she was here. He always seemed eager to see her, yet how serious could he be if he hadn't mentioned Anna at all?

Did he still plan on marrying Anna? Even if he didn't, shouldn't he have mentioned her to Sarah? And why had he left Anna hanging like that? Maybe Sarah didn't know

Jathan as well as she thought. In fact, what *did* she know about him?

What did she *really* know about him?

Jathan dropped his hands. "*Ja,* well, you may like washing dishes, but yer aunt invited me over for dinner tonight. I hope you don't mind."

"Mind?" She turned around and dried off her hands. "Why would I mind? I jest feel bad leaving Catherine with so many pans. I had to make yet another batch of cupcakes this afternoon yet." She glanced up at him and sighed. "I jest hate leaving all these dishes, that's all."

Jathan pushed back his chair slightly. He had enjoyed Sarah's aunt's meal very much, but ever since he'd found her washing dishes, Sarah had hardly said five sentences to him.

He told himself she was just tired, and he'd turned his attention to enjoying the meal — a pork loin roast, baked potatoes, Jell-O salad, and apple pie for dessert. It reminded him of the meals his mother used to make when all of them were younger. Before most grew up and got married. Before *Dat* got sick.

Spending time with all Sarah's cousins made him smile too. Three school-age boys, three younger girls, and a baby boy. The laughter around the table caused Jathan's heart to dance. Seeing it made him think he'd like his own large family someday.

The older boys were sharing a story about their geography lesson. Sarah joined in the conversation, but it was clear something was wrong.

Jathan's gut tightened with worry. What was the problem? Maybe she was missing her own home and family. Maybe there was too much work at the bakery and she was weary.

As soon as the meal was over, Jathan rose and turned to Aunt Lynette. "I hope you don't mind, but I'd love to steal Sarah away. It's been work, work, work, and I miss time jest sitting with her talking."

A grin filled Aunt Lynette's face. She waved them away. "I don't mind at all. It's a beautiful night to sit on the front porch." She winked. "And I'll do my best to keep my *kinder* from climbing all over ya."

He sat next to Sarah on the porch swing and gently rocked, yet he could have been sitting alone for as much as she was talking to him. She sat still and silent.

"Sarah, yer awful quiet tonight."

"Jest thinking, that's all."

"Is working at the bakery that bad?"

"Nothing about work is bad at all."

"The customers then?"

She didn't answer at first, and he didn't prod. The silence was broken only by the whinny of his horse, which was tied up by the barn. He had a fair ride yet and his old mare Patience was just reminding him of that. That and the fact that she should have had her oats by now.

"No, most of them are *wunderbaar.*"

"But there was one? Is that what yer saying?" He felt as if he were pulling the words out of her with a fishin' hook, one word at a time with each crank of the reel's handle.

"Jest one. Her name was Anna."

His head shot around at the mention of Anna's name. His feet stopped their rocking. "Anna?" His hand flew to his face and covered his eyes. He didn't want to know what Anna had to say. She wasn't kind and gentle like Sarah.

"From that reaction, I guess you *do* have something to tell me." There was a hardness to Sarah's tone.

He lowered his hand. "*Ach,* I should have. I'm not sure why I didn't. Anna slips my mind easy. She's a couple years younger than me, and our mothers are *gut* friends. I have heard since I was small that she's meant to be my wife."

"And you agreed?"

"*Ne.* Never."

"That's not what she said. She said you only put off yer wedding because you were going to Montana."

He lowered his head and a memory stirred.

"*Ach, ne.*" Jathan slapped his forehead.

"What?"

"I can see how she would think that. She told me about her *mem*'s garden and said they'd planned extra rows for celery. She asked what I thought of that. I told her that it was something we could talk about when I returned. I meant to talk about the possibility of marriage — which there is none — not to set a wedding date. I have no interest in marrying Anna. Do not worry." He reached over and stroked Sarah's forearm. "There is only one woman I care fer enough to want to spend a future with, and she's sitting right next to me. If she'll forgive me fer my foolishness. Do you, Sarah? Do you forgive me?"

Sarah nodded and bit her lip. Her shoulders relaxed. Sarah glanced at him, and in the moonlight he could read the questions in her eyes. *What about me? Am I someone you'd consider marrying?*

Jathan moved his legs so the porch swing

started rocking again. He wanted to settle Sarah's worries. He wanted to confess that he hadn't asked her to come all this way just for the bakery, yet the words wouldn't move past the tip of his tongue. To confess how he truly felt — how he really cared — would set things in motion he wasn't ready for yet. With *Dat* still lying in the hospital bed, well, it just made everything more confusing. He had to think of *Mem* first. He had to provide for his mother — not just today, but possibly for years to come.

As the youngest son, his parents' home was his — that's how it worked in these parts. While it would be a blessing to him and his future bride, it also came with responsibility.

Jathan cleared his throat. "*Dat* stirred today. His eyes opened briefly and his mouth opened, as if he was trying to speak. The nurse said it's a good sign, and that she's had some stroke patients who regained their ability to talk."

Sarah's eyes lowered, but not before he saw disappointment there. He was changing the subject and she knew it. "*Gut* news about yer *dat*. I would like to meet — to see him — when you think the time is right."

"*Ja.*" Jathan nodded. "I'd like that."

They sat there a while talking about

Sarah's new recipes and about the customers she was getting to know.

"I've noticed more *Englisch* coming in," she said. "A few bought big orders that they took home to share. Some wanted to know if we could ship."

"I've been thinking about that. I have to make an appointment sometime soon to talk with that man from the train. He wants to find a way to sell some of our baked goods in his coffee shop in New York."

Sarah's eyes widened, and she tucked a strand of blonde hair back under her *kapp*. "Really? How would the items get there and still be fresh?"

He smiled at the excitement on her face. "That's what we need to talk about. He's especially interested in yer cupcakes."

Her mouth dropped open, and then she smiled.

"When the time comes, do you think you can make some samples that I can take to him?"

Her arms flew around his neck before he knew what was happening. Then Sarah smiled. "*Ja,* of course!"

CHAPTER 28

Sarah approached the front door of the bakery and pulled out her key. Just when she was about to put the key in the lock, she noticed the door was slightly open and the lanterns inside had already been lit. She had been the first one there for the past two weeks, rising at three o'clock in the morning to be at the bakery by four o'clock so she could start baking. Each day seemed to be filled with more customers, and Sarah struggled to keep up. It was worth it, though, every time she saw the excitement on Jathan's face.

She hurried to the kitchen, expecting to see Mrs. Schrock or Aunt Kay. Instead it was Jathan who was pulling items out of the pantry and lining them up on the counter.

"Did you know you can make yer own cracked wheat by coarsely grinding wheat berries?" Jathan asked as she entered.

"Good mornin' to you too." She laughed.

"That makes sense, but I've never tried it before." She pointed to a sack of wheat berries on the counter and what looked to be a grinder.

"*Ja,* but don't tell anyone. I don't want them to think any less of me as an Amish man." Jathan laughed but Sarah saw something in his eyes. He didn't see it as a joke.

"Well, I have a secret too." She cocked an eyebrow. "Do you want to know why my bread is so soft and the crust so nice and brown? Instead of using water, I use milk in my recipe. I scald it first and then let it cool to lukewarm."

"*Ach,* that's the secret?" He stepped forward and crossed his arms over his chest.

"Part of it. The other part is to grease the top with butter while it's still warm."

"No wonder I can't get enough of yer bread." He pulled one of yesterday's loaves from the cooling rack and split it in half with his large hands.

"Jathan!" Laughter spilled from her lips.

With a huge smile, he picked up a butter knife and buttered half the loaf, sitting down to eat it.

Sarah shook her head and then picked up the list of items Mrs. Schrock had left her to bake today. "Thirteen dozen muffins, ten cakes, and twenty-five pie crusts," she read out loud. Sarah wrinkled her nose.

Jathan glanced over at her. "Everything all right?" He looked at her list.

"*Ach,* it's jest that I forgot that when I work in someone else's bakery I need to follow their directions. I woke up with an idea for chocolate-cream-pie cupcakes and thought about experimenting. I'm not complaining, but I'll have to wait."

"Maybe I could help?"

She glanced up. "*Ja,* of course. Why don't you make the pie crusts?"

"I'm not joking. If I gather ingredients and measure, it'll go faster."

"Should I trust you?" She eyed him playfully. "One wrong measure —"

"It was my favorite thing as a child, remember?"

"Well, you've mentioned that, but how did that happen?"

"Oh, it's a *gut* story — one I can't believe I haven't told you."

She measured the flour into a large mixing bowl. "I'm all ears now. I can mix muffin batter and listen too."

"Well, I'm not sure if I can measure and talk at the same time." He crossed his arms over his chest and leaned against a counter. "So I'll start helping after I tell my story. Remember how I told you I followed my *brieder* everywhere and climbed every tree I could after they did? Well, there was one tree I shouldn't have climbed. It was on the side of the road on our way to school. It was a large old maple. Yonnie gave me a boost so I could reach the branches, and then they left me up there." He shook his head. "They thought it was funny that I'd be late for school."

"How did you get down?"

"The wrong way, that's fer sure. I tried to swing down from the lowest branch — which was still a long way up. I slipped and broke my leg something horrible."

Sarah gasped. "Did someone come by?" She set down the measuring cup on the counter, forgetting if she'd measured two cups of flour or three.

"A neighbor, yeah, but I was already in shock. They didn't know fer a time if I would make it."

"I bet Yonnie felt horrible."

"All of my *brieder* did. But they never confessed to *Mem* what really happened, and I never told. I jest told *Mem* I was trailing behind and decided to climb the tree myself."

"And yer leg?"

"It took months and months to heal. That's when I spent time with *Mem.* I was too weak to go to school, so I'd come to the bakery with her." He pointed to the corner. "They set up a makeshift bed over there. I'd watch everything *Mem* was doing. When I was able to get around some, I started to help. I enjoyed it . . ."

He stopped then, but she could tell it wasn't the end of the story. She thought about asking more, but Mrs. Schrock and Aunt Kay arrived. Jathan's mother seemed especially pleased to see Jathan there with Sarah, working side by side, but there was something in Aunt Kay's eyes that she didn't understand. Worry maybe?

The two women got to work putting items in the display case while Sarah continued baking.

Sarah finished rolling out the crusts, setting them in the pie pans. With quickened motions, she crimped the edges and then blew out a low whistle. "Pray these don't puff while baking. I'd hate to start over."

"Well, yer not putting them in the oven like that, are you?"

"*Ja* . . . why wouldn't I?"

"When baking an empty pie crust, put a cup of raw rice or dry beans into the bottom of the crust and then bake. They'll weigh down the bottom of the crust so it doesn't puff. In fact . . ." Jathan scanned

the shelves and then found a small coffee can. He opened it and brought it to her. Sarah peeked in. Sure enough, it was filled with rice.

"My *mem* has another can like this at home. You can use the same rice or beans over and over in yer crusts."

"Really? But why didn't she say anything over the last few weeks? She's seen me making pie crusts on more than one occasion. She's seen me ruin a few too."

"*Ja,* well, I think I know why. *Mem* wants to keep you happy. She wants you to stay here . . . because you make me happy." He opened his arms and Sarah stepped into his embrace.

"I'm thankful for that, Jathan. I really am. Because I can't think of anything better than this. Than being here with you. You know me. In a strange way, you know me."

Twenty-two-year-old Sarah stood at her best friend's grave. Soft white clouds drifted across the wide blue sky. The mountains were greener than she'd ever seen them. The air more crisp. Birdsong carried from the trees that surrounded the small graveyard.

She stared at the pile of dirt not wanting to believe Patty's body was there.

Two days ago they'd held the funeral and viewing. She'd seen Patty's lifeless form, but she hadn't wanted to accept it. But today she'd woken up knowing she couldn't go over to Patty's and ask her to go on a walk. There would be no chats on the porch. There would be no Patty.

Sarah sank to the ground, but no tears came. The tears had been ever present since that moment at the lake. Now there were none.

The hardest thing was, no one knew Sarah as Patty had. Would anyone ever know her like that again? Really know her?

CHAPTER 29

It was Sarah's turn to visit Jathan's home, and what started out as a simple dinner soon turned into a full family dinner, or so she'd been told.

She'd seen the house from the outside when she'd ridden to the church service just last Sunday. The service had been at the house of one of the Schrocks' neighbors, and she'd been impressed as she'd ridden by. It was a large, white house with a beautiful front porch and garden area. A red barn filled the horizon, and next to that was a finely constructed shop. But today was different. Today she'd be going inside.

With excitement bubbling in her chest, Sarah entered the Schrock house. The walls were white, plain. White curtains hung from the window. But that didn't mean it was without ornamentation. On the kitchen wall was a utensil hook, and the brass ladles glimmered like a fine sculpture. Colorful towels had been laid out on the kitchen counter, embroidered in lovely patterns of birds and flowers and butterflies.

Mrs. Schrock hustled around the kitchen with two women Sarah soon learned were two of Jathan's sisters-in-law.

Sarah approached Mrs. Schrock, placing a hand on her shoulder. "How can I help?"

"You can help by getting Jathan out of my hair. I'm mixing up some cornbread, and if he sticks around, he's gonna put his nose where it doesn't belong."

Sarah chuckled. "Well, I would like to see the workshop . . ."

"*Ja!* What a fine idea! Now shoo, the two of you." Mrs. Schrock waved them away with her hands.

Jathan nodded and offered Sarah his arm, but when she glanced up at him, she noticed his face had grown pale.

"Is it going to be too hard . . . going in there without yer d*at*?"

He shrugged. "I spent some time with him this afternoon. I read his favorite chapter in Psalms and his eyes were on me. I could have sworn he understood. But this will be the first time I'll be going out to the shop since his stroke."

"Can I meet him?" she asked. "Before we

364

go to the shop, can we stop by the *dawdi* house?"

"Yes, of course, Sarah. *Danki. Danki* for asking."

Jathan led the way, and Sarah prepared herself for what she was about to see. But when she entered the bedroom of the small house, a smile filled her face. Jathan's father lay in a hospital bed, but his face was as peaceful as if he were sleeping. His hair was gray, but she would have recognized Jathan's features anywhere. A younger woman sat in a chair next to him.

"Sarah, this is my niece Belinda. She's Catherine's older sister."

Belinda rose and offered a quick hug. Her hair was as red as any Sarah had seen and freckles dotted her nose. "Glad to meet you. I'll leave you two to be with *Opa.*" She held up a novel in her hand. "It'll give me a chance to get another book, too, in the big house. I finished this one thirty minutes ago."

Belinda hustled out of the room.

"It's *gut* everyone is helping out."

"*Ja,* I have a *gut* family."

Sarah stepped closer and noticed Mr. Schrock's wide forehead and fine nose. "You look like him," she said.

"I get that often."

Sarah chuckled. "Yer *mem* says yer stubborn like him too."

Jathan nodded. "That's probably true."

Sarah neared and took Mr. Schrock's hand in hers. He stirred slightly and she leaned closer. "You don't know me yet, but I'd like to introduce myself. I'm Sarah, and I think yer son is pretty special." She paused and wrinkled her nose. "Yer youngest one that is. The others I know are already taken."

His eyelashes fluttered as if he were trying to open his eyes. Sarah gasped. "Did you see that?"

"*Ja,* today his eyes were open as I read. It's a good sign. He's probably trying to open his eyes now to get a good look at the woman who would be crazy enough to care fer his son." Jathan laughed, and then his face grew serious. "Or maybe to see if yer face is as beautiful as yer voice, which it is."

Sarah blushed, but she didn't look away. She soaked in his gaze the same way she soaked in the evening sunlight coming through the window.

"Thank you fer coming out here." He motioned to the doorway. "But we better get to the shop before dinner. *Mem* will have a fit if the food gets cold waiting fer us."

Sarah nodded, but she had a hard time releasing Jathan's father's hand. Tears filled her eyes.

"Are you okay?" Jathan took her free hand in his.

"*Ja* . . . it jest makes me remember," she said.

"Patty?" he whispered her friend's name.

"It's been better lately, but a memory was attached to every wooded path. So I stayed inside, and I hid away in the kitchen. I started working more hours at the restaurant. In the kitchen I didn't have to think about Patty. It kept me busy. I enjoyed the new friendships with the customers there, but . . ."

"But it wasn't the same, was it?"

"No. I got mad at God for a while. Why — out of everyone — did he have to take my best friend? I tried to talk to my *mem* about it, but she said the same thing as everyone else. That Patty is resting in peace compared to life in this troubled world. She meant the words to give me reassuring strength, but until lately, all I felt was numb."

Sarah released Mr. Schrock's hand. "Well, that's how I used to feel until I met you. Jathan, please don't take these words wrongly, but I'm glad you couldn't figure out how to get us back out of those woods that night. I'm glad we had time to talk . . .

to get to know each other better."

"*Ja,* me too." He stroked his hand down her jawline. "I'm not sure where I'd be or what I'd be doing if it weren't fer you. I'd most likely be working in the factory, completely miserable."

A clock in the room chimed five o'clock and he pulled back slightly. "Come. There's more I need to show you."

She followed Jathan out of the *dawdi* house and to the other building and waited as he opened the door to the workshop. The fragrance of wood shavings met Sarah as she walked into the shop. To her, it was the smell of her back porch at home — the place her father stored up wood for the stove.

As Sarah looked around, it was the array of colors that surprised her most. Wood colors, from light to dark.

Sarah neared the pile and eyed the wood. "I never really thought about all the different types of wood before. It makes me realize the wonder of our Creator even more."

Jathan's face brightened. "*Ja.* Some people think you can use any wood for any project. That's not the case. Beech is for carving. Pine and chestnut are best for boards. Many people like cabinets out of maple. We use a lot of maple around here."

A wistfulness crept into Jathan's voice.

Sarah placed a comforting hand upon his forearm. "You thinking about yer *dat*?"

"*Ja*. When we walked in, my eyes immediately went to his workbench. I expected him to be there — tall and strong. The man you see in the bed, curled up and quiet, that's not my *dat,* Sarah."

"I wish I could have known him . . . before."

Jathan nodded. "I wish you could have too."

In the shadows of his father's shop, Jathan scanned the quiet work area while Sarah ran her fingers over the back of a child's bench. A smile grew on her face when she pictured a young boy and girl sitting on the bench listening to their mother's story. When she looked closer, Sarah noticed initials on the back. *J.S.*

Jathan? She leaned down to get a closer look. "This craftsmanship, it's beautiful. Did you do this?"

"*Ja,* but I'm afraid I didn't get high marks from my *bruder.* I like it though, and I was saving it to give to some of my nieces and nephews — a family gift."

The wood was reddish brown and polished to perfection. The design was simple yet unique with a heart-shaped back. "How

369

could you not get high marks? It's perfect."

"That's the problem. I spent too much time on it." Jathan approached "I want to enjoy the process, but all Yonnie understands is the bottom line. The more we can produce in the least amount of time, the more profit we make. That's when it was decided."

"What?"

"That I would work in the factory. I could make more money there than I could in this shop."

Sarah frowned, not liking his answer. "I know you told me that was the plan, but when did things change? How did you end up in the bakery with me?"

"I convinced them that I could make more money there. That *we* could make more money. If we can grow our business and increase profits, it'll help the whole family. It'll also take some of the stress off *Mem*. She's getting older, and I want her to be able to have more time with *Dat*. Who knows how long he'll be around?"

"I'm happy to be part of yer grand scheme. I hope I won't let you down."

"That'll never happen. Never."

"*Ach,* I wouldn't be sure about that. I've been known to have a temper, and I like my own way. You should have seen me when my *bruder* switched the salt and sugar as a joke."

He chuckled. "I saw the jar and the snake, remember?"

"Oh, *ja.*" She patted her cheek. "Some first impression there." She remembered the humor in his eyes when she'd tossed that snake into the grass. At the time, she'd disliked the way he'd looked at her, but now . . . she imagined she would have laughed at herself too.

Jathan approached and removed his hat, scratching the top of his head. "That wasn't a first impression."

"Excuse me?"

"I saw you in the restaurant . . . often."

"I remember now. With so many ba . . ." She let her words trail off and bit her lip. "Never mind."

"I know what you were going to say. With so many bachelors, it makes it hard to distinguish one from another. I admit, I'm not one to stand out."

"*Ja,* that might be true to start, but once I did get to know you, I discovered yer someone worth getting to know. I'm looking forward to that. To getting to know you better." Sarah's fingers slid off the bench as she walked to the next piece of furniture. "As surprising as it might be, Jathan. I didn't jest come to make cupcakes."

He smiled softly, but she could tell cupcakes were the last thing on his mind.

"Sometimes I wish I loved this place as much as he wanted me to." Jathan leaned forward and braced his hands on the unfinished table as if the rough wood was his only security. He closed his eyes, and Sarah saw the ache of a young boy.

The sound of a hammering from beyond a closed side door caught her attention.

Mixed in with the pounding of the hammer, Sarah heard singing. She paused. She couldn't remember ever hearing her father or brothers in song. And at their church services, they always sat on the other side of the room.

"Does he always sing?"

"Yonnie? *Ja.*"

"He enjoys his work then?"

"Very much so."

Jathan opened the connecting door and they entered. It was another wood shop similar to the first, but much neater, with a row of finished furniture pieces lined against the wall.

Yonnie glanced up and nodded to them with a slight movement of his chin before focusing his eyes back on the task at hand. He put down the hammer and slid a carving knife down what looked to be a coatrack in the process of being built. The shaved curls of wood reminded Sarah of the way her sister Evelyn's hair dried after a bath. The golden brown was the same color too. Thinking of her sister caused a small pinch in Sarah's heart, but glancing over at Jathan soothed the sore spot.

As he watched his brother, Jathan moved his weight from one leg to the other, as if wanting to be anywhere but there.

Sarah grasped his arm, causing him to jump slightly. "Can we see the barn?" she asked excitedly, as if she'd been waiting for that very thing all day.

"*Ja,* all right." He turned and led the way.

Instead of opening the doors wide to let in the evening light, Jathan lit the lantern and closed the doors behind them. "If my nieces and nephews see the doors open, they'll be all over my horse. She's an old gal, and I'd like to protect her from that."

He took Sarah's hand and led her to the first row of stalls. "Besides, I don't think the two of you have been properly introduced yet."

The barn smelled of fresh hay and the sweat of horses. Sarah also smelled the leather of the harness too. Those scents made her ache for *Dat.*

She blew out a breath, telling herself that being here, being with Jathan, was worth it. Except for meeting Anna, so far everything was going just as she had hoped.

"This is Patience." Jathan patted the nose of a dun-colored Appaloosa that looked to be older than Sarah.

The horse smelled of grass and sweat. She smelled of hard work.

"Yer a pretty thing, aren't you?" Sarah patted the horse's nose. Patience pricked her ears. "So yer the other lady who's captured Jathan's heart?"

Patience snorted and pressed her nose under Sarah's armpit.

Sarah reached up and scratched behind her ear like she used to do to Patty's dog. Patty's family had been too heartbroken to keep the dog, but it made her happy to know that the dog — now called Trapper — had a new owner, Marianna, who loved him very much.

Poor thing. Patty's dog had wandered the forests near the West Kootenai for nearly a year, refusing to join any other home. Sarah had tried to bring him home at least a dozen times, but he'd only run away. Thankfully, the Sommer family had moved in. Trapper had quickly embraced the new family that now lived in the home of his former family.

Maybe because Marianna seemed to need him as much as Patty had.

Sarah glanced over at Jathan. Maybe that's what worked about their relationship. They needed each other. Each needed the other to believe in his or her dreams.

Sarah stepped back from the horse and opened her mouth to tell Jathan they should get back, but she couldn't force herself to say the words. Being with him, looking at this place, brought a connection to him she hadn't felt before.

He must have felt it too, because he bent his head to look at her hands.

She glanced up at the shadow the lantern cast. In the shadow, it appeared Sarah and Jathan were connected at the shoulders — a broad-shouldered giant with two heads. She smiled at the mental image, but in a way it was a perfect symbol of their growing relationship. They had different strengths and different smarts, but together they worked as one.

Jathan turned his head, and she could tell from the shadow that he was looking at her. She glanced up. His eyes were dark. The softest smile touched his lips.

"I love you, Sarah Shelter." The words were so soft, she almost didn't believe she heard them. "But there is something I need to tell you —"

"Jathan, Sarah!" a voice called into the barn. The door swung open and one of Jathan's nieces stepped in. "You in there?"

Jathan took a step back. "*Ja,* we'll be right there." He turned to the door.

"Did you have something to tell me?" She looked into his face. The deep passion from a moment before was gone.

"I will when the time is right, Sarah. It's nothing." He shrugged. "Jest something from my past I think you should know."

Ten minutes later, Sarah sat in a chair at a long dining room table filled with food — mashed potatoes, gravy, fried chicken, roast beef, dressing, corn, salad, pie, cornbread and butter.

She looked around. *Can you see yerself a part of this for the rest of yer life?* A half a dozen conversations were happening at once. Bursts of laughter rose and fell with the clinking of forks and knives on plates.

Dinner finished and the children ran out to play in the yard.

Sarah rose and moved to the kitchen to help.

"Sarah, dear, we have plenty of hands. I know Jathan was excited about showing you around our home. You've seen everything outside, but you have to see the inside too."

"*Ja,* I'd love to. If you say so."

"Of course I say so. What *you* think matters more than what anyone else does."

Sarah sucked in a breath. Warmth filled her chest. *Do I matter because they all hope it will be my home too someday?*

Sarah looked around. She looked at the beautiful wood cabinets in the kitchen and the large window that overlooked the barn. Butterflies filled her stomach when she imagined standing at that window waiting for Jathan to come in from morning chores.

The thought was exciting and overwhelming at once. Would family gatherings be held here? Would everyone expect that? She watched Yonnie's wife, Leah, move around the kitchen with grace. Leah knew what was in every cupboard. She put away the serving dishes. She returned unopened jars of jelly to the pantry.

Sarah felt envy. Would she ever feel as comfortable here as Leah did?

Mrs. Schrock gave Sarah a tour of the six bedrooms, the bathroom, and even the laundry room built in back. The house was even larger than Sarah had thought and more beautiful than she'd expected, and with each step, Sarah didn't feel she deserved any of it.

When they finished, Jathan went out for evening chores, and Sarah moved to the kitchen to visit with the other women over cups of herbal tea.

"What did you think?" Leah asked.

"It's wonderful. Far nicer than the house I grew up in."

Leah nodded. "*Ja,* me too. I have attended church services here since I was a young girl. I have loved this home fer as long as I can remember."

Sarah took a spoonful of sugar from the dish and added it to her tea, slowly stirring. "Do you live very far from here?"

"*Ja,* two miles away. We have a small home."

"Small?"

"Three bedrooms. The boys have one. The girls have one, and we, of course, have one."

Sarah's brow furrowed. "And yer husband drives two miles to work in the shop back there?"

"*Ja,* or walks."

Sarah nodded and thought again of all the empty rooms in this house. It seemed a shame that they weren't being used.

After the dishes were done, Sarah went to find Jathan in the barn. He looked up as she entered and his face brightened with a smile. "What do you think of the house?"

"It's beautiful, but there seems to be a lot of room fer jest you."

"Well, *ja,* that is correct, but hopefully it won't be jest me forever."

"That's true. It jest seems that Yonnie and Leah could use this home. At least fer a while. Until yer ready to use it." She glanced over at him and noticed he was frowning. "I mean, not that you shouldn't appreciate this beautiful place, but it jest may help with yer burden."

"My burden?"

"*Ja,* well, I am sure there are memories all around. When you sit at the table, do you picture yer *dat*'s chair? Do you see yer *mem* adding fire to the woodstove?" Sarah folded her arms over her chest, forcing herself to continue before she lost her nerve. "And the workshop is here too. Don't you want to escape it?"

"Escape my family?"

"*Ne,* never. I don't mean that. I mean allow yerself to establish yer own home. To know why yer doing what you do because you chose it, fer yerself and fer yer wife and children."

"That's not possible. My *dat* is the youngest son, who took over our home from his father, who was also a youngest son."

"There is a time for tradition, that is true,

and then . . . maybe I am wrong . . . but don't you think there is a time to seek God and ask, 'What do you desire fer my life?' "

"It's something to think about." Jathan said the words, but Sarah could see from his face that he dismissed her words as soon as she said them.

It was something to pray about, she knew. Her own mother had been an example of that. Sarah had watched *Mem* over the years — speaking what she felt she needed to, and then stepping back and letting God use those words if he so chose, maybe in a different way and through a different person than expected.

And sometimes never seeing things change as she'd like but knowing God was still in control.

CHAPTER 30

Sarah had the afternoon off, and with Aunt Lynette's birthday the following day, it was the perfect chance to make that cupcake covered with violets.

Sarah gasped as she entered the cooking store and gazed at all the pots, pans, and gadgets. In one corner of the store — near the baking pans — a television played. A woman on the featured cooking program was making what looked like sugar flowers to decorate a cake. Sarah stepped closer, pretending to be interested in a new cake pan. She watched the television from the corner of her eye. The woman on the program shaped and cut the . . . what did she call it . . . fondant? Then she shaped the pieces into little flowers and put them on the cake.

"Excuse me." Sarah approached the woman at the counter. "Do you have any of that . . . fondant?"

"Yes, dear. Have you ever worked with it before?"

Sarah shook her head. "*Ach, ne.* I never saw such a thing." She didn't tell the woman that no one in the West Kootenai made such things. "Is it safe to eat?"

"Yes, dear, of course. It's nothing more than sugar and water."

The lady took her down an aisle lined with tools, molds, colorings, and tubs of fondant.

She picked up a few items and handed them to Sarah. "Here is a tub to get you started and a small booklet. There are many colorings too. Feel free to ask any questions."

Sarah nodded. "Thank you."

Looking through the book, she didn't see directions for violets, but there were directions for carnations. She was thankful Aunt Lynette liked carnations too.

Sarah studied the rolling pins, mats, and colorings and found the items she needed. She purchased them and hurried to the bakery. She couldn't bake at Aunt Lynette's house, not if she wanted the cupcakes to be a surprise.

Mem Schrock and Aunt Kay were busy up front. Sarah washed her hands and pulled off the plastic lid of the fondant container. She tried to remember the steps for making the fondant carnation. She started with a small, flat circle of fondant and then used the tool she'd bought to spread it out from the center to the edges, causing the end to ruffle as she did. When she went around the whole circle she did the same with a second and a third circle. She then placed one circle inside the other, folding the inner ones until the ruffles lifted layer by layer. Then, like the lady on the baking show, Sarah took the paintbrush she'd bought, dipped the tip in coloring, and painted the edges of the flower. She took a finished cupcake from the cooling rack, frosted it, then placed the fondant carnation on top.

"Well, I'll be." Sarah sat back and looked at her small creation. If she hadn't just made it, she would have thought the flower to be real.

Sarah finished off the carnation cupcake and glanced out to the front of the bakery. She noticed the bakery items in the display case were getting low.

"I'll just stock up, and then hurry home," she mumbled to herself.

Sarah carried a tray to the bakery counter. On it were the maple cupcakes she'd made just this morning. As she placed them in the display case, a woman entered in high heels. Her blonde hair was as short as a man's and streaked with black.

The woman glanced at her watch and then rushed forward. "I'll have one of those." She pointed to the tray in Sarah's hand.

"*Ja,* of course."

The customer paid for the cupcake and then hurried to leave. *How can she walk so fast in those shoes?* The woman opened the door and stepped out onto the front porch before taking a bite of the cupcake. Before the door even shut completely, she turned around and came back inside.

Sarah stepped forward. "Ma'am, is something wrong?"

The woman hurriedly approached Sarah. "These are the best cupcakes I've ever had. I'd like to order two dozen for my daughter's birthday tomorrow." She glanced around the display case. "Do you decorate them at all?"

"No." Sarah shook her head. "Not really."

"What about that one?" The woman pointed to the carnation cupcake sitting on the counter in the kitchen.

"That one?" Sarah noticed Mrs. Schrock and Aunt Kay's eyes on her. "Well, I jest made that one fer my aunt's birthday."

"I know that it must take extra time, but I'll pay you double the price," the customer said.

Sarah looked to Mrs. Schrock again, hoping for a hint of how she should answer. Mrs. Schrock didn't nod or shake her head no. Her face gave Sarah no indication of how to answer. But something inside Sarah did. Excitement filled her. She'd wanted to decorate cupcakes for ten years at least, and here was someone asking her to do that . . . and paying double.

Sarah placed a hand to her chin and nodded. "*Ja,* I can do that. Will red carnations be fine?"

"Do you have pink?" The woman clasped her hands together. "My daughter loves pink."

"*Ja,* of course."

Sarah had invited Jathan to the birthday dinner she'd prepared for her aunt. They waited a few extra minutes for him to arrive, but he didn't show. During the meal, every sound outside caused Sarah to turn and search the road leading up to her aunt's house, but Jathan was never the source. Frustration mixed with worry, and she told herself that he was fine. Maybe he forgot. Or maybe his mother needed his help.

Sarah was clearing the table, preparing to bring out the cupcakes — including the special cupcake she'd made for her aunt —

when there was a knock at the door. She opened it to find Jathan standing there, hat in hand.

"I'm so sorry." He rushed through the front door. "I was up in Charm today."

Sarah clasped her hands together. "Charm? Was that the meeting with the man from New Yo—"

"Oh *ne*." Jathan shook his head. "I had to postpone it. Yonnie needed me to make a delivery for him."

She rubbed the back of her neck. "You drove a piece of furniture all the way up to Charm in yer buggy?"

"Actually, it's only four-and-a-half miles, but ne. I rode up in a van with a driver. Yonnie didn't trust the man to deliver it himself. He needed me to collect payment."

Sarah nodded and motioned to the kitchen. Jathan followed her in.

"So are you working with yer *bruder* now?" She fixed up a plate of leftovers.

"*Ne*. Jest helping where I can."

She blew out a breath and told herself not to get angry. He was just helping his family. Their community, she knew, was helping with money for his father's hospital bills, but Jathan's family was also missing his father's income. She pushed her troubled thoughts away. "You can come and help me in the bakery anytime."

Jathan glanced over his shoulder at her aunt, uncle, and cousins, as if making sure they hadn't heard. "Uh, I can perhaps do that at times. It's not something I'll be able to do often anymore."

He moved to the dining room table, greeted the others, lowered his head in prayer, and then dug into his food with gusto. "Thank you fer this," he called back to her. "I was starved."

There was a heaviness about Jathan today, a weariness, as if he'd carried that piece of furniture all the way to Charm on his back.

Aunt Lynette looked at Sarah and lifted an eyebrow.

Sarah shrugged. How could she explain the wall he had around him tonight? Maybe it was just the weariness from a long day.

Jathan finished his food in record time and then leaned back in his chair.

Sarah took his plate to the kitchen and then returned to the dining room with the platter of cupcakes. The carnation cupcake sat in the middle of the plate.

"Happy birthday, Aunt."

Aunt Lynette's eyes widened. "Sarah, how lovely!" She reached out and picked up the decorated cupcake. "Oh, my, look at this. Ivan, did you see it? Jathan?" She held it

387

out for both men to see. "Sarah, did you make it?" The children gathered around for a closer look.

"*Ja,* and the flower is made out of sugar fondant. You can eat it, if you'd like."

Aunt Lynette shook her head. "Well, I'll be. I've never seen such a thing."

The tension in Jathan's face softened and he looked at her. "That *does* look real. Can I see?"

Aunt Lynette handed it over and he held it on his palm as if it were made of china.

"Have you done much of this before?" he asked.

"*Ne,* but I really liked it. I'm going to be making some more. A woman came into the bakery today. She ordered two dozen cupcakes like this fer a birthday party. She said she'd even pay double if I decorated them."

"Oh, Sarah, I'm so happy for you." Aunt Lynette offered Sarah a quick hug. "I know what I said before about fancy things in Amish bakeries, but it is clear God has given you a gift."

Jathan placed it back onto the plate with the other cupcakes. "*Ja,* that's *gut,* but two dozen cupcakes aren't going to help much with the bills."

"Excuse me?"

"Oh, sorry. Just thinking out loud. When I

went by fer the furniture, Yonnie told me about some of the things he needed money for. There was a lumber order that he thought *Dat* had paid, but then found out he hadn't."

"I'm sorry to hear that."

Uncle Ivan cleared his throat. "I'm sure if you talk to the supplier, he can make some arrangements . . ."

"*Ja,* of course, but that's only one bill," Jathan said. "I'm afraid of what else we'll find. And even if we can get some grace, the bills still need to be paid."

Sarah glanced around the table. Seven children's faces patiently waited for their cupcakes. She clapped her hands together. "Well, now, let's not ruin this birthday celebration with rain clouds." She picked up the carnation cupcake and placed it before Aunt Lynette. "Who would like a cupcake?"

"Me!"

"Me, me!"

She passed the plate down the table and each child eagerly took one. Voices rose in delight as they each tasted their cupcakes.

Even Uncle Ivan's face brightened into a large smile. "I'm sure this is the best cupcake I've ever eaten. Sarah, you've outdone yerself."

Sarah looked to Jathan to see if he approved. He seemed to enjoy the cupcake, but his eyes looked troubled. Dark circles hung under them.

Aunt Lynette must have noticed his weariness too. She moved to the kitchen and wet a dish cloth to wipe off baby Elmer's sticky hands, and then she pointed outside. "Why don't you two head out fer a walk. It's a beautiful night. It seems like Jathan can use a bit of peace."

"Are you sure?" Sarah looked around at the crumbs on the table and the children who needed help getting ready for bed.

"*Ja,* we may play a game or read a story together. It's a birthday tradition, and you two look as if you jest need some time to unwind," she repeated. "From what I hear around town, the bakery is booming. You deserve some time to relax."

Sarah rose and Jathan did too. He placed a kiss on her aunt's cheek. "Happy birthday."

"*Ja, danki.*"

Sarah followed Jathan outside, down the porch steps, and onto the two-lane country road. Summer had planted herself deep in Berlin. Green fields stretched in every direction. Pink, yellow, and white wildflowers nodded their heads on the slight breeze, as if offering approval as they passed.

They walked for a while, shoulder to shoulder. Sarah brushed her fingers against Jathan's hand but it did little good. Jathan didn't take her hand, although she wanted him to.

"Do you think you can get more orders for decorated cupcakes?" he asked.

"*Ja,* I really do. There is a book that shows how to make roses, daisies, asters. There were other designs, too, fer ladybugs, suns, monkeys — those were especially cute."

He stroked his chin. "And do you really think we can get double?"

"*Ja,* and I have an idea. Catherine's been helping some with the baking. She can do more of that, and I'll spend more time decorating. The way things are growing, we'll be the busiest bakery in all of Holmes County!"

"Yer so confident. You act as if you've been running a bakery yer whole life, but what happens when that confident woman takes a walk down a country road with a man who worries it'll all spin out of control?"

"What do you mean?"

"Well, the bakery is changing. There are new customers, *ja,* but both *Mem* and Aunt Kay have mentioned that their faithful customers haven't been coming in as often.

And with these new cupcakes . . ." He shrugged. "We'll jest wait and see what everyone thinks."

"I believe they're going to love them. The old customers will get used to the changes, and the new ones will be drawn in!" Sarah added an extra hop to her step. "Jest look at the beauty around us. Even as we walk, my mind spins with all the ideas fer decorating cupcakes. Can you imagine one that looks like that sunset? I can picture the colors and shapes I'd use now."

Jathan's footsteps slowed as if he considered her words. "So you really like it here?"

She glanced around. "What's not to like? I love the wide-open spaces. I enjoyed the mountains, too, but the horizon is my favorite. It seems to stretch in every direction with limitless promise. It makes me think that what I hope fer can come true."

"And what do you hope for, Sarah?"

She could give a dozen answers, but only one mattered to Jathan. And to her.

"I hope that I'll be able to stay around a while. I thought I would miss Montana — my family — more, but I like this community. I could make it home, with the right conditions."

He paused his steps and she followed suit, then he reached out and touched her arm.

"The right conditions?"

She dropped her chin. "I would be too bold to say anything more than that."

After a thoughtful silence, he mused. "Yer unlike any other Amish woman I know. I appreciate that you share yer thoughts and are truthful. I don't mind boldness. It's the trying to figure someone out that bothers me."

"Well, in that case . . ." She placed a hand over her heart. Her hand trembled as she considered the words she would say. "The truth is, my staying depends on the right person."

His face brightened as if the morning sun had suddenly reappeared and lit it. She released the breath she'd held captive for too long.

His head dropped to the side. "Do you think I'm that person?"

She sighed and relaxed. "*Ja*, I do."

But instead of smiling, instead of giving her the same tender words of love that he'd shared just days earlier, Jathan resumed his steps. The light on his face dimmed. "That's the problem. I know what I want to give you, Sarah; I'm jest not sure I can. There are so many family responsibilities . . . and if my *dat* improves, well, that could change everything."

"What do you mean, Jathan?"

He closed his eyes and opened them slowly. "I'm afraid I'm not going to be able to be the man you expect. The man you need."

They walked beneath the trees that lined the road. The covering of leaves was so thick that more light came in through the ends of the natural tunnel than above.

"What do you mean?"

"Well, you know the letter I wrote you, telling you I'd be able to work alongside you in the bakery?"

"*Ja.*"

"That was foolish talk, and we both know it. My *bruder* needs me to help him with deliveries and to pay the bills. There's only so much extra money we can make on baked goods. The only solution I can think of is to reconsider that job at the factory. If I'm going to live this life and support a wife and family, then that's how things have to be."

"And how do you think yer wife will feel about that? Sure, you'll have food on the table and a fine place to live, but a husband's happiness . . . Is there anything of greater value than that?"

"Listen to you. Life is not about happiness or following yer dreams. Our ancestors showed us what's really important — family and hard work. You've worked with the *Englisch* too long."

His words wrapped around Sarah's heart and squeezed painfully tight, causing her to feel short of breath.

"I expected you'd say that one of these days. All Amish people I know usually do." Sarah crossed her arms over her chest. "I can see it now. Whenever we have a disagreement, I'll be in the wrong, and the reason will be that I've spent too much time with the *Englisch.*" When she finished spouting those words, she stopped in her tracks, wanting him to stop and talk to her. Really talk.

He didn't say anything but continued walking.

"Yer not going to answer me?"

"My *dat* always told me it's foolish to answer a woman in her folly," he called over his shoulder.

Sarah gasped. She set her hands on her hips and marched after him. "You saying that — you putting up these defenses — means I've hit the nail on the head. You know I did. You know yerself you don't want to live this life jest to earn enough money to keep a family!"

They walked out of the grove of trees and

the world brightened around them. Jathan glanced down at her, his eyes partly squinted. She wished it were only because of the added light, but she knew it wasn't the case.

"Why won't you believe me, Sarah, when I tell you that's not possible?"

"What do you mean?" She grabbed his arm, forcing him to turn toward her, to pause.

"Yesterday *Dat* said my *mem*'s name. 'Mags.' It was jest a whisper."

Sarah clasped her hands together. "That's wonderful."

"*Ja,* it is. I want nothing more than for him to get better. But when he starts talking, well, I know what he's going to tell me. He was very clear before I left. He wants me to work at the shop or work in the factory."

"What if he changes his mind?"

"He'll never change his mind."

"How do you know?"

"I jest know. Why do you have to ask so many questions? Why do you have to push fer change, Sarah? Why can't you jest accept things fer how they are?"

Sarah cocked her chin and narrowed her gaze. "I want to know the truth, Jathan. The thing you've been wanting to tell me but haven't. I see fear in yer eyes. Real fear. And I want to know where it comes from."

"I know *Dat* will never change his mind because . . ." His voice caught in his throat. "He told me when I was jest a boy and he hasn't changed his mind."

Jathan moved over and leaned against a wooden fence post, as if needing the extra support to keep him up. Sarah could tell that whatever he was about to say would be hard, and she forced herself to be still and wait for his words.

"I was working in the bakery with *Mem,*" he finally said. "It was early on a Saturday. I was feeling better and could get around on my leg jest fine, but I went in with her anyway. I loved being there."

She nodded to let him know she was listening.

"*Mem* had run down to the store to get some milk. She needed it for the chocolate pies. I was crimping pie crusts fer her, preparing to put them into the oven. *Dat* —" Jathan's voice trembled. "*Dat* came in. At first, fear filled his gaze. He'd gotten up early knowing *Mem* was away. He went up to my room to rouse me fer morning chores, but I wasn't there. His worry turned to fury when he saw me with those pie crusts." Jathan lowered his head. "Before I knew what was happening, he picked me up and threw me across the kitchen, an-and then he picked up a glass pie plate and hurled it at my head."

Jathan touched the scar over his eyebrow. "He called me a sissy. He said no son of his would work in a kitchen. And then he stalked off. When *Mem* found me, she had to stitch me up." Jathan shook his head and his words shook too. In his eyes, she saw the truth. He still felt like that little boy, trembling before his father's fury. "To this day, *Mem* believes a robber tried to break in fer the cash box."

"Oh, Jathan." Sarah rushed forward and placed her hands and her cheek on his chest.

"No son of his . . ." he repeated.

The words were no more than a whisper, but Sarah knew they cut his heart like a knife.

CHAPTER 31

It had been a week since Jathan confessed the pain of his past, and even though she'd tried to assure him that she loved him and would be there for him no matter his occupation or what he needed to do to support his family, Sarah had hardly seen him.

Jathan had come around the bakery with items they needed, like the twenty-pound bags of flour they went through so often, but he rarely stayed long. Instead, he'd chat for a moment, look at and taste her newest creations, and then run out the door again on another errand for his brother.

Sarah tried to assure him she still cared. She also tried to be understanding. Maybe she'd come to Ohio not to urge Jathan to step out in his dream, but rather walk alongside him when he couldn't. To support him no matter what.

Even though Sarah's heart ached for Jathan, her soul soared as she made more cupcakes and discovered new ways to decorate them.

Some days, *Englisch* customers brought in ideas for her, but most days, she took time to gaze at the world around her as she walked to and from work.

One time, she brought in her memory jar and set it on the counter. She pulled out the small pinecone from the jar and a smile filled her face. Inspired, she frosted the cupcakes first and set them to the side. Then she picked out different-sized chocolate buttons she'd bought at the cooking store and dipped the ends in decorating gel before sprinkling edible glitter on them. Once the buttons were dry, she layered them, lining them up in rows of threes so they looked like pinecones.

After placing them on top of the frosted cupcakes, she smiled and took them to the display case, lining them up next to the butterfly cupcakes. An Amish woman was looking at the display, lined up with the rest of the women who were *Englisch.* Sarah paused, realizing she hadn't seen her before. She also realized how few Amish women came in anymore. Maybe it was because the store seemed to be filled with *Englisch* tourists more often than not.

The Amish woman bought two flower

cupcakes and a loaf of bread. After she left, Sarah turned to Aunt Kay. "Is that woman new in town? I haven't seen her before."

Aunt Kay sighed and shook her head. "*Ne.* That's Bev Troyer. She's like one of the butterflies you put on yer cupcakes. Those *fancy* ones." Aunt Kay drew out the word *fancy* as she pointed to the display case. "Everything's sunshine and flowers, but she's not much fer practical use. Never quite knew an Amish woman like her."

Sarah bit her tongue. Sarah assumed Aunt Kay was talking about Bev Troyer, but from the look in Kay's eye, she couldn't be sure.

She was about to head to the back when a small tourist bus pulled up in front. Within fifteen minutes, all the tourists had come in and left again, large smiles on their faces and boxes of baked goods in their arms. Sarah looked at the display case and noticed that every last cupcake was gone. *How is that possible?*

Should she make more tomorrow? Would this be a regular occurrence?

Sarah was rearranging the items in the display case when another woman entered.

"Do you have cupcakes?" she asked. "I saw a lady at the fabric store, and she told me about the cupcakes. Said they were the best she'd ever eaten."

Sarah raised her eyebrows. "Well, I was going to wait —"

"Cupcakes?" Aunt Kay stepped forward, interrupting before Sarah could continue. "We have cinnamon rolls. Homemade bread too."

"Yes, that sounds lovely, but what I'd really like is a cupcake."

Aunt Kay pursed her lips, glanced over her shoulder at Sarah, and then turned her attention back to the woman. "*Ach, ja,* there's cupcakes in the back yet."

"Excuse me? What did you say?" the woman asked.

Sarah stepped forward. "She means there's cupcakes to come. I have some batter that I have chilling. If you can give me an hour and a half."

"Perfect." The woman tucked her wallet back into her purse and nodded. "I have more shopping to do. Save me two dozen."

"Two dozen?" Sarah attempted to hide her smile. Even though it was hard work, it felt good that her cupcakes were so appreciated.

She finished rearranging the cookies in the display case, then turned to Aunt Kay. "Would you like me to work on the oatmeal cookies first? They were on the list *Mem* Schrock gave me."

"*Ja,* well, I don't think the list matters now." She narrowed her gaze at Sarah. "You best get started on those cupcakes." Aunt Kay spoke the last word as if she were spitting an eggshell from between her lips. Then she turned to the back and hurried to the kitchen. "I don't know why they need cupcakes — two dozen especially — when there are other things jest as *appeditlich* right here in the case." Sarah noticed *Mem* Schrock had come in. Before the older woman even had time to put on her apron, Aunt Kay launched into a rant about the fancy cupcakes.

"Should we even call this an Amish bakery with fancy cupcakes like that?" Sarah heard Aunt Kay say. Sarah's knees softened as she saw the disappointment in *Mem* Schrock's gaze.

"Maybe not," she answered. "Maybe we've made a bad decision here."

Sarah tried to ignore the women's words and rushed forward to help another customer — an Amish woman — at the cash register.

The woman shook her head. "Kay needs to stop *brutzing.*" She patted her *kapp* and clucked her tongue. "The point of the bakery is to sell what customers want, not what the bakers like to bake. Don't they understand that?"

"That's the problem, I think." Sarah sighed. "Folks used to want what they baked . . . until I started making my cupcakes."

Jathan stepped in the front door and watched Sarah set out another batch of cupcakes. His limbs felt weary as he walked through the front door but a small smile lifted his lips when he noticed the line of customers.

Sarah finished setting the cupcakes in the display case and hurried to the kitchen. She didn't look happy. Jathan followed her in, wrapping an arm around her shoulders.

"Having a *gut* day?"

"Well, pretty *gut.*"

He bent down and gazed into her face. "And what's bothering you?"

Tears rimmed her eyes. She shrugged. "I've been wanting to talk to you about this kitchen. There isn't enough room. It wasn't made for three women, really, and now with Catherine helping to bake, we're always bumping into each other." She knelt down and looked under the counter. "Look at all this open space. If you built some racks, I could place my decorated cupcakes under here — especially the ones for special orders. Or maybe even set bread to rise. It would free up the counters."

He knelt next to her, placing an elbow on his knee, and grinned. "The bakery's really taking off, isn't it?"

"Well, it's been busy." She paused. "Not to say I do anything special, but I've seen that some customers do enjoy my cupcakes." She fixed her eyes on his. "Sometimes it's the little things that make all the difference, don't you think? We don't need to worry about expanding the kitchen, jest have to make better use of space."

He focused on her gaze and nodded. "Yer cupcakes are the talk of the town. Not only pretty but *gut*." Jathan patted his stomach. "I think I've gained some weight since you've been making them."

"The recipes are simple. Catherine's been making them jest fine. If we wanted to expand, to help out yer family, I have a new idea too."

"*Ja?* What's that?"

She looked to the cabinet that held her memory jar, then looked back at him. "Well, I can't keep up with all the decorating, but what if we put out items fer folks to decorate the cupcakes themselves? We can give them a little cup, and they can fill it with sprinkles and edible glitter. I think they'd really enjoy it."

He nodded and smiled. "I like that." Relief — joy — flooded Sarah's face, and her cheeks grew pink.

"*Ja,* that's something we can talk about. I can mention it to *Mem.*"

As he began to rise, Sarah grabbed his arm. "But Jathan, will you tell yer *mem* that it was yer idea? I've noticed lately . . ." Her eyes pleaded with him as she let her voice trail off.

"What?"

Sarah shrugged and then she fingered the fabric of his shirt. His skin tingled under her touch. "I've jest noticed that anytime I bring up an idea, yer *mem* and Aunt Kay exchange a glance. I believe they've grown weary of my ideas."

He didn't say anything. He'd seen changes too. *Mem* seemed more distant than usual, and she'd been cooler to Sarah than when she'd first arrived. There was another tell-tale sign too. *Mem* hadn't asked in the last week when Jathan was going to talk to Sarah about a wedding. That wasn't like his mother. Tension built in his chest, but he didn't want it to show.

"*Ja,* of course," he said as he rose. "I don't mind claiming a *gut* idea like that."

■ ■ ■ ■

Sarah walked home the long way from work, passing by her favorite flower garden on the edge of town. Black-eyed Susans, mums, zinnias, irises, and dozens of other flowers Sarah didn't know the name for graced the garden with golds and oranges, purples and blues. She was just about to continue on when a white *kapp* bobbing in the far corner of the garden caught her eye. She imagined the sweet old woman who lived here, kneeling in the garden, tugging at the weeds.

Sarah had the rest of the day off. Should she offer to help? It was one way to make friends. Heaven knew she needed a friend right now.

"You have a lovely garden!" Sarah's voice carried on the slight breeze. "I've not seen one like it. Do you need help? I imagine the weeds are quite overwhelming in a garden this size."

"Oh, hello!" The figure rose and stepped forward with speed and agility Sarah hadn't expected. A wide smile flashed in the sunlight and Sarah gasped. It wasn't an older woman at all. She was young and beautiful with reddish-brown hair tucked under her *kapp.* As she neared, Sarah recognized her immediately. Wasn't this the woman Aunt Kay had talked about earlier? Bev Troyer?

"I recognize you." The woman pointed. "Yer the new baker at Our Daily Bread."

"*Ja.*" Sarah nodded. She paused, forcing a smile. Should she withdraw her offer to help? It was clear the other Amish women disapproved of Bev. Should Sarah risk her own reputation by spending time with her?

Sarah released a breath, remembering her reputation was already ruined. After all, she was the one who made those *fancy* cupcakes.

"*Ja,* I am the new baker," Sarah continued. "I enjoy baking very much."

The woman sighed. "*Ach,* I wish I could bake. I make a mess of everything. My *mem* gave up trying to teach me after I set the kitchen on fire . . . twice. That's when I took up gardening. I can't set anything on fire or poison anyone from out here."

Sarah smiled. "Are you saying yer an Amish woman who can't cook?"

The smile on the woman's face faded. Her expression darkened and tears sprang to her eyes. Bev didn't answer but instead lowered her gaze and pretended to focus on the green rose leaf she pressed between her fingers.

"*Ja,* well, I do cook some." Her words

408

weren't convincing.

"*Ach,* I'm so sorry." Sarah placed a hand on Bev's arm. "I didn't mean you disrespect. I understand what it means to not fit in. I'm from the west — from an Amish community in Montana. Amish people live differently out there. My parents had a small garden where we lived in the mountains, but my biggest problem is that although I bake, it's far too fancy."

"Fancy?"

Sarah nodded. "*Ja.* I like making cupcakes and decorating them to match yer garden."

The woman's eyes widened, and she giggled behind her hand. "Yes, I bought and ate two myself, jest today. They were beautiful . . . and delicious."

Sarah leaned closer. "You can imagine the type of response I get to my *fancy* cupcakes."

"I imagine they're similar to the comments I receive about my *fancy* garden." Bev glanced over her shoulder. "No matter how often I say that God's the creator and I'm simply highlighting his handiwork, many people talk. I know what they say." Her voice quivered. "But you are right — some Amish woman I am."

And some follower of Jesus I am fer having considered walking away. Fer being worried about my own reputation.

Sarah smiled at the woman. "My offer is still open. I'd love to help with yer weeding — or whatever you may need help with. I have the afternoon off."

"Oh, the weeding is done, but I'd love fer you to come in for tea. I have nothing to serve with it but —"

Sarah patted Bev's shoulder. "Don't worry about that. I take too many nibbles of this and that at the bakery. Treats are the last thing I need."

Seventeen-year-old Sarah walked through the forest. It was Sunday, and they were on their way to their church service, but instead of walking down the country road like everyone else, Patty had convinced her to take a more scenic path. A content smile rested on Patty's lips as she walked. She breathed in deeply and glanced from tree to log to leaf.

"Sarah, watch yer feet!" The words spouted from Patty's mouth.

Sarah paused and looked down. "What's wrong with my feet?"

"There's nothing wrong with them. It's where you step, that's all."

"Nothing's there but leaves, raindrops, and a spiderweb."

"You call that nothing?"

Sarah looked down and noticed the drops of rain clinging to the spiderweb. *Mem* crocheted delicate trimming on handkerchiefs, but nothing she made came near to the intricacy of the web.

"Yer right." Sarah stepped over it and walked gingerly.

Patty seemed to see — truly see — the world unlike anyone Sarah had ever met. And through her friend's eyes, the world became a different place for Sarah as well.

If only she could learn to see in such a way on her own.

CHAPTER 32

Sarah had woken up to the memory of Bev Troyer's garden and an uneasy feeling stirred inside her. She'd found no greater joy lately than working on the cupcakes, but deep inside, she knew it wouldn't matter if she found great joy making the cupcakes. Or even found joy in seeing the smiles on the faces of the *Englisch* customers. She longed to be understood, to be appreciated. And when she went into the bakery later that morning, she longed for both of those things more than anything.

Dawn hadn't broken yet when she arrived at the bakery. *Mem* Schrock and Aunt Kay were already busy at work. They offered pleasant smiles as she entered. Sarah immediately went to the cupcakes she'd baked yesterday and frosted them. Then she set to work with the fondant, cutting small shapes, spending more time on them than she should.

Finally, when she was finished, Sarah held up a cupcake that looked as if it were a section of Bev's garden. A smile curled on her lips. The flowers looked so real. She gazed on them with pleasure. Is this how God felt after creation? She turned the cupcake in her hand. Her thumb left a smudge. Sarah didn't fix it. Instead she held it up for the women to see and allowed a sad smile to fill her face.

"What are you thinking about?" *Mem* Schrock asked.

"Oh, I had a friend once who used to touch the birthmark I have right behind my ear. My friend Patty told me that when God finished forming me, he left his fingerprint. She'd stick her thumb on that spot, grin, and say, 'Well done.' "

"That's nice, dear," Aunt Kay said.

Sarah took a step closer to the women, still holding the cupcake in her hand. "I haven't thought about that in a while."

"Why not?"

Sarah's smile vanished. She stared at the women, unblinking, through many ticks of the clock. "Well, because I used to think of that when I was sad, but these cupcakes . . . making them makes me happy."

Both of the women's mouths dropped

open, as if they struggled for words to respond.

Sarah put down the cupcake and took an embroidered handkerchief from her pocket. She turned it over in her hands. "My *oma* made this for me. It's fancy, don't you think? But it's beautiful too." She held it out to Aunt Kay. "Do you have any like this?"

Aunt Kay narrowed her gaze, as if understanding where Sarah was taking the conversation. She glanced down at the cupcake and then back at Sarah. "Food is for nourishing the body, not fer trying to make yer things appear better than everyone else's."

"Is that what you think? I don't make these things fer myself, but fer others. To give joy fer a moment. To make special memories. You don't know —" Her words caught in her throat. "You don't know when someone will be gone. The moments, they matter. Why wouldn't I want to do something to make them feel as special as possible?" Sarah took a step back and forced herself to be calm.

Mem Schrock blinked rapidly and then blew out a deep breath, focusing her eyes on Sarah. "I understand what yer saying. Unlike my sister, I do not think it's the cupcakes that are the problem. They are *gut*.

The *Englisch* like them. The problem I have is wondering if they belong *here*."

Jathan's mother softened her voice as if her whispered words would make her comments less painful. "Jest 'cause things are different, doesn't make them better. *Ja,* new customers have come in, but what about our regulars? I haven't gotten an order from my friend Marge in two weeks. I spied her this morning sneaking into The Baker's Pantry down the street. Things are simpler there. Most of my Amish friends like the old ways."

"I understand." Sarah nodded. "I was jest trying to help. I have all these ideas. How rude I've been to come in and make these changes without really understanding." She swallowed hard. "Do you want me to stop making the cupcakes? Is that what you want?"

Mem Schrock shook her head. "*Ne.* There's no need for that. Jest please try to understand, will ya? Can you consider, dear Sarah, our side too?"

Sarah went through her day like any other, but on the inside she began to understand. She didn't need to prove herself right. She was right . . . and *Mem* Schrock was too. Just because they were different didn't mean either was wrong. They both served God and their neighbors, just in different ways. The problem wasn't trying to change the other's mind, but how they could come together — benefit each other.

Lord, give me the wisdom to be giving, yet understanding too. I want to serve you in the way you desire. If yer desires match mine, then gut. *If not, help me to release my desires — release my dream.*

The prayer hadn't flowed through Sarah's mind two minutes prior when an elderly Amish woman shuffled into the bakery and sat in a chair at one of the small cafe tables. The woman's eyes were fixed on Sarah. Her white eyebrows folded down. The shop was busy this morning, mostly *Englischers* ordering Sarah's cupcakes. When the crowd slowed, the woman was still sitting there, eyeing the cupcakes. Sarah took one, placed it on a plate, and carried it over to the woman.

"I've been wanting to talk to you. It's busy today." Sarah smiled.

The woman fiddled with her *kapp* string. "Humph. Yer not from around here."

"*Ne,* I'm not. I was born in Kentucky, but I don't remember living there very well. I've lived in Montana since I was eight."

"In the Rexford community?"

"*Ja*, in the West Kootenai. Rexford is right across the lake."

"Humph." The woman focused on Sarah's face. She refused to look at the cupcake on the plate. "You don't know how things work here."

Sarah's heart pounded, and she felt as if her feet were not on the wooden floorboards but sunken into them. Her feet felt heavy. Her heart did too. She didn't know what to say. Sarah sat down in the chair across from the woman. She sent up a silent prayer for wisdom. She sure needed it.

"I'm sure you know all about how things are in these parts. How things used to be," Sarah finally said.

The woman jutted out her chin. "*Ja*, I've lived here my whole life."

"Do you remember then a time before the roads were paved?" Sarah asked.

"All mud and dirt." The woman waved a hand in the air. "In the winter, the hens didn't lay well, and we ate corn mush and ground wheat. I can't believe Amish women today buy store-bought cereal. Everything's fancy these days." She glanced at the cupcake. "There were no tops for buggies and most people hooked up their workhorses. None of these fancy horses jest for the buggies. I sold my eggs for thirty cents a dozen."

417

"And the clothes? Are they much different?"

"We didn't have Sunday shoes, and in the summer, the *kinner* ran around barefoot. I often didn't have shoes either — not until the snow came."

Sarah wrapped her arms tight around herself. "Weren't yer feet cold?"

"*Ja,* but on cold mornings, when I went to the barn, I let the cows out and then went and stood where they'd been lying."

"Did you ever go stand in a fresh manure pile to warm yer feet?" Sarah asked.

The woman's eyes widened, and Sarah wished she could take back her words.

The woman leaned in close to Sarah's ears. "*Ja,* how did you know?"

"My *oma* told me she used to do the same thing. *Ach,* I'm so thankful for socks and shoes."

Laughter slipped through the woman's lips. "Yer the first one I've confessed that to. Then again, no one's asked.

"Things have changed so much. Life around here used to be simple. Now it's not at all. With so many cars and *Englisch* folks, seems we're doing more and more to make things pretty-like for them. Seems we're getting too concerned with working to please people rather than God."

418

The elderly woman glanced down at the cupcake and then looked around the room. For the past few weeks, Sarah had been having so much fun with her creations she didn't realize how the treat looked to others. Blue frosting, pink swirls, yellow flower petals. To Sarah, it captured nature, God's creation. But to this older woman, it was simply another change. Another way her simple community was turning to fancy things.

Sarah rose and picked up the plate. "I'll be right back."

She hurried to the kitchen. She walked straight to the vanilla-bean cupcakes on the cooling rack. With a half-smile, she picked up the chocolate frosting in the decorating bag. Starting on an outside edge, she swirled the frosting around on the cupcake until it rose in a swirl in the middle. Satisfied, she returned to the elderly lady and placed it before her.

The woman eyed it curiously. "What's this?"

"I'd like to call it a cow-pie cupcake. It may look like the real thing, but I guarantee you'll be pleasantly surprised when you bite into it."

The folds that surrounded the woman's eyes faded as her eyes brightened. Laughter

419

split the air — a big belly laugh that Sarah hadn't heard in these parts until now. All eyes turned in their direction. The older woman continued to laugh until tears ran down her face. Sarah's laughter joined hers.

Gasping for breath, the woman wiped away tears that rolled down her cheeks, then, with a twinkle in her eye, she picked up the cupcake and took a big bite. Her lips curled up in a smile, and she finished off the rest of it in less than thirty seconds.

The elderly woman was dabbing the corners of her mouth with her napkin when a young woman walked in. She ignored Sarah and focused on the older Amish woman. "*Mem,* my shopping is done. Are you ready to head home now? I know it's been a long day fer you already."

"I'm almost ready, dear." The woman covered her mouth with her hand and her shoulders rose up and down, trembling. "I — I jest want you to try the cow pie first." Laughter spilled from her lips like before, and she motioned toward the kitchen. Sarah nodded, then she rose. She glanced at the woman's daughter and shrugged. How could she explain?

In the kitchen, she frosted another cow-pie cupcake and returned, placing it before the daughter. The daughter didn't seem to understand, but she smiled and took a bite anyway. Her face glowed at the taste.

"Why, I do believe this is the best cupcake I've ever eaten." Then she stepped closer to Sarah. "But you do have to excuse my mother. She does get her words mixed up sometimes. I'm sorry she called yer cupcake a cow pie. I'll have to talk to her on the ride home."

Sarah was about to explain when the jingle of the bell on the front door interrupted her thoughts. Jathan entered with a long stride, and he didn't look happy. Instead of approaching Sarah, he moved to his mother. "Yonnie said to come. Said you need to talk to me."

Mem Schrock put a hand on his shoulder. "Do you have the buggy?" she asked.

Jathan nodded.

"*Gut,* then we need to go fer a ride. There is something I need to talk to you about. Something fer yer ears alone."

CHAPTER 33

Jathan's shoulders tightened in knots. His head ached, mostly because he hadn't gotten much sleep. He couldn't stop thinking about Sarah. Couldn't forget the disappointment he saw on her face every time he looked at her lately. He loved her, really he did, but how could he turn his back on his family? They needed him. Wasn't his role as an Amish man and a follower of God to see their needs met? He saw no way to do both — to love Sarah with everything in him and serve his family too.

He helped his mother into the buggy and the two slips of paper in his pocket seemed to burn through the fabric. The first was a check from the piece of furniture he'd delivered earlier today. It was something, but not enough — never enough.

The second was a letter from the businessman in New York asking when they'd be able to reschedule their meeting. Jathan knew that would be impossible now. He barely had time to buy supplies for the bakery. How had he ever thought he could manage a bigger project like shipping items to New York?

Earlier, when Jathan had gone to pick up the end table for the delivery, he'd seen that Yonnie wasn't working. Instead, he was cleaning up the already-perfectly organized work area.

"*Mem* said to send you to the bakery when you were done with the morning chores."

Jathan glanced in the direction of the *dawdi* house. "Is it *Dat*? Is something wrong?"

"*Ne*. Nothing like that. It's about the bakery," Yonnie had said. "It's about Sarah."

Now *Mem* sat in the front seat of the buggy next to Jathan.

Mem cleared her throat and readjusted in her seat. "There's been a change of plans. Yonnie has been offered a job in Sugarcreek. He'll be working at a furniture shop there and a home will be provided fer his family. It's much larger than their place now."

Jathan tried to process the information. "What does that mean for me?"

"Well, instead of helping in the bakery at all, we need you to work in the woodshop. There are orders that need to be filled."

"*Mem,* that's not possible. You'll not be able to handle the bakery on yer own. With all the new customers . . . yer not going to be able to keep up."

"We know."

"So are you going to hire someone else?"

"*Ne.*" Mem let out a heavy sigh, and Jathan could see all of her sixty years in her worried, wrinkled face. "I've been talking with Kay. We want to keep things as they are. No, more than that. We want things to go back to the way they used to be. We didn't make a lot of money, but we enjoyed our time together." His mother released a sigh. "I didn't know how much I wanted things to stay the same . . . until they began to change. Jathan, I hate to do this, but you need to tell Sarah that we want her to find another place to work."

"Jest like that?"

"It can be no other way, Jathan. You haven't been to see him in a few days, but yer *dat* has been trying to talk. The nurse came and said the words should start coming faster." She covered her face with her hands. "It's fer yer own good too. I don't want you hurt again. He has his own mind, you know. Always has."

Sarah expected Jathan to be waiting outside

424

the bakery when she got off work. Surely he wouldn't just leave her full of questions and empty of answers. But he hadn't been there.

She hoped he'd come to her aunt's house in the afternoon, but he didn't.

Every one of her nerves tensed up during dinner.

After dinner, her uncle, aunt, and cousins walked to the pond down the road to skip rocks. She declined their offer to join them. Her aunt must have sensed Sarah's tension and didn't press.

Sarah had been tense since the moment Jathan and his mother had driven away in the buggy. From the look on his mother's face, Sarah guessed the news wasn't good.

Having given up on seeing him this evening, Sarah jumped when a knock sounded on the front door. She hurried to open it.

Jathan's face was pale. His eyes red. "Do you have a minute to talk?"

"*Ja.*" She followed him outside.

Instead of sitting on the porch swing, Sarah moved to the porch railing and leaned against it. After taking a big breath, she turned to face Jathan.

"I need to talk to you, Sarah," he said. "My *mem* and some of the other women, well, they've been talking."

"Did they tell you about the sweet old couple from Pittsburg who came by?" She pushed the words out of her mouth, pretending all was well and today was just a normal day. "They loved the cupcakes so much they put in an order for next Monday for their granddaughter's birthday. They are going to drive all the way back here to pick it up. Can you imagine driving three hours each way jest for cupcakes?"

Jathan was silent. He lowered his head and, from the way his shoulders slumped, it looked as if he had an invisible buggy parked on top of him.

Sarah's heart sank. She leaned forward and took Jathan's large hands within her smaller ones. "That's not what they talked to you about, is it?"

"Ne." He pulled his hands from hers and rubbed the back of his neck. "I don't know how to say it any better . . . it's jest they feel we've been trying to force the bakery into something it's not. My *mem* and aunt think it might be wise for you to find another place to work."

Sarah jerked her head back as if he'd just thrown a glass of cold water into her face. "So that's it? They . . . they don't want me."

"It's not that. They care for you much. *Mem* wanted to make sure you knew that.

426

She jest wants the bakery to go back to the simple way it was." Tears rimmed his eyes. "There are many bakeries in town and in the neighboring communities."

She touched his hand, but it felt cold, lifeless, under her fingertips. "Is that what you want?"

"I don't think there's another choice."

"No other choice? Really, Jathan? I thought you'd be able to figure out some way to help me. I thought you'd be on my side here. If I can continue to gain customers, we can expand. Don't you think that could help yer family?" She let her voice trail off.

Jathan lowered his head, and she understood. Sarah's lower lip trembled and an ache penetrated her chest. He wasn't going to fight for her.

"There is nothing I can offer you," he finally said. "There will be no bakery fer you to work in. And as fer me —" he set his jaw — "I'll be working at the workshop, filling orders. I may be slow, but I'm better than nothing."

"That's it?" She clasped her hands together and pulled them to her chin.

He nodded. She could see pain in his eyes — pain from hurting her — but obviously it wasn't enough to make a difference.

The ache of his indifference transformed into anger within her. Patty had abandoned her, but it hadn't been her choice. But this . . . she'd thought Jathan was someone she could marry. It was good she found out the truth now. He'd rescued her from the woods, but he wouldn't take one step to stand up for her.

What a fool I've been! Her hands balled into fists at her side.

"Are you sorry you came here?" he asked.

"I'm not sorry I came to Ohio. I love Ohio. I'm sorry I met you." A sob came out with her words. She turned her back to him. Her whole body ached. Her heart ached worse. She wanted to run away, crawl into bed, fall asleep, and never wake up.

He placed a hand on her shoulder but she pulled away.

"I'm sorry I met you, because this — this hurts jest as much as . . ." She couldn't say it. She didn't want Jathan to have the pleasure of knowing.

"As Patty?"

Sarah spun around and pointed at his chest. "Don't you dare say her name! It's not as if you knew her. In fact, I'm glad you didn't. *Ne.* Let me change that. I wish she *would* have met you. Patty had a way of seeing inside people. She could have warned me to stay away right from the beginning."

"Is that the truth? Do you really wish you'd never met me, Sarah?"

"Ja." The word burst from her lips, even though she knew it wasn't the truth. The only truth her heart knew at this moment was how much it hurt.

Jathan moved to the front porch steps. She walked to the front door as he continued down the steps. She wanted him to pause and turn. She wanted him to say he changed his mind, that he didn't want her to leave, but he didn't. Jathan continued to his buggy.

As she watched him go, his image blurred. Sarah lifted her apron and wiped her eyes.

She watched until the buggy disappeared over the crest of the hill. It was gone for a moment as it moved down into a dip. Then it reemerged as it crested the next hill before disappearing again.

Sarah scanned the horizon. She hadn't thought about Montana — she'd been so eager for the new business. She'd made friends here. She'd been hopeful concerning her heart, her future. She'd been able to imagine and dream and plan in ways she hadn't since Patty's death. But now . . . Sarah blinked hard. She should have expected such. Why should she stay? She looked up into the sky. Clouds moved in blocking out the sun.

Watching the road the buggy had traveled down, she moved to the porch steps and sat. The air was chilly but she didn't care.

"God, are you out there somewhere? I feel so alone now. I've always tried to do the right thing. I've served you, and I try to care fer others. If yer a *gut* God then why . . ." The tears came then. *Why* was all she could manage to say.

She wrapped her arms around her legs, pressing her skirt tight to her. She didn't know where she was supposed to go or what she was supposed to do.

Sarah woke up the next morning with one task on her thoughts. She had to go to Jathan. She had to apologize.

Thinking back now, she recognized the look in his eyes. He'd wanted her to say she'd stand by him no matter what. He'd hoped she'd tell him he was more important than working at the bakery, and she hadn't done that.

Sarah wasn't sorry she'd met him. Even if things didn't work out between them romantically, she'd never be sorry. He was a good man who carried his own painful memories close to his heart.

As much as she cared, even if things didn't

work out, she didn't want her harsh words hanging between them. Asking forgiveness, she knew, was just as much about herself as it was about him. She needed to ask God to forgive her for the way she acted, and she knew she only had the right to do so if she asked Jathan's forgiveness first.

She'd also woken up thinking about Patty. Her friend would take off her *kapp* and plop to the ground in despair if she knew Sarah was going to give up so easily. There were no tall, thin trees here — the types Patty had always dared Sarah to climb. She wouldn't fall to her death by going after Jathan, but she could tumble, and her heart could get scraped up pretty fierce. Still, that was the risk she had to take.

She dressed and hurried out to ask her Uncle Ivan if she could borrow his buggy. The sun had just risen, but she could not wait.

It was *Mem* Schrock who opened the door after Sarah's knock. She coughed, and Sarah knew why she wasn't at the bakery. Most likely the same reason she wasn't in the *dawdi* house with *Dat* Shrock.

Before Sarah even had a chance to talk, *Mem* Schrock held up her hand. "I'm sorry, Sarah. Jathan's working right now. You'll have to come back another time."

Sarah placed a hand on her chest. She could count on one hand the number of times she'd felt so angry. Even after Patty's accident, she'd felt more pity for the young couple on the boat than anger. They'd been on their honeymoon and had just borrowed the boat for the day. They'd been playing around and hadn't meant any harm — much less someone's death.

But this woman.

Mem Schrock swayed forward, blinking rapidly. Her lips compressed and at last she stammered. "You two are just too different, Sarah. He needs someone more . . . Amish. Who likes the old ways."

Don't listen to that. Sarah could hear Patty's voice in her mind. *You are not like anyone else, Sarah, and you don't want to be. How boring the world would be if everyone was alike.*

The memory of Patty's smiling face brought a bit of comfort, but it still did not shield her from the pain of *Mem* Schrock's scowl.

"*Ja,* I understand, and yer probably right, but can I please talk to Jathan? Jest fer a few minutes?"

"*Ne.* There's a big order he's finishing. I ask you not to go out there."

Sarah glanced over at the building just behind the barn. She knew she could walk past this woman. But she also knew it would do more harm than good, especially after what Jathan had to say yesterday.

"G'day, Sarah."

"Good day."

She walked back to the buggy. Above her, the clouds skidded across the sky. Instead of celebrating their beauty, she focused on the rocky driveway and the way the gravel bit through the soles of her shoes.

It didn't matter if she could apologize today or if it would be two months before she had Jathan alone to say her piece. They'd had a fight, yes, but every fight was evidence of something more.

Dat had always told her that whenever you got angry at another person, it was an opportunity to take a glimpse of your own faults. Yet even if she and Jathan managed to work out those faults — as she hoped they would — there was the issue of his family. They'd always be there. Their beliefs weren't going to change overnight just as hers weren't going to change.

If his family couldn't accept her — if they didn't appreciate her passion and creativity — how could she live with that? More important, how would Jathan deal with it?

She couldn't imagine putting him in that position. He cared for her, but he loved his family. She wouldn't ask him to choose.

She climbed into the buggy, knowing this was the beginning of a new path for her. To save Jathan from having his heart split in two, she knew the best thing would be to give him space to make his own decisions, even if those decisions didn't involve her.

CHAPTER 34

Sarah pushed the food around on her plate and tried to ignore the nine sets of eyes on her.

She took a sip of her water and turned to Aunt Lynette. "I heard you talking about Aunt Esta needing a *maut* when her babe is born. Do you think she'd be interested in me?"

"You? Yer more than qualified, but what about the bakery? So many *wunderbaar* things are happening."

Sarah hung her head. "Not anymore."

Aunt Lynette furrowed her brow. "I don't understand."

"They want things to go back to the simple ways. A little baking, nothing too fancy, and their old Amish customers."

"What? Really?" Aunt Lynette leaned forward in her seat. "But yer cupcakes . . ." She sighed.

Sarah swallowed hard and shrugged.

The room was absolutely still. Even though Sarah knew the baby and toddlers couldn't understand the *Englisch* words she and her aunt spoke, they must feel the tension.

"I — I can't talk about it now, but they have decided to go back to the way things were. I'd like that nanny job. I need to get away, even if it's less than five miles."

"*Ja,* I understand. I will send a note with Ivan to take to Roy J. to get to Esta that will tell her yer desire to work fer her."

"*Danki.*" Even with the crushing blow of yesterday's news, she couldn't help but smile. Since there were many Roy Yoders in Holmes County, nicknames were common. Esta's husband was Roy J., although no one knew what the J. stood for, and at the bakery, she'd heard talk of Albert's Roy, Twin Roy, and Limpy Roy, each of whom were named such because of their families or a trait.

The smile quickly faded and she hurried to her room.

What am I doing here?

In Montana, there was only one Roy, and he wasn't even Amish.

In Montana, her boss, Annie, let her be as creative as she wanted to be with her baking.

In Montana, she had to be more concerned about coming across a bear as she walked to work than she did about the number of tourists one could draw to one's shop.

Yet, even as she questioned what she was doing in Ohio, she didn't feel God releasing her to return to Montana. She thought of her friend Marianna, who'd gone back to Indiana. Marianna had said that Montana had stayed with her every moment. For Sarah, that wasn't the case.

Sarah sank onto her bed, and a knowing settled on her. Just as she knew when a loaf of bread needed an extra two minutes of baking. Just as she knew what ingredient she needed to throw into her cupcake batter. She knew she was supposed to stay in Holmes County. At least for a little while longer. She may have come to help Jathan, but she had a feeling God wasn't finished with her yet.

Sarah curled up, pulled the pillow closer to the edge of the bed, and placed her cheek on it. She just hoped she could stay on to help with Aunt Esta now. Otherwise she didn't know what she'd do.

Esta wobbled through the front door, motioning Sarah to follow. Esta's stomach looked as if she had a pumpkin tucked under her dress, and Sarah knew the time for the baby to come was close.

A week had passed since Sarah had last seen Jathan. She'd had a chance to visit with Esta and discuss the job. Esta had been thrilled and Sarah had spent the rest of the week enjoying time with Aunt Lynette.

Every day she waited and hoped that Jathan would stop by.

When that hadn't happened, she'd told her uncle she was ready to move to her new home.

Uncle Ivan had dropped Sarah off and, at her insistence, left her boxes on the porch. He gave her a pat on the shoulder before leaving.

"I'm thankful yer here," Esta said. "I thought about asking the Miller girl again, but news has it she's gonna be marrying soon. I'm sure she'll have enough preparation to do without having to help me out. Yer an answer to prayer, Sarah."

Esta led her to the stairs and looked up the tall flight. Her hand gripped the rail and she paused.

"If you tell me which room it is, I can find my own way."

"Really?" Esta let out a sigh. "It's at the top of the stairs, second on the left." Esta shook her head. "I'm so sorry though. I haven't readied up the room yet."

"Don't worry. I can clean up the room. That's what I'm here for, remember?"

That and to run away. To forget the real reason I moved to Ohio.

Esta's house was situated not far from the downtown area of Charm, Ohio. It was a pleasant walk to the grocery store and library. Sarah enjoyed taking the two older toddlers there. Helen was three years old, and Jonah was two. Both had light brown hair and large, beautiful eyes with long lashes just like their mother's.

It helped to get out of the house. To have fresh air. To keep her mind occupied on things other than her own troubled thoughts.

When the midwife arrived one morning and suggested Sarah take the children out for a while, Sarah understood. She spent two hours walking the streets of Charm and playing with the children at the park. Only when they grew tired did she decide to return.

"You got here jest in time." The midwife strode onto the porch with the newborn swaddled up. "I have to finish with Esta yet. Can you take the wee one?"

Sarah nodded. "*Ja,* let me get some cookies fer the children first." She sat them at the table with a couple of cookies and then took the baby into her arms. His face was pink and wrinkled. His hair was still coated with a white film. Sarah's soul ached. *Will I ever have the joy of being a mother, a wife?*

The baby's eyes were wide as he looked around. "Welcome to this world. Do you like what you see?" She swaddled him and tucked him under her chin. "This is a *gut* home, a *gut* community."

"Your aunt wants the *boppli,*" the midwife called from the hallway behind her.

"*Ja,* of course." Sarah rose and carried the baby to Esta. She'd only met Esta a few times before during family vacations, and she'd always had a hard time calling her aunt since she was only a few months older than Sarah.

A few months older and married with three children now. Sarah shook her head and pushed those depressing thoughts away.

"In God's good time," she whispered to the tiny babe. "All things *gut* in his time."

Jathan hummed one of his mother's favorite hymns as he sat by his father's side. It wasn't until he started the second line that he paid attention to the words to the tune playing in his head.

I need no mansion here below
for Jesus said that I could go
to a home beyond the clouds
not made with hands.
Oh, won't you come and go along?
We will sing the sweetest song
ever played upon the harp
in Gloryland.

It wasn't until he started school with the other Amish children in their one-room schoolhouse that Jathan realized the gospel songs his mother sang at home weren't typical. Singing wasn't typical for that matter. But Jathan's mother had a beautiful voice, and she often sang him to sleep. It was only as he grew that he understood her lovely singing could be considered prideful.

He looked at the still form of his father. Was what his mother said true? She'd told Jathan *Dat* had woken up and asked for him.

Jathan stared at the ashen face and the limp hands that lay at his father's sides and had a hard time believing it. Maybe *Mem* was just trying to give him a sense of hope. Since he had no hope for Sarah or the bakery, maybe she figured he'd find a bit of joy in his father's improvement.

Jathan tried to think of another song when he felt *Dat* stirring beside him. Looking up, his head jerked back to see *Dat*'s eyes open and fixed on him.

"Dat?" Jathan scooted the chair closer to the bed and grasped his father's hand. "*Dat,* do you understand me? I'm here."

Jathan noticed the slightest nod of his father's head. He started to rise, wanting to go get *Mem,* but *Dat*'s hand clung tighter.

Was he wanting this moment to be for just the two of them? The intensity in *Dat*'s eyes told Jathan he did.

"*Dat,* I'm so thankful yer here. I'm sorry I left. I'm sorry I went to Mont—"

Dat squeezed Jathan's hand again and Jathan paused his words.

Dat's cracked lips parted slightly, and his face scrunched up as if it took every ounce of energy to form a word. "Go." The word pushed through Dat's lips.

"*Ja,* I went to Montana."

Dat's brow wrinkled more, and Jathan knew that's not what he was talking about.

"Go-o-o."

Jathan leaned closer, wishing he could help *Dat,* could understand better.

"Go-o . . . to . . . her." *Dat*'s upper lip lifted slightly.

"*Mem?* Do you need *Mem?*"

Dat frowned again.

"Who, *Dat*? Who are you talking about?"

"Sarah." Out of all the words, this came out clearest.

"You know about Sarah?"

His father settled into the pillow, telling him he did.

"So you've been understanding what we've been talking about all this time?" Jathan stood. "And you heard when she came in . . . you heard us talking about the bakery?"

The slightest smile curled on his father's face.

Jathan sank down onto the bed. "That's why you wanted to see me." An electric sensation moved through Jathan. *Dat* knew of her. Accepted her. Then the weight of what Jathan had done hit him. He lowered his face into his hands. He thought he'd known what was required of him. But what if he'd been wrong?

"She's not at the bakery anymore. I was a fool, *Dat*. She's gone." Gone from his life. Gone from Berlin.

Dat's eyelids fluttered and Jathan knew the effort of talking tired him. Jathan leaned forward and pressed his lips to his father's forehead. For the first time in his life, he loved his father completely and understood that he was no different than his father. Both had clung to the traditions they knew and were fearful of anything different. *Dat*'s fear had emerged in rage. Jathan's fear had caused him to run.

Jathan leaned back, and as he did, three more words slipped out of his father's lips. "Yours. Make yours," he said before he drifted off to sleep.

What did *Dat* mean?

His life?

His bakery?

His future wife?

Maybe all three. Jathan wasn't sure, but at that moment, he knew what he needed to do and for whom he needed to do it.

CHAPTER 35

Sarah heard something clatter to the ground. It almost sounded like the tray she'd just taken in to Esta. She opened the door and poked her head inside. "Everything *gut*?"

Esta glanced up at her. Dark circles ringed her eyes.

"I fell asleep leaning against these pillows and the tray hit the floor."

Sarah hurried in, picking up the spilled toast and eggs. "Don't worry. I'll make you more. Thankfully the plate didn't break."

"The *boppli*'s been up so much in the night. I've never had this problem before." Esta yawned. "It seems I'm not making enough milk."

"Have you tried a tincture?" Sarah asked. "There was a woman near where I lived in Montana who made them. We sold them at the West Kootenai store. I can write to my *mem* and ask if she can send me some Max-

445

Milk. In the meantime, I can walk to town. There's an herbal tea with fenugreek that will help. It's worth a try."

"Would you do that?" Esta scooted farther down in bed, and Sarah could tell she was more interested in sleep than breakfast.

"*Ja,* and how're yer afterpains?"

"Worse than with the other children. Real tears come when I nurse."

Sarah nodded. "Others at the store told me that happened. I'll pick up some red-raspberry-leaf tea and a calcium supplement. It should help."

"*Ach,* Sarah." Esta stretched out her hand.

Sarah step forward and squeezed it. "The young woman I had stay after the last baby was *gut* about cooking and cleaning, but our Lord knew I needed you here this time."

Sarah nodded. "I'll get the *kinner* dressed, and we'll head into town. Should be back before the *boppli* wakes."

Thirty minutes later, Sarah was on her way. It felt good and right to walk the mile to town with Jonah on her hip and Helen's hand in hers. The rain of yesterday was gone, and warm, fresh air filled her lungs. Jonah jabbered in toddler talk, and Sarah greeted two Amish women she recognized as customers from the bakery in Berlin.

The two women paused in their tracks and

their eyes widened. The color seemed to rush from their faces and Sarah guessed why. They'd most likely gotten an earful. They obviously knew she was no longer at the bakery, but neither said a word.

"Sarah, *gut* to see you. Look at those adorable *kinner.* I hope Esta's faring well."

"*Ja,* well as can be, I suppose." Sarah smiled, telling herself that if they weren't going to bring up the subject of the bakery, she wasn't either. "I'm jest heading to the store to pick up some things for Esta — to help with her afterpains."

"She had another son, I heard? A *gut* playmate for young Jonah here, *ja?*" one of the women asked.

Sarah stroked Jonah's fine, silky hair. "*Ja,* another boy, Job."

The older woman patted her *kapp* and nodded. "A *gut* biblical name."

"Are you visiting family in Charm?" Sarah readjusted the toddler on her hip.

"Uh, my sister's sewing circle is at noon. And before that . . ." She glanced at her friend. "We're jest heading to the fabric store fer some supplies." The woman's cheeks reddened, and Sarah wondered if they were going to ask why she left. Then again, they most likely already knew. The

447

Amish had their way of spreading news like that.

She imagined their words, *"Poor dear. She had fancy ideas . . . Doesn't she know we're plain folk?"*

Sarah wanted to ask if they'd been to the bakery lately, but she didn't want to hear if things had returned to how they had been. She didn't want to hear that all her hard work — all her ideas — had been for nothing.

"Have a *gut* day then." She led Helen away. "Enjoy yer sewing circle!" she called over her shoulder and quickened her steps before they could see the disappointment in her gaze. Without warning, two tears slid down her cheeks.

A keen, sharp pain stung her heart at the thought of having failed Jathan's mother, the bakery, and Jathan.

On the way to the Charm General Store, Sarah passed by Miller's Dry Goods and Fabrics, the store the two women had been headed to. Laughter and conversation poured out of the open front door and she paused in her tracks. Could it be? She took a few steps up the sidewalk and Jathan's voice was clear.

"This fabric looks *gut* enough to eat." Tears sprang to her eyes, but she didn't know what she was so upset about. That he'd come to Charm without stopping by to visit . . . maybe to drop off a piece of furniture. Had all of Berlin come this way?

Sarah quickened her steps, clinging tightly to Helen's hand. "Hurry," she urged the little girl. "Faster."

Helen fussed beside her and Sarah looked down to see her struggling to keep up the pace.

"I'm so sorry." Sarah scooped the toddler onto her other hip and hurried on to the general store, refusing to look back to see if Jathan was exiting the fabric store yet. Tears filled her eyes and her throat grew hot and thick. He was a good man, she knew, but she couldn't have a relationship with someone who lived under the strict demands of his family. Even if he came around, she told herself not to keep her heart looped to his. When she became a wife, she wanted to be the most important person in her husband's life other than God. She didn't want to have to vie for her husband's attention. She didn't want to have to beg him to share his heart.

Patty was the first to enter the old log cabin. It was the second time they'd come here, and they'd only done so at Patty's insistence. Coming here made Sarah wonder about the people who'd left all these things. Realizing they were items people cared for and treasured caused her stomach to do flips. It didn't seem right to sift through someone's memories.

"Look!" Patty held up a small gold key. It was dusty but otherwise in good condition. "It's a strange key."

She held it out and Sarah took it between her fingers. "It looks like it's from a wind-up clock. My *oma* in Kentucky used to have one like that."

"Do you remember much about Kentucky?"

"Not much. I remember my *opa* holding me up so I could turn the key in the clock. I —"

"Look at this!" Patty's words interrupted Sarah's sentence.

Sarah glanced at the rusty piece of metal and wrinkled her nose. "It's a chain from an old bike."

"*Ja*, but I think it's beautiful." Patty took some wire that was sitting on the counter and formed two hooks. She twisted the hooks onto the ends of the chain and then, wrapping the chain around her arm, twisted the hooks together.

Sarah placed a hand to her head. A

bracelet? What would Patty think of next?

Patty chuckled as she glanced over at Sarah. "Do not worry, Sarah Shelter. I know this is jewelry and is forbidden. I know not to wear the bracelet anywhere else but in the forest. I know the rules . . ." Her voice trailed off. "I also know when to break them. When to allow myself room to explore without damaging anyone's feelings or ideas."

"Oh, Patty." Sarah shook her head. "Must you really be so dramatic over a simple piece of chain?"

Patty gasped and placed a hand over her heart. "Sarah, don't you know it wasn't a chain but a bracelet all along? It jest took me to see it . . . and to wear it. Sometimes it's the outside observer who knows the truth best all along. Sometimes you jest need to open yer eyes and see . . ."

Sarah had thought she needed to wait until she was in a settled, peaceful place to look into Patty's memory jar, but when the light of hope threatened to be blown out by her very next breath, Sarah knew she couldn't wait any longer.

Esta, the baby, and Roy J. had just gone to bed. Helen and Jonah had been sleeping for hours already. There was no better time, but still Sarah held her breath as she poured out the contents of Patty's jar.

A small compass, an old padlock, a Scrabble piece, a dog tag for a dog named Lady, Canadian coins, a locket, wooden sewing spools, and a rock Sarah clearly remembered — one Patty had been sure was an arrowhead.

Sarah laid out more of the items. Three tiny apples they'd formed out of polymer clay and painted. A brass antique whistle that was rectangular and flat.

"Patty, this wasn't how things were supposed to work out. We were going to grow up, get married, raise our children together," Sarah whispered. "I can't do this without you . . . I'm so uncertain."

She closed her eyes and gripped her fist on her lap. A memory surfaced, not of their time together, but of a dream she'd had. She'd been strolling down a country road with a wooden fence lining it. She held the hand of a small girl, and they walked with slow steps. She knew she was going to Patty's house, but the road stretched on. She couldn't see the house in the distance even when she knew it should be there. Where was the house? Her heart began to pound and just as she began to panic, she'd awakened to moonlight streaming through the window.

Had that dream been preparation for what was to come? Had God been telling her that she'd lose much for a while but someday she'd be able to spend eternity with Patty in their forever home?

Sarah was just about to put all the items back in the jar when she noticed something was wrapped around one of the spools. Her heart pounded as she pulled it off. Tears sprang to her eyes when she unfolded it.

A letter from Patty!

Dear Sarah,

If you find this letter, it means one of two things.

You're digging in my jar — maybe looking for that snail's shell you found down at the lake on your birthday. I put it in my pocket after looking at it and forgot to give it back to you. I kept it because it reminds me of that day.

If you're not looking for something, it could mean something else — that I'm gone from this earth. You, of all people, would be the one to ask for my jar. Everyone else would think it was junk.

I have no plans of leaving earth earlier than you, but maybe it'll happen. Heaven knows of all the times we've raced on foot, you've only beat me once, and that was the same day I sprained my ankle jumping down from Dat's apple tree. But deep down, I wonder if it's going to happen. Maybe that's the reason I'm writing this letter.

I'll admit this only to you, but sometimes, at night, I can hear a fluttering outside my window. For a while, I thought for certain it was the owl that lives in a nearby tree. Or maybe bats. But every time I rise to look, I don't see a thing. The night is dark as the inside of a black cow and there isn't a stitch of movement.

When it started happening more often, I prayed to God about it. And I had this warm feeling that moved in the center of my chest, right near my heart. It's felt as if God sent special angels to watch over me. Maybe it's the fluttering of their wings. Or maybe they're waiting around to take me to heaven.

If that is the case, Sarah, I have some parting words for you: Every day, you can choose to be part of God's creative process. I'm not talking about making things. Rather I'm speaking of allowing God to form you. We, God's people, are his greatest creation, but it's easier to tend our gardens than our souls. Not that I have everything all figured out, but I've been watching you. God has made you a unique design. Never forget that. Also know that God's made someone else to be your fit, to see your specialness as I do. Sometimes you're a timid thing, but if you find the right guy, be bold. Be bold! You don't want to look back at your years with regrets. Regrets have no place in your memory jar.

All my love,
Patty

"Now listen." Patty plunked down on the ground beside her. "I need you to make me a promise. We will be friends forever. We won't let anything get between us."

"Even if one of us leaves?" Sarah asked.

"Leaves? Why would we do that?"

Sarah swallowed hard. "Well, if our *dats* make us . . ."

"There's always letters and visits."

Sarah nodded. *"Ja,* there are always those."

"And there's always this." Patty took Sarah's hand and placed it around her wrist. "Feel that?"

"Feel what?" Sarah asked, thinking Patty meant her heartbeat.

"Feel this moment that you'll store away.

A moment that's as warm as my skin under the sun's warm rays. A moment of friendship. Forever friendship."

CHAPTER 36

The breeze had picked up and Sarah held the screen door so it wouldn't slam as she closed it. The aroma of Esta's coffee followed her out the door. Instead of pouring herself a cup and chatting with her aunt at the kitchen table, she escaped to the porch with her Bible in hand, sitting down on the top step.

The changes of autumn were evident in the world, especially around Roy J. and Esta's farm. Crisp air stung Sarah's cheeks, and the rustle of the drying leaves on the trees danced in her ears.

Sarah watched the orange and yellow leaves as they swayed in the breeze. She knew, with one strong gust, a number of them would blow from the trees like seeds blown off a dandelion.

She thought about her plans for her day, first of which was for Roy J. to bring up glass jars from the cellar so they could get to canning. And then she'd make cupcakes. Sarah smiled. She didn't have a big customer base, but Helen and Jonah always came back for more, and they paid with the most delightful hugs.

As she thought about these things, something caught Sarah's attention. It was a tall, Amish man striding around the side of the house with confident steps. Jathan stood tall as he walked, and Sarah's heart leaped in her chest. The pain and heartache of not seeing him vanished at one flash of his dimpled smile.

She wanted to run to him, to open her arms, but instead she continued sitting.

Jathan paused before her and then sat down. "Sarah, I've been a fool."

"Are you trying to convince yerself or me?" She blinked as she looked at him, telling herself it was okay to cry this time, with happiness, with wonder. "I'm already convinced."

"I have something to show you and it's not very far. It's jest a short walk."

"In Charm?"

"*Ja,* Sarah. In Charm. Won't you come with me?"

It only took them ten minutes to walk to town. When they got there, they approached a row of shops.

"Have you passed this place before?"

Sarah nodded.

Jathan smiled. "Have you gone up the side street to see what's up that stretch?"

Sarah bit her lower lip. "*Ne,* I suppose I haven't. Is that what you've come to show me?" she asked.

Light danced in Jathan's gaze. "*Ja.*"

He took her hand and led her forward, toward a walkway that curved around the side of the building.

He paused just before they rounded the corner.

Jathan swallowed hard. "You have to close yer eyes."

"Really?" She laughed and placed her hand over them, leaving her fingers partly spread so she could peek through.

"Yer not fooling me." He released her hand and crossed his arms over his chest.

She squeezed her eyes shut and then his hand reached out and led her forward. When they'd taken ten steps, he paused and turned her shoulders so she faced . . . whatever he had to show her.

"Okay. Now open yer eyes."

Sarah's eyes sprang open. Aunt Lynette waved and smiled. "I'm first in line!" she called.

Dozens of others stood around. Bev Troyer

and other former customers Sarah recognized though she did not know their names.

Next to Lynette, Jathan's niece Catherine wore a yellow apron over her Amish dress. She waved and smiled. "The kitchen's all ready fer you, Sarah!"

Sarah looked from the smiling faces to the building. It was a simple storefront with white curtains in the windows. There was some type of sign, but a sheet was draped over it.

"Why is that covered?" she asked.

Jathan led her up the porch steps. "That's the best part. Everything will be revealed in time." Then he led her through the door.

"It's a bakery, Sarah. A cupcake bakery. And it's all yers."

"Mine?"

"Well, ours. My *dat* and *brieder* gave their approval. *Dat* is doing better. He can talk some, and Yonnie is staying and running our workshop after all."

"Ours?" She repeated the word as she stepped through the door. No one followed them inside. It's as if they all understood this was Jathan's gift to give without all their fuss.

Inside, colored tablecloths brightened the space. Above the windows, a fringe of branches was on display. Small trinkets

460

hung from them. A pinecone. An old whistle. A wooden yo-yo. All things similar to what Sarah had in her memory jars. Emotion caught in her throat.

"Where did you get all these things?"

"Oh, I asked around. Friends shared their keepsakes. Attached to each one is a paper label and a name. In time they can each tell you the story behind each item."

She looked at the decorations on the wall. More items. More names. "Patty would have loved it."

"Just as long as you do too . . ."

"*Ja*. It's perfect."

"The kitchen isn't modern. Not as much as I'd like, but we can improve things over time. The man in New York offered to put up the money fer all this. He believes in you, Sarah. I do too. And . . . I want to show you this too."

Jathan took her hand and led her to a display case on a side wall. A counter had been set up with trays. Lining the counter were twenty glass jars. Each jar was filled with treats: gummy bears, cookie crumbles, colored sprinkles.

She clapped her hands. "What's this for?"

"You should know." Jathan bent down and kissed her forehead. "It's a decorating station. It was yer idea. My *mem* reminded

461

me. She thought folks might enjoy decorating their own cupcakes . . . making them fancy."

Sarah turned and scanned the faces looking through the window. Standing off to one side she saw *Mem* Schrock watching her through the glass.

"*Danki,*" Sarah mouthed, and then she motioned her inside.

Mem Schrock entered with open arms. "I'm so sorry, dear. I jest didn't see yer vision. I see it now, and Jathan has done a lovely job."

"*Ja,* he has. And I'm starting to understand. You didn't see my vision because God gave us each our own."

"Yer right, dear." She leaned forward and kissed Sarah's cheek.

Sarah placed a hand over her heart, not realizing how such a simple motion could mean so much.

"*Danki* . . . I love it."

"*Ne,* dear, thank *you,*" *Mem* Schrock said.

"Fer what?" Sarah asked.

"Fer helping us all understand that God made us all creative in special ways. Fer Will and Yonnie it was with wood. Fer Jathan it's numbers, baking, and ideas. Jathan needed this . . . needs to get out of that workshop. He did it fer you, but in a way, it's yer gift to him too."

"So you won't be mad if my cupcakes are fancy?" Sarah chuckled.

Mem Schrock wagged her finger in the air. "Well, I'll choose the plain ones myself, but if our God created the violets and the butterflies, I suppose he'd appreciate you honoring him by recreating those things fer people to enjoy." Then she chuckled. "Of course, I still think it's a shame that you put all the work in and someone jest gobbles it up."

"Not to me." Sarah smiled. "Because even after the last bite is eaten, the memory remains. And it's those memories we'll always carry with us. It's the things we appreciate and treasure that stay on our minds and hearts even after they're gone."

Mem Schrock gave her another hug and then hustled out to join the others.

Sarah turned and faced Jathan. "It's *wunderbaar. Danki.*"

"It's not only me you have to thank. We all did our part. Yonnie made the tables and chairs. *Mem* sewed the curtains and tablecloths. Some of yer customers came up to help too."

Sarah let out a contented sigh, and as she looked around the room, she remembered that moment at Patty's grave. She'd questioned if anyone would ever truly know her, truly understand. Jathan did.

She looked at Jathan and took two steps forward. "This is me."

"*Ja*, Sarah, it's fer you."

"No, Jathan, you don't understand. You know me. You've captured everything inside me within this place . . ." She let her voice trail off.

"If you believe that and can forgive my foolishness, I have something else to show you."

Jathan took her hand. They walked through the kitchen and out the back door. There was a small patio, a walkway, and at the end of the walkway, a little house. On the door was a wooden sign that read *Schrock*.

"What is that? Is that cottage yers?"

He glanced down at her. "It is mine, but I hope someday it will be ours."

"But what about yer parents' house?"

"I've been thinking about what you said." Jathan grinned. "Why do I jest have to accept things because that's always the way they've been? I spoke to Yonnie. He and Leah were excited about living at the house. Not only do they have room fer all the children, but he's right by the workshop, too, and Leah is there to help *Mem* with

Dat."

"So as fer us . . ."

"As fer us, Sarah, we can begin a life together. The life we want."

"Danki . . ."

"I need to thank you too." Jathan lowered his face toward hers. "You have given me permission to be myself, to pray fer and ask God to show me who he designed me to be. And the more I've gotten to know you, Sarah, the more I believe that he designed us not to work by ourselves, but together.

"And . . . there's one last surprise." Tears rimmed Jathan's eyes as he led her back around to the front of the store. Her friends waited. No one spoke. They all just looked at her with eager eyes.

"We brought someone special in today." He pointed to someone sitting in a rocking chair on the far corner of the porch.

Sarah watched as the tall Amish woman stood and strode toward her. She had Patty's smile and Patty's eyes. A longing for her friend welled up inside.

"Mrs. Litwiller." Sarah rushed forward. "You came."

"We live not many hours away. I have cousins here. Jathan found me. He's a persistent young man." She gave Sarah a hug and pulled back. "I couldn't miss this, especially not when Jathan honored Patty so by using her name."

Sarah placed her fingertips to her forehead, not understanding. "Her name?"

With a wave from Jathan, Yonnie pulled the sheet off the painted wood sign that hung above the door. Sarah read the name of the bakery and gasped.

"Patty-Cakes." Tears sprang to her eyes. "She would be so proud of this. So happy we used her name."

Then she stepped closer to Jathan and placed her hand on the back of his neck, pulling him close.

"After Patty's death, I wasn't sure I'd have a full, happy heart again, but I do, Jathan . . . I do."

"You also have someone who loves you completely, Sarah. It jest took me some time to figure it out myself."

Sarah smiled and then shrugged. "I understand. All of us get lost and wander off the path fer a time. I'm jest glad you found yer way out."

"God led me out." Jathan kissed the tip of Sarah's nose. "And he used my *dat*'s words to do so. I'm jest glad the path led to you . . . always to you."

"Me, too, Jathan." She snuggled her cheek against his chest. "I'm also thankful fer

Patty-Cakes, fer the memories past and the ones I still have to experience."

EPILOGUE

Ten-year-old Sarah didn't like to obey, but she hated disobeying worse. She always had this ache in the center of her chest that moved out in all directions every time she did something she knew she wasn't supposed to do. The ache reminded her of the time she'd gotten into a fistfight with her brother Jonathan and he'd hit her square in the chest. He said later he was only playing, but she hadn't thought so and Dat hadn't either. Jonathan had had to do her chores, in addition to his, for a week. While that punishment couldn't ease the pain of the punch, it did turn the memory from a bad one into one that had a bit of humor as she watched Jonathan try to knead bread and wash dishes.

But now . . . Patty eyed the empty kitchen as if she were the queen and her mother's workspace, full pantry, and cooking stove her domain.

Patty sat on her knees on the kitchen chair and leaned forward, putting her elbows on the table. "*Mem* said we can bake cupcakes if we don't make a mess."

Sarah shook her head. "Did not."

"Did too."

"But we're not old enough. I mean, nobody's home."

"Are you saying that yer *mem* doesn't let you bake?" Patty gasped.

"Well, when she's home she does."

"What are you, a *boppli*?" Patty stuck her thumb in her mouth and pretended to suck it.

Sarah jutted out her chin. *"Ne."*

Patty tossed an apron in her direction. "Then why don't ya put this on? I'm sure yer *mem* wouldn't like it if you messed yer clothes up."

The door opened and then slammed. Heavy footsteps sounded across the living room floor and then tromped up the stairs.

Sarah jumped. "Who was that?"

"*Ach,* my *bruder* Michael. Don't mind him none. He jest forgot something in his room."

"Does he always walk like that?"

"Like what?"

"All stomping about?"

Patty shrugged. "Guess so."

"And yer *mem* doesn't holler at him?"

"*Ja,* of course she does, but *dat* tells her that she's growing boys who will be lumberjacks, not bankers. *Mem* doesn't like it much when he says that."

"And what about the girls?"

"Girl. I'm the only one." Patty shrugged. "Sometimes I stomp, too, but *Mem* doesn't seem to mind so long as she sees me doing girl things. That's why I'm writing my own cookbook."

"A cookbook? Really?"

Sarah thought about the cookbooks *Mem* had on the bookshelf back home. They were written by older ladies who knew what they were talking about. She rubbed her eyes and stared at Patty, feeling like her friend was a woman in a girl's body.

"*Ja.* Most of them are things that *Mem* makes. I jest write them down. But I have a special section in the back." Patty pulled a lined notebook off the shelf and opened it. It was filled with recipes in Patty's handwriting. The pages were splattered with batter and one corner had an oil stain.

"See back here?" Patty pointed. "These are my own creations."

On the top of the page was only one word. *Cupcakes.*

Sarah read down the list.

Huckleberry
Lemon and Cream
Chocolate Chip
Raisin

Patty pointed to the bottom one. "Those didn't turn out that *gut.*" She wrinkled her nose.

Patty prepared to turn to the next page and then paused. "I have to know something, Sarah, before I show you the rest. You have to promise me one thing more than anything else." Patty's face was serious, and her dark eyes were fixed on Sarah.

"*Ja,* what is it?"

"First, I don't care if you use my recipes. *Mem* says that *gut* recipes should be shared. But if I share them, you have to promise me that every time you make them, you'll think of me. That you'll remember that I was the one who showed you all the best tricks, and when yer old and you have children, you'll always tell them, 'You can thank yer dear ole' Aunt Patty fer this yummy dessert.' "

Laughter burst from Sarah's lips and she nodded. "*Ja,* all right. I promise."

"Gut!" Patty pushed a chair over to the kitchen counter, stood on it, and took a mixing bowl from the cupboard. "Because if I want to be remembered for anything, cupcakes would be it."

"More than helping people or serving the poor?" Sarah didn't know why those two things popped in her head other than the fact that *Dat* had read the story about the Good Samaritan over dinner the night before and had talked about caring for those no one else would help.

"Of course we should do that. But isn't it lovely to spread a bit of happiness and beauty, too, jest like God does?"

"*Ja,* I suppose."

"Sometimes God calls us to take big leaps of faith but other times . . ." Patty looked to Sarah with a twinkle in her eyes. "Other times he jest wants us to offer a bit of love in a way another will gladly accept it. You remember that, Sarah Shelter." She waved her arm to the wildflowers that colored the field that had been frozen and dead just two months prior. "You remember that this moment is the most important one of all."

DISCUSSION QUESTIONS

1. Sarah Shelter's life is transformed after she loses her best friend, Patty. In what ways did Patty's death change Sarah?

2. Jathan Schrock is an Amish bachelor who has traveled to Montana to hunt — or so it seems. Even more than hunting, what was Jathan running to? What was he running from?

3. *The Memory Jar* is set in a small Amish community in Northwestern Montana. How is this setting similar to or different from other Amish novels you've read?

4. Sarah gets to know Jathan on a hiking trip. How did that trip change the course of their relationship?

5. Sarah has a wonderful talent for making cupcakes, yet this becomes a conflict with

other characters within the book. Why do you think some of the Amish community members reacted as they did?

6. Throughout the book are flashbacks of times Sarah spent with Patty. In what ways did Patty's influence impact Sarah even after Patty's death?

7. Jathan can't forget a painful time in his past when his father's words hurt him deeply. How did those words impact Jathan's actions in the novel?

8. When Sarah travels to Berlin, Ohio, she enters a community much different than the one she left in West Kootenai, Montana. Do you think the Berlin community had more influence on Sarah, or Sarah on the community?

9. Bev Troyer is an expert gardener, but she cannot cook. Why do you think it's easier for us to point out other people's faults rather than their gifts?

10. How did Jathan's reconciliation with his father impact his other relationships?

11. What do you think is the underlying

theme of *The Memory Jar*? How does this theme play out in the lives of the main characters of the novel?

12. At the end of the novel Sarah is given a great gift. Why did this gift mean so much to her?

13. Are you like Sarah? Do you have a dream that others are trying to squash? How can you follow God's dreams for your life? What is God asking you to do?

ACKNOWLEDGEMENTS

I am thankful for my friends who have shared the Amish lifestyle with me:

Ora Jay and Irene Esh
Dennis and Viola Bontrager
Martha Artyomenko
And Eli and Vesta Hochstetler for welcoming me to Berlin, Ohio, and introducing me to many wonderful Amish friends!

Thank you to Amy Lathrop and the Litfuze Hens for being the best assistants anyone can have. Many people ask how I do it all . . . Thankfully, I don't have to do it all with you on my team!

I also appreciate the Zondervan team, especially Sue Brower, Alicia Mey, and Tonya Osterhouse. Your insight, help, and enthusiasm have been amazing! I also send thanks to all the managers, designers, copy editors, sales people, financial folks, and everyone else who make a book possible!

I'm also thankful for my agent, Janet Grant. Your wisdom and guidance has made all the difference.

And I'm thankful for my family at home:

John, it's amazing that we're about to celebrate twenty-three years of marriage. I can honestly say I love you more and more each day. I'm so thankful for a husband who believes in me, supports me, cheers me on, and brags about me to anyone who will listen.

Cory, Katie, and Clayton . . . living so far from you is hard, but love expands across the miles. Cory and Katie, God gave you the gift of love in each other. You're an amazing couple and great parents! Clayton, you bring such joy to your papa and me. I'm excited to see who God created you to be. God has good plans for your family, and I'm eager to see what they are.

Leslie, I love your heart for God and your heart for others. You're the first to volunteer and give and serve! You are an example to the young people you mentor, and you're a model to me. When I get busy with life, hearing you play the guitar and worship reminds me what's important. I can't believe you're almost a senior in college. Time has passed quickly, but I'm thankful that you've allowed yourself to be molded and fashioned by God.

Nathan, it's amazing how much you've changed in just the last six months. You've grown into a man before my eyes, and it's wonderful to watch. Your love for God is matched with a servant heart and a gentle attitude. You aren't one who wants to be noticed, but I see — and God sees too — how you care and serve.

Alyssa, what a bundle of joy you are! Every day is brighter since God brought you into our lives! At two years old, you're my little companion during the day, making me smile and causing me to remember that laughter is just as important as any to-do list.

Grandma Dolores, I know not many people have the chance to spend so much time with their favorite grandparent. I am a blessed woman. At eighty-two years old, you keep me on my toes with your wit and surround me with your prayers. Thank you.

And to the rest of my family . . . I appreciate all of you! I'm so thankful you're in my life! God gave me the gift of you!